The
CABLE DENNING
MYSTERY
SERIES

by
James P. Alsphert

James P. Alsphert
presents

The Seven Fates
of
Kathmandu

A
Cable Denning
Mystery

**BOOK
4**

Published 2018 by Movies of the Mind

Printed in the United States of America

First printing, 2018

ISBN-13: 978-1-64056-017-8

MOVIES OF THE MIND
www.moviesofthemind.net

CONTENTS

"Seven Fates there were, called the Moirai, created from the lightning bolts and roiling clouds of thunder in the Heavens—and so it came to pass, each sister-goddess was mandated to bring the human creature his just desserts. This misshapen thing, man the treacherous, man the enslaver, man the war monger, man the wanton breeder. They came as sisters seven, each with her unique lesson to bestow upon the sons of men, BIRTH, INITIATION, CALLING, PASSION, LOVE, CONSCIOUSNESS, DEATH...the very qualities that reveal to man his own accomplishment or failure and thus does determine his fate...oh, long life or early demise, which shall it be? It matters little to the Seven Fates who await unseen...in the shadows..."

Chapter 1

DEATH BY ANOTHER NAME

Fate #1 – *Birth*

I had never jumped from an airplane before. What an experience! Crazy and scary as hell, falling out into nothingness, plunging through thin air to an unforgiving terrain three thousand feet below. Winds whistled by my ears like banshees on a bender and when I saw the ground coming up at me faster than I wanted it to, my heart ended up in my throat. It's true what they say about one's whole life flashing by when death pulls at those little puppet strings, and tucked away in the hollows of your worst fear comes the screaming horror that this might be the last few seconds of your earthly existence. I pulled the long cord and my body got jolted pretty bad as the parachute jerked and opened above me. I grabbed the mainstay ropes. It wasn't exactly floating, but at least the damn thing actually worked! I descended slow enough to know that if I landed on something sort of fall-friendly and not life-threatening, like an outcropping of rock or a nest of vipers, I might just survive the descent.

The earth was still coming up faster than I would've liked, but it seemed I was headed toward a river or its banks. It looked like it might be lined by sandy and rocky debris with small trees above. I had learned from an ex-jumper that one had to use their legs as shock absorbers when one landed and then roll. So as I came down from the sky at about twenty miles-an-hour, I guessed, I hit the edge of a bank, tumbling down into a sandy area below. Suddenly my mouth was full of sand and my hip felt like the god Thor had just slammed it with his mallet. But I think I was mostly conscious. I rolled over onto my belly, crawled to the edge of the river, and took a mighty drink. It was hot as hell. All of a sudden I heard a voice call out above me. A strange looking figure in a three-cornered hat and some kind of black robe stood looking down at me.

"Welcome, white *Hajji*, to *Parasi*. I trust you are not broken."

I turned to look at the man. He had a nice aquiline nose and bright dark eyes with a kind smile. "No...I don't think I'm broken, but the son-of-a-bitch who dumped me out didn't give a crap about that. Are you friend or foe?"

He made his way down the embankment and knelt to help me sit up. "You may call me friend, white Hajji. All creatures and beings remain unified under one Intelligent Source, but it is difficult for beings to overcome their species, or the divisions within their species. Therefore they turn against one another to destroy that which is different. Greed, lust for control, war, prejudice, perjury... this is the way of the lower ones."

I was half-listening to this shaman who seemed to have appeared out of nowhere. "And...just...just who might you be...if...if I may be so bold?" I said, still spitting out the sand in my mouth.

"I am *Limpao*. Once I was a Holy Man, but even the Buddhist and Hindi ways have gone astray. Islam is dividing itself. Now I walk al-one...with the *cosmos...* here...there, everywhere at the same moment."

He assisted me to my feet and helped me remove my parachute. "I think I might like you, stranger Limpao. I am Cable...Cable Denning...an American who just got ditched by his so-called fellow travelers. I'm on my way to *Mount Shivapuri* by way of *Kathmandu.* Can you steer me in the right direction? I'm a bit lost and I don't have a compass, plus I'm a little bummed up in my hip from a three-thousand foot fall."

"It is a long journey to Kathmandu, *Hajji Cable.* But I will help. We will go to a village I know and you may secure an animal to take you inland to Kathmandu."

I tried to shake the guru's hand but he offered only a fully sleeved arm. "That's sounds swell, Mr. Limpao."

"I cannot take your hand. You are an infidel, one who is not clean in the eyes of the sacred ones. The natives of your present land, whose homelands you have stolen, called you *White-eyes the Treacherous.* Did you know that?"

"Nope, but I'm not surprised. I know the American natives got a dirty deal. White men are shitty, shifty-eyed—and yeah, treacherous." I laughed to myself. So were members of every goddamned race. "So, if I'm an infidel and unclean in your eyes, why are you helping me?"

"Because you are a *being.* Come, stand still with me—let me look into your eyes." He stood with me and penetrated my eyes with his own. "Ah, there is fear and you run...flee from those who are both evil and strange to your species. What odd thing is it in your eyes that I see? You seek something that does not belong..."

"That's another story, Mr. Limpao. If you'll just get me to a town so I can get cleaned up. All my belongings are still on the aeroplane that dropped me off." I checked my pockets. Luckily, I still had money.

We walked for about an hour and my hip still hurt. By late afternoon we had entered a medium-sized village. "Here they will not welcome you into their homes. You will have to find refuge elsewhere, with the *Bal'kati*. With them, all who have payment are welcome."

The streets were quaint, dirty and filled with oxen and other animals, people, little vegetable and fruit stands and colorfully dressed men, women and children who looked upon me as some alien descended from the skies. Well, at least on this day, the shoe fit! Finally we got to a very nice whitewashed building with a large red awning over it. "It is here, Hajji Cable, you will spend the night. Brightly in the morning I will seek you to provide a traveling animal for you."

"Thanks, Mr. Limpao. I'll—I'll see you in the morning." I entered on a red carpet into a very quiet room where incense was burning. A lovely young woman wearing a green veil and a pretty see-through outfit came up to me. I got the distinct feeling I was in a damn brothel! She addressed me in her native language and I told her I didn't comprehend her lingo. It seemed India's influence by way of the Brits had brought English halfway around the world. "Forgive me...I have learned your language...but I do not use often. Do you wish a lady for the evening? We have many to select from."

"Well, to tell you the truth, I was hoping for some lodging—to stay, sleep overnight—I'm not too interested in one of your ladies, thanks all the same. And according to Mr. Limpao, I am an infidel, unclean, impure, certainly not worthy of your lovely courtesans."

"Oh, but if you are seeking place to stay...it is very reasonable...to include a new *Devadadi*—very little extra charge."

"No thanks, lady. I just need a room for the night—maybe a place to wash up and a bowl of rice or something?"

She said no more and led me upstairs to a very pleasant room. But it was hot as hell and I began to sweat. I showed her my money and she took about thirty-five cents equivalent from the money exchange I'd made in Calcutta. I thought that was pretty cheap for a night, a washbasin and a bowl of soup or rice. I threw all of my clothes off and flopped on a set of cushions on the floor, that I assumed was to be my bed. I dozed off with the sound of cackling chickens down the road. Suddenly I was aware of another presence in the room. Still completely naked, I sat up only to greet one of the most beautiful young women I had ever seen. She was well defined of face and body, her dark-brown eyes with very white whites looked at me and she smiled with teeth that could have been a dental magazine's poster dream girl of the month. Her shiny black hair fell to her shoulders and her wonderful young breasts stared out at me from an all-too-thin blouse made of pink silk. "*Hajji Baba Sahib*—my name is *Regini*—it means melody in your language. I am told you desire my services. First, may I wash you?"

I sat there stunned. How could nature put such an exquisite creature in the midst of a miscreant, filthy race of beings—known as the human race? What perversity was at work here? "Please call me Cable or Hajji Cable if you like. I—I, uh, can manage to wash myself, but I'd be obliged if you could fetch me a bowl of soup or rice or something. All I had was a cup of coffee this morning in Darjeeling."

"You walk all the way from Darjeeling?" she asked with amazement as those great lamps of hers widened.

"No...I didn't walk...I flew...in an aeroplane...you know...piece of metal with a propeller that makes a lot of noise?"

She didn't have a clue so I asked her to lead me to the toilet and washbasin area and she went off to procure my meal. But I didn't have long to wait. As soon as I was seated back down on the floor, relieved and all nice and clean, the beautiful vision called Regini returned and graced my surroundings by lighting a few candles in the room and then bringing me some hot rice soup with some delicious vegetables in it. I practically gulped it down and asked for a second bowl. When she had brought that and I had consumed it, I finally felt like I had something in my stomach and relaxed a bit. Regini took my bowl and soon returned. She seemed awkward and ill at ease as she approached me. "I am unhappy, Hajji Cable. I am to serve you. But I have not known a man. That is why Shivirni called me *Devadadi*. I am without experience. I was stolen from my mountain home and my family. I cannot go back, for once I am among the *Bal'kati*, I am disgraced. Will you not also shame me?"

I reached for her hand but she withdrew it. "No, I will not shame you. In fact, I didn't even want a woman tonight. But to save face with the rest of the girls, if you

6

want, you can stay with me in this room tonight—and tell your girlfriends you had a good time with old Hajji Cable here. How's that sound?"

"You would do that for me?" Then she took my hand and kissed it.

"Hey, now, wait a minute—remember, I'm an infidel. You don't want to be touching a tainted, evil man, now, do you?"

She laughed with me. "I like you, Hajji Cable. Yes, I would like that. I would like that you touch me. Yes, you are good."

That night, all became deathly still. It was decided that Regini would sleep in my room and so she curled up in a corner like a little animal in fetal position and soon was fast asleep. Or so I thought. I, on the other hand, drifted in and out of strange visions and dreams, recounting my bizarre experiences of the day, still seeing Hughes' confused face as he forced me out of the airplane to my fate below. Then I drifted deep into a land of pinks and blues, orange skies and yellow trees. Regini came to me very beautiful and very naked. She was modestly cupping her hands around her womanhood, while her solid, firm breasts stood out with those almost-black nipples I had seen on Indian women before.

She spoke to me. "You must impregnate me," she said in her soft demure voice. "I am the goddess of birth. But to give birth to your child, I must die a lifetime. It is the way." She came to me and melded into me, allowing me to hold her, possess her completely as she moaned and sighed until she awakened the fullness of my manhood and as I penetrated her, a deep red excitement pulsed through my brain and I can remember filling her and filling her with my essence until I was pumped dry. Then the scene shifted and we were both dressed in native garb and Regini was writhing on a mat in some hot shack with her legs spread, an infant's head, wet with black hair, was peeking out of her distended vagina. She held on my arm and screamed into the hot afternoon. But no one heard but me. The baby came blooping out of her body and I grabbed the little wet shoulders and helplessly held the child with one arm while Regini still clung to my other. Then her grip went limp and her beautiful face held the glossy stare of the dead. Then I heard her voice from some invisible place. *"This is the lesson of birth, Hajji Cable, one day you, too, will trade life for death. See my face. There is peace. I am released from all earthly caring. Our son will bloom as a new flower..."*

In the distance I heard a rooster crow and the village began to awaken as the sun began its day-ward journey. I awakened slowly, feeling quite well and still marveling at the dream I had experienced. I glanced over at the corner where Regini had slept. She was gone. Maybe it was all a dream. But soon she entered the room, a radiant smile upon her lips to greet me with a tray of morning tea. "Happy day, Sahib," she lilted.

"Happy day to you, too, Regini. Did you sleep well? I don't see how you can sleep on the bare floor. I've heard of some of your people get their rest on a bed of spikes—is this true?"

"It is true, Hajji Cable. It is part of the *initiation of the body*—to overcome the limits of physical life."

"I see." By now I was used to going around naked in the heat of this country, so I started to get up because I had to pee. But I glanced at my pillows. Where the middle of my body would have lain was a drying puddle of fluid. I dipped my finger into it. It smelled like my own semen. Then I saw my pubic area was crusted with dried ejaculatory fluid. I glanced at Regini. "Uh....by any chance, did you happen to visit me in the night—and did we—did we, uh, share an intimacy—?"

"—maybe you dream, Sahib. Some dreams...are magic...and take us away to new places. I, too, have felt magic during the night with you."

I was beginning to suspect something else was going on here. "Yeah, I dreamed alright—and you *were* in it and we were kind of entwined in each other and we made love—"

"—surely it is because I told you I had not been with a man before—and your body listened...and the Goddess Temptation lured us into a dream...where—where our desire—did seek refuge."

As she placed the tea tray down on the floor, I reached up under her sarong and put my finger directly up into a very wet, very warm vaginal passage. She started and pulled back, looking at me with surprise. Then I took a whiff of my finger. "If it was a dream, I think it spilled over into some physical places. How come you and I smell the same and you're still leaking out my male essences?"

She turned and ran from the room. I didn't know exactly how it happened, but as I was peeing, I started to glue it all together in my head and maybe the fact is, that somehow I was drugged and the beautiful Regini

9

did come to me during the night and literally mated with me. At least that was the feeling I had.

I washed up a bit, dressed and went downstairs. There were no women to be seen anywhere. Only the High Lord Limpao stood patiently in his black robe and yellow sash awaiting me. "I trust you slept well, Hajji Cable. I have secured an animal for us. One each. I will accompany you to Kathmandu. It is not safe without a guide."

"That's swell of you, Mr. Limpao. May I pay you something for helping me out?"

"That is not necessary. I am going your way, if I may say so. Come, we must walk to the donkeys who await us."

"Donkeys? I didn't know you had them here, too. I've never ridden a donkey before."

"It was that or a yak, as you call them. The *Sherpa* prefer the yak. Donkey more comfortable."

We walked along. "Uh....Mr. Limpao—"

"—please, simply call me *Limpao*—I do not like the European prefix you bring to my name."

"Oh, yeah, sure...okay. Anyway, I'd like to ask you a question. You see, I had this dream last night that wasn't quite a dream. One of the courtesans of the whorehouse stayed with me but told me she was a virgin and slept in a corner all curled up like a good girl. But the dream I had included this beautiful little thing whose name was Regini—and she came to me and we made very intense, passionate love."

"You call that *love*? Dear man, no, no...it was mere coupling. The sign that it has begun."

"I don't know exactly what you're talking about, but there were sure signs that a real physical something had happened this morning, if we're to consider the liquid stains on my pillows and the young lady's very lubricated and still very wet womanhood." I cleared my throat. "And that's not including the rest of the dream, in which I found myself helping Regini give birth—but she died delivering the child—and then she spoke to me in my head somewhere, telling me that life and death was some kind of exchange or something."

"As I say, it has begun." He was stoic as we walked on the dirt roads toward the center of the village.

"What has begun?"

"You are destined to meet *The Seven Fates* during this journey, Hajji Cable. I saw it written on your forehead yesterday. You have met the first of them. Her name was indeed *Regini*, the first note of harmony when two blend to give birth to a third entity. She is your lesson...she will die to give your progeny life. One day you will have a son who follows in your footsteps, as they say. Only his destiny shall be marked to take a different path, for no two destinies are the same."

"What in the hell are you talking about, Limpao? I know you people are full of superstition and beliefs. I'm just saying that somehow during my sleep this lady came and had sex with me. I'm a detective in my country, and here's how I figure it. She doped me with the soup or tea she served me last night. Then when I slept, she crept next to me, aroused me and we had great sex. That's it."

The ex-Holy Man chuckled. "That's it, Hajji Cable? In the West you make things crude and discontent your-

11

selves in all the *what ifs* of the world. Then you begin to discount the unseen worlds, where all things are formed. I am sad for your kind, for you miss the center of life—and thus in the end, you live without meaning."

"Well, that's how I saw it anyhow." Soon we entered a large stinking tent filled with flies and animals. Two handsome dark-brown donkeys greeted us. On their necks were fastened large plumes of some kind of light-brown and grey hair. "So what's this crap? It's high enough to tickle my nose if I lean over too far."

Limpao laughed. "Do not lean too far or—like life—you shall fall."

Fate #2 – *Initiation*

We traveled by donkey for two days. It was a rather uneventful ride, being jogged up and down all day until your butt's so sore it's numb. But the city of Kathmandu was bustling with energy and people. It was a colorful parade of humanity, animals, merchandise and scenery, for in the distance stretched the mighty Himalayas, culminating in the 29,000' ft. Mt. Everest, which no man had ever climbed. They said one would die from either the elements or the rarity of oxygen at such an altitude.

I told Limpao I needed to seek out a Ghurka named *Bappa Ra* who would help me to my destination. But then the one-time Lama cautioned me and said he needed to speak to me privately. We turned in the donkeys and headed for what appeared to be some kind of opium den, not unlike the dank, smoky place I visited when first I sought out Lei-Tao back in '27. We walked down into this place of great suffering and found a little room way at the back where a little man with a black cap served us tea. "You must listen, Hajji Cable. You are in great danger. Not only has your spirit chosen the Seven Fates to educate you, but enemies sprout up like bean plants all around you. They want what you have. You have seen what you should have not. Therefore, we must fool them."

"And how do you propose we do that, O Swami of Nepal?" I said, ribbing the very serious man.

"By making *two of you*. One will be *you* while the other a—a—I am not sure how you say it in your language—"

"—how about *decoy*—one who looks like the real thing but ain't?"

"Yes, *decoy*. Now, I must get you to *Innioma*, the Goddess of Initiation. Actually, she is also the Goddess of Transformation—for the way to true transformation is to go through and survive the initiations—"

"—damn, but you people sure have your gods and goddesses...what about regular people—are they recognized at all?"

"They are forming souls. They must be left alone. You see, you have already been visited by the first Fate, and that was the Goddess of Fertility and Birth. She came to you last evening. You inseminated her, now she is with child. She will bear your child and perish in the process. And one day, from the spirit world, a woman in the physical realm will bear you a child. The one I spoke of. This is the lesson of birth. Someone is born so someone may die. It is the way of the earth beings. The Fates teach us this...learn it well, Hajji Cable."

"I'm not buyin' a lot of your hokum, Limpao. This delicate, beautiful young whore came to me with her cock and bull story about being a virgin—part of her game, I'm sure—she wanted it, I gave it to her—and that's that. I'm a happier man for the experience."

He laughed. "Exactly how it should seem to you. But not all of the experiences the Fates offer shall be pleasant ones, I assure you. Now we must make two of you."

"Two of me?" I queried the smiling man. We finished our tea and Limpao led me into a back room that was filled with a sweet incense. We stood before a bright yellow curtain. A deep feminine voice called out from behind it. "Come..." it said.

I followed my guide into a darkened space where a figure stood in front of a large yellow candle. Limpao bowed graciously. I followed and did the same. You know, the old 'when in Rome' thing? "The High Lama Limpao speaks to me with his mind. He speaks of your danger." I could hardly see the lady in the semi-dark room. But I could tell she was of medium height and a bit stocky. "He wishes you to become *two* of yourselves. One will be the pulse of you as you are—the other in appearance only—emptied of your pulse. Come..."

I approached the candle. In front of it was a large brass chalice. The Goddess of Initiation pointed to it and indicated that I should drink. It contained a yellow fluid, thick and not too tasty, but I did as she said. Soon I fell into a stupor until I was seeing double. "Now..." the Goddess was saying, "capture the twin out of the shadow world and bring him here to me." In the altered state she had induced, I consciously called out to me and summoned my image. Suddenly standing next to the

Goddess stood an exact replica of Cable Denning, dressed exactly as the guy that was supposed to be the real me!

"We must send him West as you go North into the land of *Shivapuri*," Limpao spoke up.

I don't recall a lot after that except that when I came to I felt a bit woozy and Goddess *Innioma* stood above me. She wasn't all that attractive and had a rather large bump on the middle of her head. I thanked her for the decoy and asked if I could pay her something for her trouble. "You will pay by who I am—for your initiation shall be terrible and unforgiving. But you will survive it. Go now...to the Nepalese soldier. Go to the long dream, the *Datura*." Crap, that was the very name Crazy Jack had used back in the states the last time I saw him! That little son-of-a-gun had been right all along. I didn't know how he did it, but he was spot on most of the time.

Somewhere inside I could tell there was another one of me roaming around in the world. I didn't know how I knew, I just did. Limpao took me to the edge of the city. "*Bappa Ra* the Ghurka will betray you with his laughter, Hajji Cable. Be aware as he guides you to Lama *Daishi*. I wish you good fortune, little traveler."

"What about you, Limpao?"

"I am completed here. I will go back to the land of the *Parasi*, where the mountain waters flow into the river. For all that ever was, is... or shall be...is found in the river. The Great Buddha left us with this...that we travel far but go nowhere except inward...inward toward Nirvana."

"Oh, well, you could've fooled me. Here all the time I thought I was really here on this three-dimensional plane actually *doing something*."

"That...is your illusion, Hajji Cable. Walk well, walk deftly..." Then he turned and was gone, ambling down a street now forgotten in some strange memory of mine.

Bappa Ra the Jokester

On the outskirts of the town lay a military fort, set up by the British and manned mostly by Indian and Nepalese soldiers. When I asked for Bappa Ra, I was shown into a presidio courtyard and asked to sit in the shade. Soon a rather jovial character appeared, wearing khaki shorts, a canvas shirt with decorations pinned all over it and a large-brimmed hat. I figured him to be about forty. "There was a young man from Dover, who looked and searched for a lover, but how she did tease when he got her disease—and now he is less than a plover!" I arose as he greeted me. "Sahib Denning Man—you have been seen everywhere! How do you manage? I am Bappa Ra, at your service."

"How do you do," I said, looking the character over. "How'd—how'd you know my name? I don't remember signing your register when I entered this country..."

"Some come to us...pre-announced, lad. There was a hiker from Perth, who rode on his bike full of mirth—but when he had spilled, he thought he was killed—but only had fallen to earth! Ha! ha! How I enjoy to laugh, Denning Man." Then he grew serious. "What may I do for you, since you have traveled so far from America to know me?"

I was thinking of Toggth and how he had nailed this trip and my journey to Lama Daishi. I was also thinking how connected things were, how people can know one another through an invisible pipeline and when big things are at stake, it doesn't take very much time for things to travel along those lines of communication. I wondered how much "other worldly" help these guys were getting. "Well, I came to Nepal to seek out Lama Daishi in the foothills of *Shivapuri*," I said, checking out the man's glowing almond-colored eyes. "I was told by General Smedley Butler you were my man in Nepal to make that connection."

"And so I am, Sahib. There was an old General named Smedley, who sang some old songs called a medley—but when he was through, he could remember no tune—and ended up shooting a tidley! Ho! Do you like limericks, Denning Man?"

"Not particularly. But I see you do. So when can you take me to see the Lama? I'm kind of in a hurry here. You see, I've got to get back to the states in a couple of weeks or so."

"There cannot be haste in Nepal—and especially with the Lama Daishi—for he cannot speak unless that day is favorable to speak. But let's say...I return tomorrow morning brightly and we will begin our journey to the land of the *Shivapuri*. You will like it, for it is a beautiful land of rivers, hillsides, trees and pretty women. 'I cannot say she was broken, but baring her chest she gave token—that I had the brass to trundle her ass—and soon we both were a soakin'!' Eh? Tomorrow at

17

dawn, Sahib Denning." Then he saluted me and walked away. I made my way back to the city and asked around for a room, but no one understood me. Where would I find a hotel?

No one told me that Kathmandu had no visible street signs. So one fumbled one's way along crowded, dirty streets until one found what one was looking for. And that was that. By sheer chance, I found *The Hotel Nepalani* on a main drag somewhere in the middle of the city. I looked like something the dog had dragged out of the closet because I had to leave all my things aboard Howard Hughes' speedy little aircraft when I got dumped somewhere between India and Nepal. Now here I was in my bare necessities. No one seemed to mind and the hotel management seemed content to know my American identification was intact and that I spoke English impeccably. Well, sort of. I checked out my funds. I still had a lot of dough, by Nepalese standards. So I found me a little clothing shop and bought some decent duds: a pair of dark trousers, a white shirt, a nice light brown silk scarf and a thin white silken jacket, all for the price of about $15 American. I went up to my hotel room, soaked in a tub a good long while, washed up, put on my new clothes and felt like a new man. I meandered down to the restaurant and was pleasantly surprised to find I could get a good English gin and ordered fish with lots of fresh vegetables, lightly steamed. It was delicious. I had also noticed a woman with light-red hair looking at me often from her table where she sat opposite some older gentleman. She wore a light linen dress that was cut pretty low with pretty white buttons down the front. She wore her hair down over her shoulders. From where I sat, I thought she had blue eyes, very red lipstick and rouge on her cheeks, unless she was very embarrassed to see me.

After dinner I meandered into the bar. It was noisy and a small combo was playing while a very English looking woman was singing *I'm Always Chasing Rainbows* with a warm, attractive voice. It was good to hear music again. I had missed it a lot. It was about ten thirty when a voice spoke behind me. "Do you ever feel that way—that all you ever seem to find is the rain? It rains a lot in Nepal..."

I spun around in my barstool to see the same dame who was looking at me during dinner. "Yeah...I think we all feel we get the short end of the stick now and then..."

"Oh! How delightful! You're an American—and a young, handsome one at that," she said, obviously enthused that I wasn't just another dull Englishman. "I've been to New York, but nowhere else. Would you say New York is representative of most American large cities?"

"Indeed not, madam," I said, acting like a guy in the know. "New York is unique like San Francisco is unique on the west side. I happen to come from Los Angeles, California...and know a lot about *its* uniqueness. It ain't pretty."

She smiled and looked me over. I got the distinct feeling she liked what she saw. "My name is Abbey Thurston, Mr.—Mr.—"

"—Denning, Cable Denning. Pleased to meet you," I said, extending my hand. She took it and held on to it for a moment.

19

"It's a good hand, Mr. Denning. By the looks of it, I'd say you are, uh, some kind of businessman—or at least one who does not work with his hands. Are you a salesman?"

I laughed. "From time to time, Miss Thurston, I guess you could say that. I have to sell clients on the fact that they need my services."

She lifted an eyebrow. "Oh...now I am intrigued. But let me guess. You sell...ummm....something like insurance or you follow up on things—alright, I give up...what is it you do that's so mysterious?"

"I'm a private dick...the guy that cleans up after dirty relationships, divorces, murders, suicides and miscellaneous folks who have stepped over to the other side of the rope."

She giggled. "I'm sure I'm not the first to mention this, but in England, 'dick' can mean several things—"

"—I'm in a lady's company, Miss Thurston, so allow me the clarification here—'dick' means private detective. Might probably have its origin from your part of the world...that Dick Donavon Scottish detective series popular here around the turn of the century."

"Oh, yes. Well, I imagine—your chiseled features, square chin, the fearless look in your eyes...you must be like one of those tough guys Hollywood makes motion pictures about? I've seen a few...are your streets really that lawless—and is your illegal alcohol business truly run by those bloody underworld characters?"

"Yep, and then some." I looked around. "I—I noticed you had a companion for dinner—"

She looked distracted. "—that's Harvey, my husband ...not very exciting after nine o'clock, I'm afraid."

20

"Ah, then you're married."

"Well, yes—and then again, no, Mr. Denning. You know how it is, a few years with station and money and travel ad nauseam—and you're ready for some real excitement. After all, my husband is twenty years my senior."

"Why do you dames do it? I've seen it a hundred times—marrying some poor old bloke who lives in a different time and fun zone than you do. So you take on lovers, then?"

"Occasionally...I think women marry for station and wealth—a poor good looking chap is a poor bet when it comes to keeping the wolf away from the door, you know. You're a smart man, I can tell. You already know these things. And, as a private investigator, you must run into the age disparity all the time. That's how a lot of the trouble starts, right?"

She checked me out and spoke slowly. "An attractive but bored married woman meets a mysteriously appealing man in a cocktail lounge in Kathmandu, and—"

"—you got it, sister. So...may I buy you a drink and try my luck? It's a bit lonesome here in this chaotic city all by myself."

"You came alone? Kathmandu can be dangerous for a single person."

"I originally came with others, but we got separated. I'm on my way to *Mt. Shivapuri*, actually."

"Shivapuri? But why? That is such a remote area and mostly jungle, I understand."

"Let's just say I'm seeking spiritual peace, Mrs. Thurston."

"Oh, I see." We ordered new drinks and toasted. "Here's to your spiritual peace, Mr. Denning. How much longer are you staying in Kathmandu? I was hoping we might...find time...to get together..."

"Bright and early tomorrow morning. I'm being guided by a Gurkha named Bappa Ra. Now that's a hell of name, isn't it?"

"What's your room number, if I may be so bold?" she asked, knowing full well that she intended a midnight rendezvous with me.

"It's #216, at the end of the hall on the right."

"Would you like a lady's companionship a little later?"

"Not a bad idea in my book, lady."

"Call me Abbey...may I call you Cable? What a sensual, unusual name. Did your mother think that one up?"

"I don't know. I was just born with it. Those days people didn't talk a lot about how someone got a name—unless they were famous."

I was reaching for my glass when all at once everyone's glasses began trembling where they stood. A large crystal chandelier in the hallway began to sway and someone yelled "Earthquake!" I grabbed Abbey Thurston by the hand and took her to stand with me under a huge wooden transom that divided the lobby from the bar. The earth shook and convulsed. Out on the street we could hear glass shattering and people yelling and screaming as they experienced that special revelation that nothing you counted on is secure anymore!

The trembling finally stopped. I looked around. Much of the hotel was in shambles and some people in the bar had been hurt by falling debris from the walls and ceiling. The pretty little band singer got buried under her musicians when a large column had collapsed above the bandstand and crushed them. "Don't you think you'd better check to see if Harvey's okay? What floor are you folks on?"

"Bottom floor, #102," she whimpered, obviously frightened by the tumult. We slowly made our way toward the beginning of the corridor. We got to room #102 and opened it. But beyond the door, the whole outer wall of the hotel had collapsed out into the street and there was no Harvey to be seen. The trembler had cut off all water and electricity and many of the torches that lit the passageways and interiors of buildings had fallen onto the ground, now beginning a raging fire.

"This wooden city and everyone in it is going to be ashes. Including us, if we don't get out, Abbey. Are you coming?"

She looked at me and then at the empty bed where Harvey would have been. She spotted her open suitcase in a corner, quickly went to it, slammed it shut, grabbed it and took my hand. We ran through the streets amongst the crying, the dying and the dead. Then I distinctly heard a voice calling out to me, in fact, it was the voice of the Second Fate *Innioma, The Goddess of Initiation.* "*This...is the beginning of your initiation...you must transform from the old to the new...beware!*"

Somehow, through all the confusion of thousands of panicking people running helter-skelter, trampling one another, fleeing the falling buildings and raging fires, I lost Abbey Thurston. I ran toward the presidio where I might find Bappa Ra the Gurkha. Miraculously, I found him close by throwing a bucket of water on a little boy burned beyond recognition. "Bappa Ra! Bappa Ra!" I yelled through the din. "Maybe we can begin that trip to Shivapuri now!"

He looked at me strangely. "You are a foolish and determined American, Sahib Denning! All we can pray for now is rain! We have no supplies with which to travel—what do you suggest? I abandon my post to guide you through an impossible, broken land?"

"Yeah, something like that. I'm still on a timetable, Bappa Ra. If you can't come, I'll go it alone. What's it gonna be?"

He threw the bucket to the ground. My hunch was that I was this guy's assignment through whatever organization was paying him to watch over little ol' me. I doubted he'd abandon *that* task, for somewhere in him I got the feeling he was hankering for a gander at the *Fen de Fuqín*, thinking I might have access to it. "So, it will be as you say, Sahib Denning!" he exclaimed through the sounds of screaming and chaos. "Come! We will take a water route if there is still water in the river!"

We searched along the shores of a small river and found a little flooded boat with two oars still bobbing inside. We upturned it, drained out the water and then launched it upon the river, paddling at the direction of Bappa Ra. His prayers must have been answered, because suddenly the sky opened up and a deluge of rain swamped us and we were both bailing water out of the boat with our cupped hands. The fires would be quelled okay, but then the mud and filth of streets washing down dead and injured bodies and debris would commence. The rains abetted a little. Animals and people alike were strewn along the shores as we continued our way up river. But soon we were faced with another unpleasant challenge. The drenching downpours had caused huge amounts of water to pour into the rather small river and up ahead we beheld a wall of water rushing toward us. Bappa Ra indicated that we should make for shore immediately. We paddled like madmen until we reached the shore and scampered out like track runners on the final lap. My hip hurt like hell from the bruising it had taken when I crash-landed on the banks of the *Parasi*. We had run just far enough to avoid the oncoming wall of water that inundated everything in its path, wiping away any traces of animals, people, villages and anything else that was in its way.

Chapter 2

HELL DRIVES NO BARGAIN

By dawn we lay exhausted on a muddy trail, being eaten alive by insects. Down deep where I was barely conscious I was thinking this is what *Innioma* meant by my *initiation* being terrible and unforgiving. Yet she also said that somehow I'd survive it. Life's funny that way. The twists and turns you take by your own will, so you think, may lead to this—an ugly, relentless adventure made up of misfit pieces delivering you to the unknown, shoving real three-dimensional life down your throat until you choke on it because it was too far from your dream of the ideal, or too far removed from the streets of Los Angeles. I had missed New Year's Eve in Los Angeles where celebrants were strewn across my city, drunk, disorderly, loud, filled with that reckless mirth only the true escapees of the world are capable of. Yet in the middle of the night when I hear that melancholy sax playing the tune that defines that deepest inner core of my being—that lonely and neglected part of the self that seeks out refuge—and I step down into the reveling din like I had done a thousand times before, hearing the chattering of drunken souls, clinking glass—and best of all, a beautiful babe in a shimmering gown with half of her tits bulging out, singing Cole Porter, maybe George Gershwin or Irving Berlin. I could hear it now, those haunting notes pouring forth and me closing my eyes and feeling Honey or Misty or June Maye singing out to me her siren song, calling me to that elusive land of pure romance and great sex along with a glass of English gin and a Lucky Strike.

I reached into my pocket for a smoke. But everything was soggy and steamy. I looked over at Bappa Ra who was snoring away as if the insects eating away at his face didn't matter. "Uh, Bappa Ra the Gurkha soldier, we'd better be on our way," I said.

He opened his eyes wide and stirred, then sat up. "Oh! Sahib Denning...you are still alive...good! Then we travel to Shivapuri. Come."

The Living Terror of *Klatha Hum*

Best that I could figure it, the walking distance from Kathmandu to the base of Mt. Shivapuri was about twenty miles. We got up and limped along the ascending trail. The good thing was, the further we traveled from Kathmandu, the less damage seemed apparent from the terrible earthquake that must have ravaged so much of the land. Somewhere around mid-morning, we made our way into a little town. An ancient fire truck stood in the center of what might have been a town square. The faded gold lettering on the side read, "*HMS Kathmandu Fire Brigade.*" But now it was a dilapidated souvenir, a keepsake representing the richest thing these desolate people might have owned collectively. Nepal was poor. Poverty was the rule and hardly ever the exception here in this land of beauty and torture.

Money was worthless here, so I traded my scarf for some food and drink for Bappa Ra and myself. I had

27

bought the handsome silk light-brown scarf when I purchased my new clothes the day before. All I had left on me was some water-soaked dough, along with my papers, my pants, shoes, white shirt and tie and white silk coat. I'd left my hat in the cloakroom of the hotel when the earthquake began. I was wondering about Abbey Thurston. I was sorry I lost her, but the chaos and confusion of the moment made it impossible to hang on to anything except your own sanity—and even that was in question at the moment!

We thanked the people of the village and were about to leave when a tall, husky man with a very dark complexion and wild eyes walked toward us carrying a large snake wrapped around his neck. "Sahibs...travelers...I am *Yon Kahn*. The village people did not tell you there is one other price to pay for safe passage."

I looked at Bappa Ra and he shrugged his shoulders. "What might that be, O snakeman, Yon Kahn?" Bappa Ra asked.

"It is that the white man challenge and be victorious over *Klatha Hum* by honest contest," the man with the snake answered.

I looked around. "And just who is *Klatha Hum?*" I asked, almost afraid to know the answer.

"Come..." the big man said and signaled for Bappa Ra and me to follow. He led us to a shaded spot in the back of the village. There was a wire mesh enclosure with a large pile of stones, made to look like a little dwelling of some sort. Yon Kahn grabbed a long stick, went into the enclosure and stuck it in the hole used for an entrance to the stone edifice. Soon I heard a familiar hiss and as Yon Kahn backed away, out came a very large yellow king cobra! Suddenly visions of *Boak the Magnificent* rushed into the fear zone in my brain and chills ran down my spine. *Klatha Hum* had to be at least twelve feet long and his eyes were black and agitated. He struck at Yon Kahn and the man quickly extended his stick and backed away, stroking the large pet python looped around his neck. The yellow viper chased Yon Kahn to the little gate opening as Bappa Ra assisted him out. Then the big guy with the python around his neck looked at me with a wry smile. "*Klatha Hum* is sacred...*Nag Panchami*...the celebration of the divine power of the king of the vipers...*Naja naja...Klatha hannah*...he will test the true strength of your white man's poor and unfulfilled spirit."

I looked at the two of them, and thought everyone was nuts around me, including myself if I dared to enter that arena against the deadly cobra. He hissed and spit at us, rising up to a third of his height. He stood there, swaying back and forth, those beady wild eyes awaiting our next move.

"You guys must be out of your mind—what am I doing here even listening to—let alone considering—your prankster jokes—"

"—they are not prankster jokes, I am afraid, Sahib Denning. They are offended you are a white man invading their land. Your kind always brings cruelty, destruction, famine, sadness. If we are to continue our journey, Sahib Denning, somehow you must defeat the snake—or die in the process."

Suddenly I felt numb. I couldn't believe this was happening. Then as I looked at the snake, the voice of *Innioma*, the *Goddess of Initiation* seemed to come from

29

the reptile. *"If you do not fear, no fear will be shown you. You will always attract what you fear. This is the initiation. Come to me without fear and I will spare you."*

If this is what the old goddess meant by exchanging out the old for the new, I didn't want any part of it. I just wanted to get out of this land, get a boat, grab a plane, and fly away back home— now! "This is bullshit, Bappa Ra! Tell Tubby here we're on a journey to *Shivapuri* and I'm seeking spiritual enlightenment or something."

Bappa Ra spoke to the snake man in his own dialect. Then he turned back to me. "No can do, he says, Sahib Denning. 'There was a fine viper called Snake, and his bite gave a terrible ache—but much to his bane, when he struck at my brain, it killed the terrible Snake!' We have no choice...you must wrangle the reptile."

"With what?" I asked in a desperate voice. I could see at this point either I enter the terrible contest and somehow subdue the snake—or this would be the end of Cable Denning's Himalayan adventure—and his life!

"Your wits, white invader, your wits...my English remembers..." Yon Kahn snickered. Then he proceeded to kiss his pet snake.

I was glad the locals weren't as enthusiastic about this rather unfair contest in the gladiator ring of the cobra's lair. About twenty natives gathered. There were even a couple of cute young babes, smiling at me as I nodded to them. A smiling little man dressed in a white toga came to me and handed me a bottle of something to drink. We bowed and I smelled the stuff. I took a sip. It was pure alcohol! I gave the bottle back to the little man and proceeded forward towards the gate, behind which waited *Klatha Hum* with his intense black eyes watching my every move. I thought about what I had done to communicate with Boak. He ended up biting me because he had been agitated. If I calmed myself in some way, maybe he would calm himself if he felt he was not threatened in any way. I knew of no other possibility. It was control my fears—or buy a one-way ticket to oblivion!

Bappa Ra let me in the pen and urged me to take the long stick Pappa Kahn had been playing with. But logic told me the snake himself had no other protections except his body and his venom-conduits, which happened to be a sizable pair of fangs. The gate closed behind me. Funny, how alone you can feel even when people are around. Some came to see me die, others came to honestly observe the outcome, either way—and maybe the one young woman who smiled the brightest at me— maybe she knew there were powers beyond the ordinary that we all possess...if we but access them.

As I entered, *Klatha Hum* hissed at me and growled in that horrid, deep-throated snake-growl that I recalled Boak employing to warn me. Now with increasing agitation, he swung back and forth rapidly, trying to anticipate what tactic I would use to try and subdue him. Indeed, my first victory was at hand. He felt challenged. Next I very slowly and quietly bent my legs and sat on the ground about eight-feet in front of him. He stopped swaying and rose himself up until he was all but one-half his length, hovering there above me. Then I did the unthinkable. I refused to look into his eyes. Instead, I put my head down in submission to him. From that point on I was going on gut instinct and it amazed me how sight-dependent humans are. Tuning in other senses was like trying to get a clear radio station when you're out of range. Then I heard *Innioma's* voice somewhere in my head. *"You are brave. Klatha Hum desires your hands...extend your hands to the earth."* I didn't know what the hell she was talking about but I obeyed. I just kept looking at my hands and attempted to think no thought, projecting that vibration to the reptile. In fact, I allowed myself a beautiful morning in Bronson Park and some luscious babe was holding my hand. But I couldn't look around to see her, for fear old *Klatha Hum* might take a bite or two. Then I heard him lunge forward and I was ripped out of my reverie. I concentrated to make sure I had no thoughts, especially not an ounce of fear, but I was dripping with sweat that now poured down my face in rivulets. Now I was back in the snake pen watching my hands. The yellow cobra must have lowered himself, for soon I could see his black tongue go out as his smooth head very slowly approached me, like a lion in for the kill. But I didn't flinch. People outside the pen were breathing hard and gasping, but *Klatha Hum* continued forward. Then a miracle happened. The snake came up to the fingers of my left hand. I could see his nostrils dilating. He flashed his tongue out once just enough so that it touched my longest finger. I remained motionless. Losing interest in me, he did a switchback and slowly entered into his little stone house and out of the sun

Cheers went up from the locals as Yon Kahn and Bappa Ra rushed in to pick me up and take me outside the pen to safety. Yon Kahn removed his snake from around his neck and placed it around mine, which wasn't the happiest reward I could have imagined for such an act of bravery. I was thinking a bit more along the lines of that pretty little thing who had been smiling at me so much. "*Henrietta*—much proud of you, Sahib!" Yon Kahn laughed. "I am sorry to misjudge you—you are good in my book!"

Bappa Ra hugged me until most of my breath was gone. "Never have I seen such a thing, Sahib Denning!"

I was soaking wet and exhausted. Two of the native girls observed this and came over with two metal buckets of fresh water and threw them onto me, cleansing my body in such a way that I could breathe better than I had in years! Or maybe it was the lack of smoking these days. Either way, I was winner for the day!

The Third Initiation

We were persuaded to stay the night and the locals extended a fine hospitality to Bappa Ra and myself. That pretty little thing who had smiled at me so much during my ordeal with *Klatha Hum* sat beside me but when bedtime came, these folks had pretty strict rules about who sleeps with who, so the best I could get out of her was a kiss on the cheek and another one of those great smiles. But I had been about run to my limit anyhow, and sleep came like a tidal wave of sweet bliss.

But during the night not all was to be sweet dreams. In fact, I continued to dream that long dream Crazy Jack had talked about, the *Datura*. I was back in the states and in bed with some dark-haired babe, only we were drinking in excess to the point where alcohol poured over our bodies as we drank ourselves into a stupor and smoked continuously until the room was one big tobacco cloud. She was laughing and grabbing my private parts, yanking on them until it hurt. And then I saw her. Above us near the corner of the ceiling appeared a vision. This time the goddess was indeed beautiful and she approached and hovered over the two of us, watching my body move between the woman's legs. Then she announced herself. *"I am Sinleila, the Goddess of the Passions. Do not become lost in me. My sister, Amorta, is Love...but you have not learned her ways yet. Have my favors, but do not dissolve into nothingness...that is your danger...for in the end, I am empty without my sister's hand holding mine. We were born together, separate, but as one."*

I awoke with a start. The lovely young thing from the village was bending over me, offering me a morning cup of tea and a pancake of some sort. I stirred and told her I had to pee. But she didn't understand. So I got up and indicated I would be right back. On my way to the woods surrounding us I encountered Bappa Ra, who had been doing the same thing, he told me. I continued on my way until I had inadvertently come upon the wire cage of *Klatha Hum.* He was stretched out his full length in the morning sun. "Mind if I pee outside your pen?" I asked of the snake. He didn't answer, so I did it anyway. Before I knew it, like lightning he had whipped over to where I stood with my schlong still dripping. He rose once more above me, hissing and growling. "Don't you get it?" I said to him. "I'm not here to harm you—nor am I particularly interested in getting bitten and devoured by you. So...how about a truce." I finished my business.

The flanges of his hooded neck stood out as those black eyes penetrated my own like darts. "So long, kid, I leave with respect—even though I'm not so sure about the sacred part of you. I just think you heard me—and we were both helped along."

It was January 3, 1933. Bappa Ra and I continued our trek on foot. A few hours out of the village of *Debota*, we began to climb and the heat was oppressive. At the top of a high hill we paused and I looked down several hundred feet to a muddy, restless river, still swollen from recent rains. I noticed Bappa Ra was nervous and wishing to stop for a few minutes. "How much further do you guess?" I asked the Gurkha.

"Oh, Sahib Denning, not much to go. But I am afraid this is as far as *you* go."

My danger antennas went up. "What do you mean?"

"I apologize, but we are late. You were supposed to have died December 31, 1932. But here it is, Sahib Denning, already several days into January of 1933!"

"Wait a minute—the General told me you were here to help me—he informed me you were one of us and I could depend on you."

"He was wrong. I am what you Americans in Wall Street investor's market places call *a double-dipper*. Besides, it was decided some time ago, you were more trouble, Sahib Denning, than you are worth. You know too much, but too little to help the cause of the Führer. He pays well, you know. And Dr. Becker is most efficient. By the way, Sahib, what was all the fuzz about anyway? This is something you wish to die for? I was going to cut you through with my fine tiger knife, but I seemed to have lost it during our travails. Quite a shame...I truly liked that knife."

"It's not *fuzz*, you stupid shit—it's *fuss*—and you'll never know what you want to know, idiot, because *I* don't even know!"

He got that strange sick smile on his face, the one that told me he was about to tell me another limerick. "There was a young girl from Shussy, who had a marvelous pussy—but each time I approached, she stuck me with her brooch—and gave me a great big...*pushy*! Good-bye, Sahib Denning!" With that, Bappa Ra kicked me so hard I literally went spinning and tumbling down the mountainside. About a third of the way down I collided with a small tree, hanging from which was a bee's nest. All of a sudden I was rolling and being stung repeatedly by a swarm of angry bees. I struck a few medium sized rocks on the descent, banging my arms and head, but finally came to rest in the muddy waters of the little river I had seen from the top of the mountain. But the bees pursued me and my body was swollen with bee stings and I had to take a deep breath and submerge my head in order to prevent more stinging on my face. I floated downstream, barely alive. Finally the bees stopped dive-bombing me and I drifted toward a muddy shore. With my last ounce of energy I crawled up the mud bank like a slithering pollywog and caked my arms and face with it. My mother used to use mudpacks for stinging nettles—why the hell not bee stings? I ached all over my body, for some of the stingers were stuck in me and many of the stings had penetrated my thin shirt and pants. I had a myriad of painful welts all over my face. I labored to breathe, then I collapsed upon the shore.

"Are you now as humble as a flower, as simple as a drop of water?" a voice spoke to me in my delirium. I could recognize the voice of that damned cruel Goddess of Initiation, *Innioma*. *"You must be reduced to nothing to become something...you have survived your initiation. Now you may proceed. Do not look back or to the side, but straight before you..."*

Hell, look straight before me?—I could hardly open my eyes. I could feel something nibbling at my feet as I drifted into un-consciousness. When I awoke I had been dragged out of the water and found myself under an oak tree, half conscious. "He is living still," a young feminine voice spoke with a decidedly Nepalese accent. "But he is very ugly. His face and body are swollen. He does not appear healthy."

"Maybe he will not live long. We must tell the Master we have found him. Will you remain, Devi, while I inform the Master and go for help?"

"I guess so. I have never smelled a white man before. They smell strange. Please, Kusum, hurry—what if he attacks or something? Or if he dies while you are gone?"

"He is too weak to attack you. Stay quiet with him. Give him fresh water from that spring coming down to the river over there. Take your scarf and wet it, then remove the mud and wash his face often. I shall return just as soon as I can."

I heard light footfalls rustle away. I opened one eye. Bending close to me was a lovely young woman, perhaps eighteen or so, her dark eyes filled with wonder. It was difficult trying to speak. "Uh...uh...I—I, uh, want to thank—thank you—did something eat my feet? I still—still can't feel ..." The truth of the matter was that I was

37

in great pain and discomfort, but my body had shut down somewhat to tolerate the toxins that were poisoning my blood, and therefore my body had responded by swelling. I ran my fingers over my swollen, bee-stung face. It felt like a horrible case of acne had created boils and festering sores over my entire face and Cable Denning would be a grotesque monster for life!

The young woman with the shining black hair took my soggy shoes off and examined my feet. "You still have ten toes." She took each foot in hand and squeezed gently. "Maybe baby leeches have begun nibbling at your toes...or bore worms have entered your liver through the bottoms of your feet—but I cannot tell, sir."

"Bore worms?"

"They eat a person—from the inside out."

I shivered inside. "You mean that? I could be dying from a lousy...lousy infestation of pin worms?" My voice was weak, croaky.

She smiled at me as I opened both eyes and she dabbed my face with cool, fresh water, using a dark-green silk scarf. "You have good American English. I have studied both dialects. I think I prefer British better. What happened to you that you are so ill and ugly?"

"Someone...someone tried...tried to kill me...as I—I fell down a hillside, I hit...a beehive...and got stung...until I fell...into the water..."

"That is terrible! What man wanted to kill you?"

"...Bappa Ra—playing...both...both sides..."

"I do not understand 'both sides,' as you say—but I know Bappa Ra the Gurkha. He is a bad man. My family never trusted him. He came from the area of Mt. Shivapuri." Then she brightened up. "But even if you are

38

ugly, I still like your American English sayings—yet I prefer British English the best."

"Considering...considering they dominated and educated your race, that's—that's understandable..."

"Oh, but I do not dislike American English. It is hard to understand for me—lots of foreign words—I do not know what you call them—"

"—slang...Americans...famous for....inventing special—"

"—you be still now, please. Oh, I am Devi Botka. My older sister, Kusum, has gone for help, to carry you to *Bhairav Kunda* where you can rest and become well."

"Who—who's there—in—in village? No bad guys, I hope."

"It is not a village. It is a destination. You might say it is a *district*, I think is how you say it. Lama Daishi expects you."

I was rather surprised to learn the lama had advance knowledge of my arrival. But I guessed these people were in touch with other dimensions, and communication through those channels was a lot faster than Western Union. I tried to speak, but my strength failed me. I did manage a few more words before I sort of went into a stupor of nausea and exhaustion. "Would...would you prop me up against that tree? I think...rest better with my head up...and my back against it..."

Devi Botka stood about five-feet five, was very well proportioned and looked quite strong. She placed her hands under my arms and dragged me over to the oak tree. As she came near, her breath smelled of fuchsia and her body had the odor of ripe honeydew melon.

39

"What if you die when you sleep?" she asked curiously.

"Then toss...toss me into the river over there...and let the pin worms...and leeches...enjoy themselves."

"You do not wish a ceremony—a sacred burning on the pyre? Then your spirit shall be purified."

"Naw, I'm not much...for...for...ceremony..."

"Oh...I do not know your name."

"Sorry...I'm—I'm Cable, here in Nepal...better known as *Hajji Cable* or *Sahib Denning*—take your pick..."

She tittered and smiled at me. "That is a nice name. Now...you sleep...I watch for you...Hajji Cable."

"Thanks..." I whispered under my breath. Then I was out for the count, drifting off again into a restless dream state. But for a change my dreams were pleasant and I was back with Noda, Eli and the magical blue light. She was touching me with her blue fingers and it felt good. It was as if her energy shot through my body and turned me on but not in a sexual way, but rather put me in a kind of euphoria that felt sensual but covered every part of me. *"I have told you all things will be revealed in time. You must persevere, Cable...you are not abandoned during these times. Eli, Toggth and I shall be watching and helpful when it is appropriate to do so."* It was Noda's voice and a warm feeling ran through me as she spoke into some deep place where all is hushed within me. And somehow I knew it was her. Maybe there was some kind of crazy set of balances in the universe, so that guys like Bappa Ra, Becker, Hitler, the hidden wheeler dealers like Phillip Wrigley and maybe even the odd Howard Hughes, would get their comeuppance in due course. The dead ones like Sandor, Ravna and his kind

40

had taught me the blood of the world courses through all veins containing both good and bad, the beauty of higher dimensions and the low, dastardly evil of those who have no conscience and are either born with something missing, get badly warped along the way or they're not totally human to begin with. Either way, nobody is exempt from being in the mix.

When I woke up I was lying on a dried grass mat of some kind and I felt an arm around my body just above my waste. I stirred and a soft, feminine voice sighed. The lovely Devi Botka had fallen asleep protecting me. My face and body throbbed and it was hard for me to move. Then I heard other voices. Soon a couple of men came and gently turned me over, sat me up and had me sip a liquid. Even my tongue was swollen from the bee stings, so I spilled much of the bitter juice down the front of my filthy shirt. Then they lifted me onto a litter of some sort, but before I could say anything, I became drowsy and soon lost consciousness once more.

The Mad Lama of Shivapuri

It was January 6, 1933. Days had passed without me knowing it. I woke up in a cool, dark hut where a dim candle in an old hurricane lamp glass burned. There was an intense and pungent smell of sandalwood incense. I saw or heard no one.

Then as I began to focus my eyes, I saw a figure standing just inside the entrance to the hut. He was motionless and he held his hands, one on top of the other,

41

at mid-belly. His white hair was wild and full and he sported a moustache, accompanied by a long, white beard that came down to just below his breastplate. He wore a simple, sleeveless pull-over of some kind made of cotton and around his neck was a string of dazzling orange beads, the size of small marbles. The face was kindly and his demeanor reminded me of Ben Gunn in Robert Louis Stevenson's *Treasure Island*. Yet when the voice spoke, it was soft and medium-high, but very calming. "I felt you awaken..." He stepped forward toward me slowly. His almond eyes shone in the dim candlelight. "I am Lama Daishi. You have traveled far to see me. We had to make you well before we could proceed to speak together."

My voice was still dry and seemed wrapped in cobwebs as I tried to speak. "Lama Daishi...well, thanks...it's—it's good to know you."

"You will *never* know me, *Kunda Dagli*. But that does not matter."

I felt my face, arms and chest. The swelling from the bee stings was completely gone and the soreness that had crippled me had vanished as if it had never existed! "My face...body...they—they're—they're back to normal...was it—"

"—do not exert yourself, *Kunda Dagli*. Tomorrow you shall meet me on the mountain, for you have already arrived—two days ago."

I thought I didn't hear right. "How—how can that be? I'm here...just now."

"It appears there are two of you and we must determine which is the proper personage. I believe it is the work of *Innioma*, the goddess who would be ruler-queen. She is one of the Seven Fates—sisters brought from other dimensions to deal with the fallacy of human kind and help direct their destinies. At least, that is what they are *supposed* to be about. Sometimes...they are bored...and must play naughtily with the sons of men."

"You mean—you mean to say I have a twin here?" I remembered the homely Moirai had, with good intentions, created a subterfuge by summoning forth from her bag of tricks a double Cable Denning. One was supposed to go west, if I remembered right, and the real me was supposed go north to arrive here—in the mountains. So, who got their wires crossed so that we both ended up here?

"Not only that...but he says *you*...are an imposter, and *he is* the genuine Cable Denning—is that not *your* name?"

"Yeah, but—"

"—please, Kunda *Dagli*, tomorrow...we shall determine the truth."

"Just call me...uh, Cable...I like that better."

"Very well, *Kunda Cable.* I will leave you now. Devi and Kusum will attend to your needs. They are my sister's children. You will find them exceptional—and quite attractive in both spirit and body."

"Yeah...I...uh....have met only...the one who slept by me...Devi..."

"Kusum is more business-like, a good balance for the more romantic and emotional Devi." He turned slowly to go. "We shall meet on the mountain, Kunda Cable. Rest well until then..."

43

Dawn was a beautiful dream in the foothills below Mt. Shivapuri. It was the land where tropical zones met temperate climates and the diversity of plant life astounded me as I looked about. Many varieties of trees, shrubs, plants, birds and miscellaneous monkeys all somehow blended into a cacophony of sound. Incredibly colored butterflies, bright Rhododendron grew everywhere. This was also the haunt of the black bear and the snow leopard, so I heard. Great contrasts of green verger filled the hillsides—sun-lit with the early light. Surprisingly I rolled off my elevated sleeping mat and found I could stand and walk with fair ease. Someone around here must be magic, or else I could not have healed so quickly and thoroughly. Just as I was stretching my body to check out the stiff places, Devi Botka entered the little hut. "Happy day, Hajji Cable," she intoned with a softness in her voice. "Now that you are well, you are not so ugly anymore. When I wash and dress you, I find you are a very healthy man...but I think some female bees stung your dangling man part."

I felt a bit embarrassed as I cupped my crotch with my hand. "You mean to say...you...you, uh, saw all of me—and even washed it?"

"Yes, and it began to swell—even more, so I leave it alone."

"That was probably best," I said.

"You have mated with many females—or do you have a mistress or wife?"

"No...I'm not the marrying kind...I don't think."

"Oh. Well, then, again I say, greetings to a new day...and thanks be to the gods you have mended so well."

"Same to you, Devi. Yeah, it's—it's like a miracle. Even my voice is coming back and I feel okay."

"That is well, Hajji Cable, for today I must guide you to the foot of the mountain. Lama Daishi wishes you to greet him there. He is confused, for he has told my mother there are *two* of you—and the one who is with him now tells Lama Daishi you must be destroyed, for you are a *rotang*, a conjured evil."

"That sounds about right," I said, my voice beginning to sound like it's old self. "With the luck I've been having lately, by the time I get to see the lama, I'll be judged and they'll be ready to stone me to death."

Devi Botka laughed. "Oh, no...Lama Daishi, my uncle, would not do that, he is too wise."

"I hope so. By the way, if he is your uncle and he's as old as he looks, how old is your mother?"

"Lama Daishi is four-hundred years. My mother was born five years after, but they are about the same. Kusum is but twenty-six and I but twenty-four years young."

"Now that doesn't make sense, Devi. I don't understand."

"Long ago my family learned the powers of the *Ódeo nectar*. It will keep us young for many, many long years, if we wish."

Now I recalled Noda's special—and only—food, made from some plant in her land.

"Yeah...I seem to have bumped into that stuff before...Noda of the Blue Light. It was another—uh...'dimensional land', *Gwiw Faun*, I think she called it."

Devi seemed astonished. "You have seen Noda?"

45

"Well, as I, uh, understand it, Devi, she made herself appear in a human female form for my behalf. I definitely get the impression she's not a physical babe in real life."

"Oh, I like your American English *slang*, Hajji Cable," she giggled. "You are more handsome the more you talk." Then she reflected. "Something about your voice. It moves me strangely."

"Now don't get any ideas of the female kind, lady. Besides, you're much too old for me," I chortled.

"My poor dead father would slay me if I married a *tinta letto*."

"Tinta letto? Let me see, that must be your word for bourgeois American white man, right? And who said anything about marriage? I was thinking of just a good time in the sack with a young, virginal Nepalese girl," I kidded her. "You are virginal, are you not?"

She blushed. "I am not allowed to speak of such things, Hajji Cable."

Soon Devi and a young man named *Sardi Dolpo* led me up a steep wet trail with the sounds of nature abounding everywhere. We walked about two hours when the forests began to fade back and we were on a rather barren plain with only a few bushes here and there and lots of rock, like I'd imagine a moonscape to be. Devi came up to me and broke her own code and hugged me tight. "I will miss you, Hajji Cable. If you are the bad twin, you will die up here. If you are not, and you return, then will you kiss me good-bye before you return to America?"

46

"You can count on it, Devi. Thanks for everything. You know, watching over me and all. I think I'm gonna like you for a long time."

She smiled and began to descend with Sardi Dolpo leading the way. I had forgotten to ask them what I was supposed to do here on this deserted mountain plain with the winds blowing cold air down from the towering snow-laden peaks in the distance. And except for that whistling, relentless wind, there was nothing. No movement, no bird nor animal in sight, just an endless blue sky above the white mountains above me.

I walked toward an outcropping of rocks in order to get out of the damned wind. Then out of nowhere, Lama Daishi appeared in front of me. "Now how the hell did you do that?" I asked the ex-priest.

"Where word and spirit mingle, flesh is born, matter formed. Therefore I manifest and de-manifest at will."

"I'll be damned," I said, marveling at this obviously very advanced being. "So I guess before we can talk about other things, we need to get that meddlesome imposter out of the way, right?"

"Strange, that is what your twin says about you. Come. He is waiting."

We walked toward a very high escarpment. At its base there was a small entrance. Lama Daishi was slim and could easily fit through the hole in the rock, but I had to bend and squeeze my way through. Soon we were in an eerily lighted cave. It was a kind of amber light that filled the inside from no visible source. Sitting on a big stone chair I got my very first glimpse of what 1933 Cable Denning looked like from a distance. Actually, he was a pretty handsome bloke, about five-ten, cut a pretty good figure and had that unmistakable chiseled chin with the cleft women just somehow loved to trace with their fingers.

Cable Denning II got up and began walking toward me. "Now, let's get this thing straightened out right now. If you'll pardon, Lama Daishi, I think I'd like to interrogate this creep who says he's me."

"As you wish, Kunda Cable..." the Lama answered.

"Hey, wait a minute," I said, "I thought you called *me Kunda Cable*—can't we call this imposter something else?"

"Okie-donkie, as you Americans say."

"No—it's okie-dokie, Lama," I said. "A colloquial slang."

"Don't let him get you off the track—I know the kind. Detectives learn how to spot 'em quick. And this guy's definitely a see-through imitation of me," my other self commented, making me raise an eyebrow. He had a lot of nerve, I thought.

Lama Daishi reflected. "Hmmm...there is, in your Christian bible, something to the effect of '*these two born in Zion where Heaven and Earth come together...like an hourglass where the two halves meet in the center...such they are as one...*' We seem to have a genuine confrontation of differences, yet sameness. Thus my question would be, what does the real Cable Denning know from past, present or future event that the other could not possibly know?"

Suddenly Zelda Blodgett popped into my head. I didn't know why but I had to blurt it out. "Zelda Blodgett. If you are truly the genuine article, pal, then who was she to me?"

My double hesitated and walked back toward the stone throne. "You're trying to trip me, buster—well, it won't work, because I have all your memories, too—and some pretty good ones at that, wet passionate nights when you took her virginity and how you treated her like dirt when..."

All of a sudden my phony double realized he had betrayed himself.

"Ha! ha! you cheap imitation—tripped yourself up, didn't you? But, you see, even if you hadn't done that, you would've lost, Mr. Cable Denning Double. Because the one thing *Innioma* told me that made us differ was that you would not be able to inhabit my *spirit*, lover boy. So, guess what—you're the odd man out—and as much as I like looking at myself from a distance, you're outta here!" I turned to the lama. "So how do we get rid of this guy?"

Lama Daishi smiled faintly at both of us with his forefinger impressing his cheek as if he were in deep reflection. "It is true, unless you know who you are, you cannot *be* who you are."

My double scratched his head. "So, smarty ass, what was the fail-safe secret about Zelda Blodgett I could not have known? Even if I'm not you, I still think you're a pretty haughty son-of-a-bitch—and your shit doesn't stink when it comes to babes, right?" My God, I thought, he even talks like me!

From deep down inside me somewhere, feelings arose and my eyes began to mist. "That...that I actually came to love her...I mean, really love her. Not just her, the woman...but her indomitable spirit set her apart.

And what you could not have known, twin boy, is that my *spirit loved her.*"

My twin sat down on the stone seat, dejected. "So it's that way, is it? But what if I told you I'm enjoying being you—I like being in this human form, even if I don't have a spirit—who the hell cares anyway? I don't see anyone giving medals for having one, at last recall."

"You cannot be two if you are not even one whole person," Lama Daishi weighed in. "You cannot even be a muse, nor suffer the deeper hurts of this dimensional existence, that lift us up, to higher love." With that, Lama Daishi swept his hand up to the throne and in a flash my double vanished into thin air! The psychical-physical repercussion hit my chest like a ping pong paddle.

"Now how the hell did you do that?" I asked, holding my chest.

"Simple. He no longer existed to my mind. So I wished him gone. I sent him back to the point of *Innioma's* conjuring from your ectoplasm. Now you will feel stronger as well."

"Thanks for believing me, Lama Daishi—but how did you know, really?

He looked up to the glowing amber ceiling. "All things here come by semen, ovum and breath...for the birth of *the new man*, and I saw in you much *music* and how you relish music with your heart and spirit. '*Find all who seek, and thereat find all musicians are with him, for he is the new man becoming...*' Your twin could not have done that, nor did I see that feature within him. Only spirit can partake of music."

50

"You're pretty damn clever, if I may say so. If you don't mind, may I speak of why I originally took this impossible trek to see you?"

He looked at me seriously. "I already know. I've known since first you met with Noda and Eli in *Gwiw Faun*, the land of the blue light. I knew you would come seek me out for anointment." Then he picked up his orange-marble neckpiece in one hand and motioned me forward to take a closer look. "There are 144 perfect beads, representing the elements of creation, over which I have command. The *naga sadhus*...the mountain holy ones...of which I am originally, remain in ignorance because they have stopped at 108 beads of crystal. That is why I left the order. I had to continue to grow. Therefore, as for you or anyone else, your covenant is with your Source directly—and never beholden to anyone's philosophy. For philosophy, like religion, is only someone's opinion of how they would rule the world, given the chance."

This was a man after my own heart! Yeah, he saw how the shit scattered once it hit the fan and those that splattered up against the walls of humanity were the vermin that ran the world. "My sentiments exactly, Lama. Now, about my anointment—you see, I was actually supposed to be dead by December 31st—and it is my understanding that anointing someone kind of protects and preserves them—"

"—I cannot help you, Kunda Cable. You are impure and unclean, you reek of the infidel whose ways demolish sanctity and good living. You destroy your body with addictive chemicals, you denigrate women with an unquenchable sexual appetite and leave them when you tire of them, having little or no consideration—not to mention patience. Have you ever asked yourself, what might be *her* needs in your intimacy, *her* pace of coming to know herself? *It is better to be without, then to be with someone incomplete, especially if it is you who limps and stumbles. Can one cripple help another cripple up the mountain?"*

"So that's it? I traveled half-way around the world or more for this? Have you nothing that can assist me?"

But his mind was stuck on something else. "I have seen how my little niece, Devi, looks at you and cares for you. That little tickle in your male organ is all you seek, to release by selfish means into an innocent's fresh womanhood. And you would have her, then abandon her."

I got a little miffed at the lama. "Aren't you forgetting something, Lama Daishi? Aren't you forgetting the responsibility of the other party—that other 'soul' who makes a decision for herself? I've been there and back and seen it a million times, babes want it, too, Mr. Holy Man. Where have you been? Don't you remember woman as the seducer, the temptress? Well, I do—and in the dark of night under the sheets when she gets wet for you because of her own fantasy of desire and passion, no being is as convincing or forebodingly seductive as the female of the species. Yeah, you know why, too—I know you do—it's that deep desire to mate and bring offspring into the world and when girlfriend turns to lover and lover to wife and wife to mother, then the honeymoon's over, Mister, call off all bets—because the guy's gonna be spending a lot more nights listening to the radio by himself, reading the newspaper, playing pool with the boys, drinking, smoking—oh yeah, then someday he's out there whoring again because something's missing at home, something's missing that once felt so good under those sheets and gave the illusion of that intimate togetherness of Mr. and Mrs. He and She would've gone on indefinitely, but one day love flew out of the window because baby cries all night, mother is having post-partum depression and good ol' Dad's just not cut out for those things. So he limps back to where he came from, the dank, smoky lounges he crawled out from under years before, where people shout out their problems in big red letters, abetted by eighty-proof whiskey and a cigarette that's burning a hole in the lady's dress. And then there's the pièce de résistance, some gorgeous babe in a gown so low-cut, that half her tits hang out and the dress fits so tight you can have wet dreams just watching her sing up there with a little combo. But it's not just the sex, but the heart and soul of the city she's singing about—the throbbing beat of an impossible dream etched out of concrete and asphalt, noisy gas guzzlers and electric trolley cars, newsboys yelling from street corners and garbage trucks making a racket in front of your street at dawn...and humans...trying to make heads or tails out of their existence and then that lonely sax has eaten a hole through your sanity. Then it doesn't matter anymore. You know why? Because it's always the simple things that count. Money, sex, a roof over your head, food on the table, maybe a job you can live with...church on Sunday..." I paused, because I realized I was foaming at the mouth and it was going nowhere, just a bunch of noise in a resonant cave with an amber glow. "And in the end, it was all an illusion, a dreamscape, a hologram fashioned out of a cosmos too self-conscious to look back at what it did. So the experiment in birth, love and death ends in a whimper, with all the hoopla for nothing, because in the end, no one really cared. Only you. Only you cared enough to pull yourself up out of the rat-infested gutter you came from and shake your fist at the sky and vow to yourself you're gonna make something out of who you are—even if it kills you!" I stopped. I was dying for a Lucky Strike. "And you know, I think it did..."

Lama Daishi had remained patient with me throughout my tirade. But all he did was approach me, look into my face and smile. Then he spoke seven simple words: "I know you are the right twin", and walked away.

Chapter 3

THINGS THAT COME WHAT MAY

Without a doubt, I was disappointed as hell to have taken this outlandish journey for nothing. Here I was stuck in the middle of nowhere, not even sure how I was going get back home to the good ol' U.S.A. But Lama Daishi was not unaware of things. He knew a lot more than he was saying and ultimately more than I could ever have guessed.

In a few minutes he came back into the lighted amber cavern carrying a folded yellow cloth in his hand. He looked deeply into my eyes. "There is one way to prepare you for the cleansing of your spirit. You have been told of the *Datura*, but few know what it truly is. Simply stated, *Datura* is the complete state of *lucid dreaming*. There you have the opportunity to dream into forbidden lands, enter the deepest places within your being, reach in and pull out those dark and troublesome things that have been introduced into you through the damaged and malfunctioning world of humans." He handed me the yellow piece of cloth. I opened it. Inside were only a few leaves, seeds and flower parts. "You will return to the *Bhairav* district. There you will find Devi and her sister Kusum. Instruct them to boil and simmer the herbs for one full day. You will be administered them only at the instant of sunset. When you drink one wooden cup of the distilled potion, you must be alone in a hut. There, Kunda Cable, you will experience the true meaning of *Datura*, the long and continuing sleep belonging to the Masters who came before us. Be conscious. Do as I say, reach in and withdraw from you what does not belong. Now I must transport myself. I am less and less content in human form. Farewell, earth traveler..."

With that and very little fanfare, Lama Daishi vanished from my sight. I stuffed the yellow cloth into my pocket and began the long, arduous descent to *Bhairav*. I followed the same well-defined trail I had taken on the way up. I was not sure I liked Lama Daishi. He was odd, to be sure. But you know, I didn't blame him for more or less dismissing humans from the scenario of worthwhile creatures. Sure, there was brilliance and talent, kindness and beneficence, lofty thoughts and spiritual concepts—supposedly for the good of the whole—but I don't know, I still had the aching feeling in my gut that somehow along the way humans were a failed experiment and got out of balance with the rest of nature and/or creation along the way.

I reached the district of the *Bhairav* near nightfall. Torches lit the area and I sought out Devi and her sister. The mother, *Simutu,* greeted me with a cautious onceover. Devi came out, happy to see me. She introduced me to Kusum and I told them of their uncle's request that the herbal potion be prepared for me. They seemed to know the routine, so that very night they took the yellow cloth from me and began the long boiling process on a wood fire just outside their hut. Next, Devi escorted me a few huts away to the one I woke up in just two days before. "When you take the *Datura*, Hajji Cable, you must be safe from yourself. Therefore, you will be secured in the *Hole*, a dark place within the earth."

"That bad, eh? So this is my last night as an unaffected dreamer? How about coming over later when everyone's asleep and collecting that hug and kiss you had asked about?"

She blushed in the torchlight. "I have thought of it much. If I do that, I could not return to my people—nor would my mother accept me ever again. She says sleeping with you will make me unclean and no man of my own kind will ever have me."

"Well, we wouldn't want that to happen now, would we?" I said. "Yeah, I understand. So when I kiss you good-bye when I leave, it'll have to be in front of the family and friends, huh?"

"Yes. But that does not mean I do not want to. All day this day I have heard your voice in my ear, calling to me. My body has been trembling. I secretly wish to walk the *fire walk* but my punishment among my people would be—"

"—it's okay, Devi. I understand. I'm just a horny thirty-three year old ex-cop with a yen for a little Nepalese beauty, that's all. Forget it."

She took my hand and held me by the wrist. "But I do not forget it. The woman inside me has stirred for you. I know it well, for she speaks to me of desire. Now I must go, but please do not think it is my will that wishes to, but rather my obligation to my people."

"Sure...it's best that way, kid. Men are selfish creatures anyhow. I'm no exception. I would just want you because your young and lovely, intelligent and innocent. And me—ha! the man? I would pluck your beautiful flower out of some senseless momentary desire to feel you moan and pulse as I enter you between your legs.

It's kind of animal, isn't it—I mean, when you think about it? It's strange. Why are we so driven by these things?"

"You do not know? *Ondolo parma datti*...the way of life, Hajji Cable. I do not think you less, for your desire."

"You'd better run along now, Devi. Thanks for your honesty. I'm flattered that you thought of me today anyway."

"As I shall tomorrow—and perhaps even the day after that. Happy evening, Hajji Cable," she said as she reached up to touch my lips with her own. But her lips would not separate from mine and she pressed her mouth more deeply into mine. Then before I knew it, she grabbed my neck with her arms and pulled me down to her face, holding our lips together with great force. She broke away and gasped with a deep exhale and her eyes widened as if she had surprised herself with her own behavior. "I—I am sorry...you have taken my breath! I must leave now." With that she disappeared out of my hut.

What I wouldn't have given for a Lucky Strike and a tall glass of English gin just about then! I took most of my clothes off and sank down onto my straw mat. Old Lama Daishi was right. I must have a dark, unclean, evil place in me for desiring his niece. But the other end of that was a virile young man with restless balls surrounded by pretty young things whose own thoughts were secretly seeking what I had to give. Why do humans pretend so? I wondered for a while what the herbal hallucinogen would bring on the morrow and then began to drift off.

But what seemed not that much later, I heard a quiet rustling in my hut. I missed my .38 a lot. That son-of-a-bitch Howard Hughes didn't even have the courtesy to toss my bag out after me when he had me jump from his 400-mile-an-hour airplane. My gun was in that bag along with whatever else I had in miscellaneous sundries and a few clothes. Now all I had were my fists. I poised like an animal in the grass awaiting the next movement there in the dark. Then suddenly Devi's face was before me. She had crawled under a place in my rather holey hut. She said nothing, but slipped off her clothing and slid into my arms, her warm body immediately caressing my own. She was breathing hard and I could tell her inexperience made her a bit clumsy, but her instincts were dead on as she pushed her pubic area into my own, getting an almost immediate response from my welcoming male organ. She wedged herself between my legs and kissed me fervently, then took my hands and placed them upon her breasts. Out of conscience I did not want to bring upon this passionate little woman the scorn of her community, so I gave her the last out. "Are you sure about this, lady?" I asked, somewhat out of breath myself wrestling with her in the darkness.

"Yes! Yes! It is too much for me to resist it—yes! I wish to lose my purity to you, Hajji Cable. Please...now!"

Her womanhood was young and tight and when finally I was able to penetrate her, she wailed into my chest so her voice would not be heard beyond the hut. But she was ready for me and she took me into her with a fervency that only reckless youth can maintain. I don't think she reached orgasm, but she begged me to, and without speaking, she urged me and urged me until I exploded into her with all the pent up sperm my body could muster. After about an hour we were both spent and lay wrapped in each other, tangled like a couple of octopuses on a wild holiday. She quietly traced my lips with her fingers and tenderly kissed me several times, all the time smiling with the kind of ecstatic joy only a young woman fulfilled could express. Then she gently pushed me off of her and departed the same way she had entered my hut.

The next morning I awoke with blood on my groin, smeared on my thighs and a small dried pool on my sleeping mat. I got up and immediately found a way to wash everything I could. The taking of her virginity had broken the hymen and caused her to bleed. It was a hell of an experience and I, too, would have that secret smile on my lips all day.

Sheepishly I made my way out of my hut into the brightness of the new day. I was kind of waiting for the other shoe to drop if and when mother found out little grown-up Devi had sacrificed her virginity for the sake of international détente with an American adventurer, who in truth was a down and out private dick with little or no future. Maybe that was why I did it, feeling sorry for myself, feeling sorry for the guy inside there who was trapped between poverty and the big players who run the planet, domestic or alien in derivation. "Good happy day, Hajji Cable!" a bright little voice spoke up behind me. It was Devi, looking radiant and beautiful. She came up to me, smiling. I knew she just wanted to grab me and kiss the hell out of me. But she didn't. "Your brew of *Datura* potion will soon be ready."

I summoned her closer to me and spoke softly. "Good morning, sunflower. Are you doing okay? Thanks...thanks for last night. Are you still okay with it—and no one knows?"

"No one knows, and I am happy. I've not been so happy in all of my life." Then she whispered close to my ear. "I am sore down there, but I want to do that with you again—already."

"Well, thank you for the complement. But I think you've got to act normally so that no one suspects. Otherwise, we'll both be in Dutch. You'd better run along now and pretend none of this ever happened, okay?"

"But it did, Hajji Cable. I would be bold and ask to come with you to America. But I know you would not want me. In Nepal when a girl gives herself with her heart, she belongs with the man she surrendered to. That is how I feel. So now I belong to you...at the very least, in my heart."

That kind of stuck in my throat. How quickly people complicate their lives because of sex, I thought. "Yeah, Devi, I realize how simple the old ways are. I wish it were that simple for me, too. But it ain't, kid, and you know, some of us are on a through-train, unable to stop over at the local siding. I'm one of those guys. You'd better go now..."

She looked up at me with those wonderful glowing dark brown eyes of hers and then walked away. Then I heard a commotion over at the edge of the clearing. A white man dressed in brown khakis with a great white hunter's helmet on his head had entered the compound accompanied by several bearers. He was decidedly British as I heard his high voice sing over the other people he was talking to. Then he spotted me and approached me. I was still standing by my hut where Devi had left me. "Another white man, gracious!" he said in a high voice with a thick British accent. "Charles Band, here." He extended his hand and I reluctantly took it. "So rare this far up, you know—are you on government business, chap?"

"Good to meet you, Mr. Band. No, I'm—I'm basically on a spiritual quest. Just stopping over to go into the Hole."

"Oh, you're an American. That explains it. The Anglican Church of England would not permit such a thing—perhaps sadly, I don't know. But I know the Hole of which you speak."

"You do?" I said, surprised.

"Forgive me, chap, but I am a botanist—strange new herbs, roots, fruits, nuts and the like. I work for a Beecham Laboratories in England. We discover and research new drugs and remedies for relief of human maladies. You know, headaches, depression, high blood pressure, sleep disorders and the like."

"Oh," I said. "So you know what I am about to ingest?"

"Oh, yes, the Holy Men have employed hallucinogens for centuries. But I would be warned, if I were you, Mr.—Mr.—"

"—Denning, Cable Denning."

He shook my hand again. Definitely the guy was an eccentric. But to be stuck way out here in nowhere land, who wouldn't be? "You're Irish, then? Good Irish name.

Charles Band, Senior, my father, came from County Cork. So, we might even be related."

"You never know," I said with a half-smile. "So what is it I should be warned about, if I may ask, Mr. Band?"

"Well, old chap, there are possible recurrent side-effects. You will be taking herbal concoctions of *psilocybin, mescaline, atropine* and a raft of other dissociatives known only to the local shaman or medicine man as we might define him in Africa or the like. British dominion has come with its price. We are increasingly disliked by the natives, so it appears."

"Yeah, so I've heard. But I would assume it makes it easier to communicate with those who have been English schooled."

"Yes, we rather pride ourselves in bringing backward peoples our modern language and way of thinking. Progress, progress, progress. That's what I say, Mr. Denning.' He looked at me with a look of sympathy in his eye. "So, when are you going under?"

"Pretty soon here, I think. The potion has been steeping all night. Is there anything beside the stuff bubbling back up on me that I should be aware of?"

"Well, frankly, we don't know. As you must have realized by now, the reason for the potion is to place you in an altered state the locals call *Datura*, which supposedly brings on a lucidity of the brain while you are in a sleep state. But preliminary research indicates, repercussive events can also cause brain damage."

"Seems to me, Mr. Band, it's kind of like life—a risk at every step, wouldn't you say?"

"Ha! ha! Very good, Mr. Denning, very good! Yes, risk is the name of the game of medicine. We must experiment on many thousands of people before we know the effectiveness of a new drug."

"What about plain old aspirin—been around a long time..."

"Shhh! We mustn't give that one away—or else the industry would not be profitable and Mr. Beecham and your Bristol-Myers would not be able to maintain their high standard of living."

"I see. Yeah, well, I get that one. Use people as guinea pigs, and if something seems to work, shove it down the public's craw at exorbitant prices, right?"

"Perhaps something like that, chap. But I can't complain, you know, I am paid well for the field research I do." Then he looked at me, studying my face. "Are you a drinker? Smoker? Perhaps I should remain here until you have emerged out of the stupor. I do have some experience in the field, after all. If there are complications, perhaps I can be of help."

"That's swell of you, Band. Yeah, stick around if you can. I might even have some helpful information to pass on to you afterward—you know, the kind you can use in your research and all."

"Indubitably, Denning—good show! Sounds like a winning situation. I have been trekking rather extensively. A bit of rest will do me poor old feet some good, I suggest."

Just then *Simutu Botka*, Devi's mother, came out of her hut to greet me. "Sahib Denning, we are all but prepared for your emergence into the Hole." I could tell the mother was all business-like and well educated. If she was almost as old as her brother, then she'd also have been around four-hundred years old! I checked out her eyes to see if she had any clue as to Devi's sinful trespasses of the previous night. She asked me to come aside with her and we excused ourselves from Charles Band's presence.

Then she laid the bomb. "You have defiled my daughter, and insulted her in the ways of her people. But I also know it was her desire. The Fates are strange—and they haunt you this day to include my daughter in the spider's web of both your makings. I shall not interfere, for I have learned spirit's make agreements for things we cannot always know." Then she came closer to me and looked into my eyes, deep-like. "This remains our secret, if you please. Devi will have no consequence to marry after you have left her life—but no one must know, even Kusum, her sister."

I looked kindly upon the good face of Simutu Botka. "I thank you for your understanding, Mrs. Botka. All I can assure you is that my passion for your daughter was sincere—and no promises were made."

"Oh, yes, Sahib Denning. That is the way of the white man. Take but do not promise."

"What can I say? It's that survival-of-the-fittest, domination thing that's somehow written in the blood of certain races, the white race being the most outstanding example I can think of presently."

"How can one like you be so stupid and wise at the same moment? You seek the long sleep, yet you are careless with your manliness—you bring my little Devi into her womanhood without a mate."

"It's pretty easy being stupid, lady. Look around. Most people stay the same, generation after generation, stubborn in their ritual and traditions. Hard to figure it.

Look over there, Mr. Band is the future—even your people will follow suit eventually, when they see profit over common sense. Read your history. Human nature stinks, Mrs. Botka."

She didn't reply but walked away and back into her hut. I rejoined Charles Band. "Trouble among the natives?" he queried me with a half-smile. "The Nepalese are not a subservient people, unlike the people of India when the British Empire extended its hand for health and education to a backward people. Such a shame, it is...I lament them..."

"Yeah, me, too, Band. But in the end its interference from people like you and your corporate, greedy way of doing things that will further increase the poverty. As I told Mrs. Botka, it's the survival-of-the-fittest that wins in the end. Just like the natural world."

"How observant, Denning. Now we see eye-to-eye, chap. I will remain an extra day to see you out of your chemically altered state."

"Thanks, Band, it's good to have someone knowledgeable, just in case, you know."

"Yes, Denning, quite..." He said, and excused himself to rejoin and instruct his bearers that all would remain here at the encampment.

Dream Me To Death, My Love

Exactly at sunset, Devi handed me the wooden cup from which I would drink. A few curious natives looked on as the sun began to disappear and leave its orange glow in the surrounding jungle. "I will hold you, Hajji

Cable, while you take the long dream. May you emerge with my hungry heart for you. Maybe that will bring you...home to me."

I drank the bitter potion down. "Ugh! Thanks, Devi, I'll need all the good wishes I can get. Sometimes I ask myself, why in the hell do I do all this shit anyhow?"

"Why *do* you, Hajji Cable?"

"Your uncle said it would be a last resort to 'cleanse' myself of the evil and dark places I came into this world with—or had adopted along the way. Who knows? But I *do* want to be rid of them."

"The English say such a thing might be *noble*. But I do not know. For all I can think of now is your body in mine and how that longing takes away thought of all else." With her mother and sister looking on in the distance, she tip-toed up and kissed me gently on the lips. "See? I have no longer fear of truth. I have told my truth to you by giving you my body in the dark."

In that moment, I admired this intelligent, spiffy little lady a hell of a lot. Those who would know our intimacy might do well to let it pass from their memory—and those who did not know or guess the reason for the young woman's extra-ordinary radiance that day, would remain forever in the smiling bliss of ignorance.

The three women led me to the edge of the compound. A large circular grass mat was pulled away and there a deep-black gaping hole presented itself. "Beware the Black Scorpion and the Recluse Spider—for they may sting. If there is a *Black Himali Krait* in the Hole, then you will die for certain. It is the snake of death and its bite is always fatal. But we have not seen them lately in the Hole," Mrs. Botka cautioned me.

I got a queasy feeling inside but said nothing. My last sight of a human was Devi's face filled with tears. There was a rope ladder and I was urged to descend slowly. Perhaps twenty feet down, the ladder ended. I felt for solid earth. It was cold and smelled like a marvelous earthen garden. Suddenly I heard a voice inside my head and I knew the potion had begun its journey through my brain and body. "*I am Sinleila, Goddess of the Passions. Punishment for your trespass of experiencing passion without my sister, Love, is Fear. She is a close cousin. Sit your body down and let your spirit float out to meet the experience. You shall not die with this journey, but you shall be altered and not be able to return again to your places of false comfort. Ready yourself for this that I tell you...*" I sat against the circular, damp wall and soon I felt myself being slowly pulled out of my body and watching it at the same time.

When there is no precedent for an experience, your fears go wild and suddenly you feel yourself being ripped apart into tiny little shreds that feel like you but maybe aren't. Yet something holds you together in your head, some kind of consciousness 'beacon' that shines out into the dark, lighting your way into an unknown territory of space and time—and yet not. There are no signposts, no road maps, no street lights and the vast vacuum of nothingness invades you like an invisible plague, eating at your spiritual cells that previously held you together, that told you heretofore you were intact, a whole person, someone you could count on to add up two-plus-two and have it come out as four, or take in a real nice little combo with some babe singing *Nice Work If You Can Get It* while a noisy crowd drinks, smokes and cavorts in another kind of darkness. But instead I was ripped back into my childhood, it was 1914 and I was listening to Ray Bourne play his solitary trumpet through that darkness, playing a soulful rendition of Jerome Kern's *They Didn't Believe Me*, a tune I recalled Misty Sheridan singing to me one day long ago. The music turned me over and under like a hand-plow churning the soil, interring me into the land of forgetfulness, beyond or above memory, in some dimension of new colors, and sounds and lights and strange feelings that lit up my cosmic body like the flashing neon tubes at the *Blue Gardenia*. Incredible pinks, greens, oranges, reds, golds and blues intermingled like confused thoughts in a mind that couldn't think anymore, but could experience only the present moment without looking backward or forward. But even that didn't last. Something went off in me like an air-raid siren and told me I was entering the scariest places in me, and that I had reached the point of no return. My life—whatever it was or would be in that instant—dissolved into nothingness and wholeness at the same time.

When my altered and distorted vision brought me through that point of no return, suddenly I was on top of a huge silver-painted water tower, hundreds of feet above the ground. But one thing was very wrong, for the surface was wet and I was beginning to slip toward the edge. There was nothing to hold onto and as I got closer to the precipice, my body gained momentum and giving out with a blood-curdling scream, I fell to a certain death below. But then mid-way down I was stopped by an invisible force and a bright-yellow dragon's head started singing *I'm Sitting On Top of the World* to me and someone was opening a box of Cracker Jacks and handing me the prize in it, a little pot metal key. Holding the key in my hand, the same invisible force lowered me to the ground slowly, but my feet were numb and I began to sink into the earth. I kept going, down, down, down until I could feel the heat of the lower earth surround me. I bumped to a stop, sitting on a warmed floor of some sort. Then this little red devil approached me and asked me for the key from the Cracker Jacks box. For whatever reasons I refused and the devil and I were in a tug-of-war over the stupid pot metal key. But I won and went tumbling back into a wall that wasn't a wall but a bottomless pit. Again, I kept falling and falling but as long as I held the little key, I knew everything would be all right.

Snakes hissed at my sides, wolves growled in the darkness, until finally I broke through to some incredible paradise of light and sound and color. Beautiful angelic figures in whites and pinks floated by and two of them gently picked me up by my shoulders and carried me aloft. Now we were traveling up, up into an incredibly azure sky, then into orange and green and yellow and finally a color I had never seen before. It was like purple or violet, but not. It glowed and seemed to know me. But as it approached it turned an incredible deep red and entered into my chest. I welcomed the feeling as the two pink angels held me in place. Then a strange thing happened. I knew I had died. Or at least the old Cable Denning kicked the bucket. Yet like under an old snakeskin, there was another—a new—me!

The next part of the trip that damn hallucinogen brought me into wasn't nearly as fun. Now I was inside somewhere, and when I opened a light-green moss colored door I felt sick as floating by me with phony smirks on their faces were Honey, Adora, the reptilian Rusty Wilson, Jane Slaughter with no hands, Ziggy Thompson—all those who had met an early death because of me! I must've harbored a lot of guilt down deep somewhere, and maybe, just maybe, that was part of what old Lama Daishi was talking about when it came time to purge, cleanse and purify Cable Denning. Maybe that time was now. I tried to speak to the women as they floated by me, just barely off the ground. But for some reason, I couldn't get any words out, and as they moved through the door I had opened and continued down a dark hallway, something kept me from following, like a force against my shoulders. Another thing about this hallucinatory shit was that my body felt light as a feather. This weightless phenomenon cramped my physical style, since I was a hands-on, knock-'em-out kind of guy.

Then I heard the voice of Cronus-Gor. I looked around but could only see some dim orange-yellow light coming out of a cathedral ceiling above me. His deep, dark voice rang out: "*Do not meddle, Denning, in my happy covert activities, especially when regarding Hissler, my earth-son and current representative. They should have killed you, but failed, I see. You are slippery—and still have what I want—still have what I want...still have what I want...*" Then his voice trailed away. Yeah, so I still had what he wanted. He was still pronouncing Hitler as "Hissler." It goes to show, all brains mal-function, like it or not, alien god or not...

It seemed no one ever set the boundaries for *Datura*, but I will say one thing...it sure in hell was *lucid*. It was as if my lightweight self was really there experiencing first-hand in the present tense the whole damn thing. Next I saw Joe Lorena coming toward me, smiling as best an alien can smile when in human form. He was Honey Combes' alien sire—his human lover died of complications trying to implant a twenty-million year head-start discrepancy into her womb—and was as good a person as ever I met. I still liked Joe and missed him a bunch. Far as I knew he was still re-doing himself after Honey got killed by someone he knew quite well. Joe came up to me and hugged me. *"Cable, I've been thinking about you...I have discovered you are too advanced of your time...they will kill you, sooner or later...yet we must together be specialists, we must welcome the good ones working for your kind...we need to let them know they are welcome to help us by opposing the manipulative, demonic ones like Cronus-Gor. In our research laboratory, we have documented that your Government already has 224 photographic proofs of alien craft in and around the vicinity of Washington D.C. alone! It will be difficult to separate out which politicians are the demonics, and which are the humans simply being manipulated. The atmosphere around your White House is thick with 'amnesic frequency' that clouds the minds of the susceptible politicians. Beware, Cable, beware...leave this hot jungle land as soon as you can...the danger comes from all sides now...you are living on a prison planet. Coming to your own evolution is the only way out of the darkness. You are dwelling in the forbidden archeology."*

Prison planet? Forbidden archeology? Now I knew I wasn't just dreaming. I was tuning in on Joe Lorena actually speaking into my mind. But how? Of course it

72

wasn't as if he were telling me something all that new, especially that last part about my being in deep shit. As Joe's form began to fade away, I began to come apart. Every cell of my body was escaping from every other and the first-impulse insanity of trying to re-gather them drove me into a nervous frenzy as if I had to scratch an itch in places I couldn't even define—let alone locate! As I began to fragment and feel every trace of me disappear behind the walls of the room I was in, I screamed and yelled and suddenly woke up, writhing and trembling on the cool, damp earth of the Hole.

Someone must have heard my desperate sounds, for soon two young men had descended the rope ladder and literally dragged me up out of my dream prison. I had been in that hell-hole right through to late the next afternoon. My eyes now unaccustomed to light, that intensely bright sun seemed blinding and I shielded my face with my arms as they carried me to my little hut. I must have been there for hours, for I guessed it was very late when I finally came to enough to see Simutu Botka standing quietly in the candlelight, awaiting my arrival to semi-consciousness. She came over and instinctively knew I needed water. She held my head and gently let me drink from a wooden cup. "Thanks, Mrs. Botka," I said, falling back on my floor mat. She looked sad. There was anguish on her face. "Where—where's Devi? I thought she'd be the smile I would first see, not that you're not still a lovely woman..."

Still kneeling beside me, she grabbed my wrists. "They have taken her! They have stolen my Devi! I hear a ruckus last evening, but thought of it very little. This morning I found that Devi had disappeared! Please—

please—Mr. Band told me you were a police inspector in America."

I was trying to come awake and react to this new development. "Now, wait a minute—who would want to take Devi? And for what?"

"They do not know yet she is not a virgin. I am certain Bappa Ra has taken her to the slave marketplace for women in Kathmandu."

"Why Bappa Ra? Yeah, granted he's a no good s.o.b., but—"

"—he has always desired Devi. Since years before. When she came of age, he asked for her hand in marriage. But Devi wanted no part of it."

"So that means they'll sell her as soon as they can because she's a hot item. " I sprang up from the floor and all the blood in my head went catawampus. "How much of a head start do they have on us?"

"Several hours, at least. I will come with you. You are too weak to travel quickly, yet we must have haste." She looked into my eyes with her pretty, dark orbs. "Thank you, Sahib Denning, thank you. I know you do not love my Devi, but for the sake of her love for you and her family's love for her, we do this together."

"Together, Mrs. Botka—" I said, knowing this thing I would have to do not because I had to, but because I wanted to. Devi was a swell gal with a lot of good everything in her. Damn, those bastards!

"—call me *Simutu*, please."

"Alright, Simutu—gather quickly what drink and food we'll need. I'm going to ask Charles Band for a gun, if he has one."

"Most assuredly. He was brandishing just last evening when he drank into his cups too deeply and began to be a braggart."

"What about Kusum?" I asked.

"She and a young friend have already begun the long walk to Kathmandu. We will stop by *Latatu* and find some donkeys to ride."

Well, at least I was used to that.

Just then Charles Band walked up to me. "I say, chap, how are you feeling?"

"A little the worse for the wear, Band. But I awakened to find another twist, maybe even a little worse than my bad dreams."

"Oh, have no fear, Denning. The hallucinogens will come back on you, again and again, until you wish you had never taken the damn brew. Remember what I said about them before you went ahead and took that leap. And they say Englishmen are mad. Ha!"

"Yeah, ha"......I mused....my mind more on Devi at that particular moment. "Oh, by the way, I need to borrow a weapon—do you happen to have a spare .38 hanging around?"

"I personally hate guns. But I do have an old .32 caliber. It works okay and I have about sixty rounds of ammo. You can have the silly thing, if you wish. If it's ever needed, I'm a rifle man myself—high-powered firing accuracy appeals to me far more than that little 'pop' of a pistol."

"Yeah, well, thanks, Band. I could sure use that .32. But I can't guarantee I'll be coming back this way anytime soon. And I have very little money to pay you with since—"

"—take it away, Denning. It's yours. Consider it a gift—in case your nightly recurrences make you want to shoot yourself in the head from the horror of it all."

"Oh, that's encouraging."

"I told you, *Datura* guarantees some dandy recurring dreamtimes, old chap. Try some seltzer water before you sleep at night. It may mitigate the situation."

"How about taking some whiskey or gin with the seltzer?"

"I wouldn't recommend it. Alcohol is a drug as well, you know."

Again I thanked Charles Band, collected my gun and ammo and went back to my hut. I collapsed on my floor mat and soon was out like a light. But this time in my dizzy dream state I was floating in some euphoric place that had a large room with pillows strewn everywhere. On each pillow lay a gorgeous babe dressed in a lot of see-through silk and my libido hit an all-time high. Each one beckoned to me, but by the time I reached a knock-out brunette of my choice, I woke up with Simutu Botka shaking me. "Sahib Denning! Sahib Denning! You must awaken now. The *Datura* has taken you away. We have far to travel this day."

At first light we left the village and walked a good two miles before Simutu turned onto a fork on the broad trail and we came upon a clearing with a large hut, some smaller buildings and a fenced corral. We picked up two young donkeys here and began now to travel in earnest. Just before we mounted our little steeds, Simutu took my wrist again. I guess that was her way of punctuating. "How was your journey, Sahib Denning—your *Datura*?"

"Last night it was pretty sexy. But the original trip was lousy, terrible, in fact....frightening. Let me remind myself never to do that again. I know your brother meant well, but the crap I saw inside me was enough to kill ten men and toss me into purgatory for the next ten-thousand years!"

She laughed. "Oh, it is not all that bad. Under *Datura*, everything is—how you say—*magnified* to help you clear and cleanse. But beware and understand, *Datura* will come again until its spell has worn off."

"Yeah, well, Mr. Band sort of told me the same thing. Just in case you ever want to try it yourself, make sure you aren't responsible for the death of some real fine people in this world, and despite your brother's kindness, I think your old Lama Daishi made up too potent a dose for this gringo here. Those damn hallucinogens could be a lot of fun if it weren't for the fact that we're so loaded with all that heavy emotional crap and those dark and dirty corners inside."

The Tightrope Walker

A few hours later, we entered the battered remains of what once was Nepal's fair city of Kathmandu. It was pretty much a shambles, yet people got around quite well and many buildings still stood, including the notorious white slave marketplace and trading center. Simutu looked into my eyes as we got off our donkeys amid the busy, crowded streets. "I have a cousin here. She will take us in."

"I'm gonna check out the slave marketplace. Is that it—over there? Seems to be a fair amount of activity in that vicinity."

"Yes, and I shall come with you."

"No, Simutu. You're a woman, remember, and I don't think it's safe. Where does your cousin live?"

"Please take care, Sahib. Her house is quite far. You will not find me. I will find you." She came up and hugged me. "Please...find my Devi and return her to me. If she wishes to go to America with you, will you convince her otherwise? She is not meant for such a life."

"Of course. I had no intention of taking her away from her district, you know that—so where will I meet you?"

She looked around at what was left of the old hotel I had stayed in previously. "There...I will be there tomorrow...in the daylight."

I said good-bye and started on my way. The palace of slave traders was located down an alley between two collapsed smaller buildings. I made my way toward it, but half-way down the debris-strewn walkway, three men suddenly came out of the shadows and stood in front of me. One of those men was Bappa Ra. He was pointing his trusty Gurkha gun at me. "Sahib Denning, you are a difficult man to eliminate. How did you survive your fall down the cliff?"

"Luck, I guess, Bappa Ra. Now it looks like you and your two goons have the upper-hand again. So...why did you kidnap Devi?"

"Since she refused my many years of pursuit, I thought I might at least profit from her in some way by selling her off, in her virgin state, to the highest bidder in the marketplace. You know, it pays to fraternize with men in higher places. More than I can say for you. I understand you have taken the herbs of *Datura*. Only a true Nepalese can deal with these drugs. You are as good as dead, anyhow. But I shall not be as messy as before. So we shall dispose of you in a slightly more, how shall I say, *remote area*. It is well that *Jhor* shall welcome you." The two other dunces who accompanied Bappa Ra looked at each other with sick smiles on their mugs.

"*Jhor?*" I asked, knowing I was in for something real special.

"Yes...Jhor. For the English, she is called *a place near forest.* But it does not matter, Sahib Denning. Soon you will have no memory of this world. You see? Nothing matters after that. 'There was an old hunter from Kent, who disappeared from his fine British tent, but when he was found there was nothing left sound—and his arms and his legs were all bent.' So it is also for you, Sahib—your own fate be sealed."

They led me deep into the forest outside of Kathmandu. By dusk we came out onto a trail along the edge of a deep canyon. Soon I could hear a roar in the distance. We climbed up a side-trail and as we came closer I realized it was the sound of rushing water and sure enough, we suddenly arrived at the top of a thunderous, huge waterfall. "There are 277 wonderful waterfalls in Nepal. So few are known to the outside world. But for our purposes now, it is the *Jhor Mahankal* that is close by and most foreboding. You see, at her base there once was a crocodile farm. Somehow the caretakers got eaten by their keeps, and now the hungry, ferocious creatures lurk at the bottom...of the waterfall."

I dared not peer over the edge, but I did—and sure enough, there they were waiting down there in the waters just beyond the spray where the massive falls hit the rocks below. They urged me to a place near the falls' edge. I noticed a stout cable traversing the waters below just barely on the falls' side of the abyss. "It is not enough for you to die without fright, Sahib. So you will have all night to experience the heights you see now and gander at the gaping mouths below—waiting...and when the moon comes up tonight, you may contemplate your fate upon the morrow."

The three men tied my feet securely. Then they fastened another rope from those bonds up between my legs, exerting pressure on my crotch, then threading it up my back until they had tied the other end around my neck. Strangely, they left my hands freed up. One of the men withdrew a pair of handcuffs from his pocket and Bappa Ra undid the metal cable long enough to slide the cuffs—and me—onto the cable. He re-secured the guy wire and with a long pole they obtained from one of the surrounding bushes, they pushed me out until I hung suspended in the middle of the falls, maybe ten feet from the top of the cascade. The metal cuffs bit into my wrists from my suspended weight and it hurt like hell. I dared not look down, for my fear of heights would have certainly done me in then and there. The three men stood by and talked among themselves. It occurred to me that this is the second time in one year that I find myself hanging from a great height. First, Becker had me dangling from that steeple in Chicago—now clear at the other end of the world, here I am dangerously dangling again. Maybe this is just part of that Datura dream and none of this is real.....

Bappa Ra stepped forth to yell to me over the thunder of the falls of the *Jhor*. "Rest well, Denning Man, for if you do not cut through your wrists from your American weight, I will surely cut you down bright and early in the morning. Enjoy the moonlight." Out of nowhere came the figure of *Yon Kahn* flailing a large machete! In a flash he had decapitated the two mugs Bappa Ra was with, but the fast-thinking Gurkha drew his pistol and shot the snake man through the chest. He staggered and fell beside the bodies of the now headless henchmen. Before Bappa Ra could rally himself, another figure jumped out of the bush and clobbered the Gurkha on the head with a large stone. Blood gushed from the wound and Bappa Ra dropped his gun and sank to the ground. Quickly, a medium sized white man with wild eyes, dressed in tan khaki clothes ran over to the downed man, picked him up bodily and tossed him over the edge of the great and hungry waterfall. There was a terrible scream and from my vantage point I could see the crocodiles rip the Gurkha apart as blood and pieces of flesh bobbed in the water in front of the falls. And that was that.

Then to my astonishment, the agile older man, holding a balancing pole with a cane-like hook at one end, began to walk out on the cable! He skillfully hooked my bound and bleeding wrists with the staff. Then slowly he backed up, pulling me along with him inch by inch until we were both at the edge of the falls. Carefully, he undid the cable with one hand while holding me with the other and then yanked me safely onto terra firma. "Bleedin' Jesus, lad, but you live a dangerous life!" he exclaimed with a decidedly Irish accent. "But as I'm always sayin', life itself is but a short walk on a high wire—and all the rest is the waitin'."

I was thankful and exhausted all at the same time. "Uh...thanks, buddy, whoever you are. You're like a Saturday afternoon matinee hero—saving me like that! Who in the hell are you? Should I know you?"

He shook his head...."Nope—I'd be knowin' who *you* are, though." He scratched his short, dark beard. "Now I'd be sayin' without hardly a reservation, we both happen to have the same name—and I'm thinkin' it can't be no bloody coincidence!"

I sat there on the ground, baffled. "What—whatta ya mean?"

"Well, your lovin' mother was ashamed of me, I'm a guessin'. So the name of Cable was seldom mentioned, was he now? And your good Dad died in the process of raisin' and providin' for ya."

I shook my head in disbelief. How in the hell in all the world could a supposed relative of mine show up in the middle of nowhere, rescue me from the very jaws of death and claim to be my long lost Uncle? "I don't understand," I said, trying to gain a semblance of composure. I was in awe of the intelligent dexterity of this man.

"Of course you don't, lad. Let's get you straightened up a bit before the night swallows us up in its entirety." He cut the ropes binding the lower extremities of my body, then searched around the dead bodies for the key to the handcuffs. Soon he approached me and turned the small key into the lock and off popped the cuffs. "You'd better be followin' me this night. I know a small village where the native folk are friendly, if you know what I mean."

Like a father, he took my arm and helped me through the thickets until we reached a small clearing with a few dozen huts. We were greeted by the Nepalese inhabitants with courtesy and hospitality, and soon we were sitting before a fine fire.

"Take your clothes off, lad, and hang 'em on those branches near the fire. Don't be bashful on my account—nor that of the natives. Nakedness is a good and natural thing. As if you didn't know that, the way you've been covortin' with the ladies in your life, I'd wager."

I did as he bade me and through the night we talked. He told me he was my father's only brother. Twelve years his junior, he had gotten into trouble by accidently killing a man one night during a terrible fight. From that time on he was a wanted man in the United States so decided to live abroad, teaming up as a younger lad with the Wallenska family and learning the art of tightrope walking. Since then, he'd adventured around in the world.

But something else was niggling at my head. "Is that the only reason you left the family?"

"No, lad, it weren't that alone, though that would be enough—there was more. You see, I was as surely in love with your beautiful mother as fresh lamb stew with a sprig o' mint. Your Dad had been ailin' a bit—and even had to go back east for a spell of curin'—and I knew if I stayed to watch over your mother—well, let's just say,

Cable, I'd have violated that coveting thing in the Ten Commandments, I would."

"Did she love *you*?"

"I'm a thinkin' that's the case, lad. But ya never be knowin' about a woman now, would ya?"

"So because you were too tempted by desire for my young and beautiful mother and wanted for accidently killing some bloke, you decided to disappear. And you told no one?"

"Nary a soul. A broken heart travels a lonely path until it heals, lad. And so I traveled the oceans blue, and the lands so green and fair. I spent two years before the mast and trekked me bones to the highest mountains until I could no longer breathe the air. So, ya see, at some point it was inevitable we'd be meetin' up, if indeed you had any of me blood in ya. Quite by accident one night—in fact the very same night the earth started a tremblin'—I was stayin' at the same hotel in Kathmandu that you were—the *Nepalani*—and as I was signin' the register, I noticed my own name written twice. Once by me own hand, and the other by yours. It wasn't hard to spot ya, lad...you have the, uh, family resemblance I would be sayin'—written all over ya."

"So how much do you know about me—my mother and the family?"

"Well, as I said, I fell in love with your darlin' mother, what more can I say? She was such a beauteous creature when your father cornered her. I had all kinds of carnal thoughts about that lovely bein' for many a year. But that's all water under the bridge now, lad. Bein' so far removed and roamin' the world as I did, I lost track. And ya know, Cable, the truth is...out of sight and out of

84

mind...and I, too, was soon forgotten, I'm sure of that now."

"Maybe not by Mom. She's a constant person. I wish she would've told me about you." I looked him over. He had the same dark eyes and eyebrows as I had, the same nose and intense, chiseled looks and a body-type very similar to my own. "I mean, there's no doubt you're my kin, Uncle Cable."

"Ha! *Uncle Cable*...never been called that, lad. But if it sticks, then I'll gladly wear the moniker." He checked out my eyes in the firelight. "So beside bein' a private detective and all, an' chasin' around pretty women— what else do ya know about this world you're livin' in?"

I laughed to myself as I peered into the fire. "Enough to know I've seen and heard too much...all of it. We ain't all native to the planet earth, I've discovered. How much do you know?"

"All of it as well, lad."

"You mean the other dimensions, the world being run by demon aliens who look like us—and the *Fen de Fuqin* and all that stuff?"

"I'm not knowin' 'bout the last item on your menu, but to be sure it is that I've seen and witnessed first-hand the risin' world of alien storm troopers, politicians who ain't really our kind—and beautiful creatures as well who come disguised as friendly sexual bein's—but are as deadly as the most venomous viper in these here exotic and mysterious lands. I've seen human dissection, mutilation, experimentation and the likes of which I cannot even repeat to myself for fear of internal damnation. Crap, man, b'Jesus—they're all fuckin' aliens!"

85

By dawn we were exhausted and I needed to sleep. By noon we had both recuperated sufficiently to gain our senses and make a game plan. We ate heartily with the natives—roast crocodile, ironically! Talk about the perversity of things...seemed like Bappa Ra and his kind got their just dues. I felt bad about losing *Yon Kahn*, for in the end he came to my rescue—and valiantly gave up his life trying. I kind of put two-and-two together by figuring he'd pursued Bappa Ra because I was declared 'approved' by *Klatha Hum* and therefore one of the 'good guys'. Probably Bappa Ra's moral trespass by kidnapping Devi Botka also contributed to the manhunt. "So I'm on my way to save a young damsel from being sold off in a sex-slave marketplace in Kathmandu—wanna come?"

"Did ya sleep with her now? If you did, once they discover she's no longer a young virgin, her sellin' price will be diminished greatly."

"That's what I'm afraid of. So, are you coming?"

"I'm afraid not, good lad. My trail leads to other lands, other adventures. But I am nonetheless happy of our acquaintance. And if ever I catch a tramp steamer to the west coast of America, I shall look you and your mother up."

I felt bad. My uncle was the only living relative I had except for my mother. "There aren't very many of us, you know—doesn't that bother you? We're all we have. It gets a bit lonely fighting that battle out there mostly by yourself—I could sure use your sturdy Denning brain and hand."

"I'm fifty-five years young, Cable. I've a little lass in Polynesia who strokes me back and a few other places each mornin' and evenin'. I'll be returnin' to her one day, lad. Thanks all the same—and I do know your sentiment. Seldom is there much room, though, for the sentimental fragments of my family past. I dare not walk there for fear me heart would be pulled back down that lane of memories—and your mother."

"I'm sorry you feel that way, Uncle Cable. I was hoping—"

"—but ya know, do me and yourself a favor. I'd like ya to look up and old pal of mine in Los Angeles. A good man, is he, an Irishman named Blake—"*Boots*" Blake, a retired old lawman. Perhaps it be that he'd be better takin' the place of your absent father. He's an old western sheriff—I mean from the rough, tough days of California. You won't be sorry to be a-knowin' him, lad."

"I'll do my best to find him for you. L.A.'s a pretty big town now. Are you sure you won't come with me? Son-of-a-bitch, it doesn't seem right, I just got to know you a little—"

"—no, lad, it's best we part this way. But it sure is good with the knowin' of ya—and I'll bet your dear father would be cock-proud of his quite unique son." He scratched his head. "Uh...I'm a thinkin' I should tell ya it's also your dear mother, lad. As I said, I was overly attached—and I'd just as best keep that sleepin' dog lie, if you know what I'm meanin'. This ol' Denning here has got a big part of his heart wrapped up in Flo Denning. It's too easy for me to be one of those foolish romantics, ya know. I'd rather remember me lovely Flo as she was, one lovely evenin' just standin' in front of me smilin'— there...in all her youth—'twas a beauteous thing."

I took in a good deep breath and exhaled. "Yeah, I guess there's something to that, too. I must have a bit of that romantic nonsense in me as well. Every once in a while I get the feeling I can actually love a babe."

"Love is good, lad. It's what makes it all go 'round in this daffy world. So don't be runnin' from it—if it's real." He looked down at the ground and then up into the sky. "Like I did…I ran, Cable, ran from love and beauty. An' to this day, I'm still a thinkin' your mother's heart and me own felt linked up together, as if we were twins or the like."

"So what's to stop you from going to her now? I'm sure she'd love to see you."

He didn't respond, but looked down at the ground. "Well, I'll—I'll try to remember that, and keep it all together—inside here. I'm considerable proud of ya, Cable Denning, esquire. Ha! An' you be thinkin' of your ol' uncle now and then. I'll be sendin' ya some strength when you'll be needin' it most. And don't be surprised if some bright evenin' star one day leads me to ya door."

We embraced good-bye and I actually felt tears running down my cheeks as I left the little village. The natives had sent along a guide to help me find my way back to Kathmandu. After all, it'd been a hell of a couple of days!

I spent that night in a cheap flophouse with bedbugs for company. A morning shower consisted of a sulfur rinse in a bathhouse down the way and a breakfast that consisted of a smelly cake of fried fish and chicory brew. I got out into the morning sun and squinted my eyes. I was kind of beat up and looked like a guy who had been lost in the jungle for a year with cuts, bruises and sore muscles enough for several boxers who had just gone fifteen rounds with Tunney. I made my way over to what was left of the *Hotel Nepalani* and found a patient Simutu Botka awaiting me.

"What happened to you, Sahib Denning? You look terrible! Did you find Devi?"

"I haven't gone yet. Your old neighbor Bappa Ra and two henchmen caught me on the way in and were about to toss me over one of your sight-seeing wonders, they called the *Jhor* falls, when I was miraculously rescued by Yon Kahn and another fellow who turned out to be my long-lost uncle."

She looked at me, in utter disbelief. "You were afraid to enter?" was all she asked. "Please, we must go to Devi now!"

"You don't understand, Simutu, I was kidnapped at gunpoint. Then hung from a guy wire over the falls to become crocodile breakfast. But one thing, you won't have to worry about Bappa Ra anymore. He took my place on the menu."

She placed her hand over her mouth. "Oh! How terrible! Now I see. I am sorry. That is why you look so terrible."

"You already said that." I took the .32 out of my pocket and checked the mechanism and loaded the gun from a bunch of bullets bulging from my other pocket. "*Now* I'm ready to go in there and get Devi. You...you stay here." I started to walk away but she grabbed my arm again and threw her body into mine, hugging me intensely.

"You are brave, Sahib Denning. I can begin to know why my daughter desired you so."

"—thanks, but it's time I get this thing done. "

I walked the distance once again between the two collapsed buildings to the entrance of the pleasure palace and slave-trading center. This time no one got in my way. I entered and a big guy with a baldhead and arms big enough to squish five guys greeted me. "I'm looking to buy a little companionship. What have you got for a lonely tourist from America?"

He looked me over and saw how shabby I appeared. "You show money first, Sahib."

I pulled out what I had left. Then he led me to a large room that had candles glowing everywhere and just like in my dream, pillows on the floor with whores of all description smiling at me. I went down the rows and finally found one who also looked like the brunette in my dream. But she did not appear to be all that much Nepalese. I'd say she was a cross between English and native. I motioned to her. She got up and came over to me. "You are desiring my company?" she said, forcing a smile. It must have been hell for these women, waiting around all day to spread their legs for some guy they didn't know.

"Yeah, I think you'll do, toots. Take me to your boudoir."

She led me down a hallway and turned into a curtained doorway. The room was semi-lighted with tallow candles and incense burned in a large brass pot in a corner. A thick red mat lay on the floor and that was it. She began to undress. "How would you like me?" she said softly.

I put my hand up. "Save it, sister. Now listen…I'm here to rescue someone. Can you help—or at least point me in the right direction? I'm looking for a young Nepalese girl from the Mt. Shivapuri district—came in about two days ago."

She changed color and began to show alarm in her eyes. "They are kept below. But I cannot go there. They will kill me. You must pay me and go now."

I shoved some money in her hand and walked toward the end of the corridor where the comely brunette had told me the entrance to the downstairs quarters was. It was a big mahogany door with another one of those big guys in front of it. I went up to him. "I need to see the main boss man. I want to buy."

He checked me over. "You cannot afford to buy. Go away—it is not for you."

"Ten to one I can, buddy." I showed him a handful of dough. He opened the door without another word and I descended a flight of stairs. The place smelled somewhere between urine and perfume as I reached the bottom and cells filled with young women lined both sides of the place. A slick looking Nepalese came up to me. He was short and his eyes were a bit crossed, so you were never sure if he was looking at you.

"I may help you, Sahib?" he said in a nasal, broken English. "I see you are Englishman. You can pay?"

"Yeah, I can pay. Now show me what you've got."

"Show me money first," he demanded. Again, I reached in my pocket and showed him a handful of crumpled dough. "That is not much for a lovely young girl. You cannot afford eight to fourteen year olds. And

91

surely, you cannot afford to purchase a virgin. Perhaps a girl slightly used?"

"Yeah, slightly used will do," I said, checking out every face as we walked. "What's—what's, uh, the turnover rate here? How long do you keep them before they're sold off?"

"It matters not. The very young are sold quickly to the Chinese. White women, very valuable. Nepalese, so-so."

Finally I saw Devi crumpled on the floor of one of the cells near the end of the corridor. There must have been twenty young women crammed into that small cell. One filthy toilet was in a corner and the ages must have varied between six and eighteen! It made me sick seeing the very young sold into an unknown fate. Many, I had learned, ended up dead before they were twenty. If a new master is not pleased with his purchase, he may kill her for that reason alone. Obedience was the one thing the girls were taught. At least it gave them a fifty-fifty chance of survival. But...survival for what? I asked myself. Who would want to live that way, a sex-slave to some strange man who had no other design than to use her for his own pleasure any time he desired.

"This one...over there...the dark-haired one with the big eyes."

Devi saw me, looked surprised, then played the game and looked down to the floor. She was intelligent and I felt she'd go along with me to the hilt. "She is not a virgin, Sahib. But not over-used, either. You can afford her, perhaps."

Again, I showed him my money and he took it all and counted it. "This is not enough. She is pretty—good bulb and tits, Mister—no, I cannot sell her for so little money."

I took out my new .32 and held it to the little man's head. "Now you see, you ruined it for yourself, buster. I'm gonna walk out of here with both my money *and* the girl—with you in tow for insurance. Eat them apples, buddy boy!"

The little man was astonished but frightened. He quickly unlocked the cell door while the other girls looked on in disbelief. But they remained silent as Devi stepped forward and came to my side. "You will die, Sahib. You cannot leave here with unpaid merchandise. It is the rule."

"Well, fuck your rule, buddy boy and show me a back entrance." He did as he was told and unlocked a door leading into another building immediately adjacent. I scurried Devi into it with my gun still pointing at the man's head. We got inside. It was a damn bank! Well-dressed people looked at us as if we had emerged from a sewer below. And I guess maybe we had after all. "Now," I said, turning to the little man with the crossed eyes. "You take me directly out into the street, quietly. If you try to make a break for it, I'll plug you with about six American made bullets. Is that clear?"

He didn't say anything but the three of us walked toward the main entrance to the bank and out into the busy, crowded streets of Kathmandu. I found an alley and we walked down until the shade was dark enough. "I should shoot bastards like you because what you do is beyond reprehensible and one of the horrors of this world. But you're just a poor shit, a cog in a wheel run by the big players. So have a nice nap!" I gave him a good whack on the head with the gun butt and he went down to the pavement like a sack of potatoes.

Immediately Devi clung to me as if she never wanted to let me go. She began to sob as she held me. "I love you, Sahib! I can never forget what you have done! Please—take me with you so I may belong to you for all my life. Even if you do not love me, my love for you is enough for both."

I didn't say anything but took her arm and led her down that long block that took us to the *Hotel Nepalani.* She was so happy to see her mother that she ran to her as the two women embraced. By the time I caught up with them we decided we needed to find those donkeys and get the hell out of town. It wouldn't be long before the word got around that one of the girls was stolen and all hell would break loose looking for us. Life on these streets had little or no value and I knew it.

By dusk we were at the edge of the city and I was saying good-bye to the Botka family, for by then Kusum and her friend had been located and the four women and an armed friend stood with them. Devi pulled me aside with tears in her eyes. "What am I to do with all the love I have for you, Sahib Cable?"

"Save it for someone who deserves it, kid. Look for a man who will be there when you need him. I wish I could say that life was really all about love, but it ain't. It's supposed to be, I think. But people get lost along the way in the things humans do, how they treat each other and the messes they create by making the wrong decisions for themselves that usually affect others. My advice to you? Keep it simple, Devi—and don't look back."

Kusum Botka knew the score and pulled her away from me. I knew in that moment Devi Botka would have followed me the rest of her life, been a faithful lover and companion and lived out her days in that contentment. People have a tendency to under-rate the significance of someone devoting their lives to another. Maybe it was the thing of a young woman's first love, the man to whom she surrenders her virginity. I think its significance is underrated, perhaps even by the woman herself. But it means a lot and will affect her the rest of her womanly days. Yeah, I would remember this chapter in my life, the one that took a thirty-three year old gumshoe half way around the world to a land as strange to him as another planet, one teeming with great populations, sweating in a tropical setting beneath the great Himalayas. As I watched them ride off on their donkeys in the fading light I was saying good-bye to all I had experienced in this country of mysteries and bizarre events—all the things that made up my great Nepalese adventure. I think, in the end, I might prefer my own brand of homegrown mystery, mayhem and murder. You know the old saying, *familiarity wears well like an old shoe*. Yeah, that's where I was going, back to the land of the familiar. So what if the world was changing?

Chapter 4

TWISTS AND TURNS

It was February 11, 1933 by the time I got back to Los Angeles. I'd been gone over two months. I won't even attempt to fill in the details of all that transpired during that month in hell it took me to get back to my particular brand of civilization. In a nutshell, my perilous journey saw me get waylaid by the traitors Wrigley and Hughes—I was still uncertain about Smedley Butler but felt he was okay in the end. I did not receive that anointment from Lama Daishi, but I did rescue the lovely Devi Botka from the devil of sexual slavery...sent her, her sister, mother and a friend back to their district to live happily ever after. Or so I'd like my story to go. All in all, the Nepalese affair was one of those outlandish nightmares that constantly teeter between fact and fantasy, in this case, mostly fantasy. How could one believe all I had experienced? I mean, just to think how close death stalks some human beings is enough to want to make you crawl back into the womb. Besides the treacherous American snakes who betrayed me, there was the genuine article in the person of *Klatha Hum*, the twelve-foot deadly King Cobra who spared me because of—of what? Something I did? Something I didn't do? Or was it simply set to be that way no matter what I did? Then there were the characters right out of a Saturday afternoon matinee at the local movie house...Yon Kahn, Bappa Ra, the magical Lama Daishi or even the ex-holy man who first befriended me, Limpao. Strewn along the way Abbey Thurston came to mind—along with a host of those nearly invisible creatures called humans who live and hide in the shadows of society. But maybe most of all, encountering Uncle Cable Denning was what I'll recall most. There's something about your own blood that calls to you, something that wants you to bond with it, feel kin to the kin, to accept, love and be loved by them. Just before I left, a package containing a bundle of hard cash was delivered to me, but the envelope had no return address. I always suspected it was Uncle Cable's way of wishing me *bon voyage*. But, alas, for Uncle Cable and me, it wasn't to be. He was a loner, like me in some ways, a man who would spend his vitality in this life chasing down that rainbow over the next hill, living on the edge of adventure and danger, being fed by it like a drug that won't quite leave you alone.

And speaking of which, I had been told the drugs I had taken for my journey into *Datura* would come back to haunt me until they were eventually dissipated out of my bloodstream. It was unsettling to experience it, for now and then out of nowhere a lucid dream would pop up, a dream in which I found myself in new and strange territory. And some were nightmares, dark and sinister things creeping out of the dark corners of my subconscious mind, hidden there in the layers of memories stuffed back to keep me from going completely nuts and having to be committed to the local insane asylum. Lord knows, I was crazy enough as it was!

Oh, yeah, and I almost forgot. Somehow along the way, I picked up the inescapable Moirai, the Seven Sisters of Fate. I'd already been ripped through the lessons of *Birth* by the illusionary goddess *Regini*, who would

97

illustrate to me that sex was only the tip of the iceberg of destiny, and for every life given to the world, one must be taken. *Initiation*, a rather homely female figure named *Innioma*, had shaken me to my roots with twin *'me'*s, an earthquake, a deadly game of chance with a poisonous viper, an attempted murder of my person wherein I plunged down a very steep cliff and half way down collided with a hornet's nest, and stung to an inch of my life. Oh, *Innioma's* list goes on until finally she had her last test for me and now I would face her dreaded sisters, *Atropa, the Goddess of One's Calling, Sinleila, the Goddess of Passion and Amorti, the Goddess of Love.* Two more waited in the wings: *Consciousness* and *Death*. But I neither knew their names nor cared at the moment, thank you. My plate was loaded like a lopsided pair of dice on a gambling ship.

Memory Turns a Twist

February 1933 would be a month when Cronus-Gor's alien son *"Hissler"* would dissolve the German Parliament and then proceed to burn down the Reichstag. Near Manila in the Philippines, the world's largest ocean wave was recorded at one hundred and twelve feet—and here at home, the first attempt to assassinate our new President FDR failed and Blondie finally married Dagwood in the Sunday comic strip. Now tell me *that* is an uneventful start to a new year!

During my absence my new secretary, Mandy Simpson Foster, had done a bang-up job of running my office—plus she'd cleaned up the place and my dilapidated bed was even made and a small vase of flowers sat on the beat up dresser across from it. I thanked Mandy profusely. So, on February 15, 1933, I officially took over as captain of my Cable Denning Private Investigator ship once more and gave Mandy Simpson a week off for good behavior. She was grateful and told me how much she had enjoyed the business and she'd saved enough money to rent her own little bungalow in back of a nice house on Bronson, near Franklin, within walking distance of my office.

One of the first things I did was to call my mother. She was overjoyed to hear my voice and that I was okay. We wanted to see each other, so that next Saturday afternoon I did the short walk up the Ivar Circle to Vine Street and on to 2166, the last house on the corner. Things seemed in a lot better shape than when she inherited the house from her deceased sister a year or so ago. I knocked on the door and my mother answered. She looked a little pale and drawn, but her smile lit me up. I took her into my arms and embraced her. "Mom—it's great to see you—I missed you! Sorry about not writing or anything."

Her eyes misted. "I missed you, too, Cable. I was so worried when I didn't hear from you. But then, I knew you wouldn't write. A cup of coffee?"

"Yeah, sure..." I said, looking around. She brought the coffee and cream to the table I could see something had been both draining her and elating her at the same time. I had never quite seen that expression on her face.

"Are you sure you're okay?"

"I'm okay, Cable. Just some chickens coming home to roost, that's all."

I didn't have a clue as to what that meant, but maybe it didn't matter. "Yeah, I suppose as we get older, we start re-running that movie inside us and not everything plays back as we remember, huh?"

"Something like that, perhaps. I don't know. I'm very happy you're here. You look so emaciated though, son....thin and worn."

"Let's put it this way. Nepal wasn't all it was cracked up to be—but in some ways ended up being a lot more."

"I don't understand. That sounds like the kind of jibberish your father used to talk."

"It doesn't matter. It was fulfilling in some ways, and disappointing in others, that's all."

We sat and did some idle catch-up chat. But I hated that kind of crap, so I got down to what was really on my mind. "Mom...why haven't you ever told me more about Uncle Cable? You mentioned him once casually, last Thanksgiving, remember? And that was it. I mean, he's the man I was named after, for God's sake. Well.....you won't believe this—I hardly do myself—but we...he and I...uh...happened to bump into each other near Kathmandu! You see—I was tied up and suspended over a waterfall and he suddenly appeared and saved my life!" Even as I heard the words coming out of my own mouth, they seemed so unreal—as a matter of fact that whole damned trip was beginning to seem unreal.

While I had been speaking my Mother's face turned pale—she was obviously stunned by all of this. "You what?! You met your Uncle Cable—how?—how could this be?—I wasn't sure he was still—did he ask—?"

"—yeah! I really did!—Can you believe it? Small world...eh? Mom....He's a real hero type.....you should have seen him! There I was....helplessly hanging from this sort of cable wire over a buncha hungry crocodiles....and here this stranger appears....dispatches the guy that put me there, and tosses him over to the crocs below—then.....well, *then*....he grabs this long pole and walks out onto the wire like a damn circus performer and uses the pole to drag me back to safety!" Strangely, as I was relating this, I watched my Mother's expression change from complete shock to an actual soft little smile as she listened. "I wish you'd told me more about him."

She looked down. "I'm sorry, Cable—I didn't really know! Your uncle is a good man. He was your father's little brother, the kind with a lot of crazy ideas and boundless energy. But he never quite fit in. At one point, your father and he had a falling out."

"Is that it?" I probed, wanting to know what was really in my mother's heart, because it was difficult for her to look at me as she spoke. "He uprooted himself forever because of a falling out with Dad?" I knew from my uncle's and my talk that there was more to it. But I wanted to hear it from Mom.

"What did you and he talk about? Did he ask about—ah....never mind—No, son," she sighed, "if you must know, he was in love with me." Then she looked up and checked out my eyes. "And being young and foolish myself, I found myself attracted to him, also. He had that Irish sparkle and good looks—a sense of romance and adventure. Your father was more practical and even keeled—an honest hard-working man."

"Were you in love with Uncle Cable?"

It was the first time I ever saw my mother blush. "Yes, Cable, I was in love with him. Shortly after your father and I were married, your father had a bad bout of health because he had worked in a Pennsylvania coal mine and had a touch of black lung. He was sent by train to a specialist in Minnesota for treatment at the expense of the coal mining company."

"Yeah, I've heard of it. But I didn't know—"

"—your father had asked Cable to look out for me while he was gone, and one night he came over for dinner. We had too much of his Irish whiskey to drink. We laughed together until we cried. He was so alive...so much fun. We even danced on the kitchen floor. Then he kissed me. That kiss, Cable, went right through my whole being and I melted into his arms. Your uncle broke away from me out of good conscience because of the decent man he was, and told me he'd best be leaving. But I was young and head-strong." My mother's eyes began to glow with a happiness I had never seen in them before, and her voice became intense and urgent. "I remember pulling on his arm, not wanting to let him go. As drunk as he was, he kept reminding me he was my brother-in-law and he loved and respected your Dad. But as I said, I was young, beautiful, sexy and impetuous. And so we made love...and that night...you were conceived...my darling son..."

I felt a jolt that sent me back on my chair. I thought I had heard it all, done it all and seen it all before. But this! I was nonplussed. But I found I wasn't really unhappy. In fact, seeing that glow in my mother's eyes made me realize that her happiness that night probably lasted her a lifetime. Not that she didn't love my Dad—even if he wasn't my sire. Hell, you hear about these things all the time—but it's always a surprise when it happens to you! "And Dad? Did he ever know—or suspect?"

My mother wiped the tears that had started forming in her eyes. "I don't think so. Your Dad and I had made love before he went away to the clinic. I conceived you shortly after. I loved your uncle so much, I convinced your Dad we should name you after the uncle you would most likely never know. Your Dad was fine with that. He loved you—and if he ever suspected anything, he was too proud to acknowledge that dark corner, and thus we lived our lives." Then her voice lowered and she smiled a glowing little smile. "But I'll bet you look a lot more like Cable—am I right?"

"Yeah, Mom, that's right. In fact, when I saw him, I thought I was looking at an older version of myself." I looked deeply into my mother's eyes. "So, then, it's—it's really true, he's—he's—"

"—*he's* your father, Cable. I'm so sorry if I hurt you by telling you. But you wanted to know. Now...you know..."

I leaned forward and put my elbows on the table. "No, Mom, I'm not hurt at all. In fact, you know how I am about truth. I think you just cleared the air for both of us. And you know, I saw a happiness cross your face I'd never seen until now. I'm convinced you loved the guy."

Again her eyes misted slightly. "I'll never stop loving him. Is he well? He was always such a restless, hard-living man."

I took a long breath and exhaled. "Do you mind if I smoke?"

"Please, not in here, my dear—the odors linger for days."

"Okay. Yeah, he's as well as any man who's been an endless adventurer *can* be, I guess. That first night we met, we sat by a village campfire and he told me he had fallen in love with you and felt it best that he leave your life because he loved his brother as well, just as you said. Of course, what he didn't tell me...was that the two of you had made love—do you think he ever knew I was his child?"

"No...he left the states shortly after that. He had had a violent confrontation with a pretty bad sort of fellow, so your Dad told me. Your uncle was not one to take a lot of guff—and quite by accident, he killed the man during a fist fight in some bar on Figueroa Street."

I was trying to swallow the whole thing and it went down okay. I was hoping I wouldn't have a case of emotional indigestion later. After all, it's not every day a young gumshoe from the ghetto learns that his uncle was really his father—and the poor hard-working man he came to know as his Dad was there by unintended proxy and went to his grave believing I was his flesh and blood son. But there was another quality in me, the one that had great empathy for the human condition, as rotten and treacherous and deceiving as it was. I got up from my chair and came over to where my mother sat and put my arms around her. "You know, Mom, at least you kept it in the family."

She clutched my arms with her hands and laughed and cried all at the same time. "Thank you—thank you, my son. I am proud of you. You might say I loved both men equally, in their own way. I would like you to live with that truth, if you can. In my heart there was no dishonesty."

I excused myself and went out on the painted wooden porch, surrounded by honeysuckle and lit up a Lucky Strike. Years peel off us like old snakeskins and with each new shiny coat I began to see that birth and death, good and evil, lies and honesty were necessary balances for each other. I would never judge my mother for what she had done. Decade after decade we torture ourselves for the sins of our earlier lives. When does it end? When do we let go and stop persecuting ourselves out of moral guilt? When does that shiny new skin, the *present*, radiate out like a glowing beacon from our souls and make us know all is as it should be?

A big abalone shell sat on the railing and I put my cigarette out in it. When I entered the house I saw someone coming down the hallway to my left. "Hello, Cable..."

I did a triple-take. "Zelda? I—I don't get it—what are you doing here?"

She was wearing very loose-fitting clothing and there was an atmosphere in the room I sensed, something that told me both women were defending something, hiding it from me and that they had secretly agreed to draw in their flanks together, as women do, to further conceal something I wasn't supposed to know. Or at least it felt that way. "There's something else I have kept from you, Cable, because—well, because Zelda asked that I should not reveal—"My mother's voice was gentle, apologetic.

"—it's all right, Mother," Zelda interrupted. "He needs to know." She approached me and extended her hand to me. "How are you?" Then she looked me over. "Gees, Cable, you look terrible. You've gotten skinny. You look drawn....haggard."

I laughed. "What is it I need to know? And as far as how I look, if you keep up the compliments, I'll get a swelled head," I laughed. "Yeah, I'm okay, Zelda. I just got back from that trip to Nepal...Kathmandu area, to be more precise. So how are you doing?"

As I looked into her warm, loving and sincere face, some part of me felt I shouldn't be standing across from her, but be beside her, holding her, loving her. She took both my hands in hers. "I'm okay, other than the fact that I'm going to have your baby."

Suddenly the second ton of bricks of the day hit me. "You—you wha—?"

"—I'm going to be a grandmother," my mother said proudly. "I've prayed so long for this, Cable. Please don't put a damper on it. Zelda and I have been corresponding and as a result, we've grown closer. When she told me, I was elated. Neither of us had anybody to bring us through these times, so we decided to do it together."

In that instant I felt like a chump. Where had I been? Here it was, my mother sitting in a big house all by herself day in and day out, Zelda pregnant with my kid—and me gallivanting eight thousand miles away from the two women in my life I knew I loved for sure. "And we've decided we don't even need you to have it," Zelda commented, her scientific voice coming to the fore.

"Wait just a frickin' minute here," I said. "You mean to tell me you get all upset one day and tell me you're leaving me because my life's too complicated and dangerous for you to stick around, right? Then you find out you're pregnant and don't tell me—?"

"—It was September 13th, to be precise," Zelda said matter-of-fact. "Remember my surprise birthday present in Santa Monica—that quaint little room by the beach?"

"Yeah, some birthday present! And you never even—"

"—please let me finish. I told you the next morning it felt like little lights and all, going into and all around my tummy?"

"Yeah..."

"So that was it."

"That was what?"

"The morning after I conceived our child, silly man. He's due in June—if I go the full term."

I stood there between the two women, puzzled, confused, wanting to run on one hand and wanting to take Zelda's hand and rush to the nearest preacher on the other. "Perhaps you two should step outside on the porch or stroll in the garden while I prepare something to eat?" my mother suggested.

"Yes, thank you, Mother." Zelda looked at me as she gave me her hand. "Shall we, Cable...?"

We found a quiet little spot deep in the garden area and sat on a small wooden bench. Zelda took my hand

and placed it on her stomach. "Feel that? That's you and me...us, Cable." She bent up and slowly kissed me. "And that's us, too." Then she began to weep as her mouth curved down and I could see all the loneliness she must have suffered keeping her secret from me. "I just didn't want our baby to wake up some day and find a bullet hole in his Daddy's body—or his own!"

I grabbed Zelda and held her to me and her whole body let go into mine. God, how I loved that woman in this perfect moment! I rocked her gently for the longest time. Finally she turned her face up to mine and I threw my lips onto hers and kissed her deeply, unable to fence in my own emotions anymore. "Zelda—oh, Zelda! Damn, I missed you so...for the life of me, I couldn't understand why—"

"shhhh...!" she said as she kissed me again to shut me up. "I told you I would love you for all of my life. I do, Cable—and I will. But you must know that nothing has changed, especially because of what I now carry in my womb. Had it been just me, I would never have left you. I cried for you every night...forever, it seemed. Then as the baby grew inside me something else happened. I realized I was an adult woman who had to grow up and face the fact that I was going to have a child—a child who mustn't ever be exposed to the violent world of his father—and live an upright life and have a fine education, even a loving grandmother."

In that moment, nothing popped up in my numbed-out brain to say. "I—I guess you're right, kid. But it seems as if everyone's considering mother, baby and grandmother in this scenario—but so far no one's asked me about my take on this—did that even occur to you?"

"By virtue of what you do, Cable, we are—you and I—doomed. I'm sorry, my beautiful, darling man, but you have no voice in this. You can't. There's no way that you could go with any decision concerning your son, as long as you live the way you live...and I fear it is too late to change."

"Son? How do you know it's gonna be a boy?"

"I just know. Don't ask me how. Trust me..."

It was getting on to dusk and we still walked and talked in the garden. That was one of the best qualities I found in Zelda Blodgett—that hours and days went by and I never tired of her. She always brought a positive, fresh, strong attitude to the table of our conversations. It even showed in our lovemaking, which was pure and good and extra-ordinarily potent. "Don't you ever miss the great sex we had? I mean, I was your first, wasn't I?"

She stopped and snuggled her head into my chest. "Cable, if things were different, I would pull you to the ground right this instant, take my clothes off and make you love me every day and every night for the rest of our lives. In fact, I'd wait for the perfect timing, the one when I knew I could conceive our next beautiful child...that's how I feel about you, Mister."

Just then my mother announced that dinner was ready and hand-in-hand, Zelda Blodgett and I walked up the stairs into the house. Dinner was a simple and rather quiet affair. I learned that Zelda was still living in Arizona and she was returning soon. They both assured me that everything would be okay and if I could help out financially now and then it would help them a lot. Of course I would do that. Yeah, me, the stupid, restless male animal who could never keep it in his pants long enough for the dust to settle. I felt confused, duped, put upon and hog-tied all at the same time. I think love gets tested when all the gold luster wears off after sex calms down to routine and you take a real good look at what you've *really* got with a babe, the big picture. I still felt that of all the women I'd known, Zelda was the easiest to be with, and also the most satisfying woman in the bedroom. But I didn't know why. And besides, the tally wasn't in yet. Hell, I was only thirty-three! What kind of crap was I talking myself into?

Feeling overwhelmed, I said goodnight to the two women and started for the door. Zelda followed me out onto the porch. "Will you run again, Cable? Please don't run from me. Even if we can't be together, don't run. I'll need you when the child comes."

I thought for a minute. "You said earlier you didn't want the kid having a dangerous chump for a Dad, didn't you? Well, I'm that dangerous chump, lady—find a qualified bloke to be a worthy father to the lad. Yeah, sure I'll send in the money when I can and take a lot of the punches on the chin because I'm the one who got you this way. But I wouldn't look to me for the role of Mr. Domestic and quiet Sunday evenings rocking on the porch with mom, pop and junior. It's not my style. If you loved me, Zelda, you loved a wild animal...one who couldn't quite be caged and conform to that conventional everyday sickness that plagues the human race with sameness." I paused and licked my lips. I was sorry I had blasted my vitriol at Zelda. What the hell was the matter with me? "I'm sorry, kid...I—I, uh, got up on my soapbox, didn't I?"

"Don't worry, Cable, I won't look to you to play any role that you can't. It's okay…we'll get along somehow. I guess it was that wild animal I fell in love with, the one who was a round peg and would never fit into all those square holes. Which reminds me, I do miss your warm, round peg, Mister. Don't forget me…I'm still a woman."

There was just nothing more I could say. I hugged Zelda Blodgett there on the porch and walked away down the hill to Hollywood and Vine. I bought a pack of Lucky Strikes at the Owl Drug store on the corner and grabbed the yellow streetcar. I felt restless, unfulfilled. Some of those hallucinogens seemed to be popping up in my head uninvited like Charles Band said they would. I had to numb myself. I had a flask of gin in my coat pocket. I needed to go bury myself in my favorite brand of 'fresh air'.

June in February

It was one of those Saturday nights when everyone and their sister decided to go bar hopping, whooping it up with loud voices, booze, cigarettes and exchanged secrets in the dark. *Signorella's Bistro Club* was packed. I thought I saw a shadow across the street before I entered, so I knew it'd only be a matter of time before Becker and his gang would descend on me again and make up for their failure to kill me in Nepal. It was a game. Both sides knew that. Only they were the cat and I was the mouse!

That most attractive young woman singing up on the bandstand was giving out with an up-tempo treatment of Gershwin's *How Long Has This Been Going On?* It was the same song she had sung on the first night we met, before Kathmandu. And this babe was selling the music...again. She stopped me dead in my tracks with her sexy version of the song. I can't tell you how great it felt to be able breath in the music again. I had been on a two-month starvation diet and now I was going to make up for it. June Maye was wearing a very sexy light-green gown with those more than ample breasts of hers about to fall out of the dress. It seemed every move she made had the word 'sex' written on it and her warm, full mouth made me want to go up there on the stage and kiss it between breaths. There was an animal magnetism about the doll. She was the magnet, and I was the part that got pulled right to her. I was standing at that bar taking all of her in. Just before she finished the tune she stopped the tempo and looked over at me and I could swear, she sang those last three or four bars directly to those things that hung between my legs.

She finished and I applauded along with the rest of the raucous crowd. I stood three-deep at the bar. Booze was flowing again in Los Angeles. FDR had lifted the ban and it was to be signed into law come December. But people were already beginning to celebrate and I realized that I brought my flask of gin for nothing. I could actually order some alcoholic libation at the bar. Ah, yeah, happy days were here again!

I knew June Maye wouldn't come looking for me in this crowd, so when she stepped down off the stage, I fought my way through the crowd until she was within earshot. "Hey, there, Miss Maye. It's me—Cable Denning—remember—the gumshoe?"

She looked at me. I could tell she had been drinking a little. She squinted to recognize me. "Oh, yeah, the guy in the hallway."

"Yep, that's me. I really enjoyed your music. I think the Gershwin tune has become my favorite. Especially the way you do it. Can we talk for a minute?"

"Sure..." She took my hand led me down that same hallway where I had met her in December 1932. This time, though, we opened a back door that led into an alley. The air hit me like a cross between shock and stale garbage. "Well, well, well...so how's the guy who dropped his comb in order to meet me?"

"That really was accidental. But I'm sure glad I did it."

"Yeah, that's what they all say—uh, Cable? Wasn't that your name? It's been a long time."

"It has...I was the guy going to Nepal—Mt. Shivapuri, remember?"

She looked me over. "I don't recall you being so skinny. Your face is kind of drawn in. Are you okay?"

"Yeah, the general cuisine wasn't so hot there—and I had some pretty rough times along the way."

"I see. So...Cable..." I could feel she was still attracted to me. "What can I do for you before I go back and warble my next set?"

"Well, to be honest, I was hoping we'd have that dinner you promised me before I left in December."

"Was it that long ago?" She checked me out again. "I don't know. What makes *you* different from all the other guys who wanna fuck me?"

She smiled a wry smile. I winked at her. "Because I'm honest about it. I can feel those same sparks fly between us as that night we met in the hallway. Have you forgotten so soon?"

"You're pretty sure of yourself, lover boy. Well, to tell the truth, I have forgotten. Plus I've had a few too many drinks tonight. I'm celebrating."

"Celebrating?"

"Yeah, six months in this noisy hole. But it's all I got. Sometimes I just wanna run, Cable, get out of it, a million miles away from this stinking city and the stinking men who paw me as I walk by—and all the rest, including the club owner who wants to own *me*, too."

"Okay, June Maye, let's just cut out all the bullshit. I'm the guy who was in a hurry to waste you, remember? Going to Nepal to a Holy Man, a stupid quest that ended in—well, who the fuck cares? I saw you as good looking, sexy and intelligent. I'd love to get under that dress of yours and explore another kind of holy, though."

She chortled. "Yeah, I'll bet you would—you and a hundred other drunk guys out there. I guess I do remember—you were the guy with the clever patter. No doubt it's how you seduce your women. Well, I'm not falling for it, buster. Besides, there's some new guy on the block who's hotter for me than Chinese firecrackers on the Fourth of July. Plus he's got money. Weren't you a poor policeman or something?"

"Yeah, a private dick...the guy who doesn't count, the one you forget in the corner because he came up the hard way from oblivion and that's where he's eventually headed back to. But in the meantime, he lives and breathes and desires like the rest of the blokes in there sucking up the drinks and hoping to get lucky—with one exception, that is. This thirty-three year old gum-shoe has seen too much to stay alive for much longer in this world, so he desperately limps into a dive like yours on a crowded Saturday night and sees this babe whose chemistry feels like a hot night in Rio during the Carnivale. Then he wants her. He wants to get lost with her, *in* her...even if she's married to the Goddess of Music—because he needs to forget the banging at that door in his head that tells him time is almost up and you gotta grab what you can while you can as long as it fits—and you fit, lady, you fit because you're falling the long fall, too, you're pulled to my groin and my kisses because it's what it was supposed to be, a one-way ticket down the upstairs...something you can't forget because it was always branded on your brain and when you really think about it, I mean really let it happen inside you, you can feel your breasts swell and your pussy pulse because he's the other part of you, the one you never had but always suspected existed, and that he might come in one night like me and walk into your life, walk into your lips and take you down with him into that land of sensual nirvana with no questions asked." Then I calmed. "You said it yourself that night, that maybe it was fate—and things happen when you're not looking. And then suddenly, he's here, looking right at you."

June Maye stood there, her eyes wide with wonder. "I—I have never...never heard anyone talk like that. But I'm afraid to go there, Cable. I may seem tough and a bit callous to you, but I'm a woman and have a heart, too. Don't force me down a pathway just because it vents your restless balls and discontentment with your own life. Maybe I can feel passion for you, I don't know. But somewhere along the way a girl wants security, if not love. You don't offer me either, as I see it. And I'm not getting any younger. How many good singing years do you think I have left, Cable? A woman's best years are brief. I don't want to lose mine."

The babe made sense. I was being selfish and pushy. "You're right, June...it's those restless balls and a pull from my gut to take you in my arms and press your body into mine until all I can feel is us."

"So why don't you?" she said, looking up at me with almost innocent eyes. She stepped toward me and lifted her mouth toward mine.

I enveloped her with my arms and our lips met like strikes of lightning in the dark. We both felt a jolt of that electricity go through us as though suddenly we were the conduits for the city power station. She pulled back, her eyes wide with surprise. Then she let out a big sigh. "Now...can you feel what I was trying to tell you?"

"Yes! yes!," she exclaimed under her breath. "I've got to get back now—but can you stick around a while?"

"Well, I don't know, I get more expensive after midnight, you know."

She laughed. "I think I'm going to like you lots, Mister. Will you stay?"

"What about that dinner sometime?"

"Fuck the dinner—take me home when I'm finished tonight. You just started something you need to finish, buster."

I laughed. "You know what they say about first times..."

"No, what do they say about first times?"

"Some begin kinda slow and take time to grow, some go off like a stick of dynamite—"

"—too late, Cable, you already lit the fuse." Then she walked off, leaving me there in the alley with a bulge in my pants and a big yen to light up and have another drink at the bar.

When June began her next song, I was poised at the bar, my eyes glued to this lovely young thing and her bulging breasts. And now I knew what was under that wonderful gown of hers. It was one of the sexiest versions of *Taking a Chance On Love* I'd ever heard and I knew exactly where it was coming from. In that moment, her loneliness was my own, her breath the same one I was breathing. Two lost souls had found each other. *'Things are mending now, there'll be a happy ending now...on the ball again, I'm riding for a fall again, I'll give my all again, taking a chance on love'* she sang and melted into my tightening balls. Now I knew *she* knew. As she glided her way through the tune, I kept hearing another voice chattering in my ear. *"It's me, Cable, Sinleila, the Goddess of Passion. Come know me...but don't say I didn't warn you. Without my sister, Amorti, the Goddess of Love, I will abandon you one day. Take the lesson well. Learn the layers of ecstasy that must one day tear you apart...and that they will. Beware, Cable...beware..."*

Just as June finished I heard a voice next to me that had an unmistakably familiar accent. "She singss viz a lot of...sensuality, don't you sink? Too bad she iss a young Chewish girl."

I turned to look into the face of Helmut Becker. "Becker...I kind of figured you'd turn up like a bad penny sooner or later—but always too soon. Jewish or not, she delivers the song, and that's what counts."

"Speaking off *delifering*, Herr Denning, I almost lamented our people's failure to, how iss it your quaint language sayss, 'do you in' during your sojourn in Nepal. But you are bos lucky und cleffer. But as it turned out, ve don't vant you terminated at zis time. My higher-ups insist on extracting ze knowledge off ze you-know-vat from you still. So...you see...sings change. Und our Führer iss now in complete power in Deutschlandt."

"Yeah, so I noticed—he managed to eliminate the Parliament and burn down the Reichstag all in just one month—a fast mover, I'd say."

"Ya..." He chuckled, glancing up to the stage where June had launched into a fast-tempo version of *Mean to Me*. "You Americans und your foolish, sentimental music. Mostly written by Chews, a pity. But zose words...do you sink I am mean to you, Herr Denning?" he chuckled.

"You could say that, Becker—but you know, as they say, it's not over until the fat lady cries."

"I don't know zat one. You stupid Americans, so full off colloquialisms—one day you vill run out of zem, you realize. Zen vere vill you be?"

"It's kind of like pay-as-you-go, Becker, you make up what fits the moment. You know, like *your* little moment in history. As soon as your little alien madman bites the dust, some other power-mad dummy will come along to take his place in some other country."

"Ve vill rule a sousandt yearss, Herr Denning. I find your rude comments distasteful. You are a little cog in our veel off fortune und domination ofer inferior races. Especially ze veak, mixed races—zey vill be our slaves und do our bidding. Vell, in fact, zey already do—only it iss yet to be implemented sroughout ze vorld—vun day, vait und see, just vait und see."

"Look around, Becker, humans are little electrical machines, that run on willpower and chemistry—do you think you can subdue a whole race of these beings?"

"Ah...to be sure...becausse ve haff help. Ze greater powers that lay beyond efen ze Führer...beyond ze *Oculus*....and more influential zan zose meddlesome Roman Casolics at ze Vatican."

I looked around the crowded, noisy room. No one had a clue that we were talking about them, their fates and the terrible creatures that rule the planet Earth. And they didn't care. People only really cared about themselves, their own piddley problems—I was surprised everyone wasn't cross-eyed! Nope they were concerned about who sleeps in their bed, how the rent gets paid, the food gets on the table. "Who was it—uh, P.T. Barnum, I think, who said *'there's a sucker born every minute'*. But the other side of that coin, Becker, is you can't fool all the people all the time. And you forgot one important element that I've discovered along the way."

"Ya? Und vat might zat be?"

"Even if humans were altered down twenty thousand years ago—I believe there is a universal mandate that everything evolves back to its original form and potential. Add to that, that *nothing* remains the same—and so guys like you and your kind will eventually be plowed under by the next wave who will be stronger and more intelligent."

"You are too smart, Herr Denning. As I said vun day to you, privately I might concur viz you, but politically I cannot." He put his hand forward. I shook it. "Vill you valk me outside?"

"No tricks? I wouldn't want to lose my amateur standing with you guys now, would I?"

"No tricks. I simply vish to convey somesing to you in a more respectable—und private—environment."

I followed him out the door, my new .38 revolver pointing at him through my trench coat. We got to the sidewalk and I stopped. "This is as far as I go, old chap."

He took my arm and led me aside. "Everysing evil iss connected, just as everysing goodt iss connected—if, as you Americanss say in cowboy language, 'you get my drift.' It appearss a new evil hass appeared on our horizon zat vishes to influence ze Asian populations. It is my personal view zat ze Japanese vill appear to choin Germany as an ally at some juncture—zen turn aroundt und vant ze vorld for zemselves."

"So...do you have a clue as to who these critters might be? After Cronus-Gor and his *Oculus* buddies, I didn't think it got any worse."

"Oh, ya....singss are destined to become vorse—before zey can get besser. At least zat iss an old fairy tale you Americanss tell your children. But ve bos know, Herr Denning, such is not ze case now, iss it?"

I took a deep breath and let all the air out. I put a cigarette to my lips and Becker lit it for me. "I don't like you, Becker, but I suppose you're better than nothing. At least you can communicate."

He put his lighter away. "Zat iss unfortunate. For I am actually fond off you, efen if I killed you right here, right now...I vould alvays regardt you as an exceptional survivor viz a goodt head on hiss shoulders—a charming example off ze male of our species, valking among ze minefieldt off beautiful vomen who are attracted to you, if for no ozer reasson zan *dangerous passion*, shall ve say?"

"So *are* you?"

"Am I vat?"

"Going to kill me here and now?"

He laughed heartily. "Nein, no, Herr Denning!—you are more valuable to us now zan efer before. Ze good news iss, zat ve haff devissedt *new* messods off *extracting specific information* from ze human brain."

"That's good news? My, how times change, Becker. And here I thought you might be inviting me to an Easter Party or something."

He laughed again. "How you are able to be humorous at a time like zis surpasses my ability to decipher your motivations."

"Awww....just chalk it up to stupidity. Now, is that what you wanted to tell me confidentially?"

"Ya...for now...off ze record, ze *neural extractor* vill begin to be employedt in about sree months' time. Zen, I am afraid, *your* time vill finally be up. But it has been a noble contest, has it not?"

"I suppose you can look at it that way. Yeah, me against a thousand of your kind—noble?...or maybe just a stupid—"

"—Cable?" a feminine voice called out from the doorway of the club. It was June. "I'm finished up now..."

"Okay, June, I'll be right there, thanks."

Becker looked June Maye over. "You see vat I mean? How do you attract such lovely creatures who—who must in time...desire you?"

121

"Just clever patter, Becker. I'm really a phony with some good lines. You see, I talk fast and hit 'em where they live. That's it. Good night, Dr. Becker," I said and walked away.

Neither June nor I had an automobile, so we took the streetcar out to her place. She lived in a cozy little bungalow up on North Wilton Place, not too far from my Franklin office. On the ride to her place she didn't say much but for whatever reasons, held my hand tight. Finally she spoke. "That man you were talking to—a friend? I'd never seen him in the club before."

"Not exactly a friend. You might say an uninvited business associate."

"Oh. I got a creepy feeling just looking at him."

"As well you should. He's a dangerous man."

"Are you in some kind of danger, Cable?"

"You might say that."

"Care to explain?"

"Can we wait until we get to your place?"

"Sure."

Four large stairs led up to an over-sized hardwood door. She put the key in the lock and we stepped into a cozy 12' x 12' living room. A large green and beige sofa was up against the west wall with a coffee table in front of it. Pictures of beautiful classic nudes lined her walls, except for one. It was a painting of a little girl wandering in the forest like Little Red Riding Hood. But this little girl was being followed by happy little cherubs floating above her head, and fireflies darted around in front of her. A matching comfy chair sat across from the sofa on the other side of the room and a tiny kitchen smelled of coffee grounds and parsley. "Well, this is it, Investigator Denning. Does it pass the inspector's test?"

"I don't know yet, I've got to check out the bedroom first," I kidded her. She smiled, took my hand and led me into her bedroom. It smelled like her, the savage beauty of her skin when I kissed her earlier in the evening and smelled the nape of her lovely neck. It was a large double bed with a light green comforter and one very large matching pillow. "Well, so far so good. But I only see one pillow."

"Who says you're staying overnight, big boy?" she said.

"I stand corrected. I guess that was a fool's assumption."

Then she slowly put her arms around my waist and looked into my eyes. "Cable...don't get the wrong impression. I don't take guys home. You're the exception, okay?"

"Okay. I feel privileged."

"You should." Then she began unbuttoning my shirt and loosened my tie. "What do you like to drink?"

"Good English gin, if you've got it."

"I'm not sure it's English, but I've got some gin."

She took my shirt off and had me sit on the bed. Then she took off my shoes and socks, unbuckled my pants and pulled them off. "Is this what's known as curb service?" I asked.

She didn't answer. Instead she turned her back to me so I could undo her gown. I did and it dropped to the floor. She was totally naked as she turned to me. "I took my bra and panties off in the bathroom at the club. Now as soon as you take off your boxers, we'll be even." I got up, took off my shorts and stood naked opposite June Maye. She slowly came toward me, licked my nipples, then kissed me. "Now, don't go away—I'll get the drinks. What are you smoking?"

"Lucky Strikes—want one?"

"Yeah, light me up, baby. As if you hadn't already."

I went to my shirt on the floor, got out a pack of cigarettes and lit up a couple. I went out to the kitchen to where she was and gently placed the smoke into her lips. "It's nice to have a woman around who smokes."

"Well, I'm a smokin' fool."

"And it doesn't injure that wonderful voice of yours?"

"Nope, just makes it sexier."

She handed me my drink and we toasted. "Here's to you, June Maye. I'm glad I'm here. I'm glad I know you and I like your place."

"I'm glad you're here, too, Cable." We walked back into the bedroom and we sat on the edge of the bed as she spoke to me. "Remember what I said about how many singing years I have left? Well, that goes for how many passionate years I have left in me as well. Tell me there's more to us than just tonight? I haven't cooled off an ounce since you kissed me. I don't want to ever cool off with you. What do you feel? Sorry, but I've got to corner you on this one."

It was kind of hard to focus on anything other than those luscious naked breasts and her slim stomach tapering to those marvelous hips and at last an inviting, black mound between her legs. But I knew I had to level with her. "June...I don't know if there would ever be a proper time to say this, but here goes, even at the risk of losing you."

"Go on, Cable, I like truth a lot..."

"Well, it goes like this. Inadvertently, I'm in a lot of deep shit. It's too complex to give you a detailed description, but in brief, I got mixed up with a bunch of spies who want something I have in my head, so they say—the knowledge of some fantastic thing I saw once, called *God of Our Fathers*. It was a golden capsule the size of a small egg, you know, one of those ancient collectibles?"

"Yeah, go on..."

"They've tried to kill me several times and failed. That guy you saw tonight, he's one of the big shots working for the Hitler underground here in the states. They want it real bad. Long story short, he informed me, just before you came out and called me tonight, that they have a new device called the *neural extractor*, and in about three months it will be ready for use. Once they've sucked whatever it is I know out of my brain, they plan to kill me as the man who knew too much." I took one last drag on my cigarette and put it in an ashtray by June's bedside table.

"Jesus, Cable, if I didn't detect a genuine sincerity in your voice, I'd swear you were reading out of a Phillip K. Dick science fiction novel. And you live like this? No wonder you're full of urgency. I'd be, too."

I took her hand and placed it on my naked leg and stroked her arm. "So it's now or never, babe. I'm giving you an out here. Our love affair to remember may not be long enough to remember much."

She looked into my eyes and put her head onto my chest. "I don't want your out, Mister. Instead, I'll *ride* it out with you all the way, Cable. That's how much I want you." She moved her lips up to mine and kissing me, lowered us onto the top of the bed. Then she took her hand and slowly moved it up my leg until she was encompassing my very anxious and hard member. She moved her breasts into my mouth one by one as I slid a finger between her legs up into a wet, warm woman pulsing for my touch. Then we ignited and all hell broke loose as our passions tumbled into a forbidden abyss of every sexual move in my lexicon of lovemaking. Our bodies sopping wet with perspiration, I entered her again and again and all she could do was beg for more. "Promise me—promise me you'll never stop taking me! Ever! Please, never stop taking me, Cable!" she sighed in the dark of her room. "Take me until there's nothing left of us—nothing except this—just this!"

Chapter 5

KILLING BEAUTY

Of that there was no doubt. June Maye and I had gone and left together on a fast train to sensual perdition. I kept hearing *Sinleila*'s breathy voice whispering, she the Goddess of Passion, reminding me this was one of my next lessons taught thoroughly, if not gracefully, by the *Moirai*, those not-too-pleasant sisters of Fate who had attached themselves to my trial and trail of destiny.

By the time I got back to the office that Sunday morning, there were other fish to fry. I nonchalantly put the key into my door lock when the damn door swung open. Sitting on a chair reading the Sunday paper sat a rather slim, handsome man. He looked a little familiar—seemed like a gentleman and got up the minute he saw me come in. "Ah...Mr. Denning, please forgive the intrusion but the door was open and I thought this to be your waiting room."

"On a Sunday? Maybe I did leave the door open when I left yesterday, but that's still not a good reason to make yourself at home, Mr.—Mr—"

"—Ness, Eliot Ness. I'm from Chicago...an agent with the United States Treasury—"

"—yeah, I've seen your mug in the paper, I know who you are—the question is, do *you* know who you are? You're not exactly a cop, not really a politician. I see you guys as the *secret police*, the kind of men who could easily turn into those thugs like the ones who run Hitler's hidden army of assassins called the S.S. or Gestapo or whatever they call it over there." I went to my desk, sat down and lit up a Lucky Strike. "Sit down and tell me how Al Capone is nowadays. And how sheepish you must feel when all you could get him on was income tax evasion."

He sat back down and glanced down at the newspaper. "Blondie finally married Dagwood, you know."

"So I've been told. I'm not really a comic strip kind of guy, Mr. Ness. There are enough cartoon characters in my real life to keep me busy. What was the real scoop on that Capone conviction?"

"The whole thing was pretty cloudy. We caught him trying to fix the jury and got the judge to use a second jury unknown to Capone and his defense team so at least they put him away. He was ultimately convicted on about 5 out of the 23 counts. Two misdemeanors and three felonies. He got 11 years in an Atlanta prison. You know, his net worth, was estimated at about one-hundred million dollars. His fines, court costs and back taxes, hardly made a dent"

"A hundred million, eh? That should buy a lot of Tommy guns. Those fines, costs and back taxes oughtta go to his victims' families or poor people instead of the idiot bureaucrats. They'll only line their pockets with it and save the lint for us further down the ladder."

"I see you don't trust your government."

"No, do you?"

"We all have our moments, to be sure, but it really depends—"

"—on what side your bread is buttered on, Ness. It's called *job security*, if you want a name for it."

"I'm still not as pessimistic as you. I believe we've got the best government in the world and the best system."

"Does that include the justice system? Be careful how you answer, Ness, remember, I was a cop downtown and saw between the cracks. I do have to say...you do your job, well and with integrity."

"Thank you, Mr. Denning. That is of the utmost importance to me." Then he looked at my white shirt under my suit jacket. "Uh...you've got a smudge of lipstick at the side of your breast pocket. You might want to change shirts later."

"Who are you, my Dad or something?" I glanced down at the tell-tale sign of light red on my shirt. "Must be the babe I was with last night. You know how women are, full of that lipstick, rouge and crap."

"Yes, I was married. I understand."

"So what happened to happily ever after?"

"She couldn't take my being gone so much—and the pressure of my job. As you know, it's dangerous chasing down hoodlums."

"I couldn't say it better myself. So...what can I do for you?"

"Your name came up on my Chicago records when I was looking up the death of another well-affiliated gangster—a man known as Jessup P. Matrangas—and his sidekick, a little fellow known as Jinx Machado. Do you remember them, maybe two or three years ago?"

"Oh, yeah. Matrangas was intelligent, smooth, definitely not West Coast. But he bankrolled Jack Dragna and his gang out here. Those two got it in a vault at the County Morgue. Nobody knows who snuffed them, right?" I said that, knowing it was Lei-Tao's people who had eliminated them as they regained possession of the *Fen de Fuqín*.

"That's right, Mr. Denning. Nobody knows. Do you have any idea who Matrangas was pursuing? We know it wasn't money or a trip to bump off any of the Los Angeles gang."

"I would leave that alone if I were you, Ness. Take my advice, stick to racketeers and gangsters. You'll live longer, believe me."

"Curious you would say that, Mr. Denning. I was warned by some ominous note a few days ago when I sent a wire to inquire about you. Someone is tapping in on the Bureau's wire service."

"The German underground. Wake up and smell the roses, Ness. Our threatened country is still under the influence of The Noble Experiment, Prohibition—while the truth is, other factions are out there planning a takeover of our beloved stars and stripes. Go back to Chicago and live longer, Mister, that's my counsel to you. Believe me, these guys are even out of *your* league—and *your* league is right up there, at least according to the press."

He paused for a minute, checking me out. "I can read faces pretty well, Mr. Denning. I believe you're telling the truth. So why do you tell me this? I could find reason to subpoena you all the way to Chicago."

"Because I'm a dead man, Ness. Subpoena me all you want."

"May I ask why?"

"I know too much and I've seen too much. So they tell me."

"We could protect you, Denning. Tell us what you know and we'll take over from there. Larry Clarkston is our head of operations here in L.A. He could be your new best friend."

"I'm not permitted best friends, or haven't you heard? Besides, I'm a loner, Ness, and don't take too well to official anything. As I told you, I was a cop once and kind of lost the stomach for law and order, big city style."

"I understand. It's true, Chicago's police department contains a lot of corruption, too. But that's the way of the damned thing. That's why Mr. Hoover believes in that extra eye watching over our citizens."

"Hoover? Yeah, like you and your boss botched Charlie Lindbergh's case last year. How many dummies does it take to let a kid get killed five miles from home when you know about it ahead of time? You, and Hoover and the rest of you blokes on the public dole—I've always wondered how many of you actually earn your salaries."

I could see Eliot Ness took offence to my statement. "Much is hit and miss in your line of work, as in mine, Denning. We have to be grateful for the successes. I wouldn't be so self-righteous."

I put my cigarette out. "Go home, Ness. You can't help me. I can't help you. It's not that we're on different sides, it's just that I've got more shadows in my world than you do."

"I do have to tell you the truth, Denning. From now on the Bureau of Investigation will be watching you, making sure you are not involved in covert operations with any foreign and hostile governments. You were

131

watched last evening with Dr. Becker at the *Bistro Club*. You were also followed to that very attractive young singer's bungalow on Wilton Place."

"Well, do tell, Ness—did you see us do it? Watch all you want, take some photos of us in her bedroom and show 'em to the boys back in your locker room in Chicago for a few laughs."

He got up and looked serious. "We wouldn't do that, Denning. You *will* be under surveillance, though. Just thought I would tell you." He looked at me, up and down, noticed my disheveled hung over look and shabby clothes. "We're both still cops, Denning—but you smoke, drink and involve yourself with women too much. It'll be the death of you."

"You got it wrong, Ness—naw, that won't be the death of me. Stupid, greedy, power-mad *men*, politicians and miscellaneous aliens will be the death of me." I waved him off. "See you around, Ness…"

"Aliens?" he inquired, wrinkling his brow in confusion.

"Just a term," I lied.

Eliot Ness said no more and left my office. I heaved a big sigh. That was all I needed, one more group or agency breathing down my neck, watching my every move until I was finally playing harps with the angels—or down there pitching forks with that other guy.

Dancing on the Brink

It was early, but I decided I needed a drink. I reached into my top drawer and took out that bottle of smooth gin that warmed my gut and numbed my brain. I took a full shot and sat back in my chair just as the phone rang.

"Yeah, Cable Denning here…"

It was a soft, very feminine voice at the other end. "Mr. Denning, your name was given me by Mr. Bruckner at the Los Angeles Academy of Dance. I—I really need to talk to someone. I'm being followed day and night. I'm quite frightened, Mr. Denning. Will you see me?"

"It's Sunday, Miss. I don't keep office hours seven-days-a-week, you know. Call back tomorrow and I'll be glad to hear your story. Everyone has a story, lady—"

"—but you answered your phone," she insisted.

"That's because I live in the back of my office and I was doing some bookwork. By the way, who am I talking to?"

"Lily Norwood. I'm a dancer at the Academy. I—I would very much like to see you today, if that's possible. You see, it's my only day off from the ballet."

I thought for a minute. I could use the dough, although I was doing okay these days. Still, what was I about, anyhow? Helping people who really needed it when they needed it, right? "Well, Miss Norwood, I just got in from an all-nighter, so I'll need to clean up a bit. How about three this afternoon, my office here on 6400 Franklin Avenue—Suite B"

"Thank you so much, Mr. Denning. I will be there—punctually."

133

She hung up and I sat on my chair wondering what challenges might be next in my bag of earthly experiences.

Punctually at three p.m. there was a knock on my office door. Boy, was I glad I bathed, shaved and changed clothes when I beheld my first view of Lily Norwood. She had jet-black hair cut to the bottom of the neck, warm brown eyes, a great face with a delicious smile. She wore a dark purplish-blue blouse with a very tight grey-black skirt split on both sides up to the outside of the knee. She must have stood about 5' 7" flat-footed and had great legs. She was medium-busted and possessed very attractive hands with long, tapered fingers. "Miss Norwood, welcome, I'm Cable Denning. Won't you come in and sit down?" I escorted her to the client's chair and came around behind my desk to sit opposite her.

"Thank you for seeing me, Mr. Denning. I was nervous just getting in and out of the taxi on my way here."

"Sounds like someone's trying to spook you. Suppose you fill me in a bit. As I said on the telephone, Miss Norwood, everyone has a story. What's yours?"

"Well, I'm a professional ballet dancer. I studied since I was twelve. I was coached by Bolm and Nijinska, toured with newly formed *Ballet Russe de Monte Carlo* and I have been asked by Warner Brothers to perform a classical selection in a new talking motion picture. I'm twenty-seven, unmarried and my father is Joseph P. Norwood, after whom Norwood Avenue in Hollywood is named."

I could tell the dame was classy. She had one of those faces you would never forget because it oozed goodness and sensuality at the same time as she spoke. "Well, a lady from the local aristocracy. So far so good, Miss Norwood. Now all we have to do is get a line on who would want to frighten or hurt you. Tell me how long this guy has been shadowing you and if you have any clues as to who it might be. That might save us some time and get me started on the right foot."

"Of course. He follows me almost everywhere I go. There was even a mysterious painted black rose left on my dressing room table at the theatre. That frightened me most, I think."

"Black rose? When was that? Do you still have it?"

"It was a week ago Tuesday. No, I threw it in the garbage immediately. It had a horrible feeling about it."

"Hmmm... Whoever it is has a flair for the melodramatic. You say 'he...' could it possibly be a woman who's pursuing you?"

"Why would a woman threaten me—aren't these terrible people usually men? I mean, they're the strong, violent ones..."

"Generally, I would agree with you. But in such cases where the arts are concerned, women have an even chance at intrigue and violence—even murder. I don't know your personal life, of course, but if for some reason you've had an intimate relationship with a woman who is now jealous of you—I don't have to paint you a picture, do I?"

She looked at me strangely but kept her calm. "I understand what you say, and I suppose it's necessary to bring up things like that in your business. But my intimate preferences do not include women, Mr. Denning."

"Sorry about that, but I have to kind of know these things." I took out a cigarette and put it to my lips, then had second thoughts. "Mind if I smoke? I suppose a dancer's lungs are important to her, right?

"Aren't yours? Yes, you may smoke, just don't blow it over here in my direction, please."

I lit up and took a deep drag, blowing the smoke up at the ceiling. "Yeah, I suppose we all need our breathing apparatus. But for me, the nature of my business doesn't have a long life expectancy. So what the hell, I say, and so I smoke, drink lousy gin or honeyed whiskey and chase pretty skirts late at night down in smoky nightclubs where the music is healing and some babe in a low-cut dress pours her heart out to me."

"That sounds like a destructive life style, if you'll pardon my saying so. And all those women? Aren't you afraid of disease or something? My Uncle Theodore is a biological chemist. He says people abuse themselves something awful with what they take into their bodies—and perhaps in your case, additionally take unnecessary risks with questionable women."

"I'm afraid I presented myself a bit on the rough side, Miss Norwood. You see, I'm not a one-night stander—or at least not very often—no, I like to savor a beautiful babe..." I was looking her up and down. "And then...if she's mutually attracted to what she sees in me—then the game is on."

"Game? I don't understand. Women are a game to you?"

"Hey now, Miss Norwood, this meeting isn't about me. So, if we're going to work together I get thirty-five bucks a day plus expenses, you know, like film if I get pictures of your shadow, legal filings and miscellaneous shoe leather."

She laughed and I loved her smile. "You can be very funny, Mr. Denning. You're able to take life so—so carelessly..." She cleared her throat and looked at me. "You look strong and intelligent. Why are you wasting yourself?"

"You know, someone asked me that about themselves not too long ago. Maybe it's because there's nowhere else to go. I don't know."

"Have you ever heard of *Tchaikovsky*? I'll be dancing his *Swan Lake* this fall. I'm in rehearsals already."

"Lady, I don't know Tchaikovsky from Beethoven— but I did attend the Brahms Piano Concerto #2 not too long ago at the Hollywood Bowl....and if I remember rightly, they started the evening out with this Tchaikovsky guy. Frankly, I was blown away. I had never heard such music." I was thinking of that wonderful evening I'd spent at the Hollywood Bowl with my secretary Mandy Foster Simpson and how moved I was listening to that fantastic music that lifted me up out of the common, everyday shit Americans are indoctrinated with.

"So you are somewhat eclectic..."

"Well, I don't know about that. But if I hear a band let out with *Gershwin, Porter, Johnny Mercer, Kern or Berlin*—then I'm in home territory. We both love what we do and hear, Miss Norwood—they're different parts of the same world—the world of music, that's all."

"I never looked at it that way. I dance for a living. My family has money, but I would do what I do even if I were poor as a church mouse."

"That's a noble attitude, if ever I heard one," I said, grinding out my cigarette in the ashtray in front of me. "But...do you dance for *fun*? Do you put your arms around some man you care for in the middle of a dim-lit lounge and dance with him because you're doing a ritual, that rhythmic and sensual dance of love that people long for when lights are low and the music seeps into their souls and melts away all the crap that the outside world builds up in them...do you do that?"

She looked down at the floor, a bit embarrassed. "No, Mr. Denning. I have never done that. It was considered below my station. My family would never have permitted it."

"What about you? Would you permit it? Would you give yourself the opportunity to let your hair down and spin around on that floor until you were dizzy from the glow and excitement of the moment and the music—not to mention being touched by someone you wanted to be touched by?"

She looked into my eyes with those warm, glowing browns of hers. "Are you testing me, Mr. Denning, or propositioning me?"

I sat back and looked at her. "Well, to be honest, maybe a little bit of both. It's not every day a doll like you walks in through my office door. But I am a professional man, and we need to get on with it."

"You talk a good talk, private detective." It was the first time I heard a little sexy frankness peek out of the

138

dame. "Maybe someday I'll meet a man I might wish to dance with in one of your dark, smoky nightclubs."

"Let me know and I'll guide you in the right direction. Now, I'll need a list of all the people you know who might be suspect. Not to alarm you...just being practical...I also need the names and phone numbers of pertinent family members I could contact in the event you get kidnapped or something. Who in your family is the most sensible?"

"Not my father. He's too busy being Joseph P. Norwood. He's never home and besides, he's a philanderer."

"Yeah, money corrupts—and some guys just can't keep it in their pants—hell, I ought to know, I'm one of them!" I said, realizing I was over-stepping my discretionary boundaries.

She lifted an eyebrow. "Mr. Denning—I think your comment hardly tactful—and certainly judgmental in regards to my father."

"Sorry about that. But it's true, isn't it? If we're gonna work together, two things you'll learn about me. One, I'm truthful, even if it hurts—and two, you gotta trust me and let me do things my way even if you think I might be a little crude at times."

She ignored the comment. "My mother lives in New York. I would say my Uncle Teddy is the most knowledgeable and accessible. I'll have to think about that list of other people. I have a few girlfriends, a couple of men friends, several acquaintances at work—and of course my dominating and demanding ballet coach, *Nico Siderova*."

"Sounds like a lot of borscht to me. Demanding and dominating, eh? Is he in love with you? Could he be the one?"

"He hasn't the time—and I do believe he is homosexual. He may be in love with my dancing, but that's all."

"Don't be so sure. Sometimes sexual frustrations get pent up inside, like a bad boil needing to burst, and sexual persuasion, one way or the other, makes a person dangle on a string like a magnetic compass—which pole is north—the attractive one?"

She got up and walked away, then turned to face me. "Why is everything so sexual to you, Mr. Denning? Aren't there other reasons why people might like you, desire your friendship or enjoy working with you?"

"Yeah, you're right except for one thing. Read up on your Freud. Sure there's money and power, control and sick egos out there—but down deep the world is run by restless hormones kicking up against the brain, nature's desire to attract and mate, preoccupy itself with propagation of the species. Where have you been—locked in a cold, dark room somewhere, obeying the disciplines of your calling?" Then I stopped. I realized I was talking about myself, too. I knew just around the corner that *Atroppa, the Goddess of One's Calling* was gonna call on *me* pretty soon, call in my chips to see how much I'd gambled on the table. "I'm sorry, I kind of stepped out of line there," I said, opening my drawer and taking out my reliable bottle of gin. My hand was shaking. "Would you like a shot of gin, Miss Norwood? I think better with a little shot in the afternoon."

"No thank you, Mr. Denning." I could tell I upset her and she was breathing hard. "Yes, as a matter of fact, that's exactly what I have been doing, 'obeying the disciplines of my calling,' as you say. I haven't had time to expand myself as I might have wanted to. And a prima ballerina has only a few good years. I told you I'm twenty-seven. The years go by swiftly...and then there are just brittle bones and stiff muscles. Dancing takes a hard toll on the body, just as your cigarettes, drinking and womanizing do. You see, we are both our own victims because we love what we do and for us, there is no other thing in this world we'd rather be doing. Am I right?"

I poured myself a full shot. "I couldn't have said it better myself." I toasted her. "Here's to you then—and the resolution of your current dilemma."

She came and sat back down opposite me. "Frankly, I'm not certain about your abilities, Mr. Denning. I know you come highly recommended, but what I have seen today—well, it makes me wonder, between time out for tobacco smoking, drinking too much and beautiful young women—will there be time for you to prioritize on my behalf?"

"Call the shot any way you like, Miss Norwood. You see, I've heard it all, seen it all and done it all before—so I really don't care if you want to hire me or not. Oh, it's not that I wouldn't do a good job for you. I know my stuff. And I put my life on the line every week when I'm out chasing down murdering wife beaters, rapists, errant husbands and wives sneaking around in peek-a-boo lives hoping no one notices, or solving the case of the mysterious stalker who threatens the well-being of some beautiful dancer. Yeah, you can call it off and go out that door and find some other upright bloke selling his wares, telling you all will be swell once he nabs your man. But you know, it doesn't always go that way. Remember what I told you on the phone—that everything has a story attached to it?"

"Yes..."

"Well, guess what? This creep of yours isn't a recent Johnny-come-lately. He's been building up something for a long time and there's something in *you* he either wants—or wants to destroy. Now, the question is, which of the two *is* it? If he just wants to scare you, he'll make up stupid moves, like eventually breaking into your house and taking something that you'll notice, but won't have any particular attachment to. This is the kind of guy who gets his kicks by frightening people. He's not a killer, in fact, he's a coward. So he won't leave a black rose in your dressing room. No—that's not his style. But the guy we're looking for hurts a lot, his pain goes deeper and darker, and there's something he's got against you, against you living, maybe, or against your family with you ending up as the fall guy." I took the last sip from my dirty shot glass. "So as I see it so far, you can rule out the play-for-fun variety of stalker, and pick the one that wants to play for keeps, blot you out of his world, get you out of his heart and mind—and if he's a man—wipe you out of his aching balls, because his desire for your beauty, your woman-hood and your willingness to submit to his favor, smack of the unavailable in this world, that sublime frustration, the itch you can't scratch deep down because all the pieces never quite fit in his own life." I stopped and looked across at her. She had tears in her eyes. "So...that's my present assess-

142

ment, based on my gut feeling and a few years of experience as an L.A. cop—*and* a private dick."

Her wet eyes widened as she took a handkerchief out of her purse and gently dabbed them. "I'm sorry...a private...?"

"Dick...private dick, Miss Norwood. It's short for private detective—and I've forgotten its derivation, I think it's something about a popular fictional British detective."

"Oh..." she said as she settled back down in her chair.

"So you can get up and walk out that door, Miss Norwood, no questions asked. Or we can roll up our sleeves and get this job done before someone conks you over the head, drags you into a dark alley, has his way with you—and slits your throat so you can join the Heavenly dancers up *there*."

Still a bit disconsolate, she reached across my desk and took my wrists. "Yes...please...I'm sorry...I do want you—I mean, I want you to work for me. Forgive me if I seem stunned, Mr. Denning. I—I never heard anyone speak as you do, nor give an assessment with so many layers. I see now why I might be in grave danger." She withdrew her hands.

"That's just how I see it for now, Miss Norwood—"

"—please, will you call me *Lily*? I believe that is a way I can tell you I trust you."

"Thanks, Lily. Then you can call me *Cable*."

"Cable...that's a strong name, it sounds like your chiseled looks and that cleft in your chin." She handed me her written list of family names. There was only one.

I laughed. "That's a new one. Haven't had my name described quite like that before. So when can you get me a list of the folks you work with?" I checked over the name on the list I had. "So is Dr. Theodore Norwood an agreeable sort, or will he give me a bad time?"

"Oh, no, Uncle Teddy is gentle—just a bit eccentric. He lives most of the time in his laboratory. Always working on some new chemical formulas that help define the bio-chemistry of the human body."

"Talking about human bodies, did I tell you, Lily, that I think you've got a swell body? And I would like to come see you dance that *Swan Lake* ballet. What's it, uh, all about?"

"Thank you, I'd like that. I'll see if I can get you an advance ticket. *Swan Lake* is basically about an evil one, a white swan who is also a beautiful young maiden, a black swan and a handsome Prince. The maiden and the Prince love each other, the black swan seduces the Prince pretending to be the white swan....and.....well I won't spoil the ending for you, but the combination of love, desire, evil and deception....leads to death."

"Ha...I'm already confused and I haven't even seen it yet. Sounds a bit like life, though, wouldn't you say? It's like killing beauty." I chuckled.

"I've always maintained that great art reflects life." She dried her eyes. "I'm very grateful that we've agreed to work together." She reached into her purse and took out a wad of dough big enough to get me back to Nepal and then some. "How about if I give you five-hundred dollars as a retainer? I'm terrible about keeping books. I will trust you to make the proper accountings."

"Yes, ma'am, and thank you for your confidence." I got up and led her to the door. "In the meantime, Lily, watch everything and everyone. Trust no one. Call me, day or night, if you're in trouble. And make sure you're in busy, well-lighted areas when you're out. Keep an eye on everyone down at the theatre and report anything suspicious to me immediately, understood?"

"Understood, captain," she chuckled, saluting me. "Can I trust *you?*"

"Not on a dark night when your eyes are sparkling the way they are now and the music's just right..."

She smiled one of those sunbeam smiles at me. "Oh, and by the way, if you're not too busy chasing one of those skirts you were talking about, maybe some night you can show me one of those tribal dances to the music of Gershwin or Porter you were talking about."

I was rather surprised at her boldness. "Really? So what made you change your mind?"

She was reflective and spoke slow. "Your voice...I could hear it in your voice...how much I've been missing...I don't even socialize with men—I mean, on official dates."

"Have you ever been in love?"

"Yes, once...he was one of my few dance partners who was heterosexual—and how. I almost had his child, but I lost it dancing."

"Did you want it?"

"Yes—and no. You know how it is with a professional woman—she wants everything—both—a little cottage with hubby and baby, and a full-fledged career with all the trimmings."

"Yeah, I've heard that can be rough on a woman. Are you okay with not being that wife and mother now?"

"Oh, sometimes...I get that longing in me. But as my Uncle Teddy says, it's just chemistry. Something he calls the *biological clock*. I don't know." Then she reached for my hand. "But if we can keep it simple, Cable, I'd very much like that dance sometime."

"That's a date, kid," I said. She turned and left.

The Saga of Boots Blake

I had to admit it to myself after she left. I was definitely attracted to the doll. I already had fantasies of those lovely long legs wrapped around me in a dark bedroom, her warm breasts pushed into my chest and my lips pressed onto that wonderful full mouth of hers. What is it they say, a guy thinks about sex every few seconds or so? Yeah, don't blame me...I couldn't help it. Babes and their marvelous feminine accessories just kept coming up like water bubbling from an Artesian Well.

I fumbled around on my desk until I had found the name of some old bloke my Uncle Cable had asked me to look up. I wanted to follow through on it, if for no other reason than...he's my Dad. *Boots Blake* was his name and I went leafing through the L.A. phone book until I found a B. Blake over on Atwater. The phone was ringing at the other end.

"Yeah? If this is that goddamned delivery man again—I told you the *fifth house* on your left—not your right!" he complained. The voice was low and gravelly like his vocal cords were lined with sandpaper.

"No, this isn't the delivery man. Mr. Blake, I presume. My name is Cable Denning. I am Cable Denning's nephew. I met him in Nepal recently—and he asked me to look you up."

There was a long pause at the other end. "Which is it now? You're Cable—or he's Cable—I don't comprendo, Mister."

"I was named after my uncle—we're *both* named Cable Denning."

"Oh. Why didn't you say so?"

"I did, you just didn't hear me."

"So, getting wise-guy on me, huh? I was riding posse long before you was born. Only it was on horseback and we ate guys like you for lunch. You're soundin' city bred and born, boy."

"Yes, I'm a ghetto rat—East Los Angeles. My Dad died when I was five or so and my mother—"

"—is your mother named Florence, by any chance?"

"Yep, you got it."

"Well...I'll be damned...then you must be Cable Denning, Jr."

"No, my Dad's name was Ted. As I understand it, my mother prevailed on my Dad to name me after my uncle—who she thought I'd never meet. Sort of to keep his memory alive, I suppose." I was thinking of how much in love my mother had been with my Uncle Cable. And how things can get turned and twisted, so happiness eludes us and leaves us with a bag full of memories.

"Oh. Why didn't you say so?" the gruff voice at the other end said.

147

"I just did, Mr. Blake."

"Call me Boots. I hate formal crap. So what can I do for you?"

"Nothing. I just promised my uncle I'd look you up, that's all."

"Well, so you looked me up. Now what? I ain't good at socializin' or sparkin' up acquaintances and the like, you know."

"That's okay, Boots. I'm a busy man anyhow."

"Oh? Just what is it ya do, then?"

"I'm a private investigator—you know, taking photos of shameful lovers who happened to belong in other beds, chasing down hoodlums, solving murder cases..." Then I thought of Lily Norwood. "And finding stalkers who frighten young women..."

"I used to be a lawman, at one time," Boots Blake said. "But in them days it was desperados, drunks and dandies breakin' the law. Then I became sheriff of a one-horse town on the Central Coast. Now I'm retired. But damn, I do miss sniffin' out one of those fancy-like crimes they're committin' these days. If you need some help, common sense is my specialty. That's what it always is, you know...common sense...think like a criminal to catch a criminal, I always say."

"Well, thanks, Boots. If I ever call you again, just call me Cable. It's easier that way, huh?"

"I liked your uncle. He was a hell of a hard-livin' Irishman. The ladies loved him because he acted like he didn't care." He laughed. "They love that, ya know. But I recall him tellin' me how enamored he was of your mother. He wanted her somethin' fierce—but respected your Dad too much to get in the way. Then he left the country, he did."

"Well, nice talking to you, Boots—"

"—before you go off half-cocked, young man, give me your telephone number, just in case. Maybe one day you'd like to come out here and visit me. I can catch you up on that mischievous uncle of yours." He coughed and spat up something. "I chew tobacco, you know. Got orange and black teeth to prove it, too," he chortled. "Anyhow, your uncle and I used to put away a lot of liquor."

I gave him my phone number and said good-bye. Right now I had two things on my mind...Lily Norwood's case—and June Maye. I was getting a bit horny for her already. Then I thought about those sisters, the Fates who were bombarding me two at a time. Both the Goddess of Passion and the Goddess of One's Calling were invading my mind, my spirit, my body, forcing me through the eye of the needle by teaching me pain through ecstasy, duty with my nose to the professional grindstone and being able to deliver by solving the penultimate case. Just then the phone rang.

"Yeah, Cable Denning here..."

"I'm still oozing you...slowly...and I love it. I woke up addicted to you, Mister. Can you come over and give me another shot of you? My belly and a few other places are aching for you. I'll have some fresh cigarettes, good English gin—and me...all of me, Cable, would you like that? Please say yes..."

I looked around my office. I knew I should be doing a couple of other things. But the hell with it, tomorrow was Monday and I'd get it done then. "Yeah, babe, it sounds like a good bargain, especially with you thrown in for good measure. When do you want me to come over?"

"Now...it's as if I can't breathe without you in me. I want you. I don't know *what* you did, but you did it. Come and get it..."

I grabbed my coat and hat and went for the door. Then suddenly I was turned around by some invisible hands and up in a corner was this incredible vision. It was a beautiful dark-haired woman with a gossamer deep-red gown, full red lips and very large emerald green eyes. *"It's beginning...she will take you down into the Nether Worlds...and you will take her down...sensual days, nights, weeks, months...until you are lost in each other...and then, eventually lost in yourselves...until you can no longer find the other...that is me, Cable— Passion's calling to you...go to her...go to her, embrace her fully, taste her, caress her, live in her until you have spent all the savings in your loins...but beware...there is another ending to it...that is the price I extract...when my sister is not present..."*

I broke away from her gaze and went flying out the door. Maybe I was going crazy after all. I got to June's place and found the door open. All the shades were drawn and I knew exactly where she was. I started peeling off my clothes and by the time I reached the bedside and saw that lovely, naked young woman lying there, a rush went through my loins and I slid over onto the top of her. Neither of us said a word as we began working the sensual magic on each other. We were like addicted animals, crashing our flesh together in seemingly unquenchable hours that turned day into night. When finally the passion was spent for the moment, we lay there exhausted and wet, glued to each other.

Finally we sat up in bed. She had a pack of Lucky Strikes and a bottle of gin on the little table next to the bed. Silently, she lit us both up, poured us a generous amount of alcohol and we toasted. "Here's to you, lover, the only one who can make me fly. You take me away, Cable. Don't ever stop taking me away...take us higher and deeper every time I swallow you up between my legs—and don't let it end..."

I clinked glasses with the lovely young woman with the large warm breasts and sullen smile. "Yeah, babe, I'll—I'll keep doing my best. You're something, you know. I don't seem to be able to keep out of that warm, wet place there," I chuckled as I took my finger and felt her. She sighed and I knew it re-stimulated her. As soon as we had finished our smokes and drank up, she pulled me onto her and again we sank down into that sensual abyss.

It was all happening too fast. It wasn't like the Cable Denning I was used to. Dolls came and went in my life and I was always able to control the moment, no matter how much I might teeter on the brink of that sexual addiction with one babe. But with June it was harder. It was almost as if her passions personified sex itself and there was no room for *love* because that hot obsession dominated every moment...every move...tangled up in each other. Just then, I was reminded—it was just like she said—the Goddess of Passion.

Chapter 6

MASS AMNESIA

Two days later I was thinking about other things. You'd think that after many thousands of years upon a planet, a race of cognizant beings would improve. Such wasn't the case for humans. If I were a P.I. from another planet, I'd definitely have to say there was something pretty stinkin' in the way humans conducted themselves on planet Earth. It was as if a cog got stuck on the ratchet of time and kept slipping back, so the gear never moved forward. War, pestilence, famine, greed, power-mongering, the cancer of politics, the ominously dark veil that science and technology threw over the eyes of the populace—and all in the name of 'helping the people'—it all added up to control, if you ask me. And above that I sensed some kind of *mind-* control, as if someone was spreading a kind of mass amnesia over the tuned out consciousness of mankind, like the sandman who tosses invisible stuff in your eyes once you're asleep. And the human race *was* asleep, as far as I could figure. Day to day existence in the trenches of survival cancelled out the possibilities of ascending to nobler, higher places. The great poets languished in this realization. "*Let us take our bloated nothingness out of the path of the divine circuits,*" Emerson said. "*Let us unlearn our wisdom of this world...and learn that truth alone makes us rich and great.*" Maybe that's why I was a truth guy, because I couldn't stand the bullshit I was standing knee-deep in most of the time.

It was Wednesday and the garbage man came down the alley next to my office building. It was always the same, the husky guy with the canvas apron tossing everybody's crap into the back of the dirty, smoking truck, revving and roaring its engine like a lion announcing its domain. A cop car sped by on Franklin with its siren cutting through the rest of the din that was the city. A couple of days ago two thugs had robbed a dry goods store down near Gower. They got away with fifteen bucks and hit the owner's wife on the head with the cash register drawer because she couldn't come up with more dough. What's the matter with people?

I sat alone at my desk, smoking a Lucky Strike and sipping my first gin of the day. Out of the clear blue I was thinking about Zelda and the child she was carrying in her belly. My child—perhaps my *son*. I was well aware that when I left her and my mother that night, I was running...running to a safe haven... running into the world that let my spirit run free and my imagination get transported by a great song, a tuneful passport to travel on the wings of illusion—by Jerome Kern or George Gershwin or Cole Porter. But I also realized that someday there'd be a comeuppance—a penalty would be extracted for my putting my head in the sand and up too many female crotches. I felt guilty for not being accountable to all the things I helped cause. But that's a long list, why start now? But there was another truth as well, the one that Zelda was standing by—that I couldn't be with her and the kid even if I wanted to, because my life was a marked red zone and anyone connected with me in an any other than casually, ran the risk of sudden death. June seemed to be pre-approved—I guess those that were keeping a watch on me must've seen her as a fun fuck on Sunday afternoons, so they left us alone. Whether it was Ness or Becker or whoever else was spying on me, I knew the day would come when the curtain would fall and down I'd go for the count.

Deep inside me somewhere I knew I loved Zelda Blodgett. She was pure, special, intelligent—and made-to-order for me in the bedroom. And she would be a faithful woman to the end of her days. I knew that also. Then I thought of Becker's last warning—three months when the great *neural extractor* would be sucking out that part of my brain that knew about the *Fen de Fuqín*—and who knows, maybe they'd extract some of the rest of my brain so I'd become an unthinking dummy like most of the other unthinking dummies walking the streets.

Then the phone rang. "Yeah, Cable Denning here..."

"It's been two and a half days, Cable. Have you forgotten me already? Was I only a two-night stand?" June Maye said at the other end of the line. Her words brought a new wrinkle to the intimate scenario we were painting. She sounded very insecure. I hoped this wasn't a sign of things to come because babysitting was not one of my fortes.

"Naw...I think we can make it at least a three-night stand. In fact, I was kind of hankering to catch your act down at the *Bistro Club*. You are there tonight, aren't you?"

"Yep. Will you be? I've got a new song I want to sing for you."

"Yeah? Great...what's it called?"

154

"*Love for Sale*, I think you'll like it. Then, afterwards, can you come home with me and get it for free."

I laughed. The dame was gutsy. "Well, at least you say what you think—and what you want. I like that." I said. "I've got a few things on my desk I gotta attend to, June—see you tonight?"

"Yes, mister sexy, yes...I can't wait to see you again, Cable. Bye."

She hung up and something didn't feel quite kosher. I was getting this feeling that as much as I enjoyed June, her passion, her body and her extremely sensual nature, I didn't want someone assuming when or how I might be available. I had to break the pattern, any habit she might form in expectation. Let her wait a little while for it during the week. She'd be all the more horny as the days went by.

The phone rang again. "Yeah, Cable Denning here..."

"Cable—it's Lily Norwood. I've just been frightened out of my—my dress and wits!"

"Well, that's not such a bad thing, I wouldn't mind seeing you out of your dress," I joked, trying to lighten her obvious angst. "What's up, Lily?"

"I went into my dressing room, and as I was un-dressing, I looked over and saw that someone had painted on my mirror with a horrible red paint. "*It's only a matter of time...*" That's what it said—Cable? Did you hear me?"

"I heard you, Lily. Seems there's a lot of activity in your dressing room lately. Do you have anyone hiding in your wardrobe closet?"

"Don't even joke about it, please. I don't know, I'm frightened and confused. It's as if I've become paralyzed from living a normal life. What shall I do, Cable?"

"Where are you now?"

"I'm still here at the theatre. Mr. Bruckner is with me—the man who gave me your name when I was looking for a detective, remember?"

"Does he say he knows me? And is he suspect?"

"No—on both counts. He told me he heard of you through someone you did some work for last year. He's my stage Dad."

"Have you compiled that list I asked you for?"

"Yes. That's one reason I called. When can I get it to you?"

"Well, maybe I can pick it up. Say, I have a proposition for you."

"Didn't you give me one of those before? And what did I say?"

"That you weren't sure about me, wasn't that it?—that you might want to trade me off for another private eye because maybe you didn't trust me—and my life style put my ability to deliver in question."

"That's not true anymore. I trust you. I told you, I heard something in your voice. It made me trust you."

"That's nice to hear, Lily. Anyway, my proposition is this. If you're willing to see Crazy Jack with me tomorrow sometime, and risk hearing what he says and taking it with a grain of salt—we could have dinner later and maybe have that dance you were talking about."

She hesitated at the other end. "Crazy Jack? That's all I need. Is he really crazy?"

"Some people think he is. But he's usually dead-on when it comes to seeing things ahead and down the road. He might have some other visions as well. What do you say?"

"Oh, dear, I guess it's okay...as long as I'm with you. What time? I don't get through with rehearsals until about six or so."

"Where do you live?"

"I rent a cottage at the back of a house just this side of Silver Lake Boulevard on a little street just off of Sunset, called Westerly Terrace. It would be a long ride, but at least it would be just straight down Sunset. You'd have to walk up the hill, though, since you don't have a car. You know, I could meet you at seven thirty at the bottom of the hill right where you get off the streetcar."

"No, I don't think so. What did I tell you about being out in the light and definitely not alone in dark places?"

"Okay, then, my place at seven? It's 1205 Westerly Terrace just past a street called Hamilton Way— almost on the corner—just walk up the stairs."

"What about tonight? Do you need someone to take you home?"

"No, thanks, Cable, Mr. Bruckner is driving me."

"Okay, as long as he's okay in your book. I'll—I'll see you then...in the meantime, babe, don't forget the list and keep your eyes peeled at all times, got it?"

"Yes, Cable...it's so nice to know I've got you looking out for me. I'm glad we met and that I hired you."

"Yeah, me, too, Lily. See you tomorrow night."

The *Bistro Club* was as noisy as usual. As I walked down the stairs I could hear that the place was jumping and June's strong, raw and sensuous voice was punching out *On the Sunny Side of the Street.* Elmo Shay's little combo put out a hell of a lot of sound. Shay's piano, sax player Eddie Hauk's superb blend of jazz and smooth ballad style was perfect for June's sexy delivery. I also like the bass man, Ronnie Aldrich. Yeah, he could make love to that big fiddle as he plucked those large catguts. I didn't know the trumpet player or the drummer, but they were good. The place came apart when June finished. Yeah, it was probably me and the other twenty guys lined up at the bar ogling her naughty pert face and those large breasts that came pouring half out of her dress. Tonight it was red. Just the way I liked it, shiny red sequins on a tight-fitting gown with thin straps.

She saw me wave to her as she took her bows. Soon she made her way through the crowd and was standing by my side. A young guy with too much whiskey sour in him started toward us. "I'll tell you...I'll tell you...I'll tell you something—"

"—you already said that," I growled at the man.

He looked at me queerly. "Are you her manager or—hic!—something? But if you aren't, what I—what I have to tell her—is—is for her—her ears only..." He bent over to look up into my face. "So...you don't look like a manager to me...so now I need to put my arm around the young lady and whisper in her—her—hic!-ear..."

"I don't think that's such a good idea, Mister," June spoke up.

"Whatta ya mean? Why not? Don't you want...don't you want to hear—hear that I'm a big fan of—of yours...so let me bend that pretty ear—ha ha! —Even if I'm—I'm a little—hic!—drunk."

June looked at me like she wanted to me take over. "Miss Maye appreciates that you're a fan of hers. But you're drunk and not very pleasant to be around—especially for a lady." I grabbed him by the back of his jacket collar and pulled him over to the bar. "I'll tell you what. When you get all sobered up, come back and tell Miss Maye how much you appreciate her, okay?"

He was obnoxious. "But that—that isn't *all*...between you and me, buddy, I'd like to screw her...cause I think she'd be really good—good—hic!—between the sheets."

I was within an inch of punching the guy's lights out. But I knew June's customers were important to her, so I held my ground. "Well, that's something you take up with her when you're not slobbering all over your tie, buddy. So sober up and come back another day."

I left him there and re-joined June. "Thanks, Cable. I get a lot of horny idiots like that."

"Yeah, I'm sure you do. I don't know what his sweet nothings in your ear were, but he did confess he wanted to fuck you."

"So what else is new? I can handle it. Actually, it's rather flattering, as long as it's from a distance. I can't stand them touching me." Then she bent up and whispered in *my* ear. "But I love *you* touching me...I got hot just seeing you tonight and imagining what you'll feel like tonight after we get home—"

"—tonight?" I said, not remembering whether or not I had promised her that we'd get together after her work.

"Oh, yeah, mister, I know someone who's aching for you right now, as a matter of fact. We *could* go into my little dressing room backstage and we can do it on the floor—or just prop me up on the dresser and shove it in me."

Whew! June's way of saying things made *my* temperature rise along with another part of my anatomy. "Why not? How much time have you got?"

"Not enough. When it's crowded like this, Elmo only gives me about ten minutes. So I'd better be getting back. Oh...and the song I told you about? You want me to sing it first or last?"

"Surprise me. When you feel it, kid, then that's when you should do it, right? By the way, you did a hell of a job on that last number."

She looked at me with those warm, sensual brown eyes. "Thanks. I always feel it with you, buster, and right about now I'm on *high simmer*—can you get your male member to join the party later?"

"Okay." I said that knowing I would go home with her afterwards, smoke, drink and have incredible sex. Those were the best things we did together. I bent down and kissed her on the nose. "Don't wanna mess up that wonderful makeup. I'll be listening over there by the bar, trying to keep those blokes quiet while you're singing."

She looked up at me and smiled a very warm smile. "If I could love a man, Cable, I think it would be you. I just don't want it to get in the way of the sex. Do you

160

know what I mean? You know, all the everyday things, like personal problems, family, bills, kids...I don't want that to happen to us."

"Sure, June, sure...yeah, I get it." I watched her walk back toward the bandstand. I thought *men* were supposed to be unemotional about sex, not babes! I remember the old adage, *"Women give sex for love, while men give love for sex."* I was beginning to think June Maye had outdone ol' Cable Denning in that department!

As June's voice purred on in the background, I remembered how Honey Combes used to be like a racehorse, ready at the gate for that first note of the night and away she would warble. There were a lot of things that hadn't healed yet. And that one was one of them.

I glanced around as three women and two men made their way through the clogged room. Even the dance floor was mobbed with people, spilling out and brushing by tables as they danced. Suddenly the world stood still for me. The most gorgeous redhead I'd ever seen was no more than fifteen feet away from me. Be still my heart! Why does God allow such beauty—only to let it wither, grow old and die one day? She stood about five-six and wore a tight shiny maroon dress. Her full, beautiful hair came down to her shoulders and her white, full breasts were tucked just right into that dress. It was too dark for me to see the color of her eyes, but they were full and bright and her smile lit up the area where she and her friends stood awaiting a table. She

161

carried herself proudly and from my vantage point she was a classy doll with good taste.

June began to sing Cole Porter's *Love for Sale* and breathed it through her microphone as if some deep melancholy was surfacing in her. I was watching this talented and pretty lady sing her song between glances at that doll who had just walked in. Finally they got a table not too far from where I stood at the bar. She was even more beautiful up close. There was something un-touchable about her. I knew dames like that could never be bought or owned. I did wonder, however, if there was a man in her life and if so, who was he, what did he do, how did he treat her in or out of the bedroom? Or was she looking for someone? *"Love for sale, appetizing young love for sale, love that's fresh and still unspoiled, love that's only slightly soiled...love for sale..."* June sang those lyrics with conviction. It just hit me that if she weren't married to the Goddess of Music, as she told me, June Maye might very well be a high-class prostitute, you know, the kind that spends the whole night with the out-of-town married executive and gets paid big bucks? Yeah, that one, especially in light of what she'd just said as she walked away, that she wanted to make sure love didn't get in the way of our sex. Now tell me *that* isn't kind of weird coming from a woman.

June finished, the applause died down, and as she started up her next number, I suddenly noticed that gorgeous redhead was looking right at me. Yeah, sure, I was okay handsome for an ex-ghetto bloke, but there were better looking guys lined up next to me at the bar. But she definitely *was* looking at me. I squinted in the semi-lit clubroom to see if she really was checking me out, or if it was my imagination. I couldn't tell for sure.

Then an interesting thing happened. One of the men in her party asked her to dance, and they made their way to the dance floor. She jitterbugged okay out there and you could tell she was having a good time. When the song was over, a gal about the same age as the red-head came out onto the floor and stole the guy to dance with. Some instinctive cue hit me on the head and I immediately walked out to the dance floor. June had just started up the last song of her set as I reached the beautiful babe. The song was fresh off the press and it couldn't have been more appropriate. It was called *My Romance*. I could tell in some weird kind of way that this lady and I were supposed to be doing this and we were being drawn back into a memory of some kind. "I hope you don't, uh, consider me out of line, ma'am, but I just couldn't see a beautiful young thing like you stranded on the dance floor. Would you like to spin around a little?"

She smiled at me with those bright warm eyes. They were a kind of speckled hazel-green. "Do I know you?"

"Not in this life, but you *were* looking my way earlier, were you not?"

Her face drew serious. "I'm sorry, when I saw you across the room, I thought you reminded me of someone else."

"My name's Cable...so shall we?"

She extended her hand. "Well, I can see no harm in it. I'm Laura Allen." We took each other's hands and spun around slowly to the music of Rodgers and Hart. "Do you frequent the *Bistro Club* much?"

We moved well together. "Not until recently. I—I, uh, know the singer warbling away up there on the stage."

"Is she your girlfriend?" she asked. I thought it a bit nosy.

"Well, I guess you could say that. We're, uh, well—an item, let's put it that way."

"She's very pretty—and talented. I love that song. It takes me away." I wanted to draw her closer and do the cheek-to-cheek bit, but I had second thoughts. Plus I didn't want June to see me hugging up to some other babe.

"Yeah, me, too." I started singing a little of the song to the lovely señorita. "*My romance, doesn't need a castle rising in Spain, nor a dance, to a constantly surprising refrain, wide awake I can make my most fantastic dreams come true...my romance...doesn't need a thing...but you...*"

Her eyes filled with a sentimental mist. "That's beautiful...you have a pleasant singing voice, Cable." She studied my face. "You sure look familiar."

I laughed. "Yeah? Well, maybe we met once upon dream. Thanks for the compliment. I just felt like singing it to you. Maybe I'm one of those incurable romantics people hear about. Especially since it's not every day that a two-bit gumshoe gets to dance with a knockout dame like you."

"Did you say gumshoe? Are you a private detective?"

"Yep, that's me."

"Did you ever know a family named *Royce*?"

I laughed to myself. How life is full of ironies. I was thinking of those ill-fated people and that incredible adventure I lived through with them. "As a matter of fact it

164

was Benedict Royce who hired me. And I knew Zephyr, Lexie and Eden. I even met Mom."

Her eyes grew wide. "My God, Cable, life is so strange! You *were* the one Eden spoke of before—well, before she died. I saw you at the funeral. I thought you had a rugged, handsome look then." She looked me over. "And you still do."

"You're too kind," I chuckled. "I haven't been in touch with whoever's left. I know Benedict got a bullet with his name on it."

The dance ended but we remained facing each other on the dance floor. "They're all gone now. The mother died recently, Zephyr drowned in the ocean near her little house. No one knows what happened to Lexie. Poor thing...he was so gentle, loving..."

A cold rush went through my body. Zephyr dead? It hit me hard for some reason. "That—that, uh, makes me feel really bad. She was such a rare girl. So what was your connection with the family?"

"I was a friend of Eden's. We went to school together years before. I was devastated to hear she died in her sleep so young."

"Try strangled and then hung upside down in a cave at Bronson Park. I ought to know...I found her."

She grabbed for my hand, holding it tight. I loved this woman's touch. "No! That's not what it said in the papers."

"Newspapers lie, Miss Allen. They tell you what *they're* told to tell you. Murder is murder by any other name, at least in my book. I liked Eden. She had gump- tion, real get up and go, even if she was a whorehouse madam." I was recalling our brief toss in the hay.

"How can the world be so beautiful with such horrible people in it?"

"I've been wondering that for a long time myself. May I ask what *you* do in this world?"

"Oh, I'm rich, and the world can get boring to the rich unless they create something to do. I've played around at acting and dancing, but my real interest is *ornithology*."

"You mean birds?"

"Yes, I've loved them since I was too young to remember."

"How odd! A beautiful babe getting herself all scratched up in the bush gazing at birds through a pair of fancy binoculars..."

"What's odd about beauty, Cable? Birds are the most exquisitely beautiful creatures on earth."

I was thinking of her and how exquisite *she* was. How her feminine soft voice sang in my ear. "I never looked at it that way. But you're right. Sometimes what keeps me going is the thought that tonight I'm gonna be listening to some great music sung by a beautiful babe like June all dressed up on that stage like a pretty bird trilling her heart out."

"Humans are a bit artificial, though, I think. But nature hits you with her direct impact. Did you know birds are very proud of their beauty?"

"Yeah, I could guess that. Look at a male peacock, huh?"

"Yes. You must take a field trip with me one day. I'll show you the wonders of things maybe you didn't realize even existed."

"That'd be swell, Miss Allen."

"Call me Laura."

"Okay, Laura. I'm—I'm in the phone book under *Detectives, Private*—Denning, Cable Denning..."

"I'll remember that." I walked her back towards her seat. She stopped and looked earnestly at me. "So that's why I thought I recognized you, Cable. You *were* the mysterious man in their lives. I think Zephyr was in love with you. Weren't you supposed to protect them as they moved to an island somewhere?"

"Yeah, but things kind of fell apart before we could make it happen. Royce was mixed up with some bad guys and when he quit them, they wanted revenge, so they plugged him."

We got to the table, I took her hand as she sat down. "It was a frightening experience for all of us." She introduced me to her friends. "Perhaps we'll meet again, Cable," she said with a warm expression in her voice. "One never knows...and thanks for the song. I love to be sung to."

"Yeah, one never knows... Oh, you're welcome, I enjoyed being the mysterious romantic partner—at least for one song and dance."

I walked away back toward the bar. A babe like that was one in a million, I thought. She was the kind of woman guys would put up on a pedestal, worship and adore—but you know what? She'd never belong to anyone because no man could own such beauty, intelligence and exceptional grace and movement. Yeah, men who attempted to own someone like Laura Allen would crash and burn on the rocks below her altar. And maybe nobody would be around to pick up the pieces.

I saw June approaching me. "One more set to go—and then *we* can go," she said, glancing over in the direction of Laura Allen's table. "That beautiful woman you were talking to, did you know her?"

"Yep. I was involved in a case with a wealthy family some time back. Laura was a friend of one of the daughters."

"Did you want to fuck her?" June asked in her matter-of-fact way.

"Yeah, the thought did occur to me. You have to admit, she's quite a dish."

"I'm glad you tell me the truth, Cable. And I can tell when you are. It's refreshing to hear you say you might desire another woman, but I'm hoping I'm enough for you. Just don't mess around on my time, okay?"

"What about you?"

"Lord, man, how could I want to screw another guy when I've got you? A girl would have to be nuts."

I smiled and hugged June. "Thanks for that, June. Just for that I'll be extra tender tonight."

"Who says I like it tender, big boy?" she laughed.

Uncle Teddy and the World's Greatest Secret

It was Thursday about ten a.m. I had slept well, considering June and I went several rounds before the bell rang and I needed to get home or perish from making love. I thought I'd look up good old Uncle Teddy and try and see him before I took Lily to see Crazy Jack. I used the phone number Lily had given me and a quick-spoken gentleman with a pleasant, high-toned voice came on the phone. He said he was too busy to see me, but when I mentioned that Lily might be in danger, he agreed to meet with me immediately. He worked out of a private lab in Glendale. The place was white, glistening marble and the man at the gate delayed me until he had called Dr. Theodore Norwood and the good doctor approved. Then I was led down a long corridor, got into an elevator with a security guard and went down two floors. Finally we knocked at a door that read *Eugenics, Dr. Theodore Norwood, o.f.c.*

Soon a medium sized man with thick black-rimmed glasses opened the door. "Mr. Denning," he said in his brisk voice. "Do come in immediately. Thank you, George, I'll call you when Mr. Denning is ready to depart." The officer disappeared and I looked around the laboratory. As were most chemistry labs, this one was filled with test tubes, Bunsen burners, glass distillers, small metal tanks and the like. But there was one door on the west side of the room that caught my attention. First of all it was circular. Second, it had a huge circle painted on it, filled in with pie-shaped wedges of bright orange, white and black.

"I'm glad to meet you, Dr. Norwood."

He took out a cigarette and offered me one. I took it. He lit me up and did the same for himself. I estimated him to be about sixty. "Hell with formality, Denning. I go for simplicity. Call me Teddy. Lily does, you know. I've been her uncle for some time now—and I ought to know."

"You mean since she was born, don't you?"

"No—I always cut to the chase—don't like to waste time, I do not—no, sir, I do not. Lily was adopted when she was three. I cannot imagine a gorgeous creature like that being abandoned on a soup kitchen doorstep with a knapsack and runny nose. Now...can you imagine that, Denning? No, you cannot, can you? Lily is a spectacular specimen of female perfection—at least as far as our biological evolution has come. More to come, to be sure—always more to come."

The guy smoked and rattled on. He was a very nervous man, but I could tell he had a genuine fondness for his niece. "Yes, you have a nice niece.....but she may be in danger. I've got this gut feeling she's being stalked by someone who genuinely has an ill intent toward her person."

"*Nice niece*—I like that. How fast can you spell it without thinking twice! Ha! ho! I've got you, don't I? Stalker, you say? Humph! Blat! It is probably some jealous male full of testosterone, unhappy and easily frustrated because Lily does not bend easily to the sexual whim of a male of the same genus. What would you say, Denning? I know for a fact that testosterone is the most singularly dangerous hormone known to mankind. It's what causes uncontrolled sexual impulse, greed, lust, war, regrets—and bad memories. I ask you, what else is wrong with this planet except that—and the existence of the male population? Oh, then there's the terrible crossbreeding humans are doing in this so-called 'modern' era, the twentieth century. Oh, my, Nordic blood with black blood, Asian with Hispaniola blood, Arabs with Canadians—ayi! If it were not for disease, just think, we would be so populated that no one could move an inch in this world."

I was getting a little impatient with Uncle Teddy. "Do you think you could tell me all you know about Lily and why you think she might be being tailed—I mean, beside what you've already told me?"

He paused. "Hmmm...besides my original hypothesis? Let me see...simple logic. Upon her arrival in the states, Lily becomes employed by a local ballet company after a long tour with some European concern, she rises fast, is most likely envied by some. Of course it could also be her involvement in *Remoh*. That's Homer spelled backward, a little joke of mine. Ha! Got you, didn't I? But without a doubt, Lily is involved in some religious sect—or the like—blat, I don't really care for those things because they're so unscientific it's not worth my time to think about them. Are you a religious man? I would hate to hate you because you are, you realize. Poor Lily is in enough hot water."

"Now...this is for real, Teddy? Do you know this sect's real name? It could be important. It's another angle, we might find someone was pushed out of shape by something Lily did or didn't do, said or didn't say. Come on, man, think...what else might you know?"

"That about covers it, doesn't it? I think you're a bright man. Lily would probably be attracted to your pheromones if you gave her a chance to smell you up close."

I was beginning to think the doc was a little on the nuttier-than-a-fruitcake side. "What? Smell me—what in the hell are *pheromones*?"

"Units of released glandular gases coming off your skin and pores—in ancient times, we may have traced you by your scent in this manner. So, getting back to my charming Lily—a woman is either attracted to, repelled by or neutral regarding a man's pheromones. It is that scent of familiarity that animals recognize and accept—or reject each other by. We are no exception. Why do humans always want to be an exception to nature when they're in nature and *depend* on nature for each and every breath they take? Anyway, ask Lily to smell you and let her tell you what kind of response she has to your Denning scent."

"Ya know, you're not helping me much here, doc. Do you have any clues except for that sect or religion you were talking about?"

"Not a one. But you're a curious sort, I suggest. And I'll just bet you've seen things most people have not. Am I right?"

"Yeah...how would you know that?"

"Ha! ha! Because my own life was threatened the moment I hung up from talking to you this morning. That's rich, eh? Hee! hee! You see how dangerous you are wherever you go? What am I talking about? No, no, no, you are naughty to imply they may catch up with me and depopulate the earth by one—namely me! Ha! Blat! But now I am a prisoner in my own laboratory—but do not, I say, do not lament me. I am more at home here than anywhere. Frankly, people bore me."

I was thinking about Becker, his goons and the *Oculus*. My phone was tapped! And they could trace any call I'd make to anywhere. But they couldn't trace a call that came to me...yet. I knew that because Ken Cole, a friend of mine from high school, worked for the phone company and told me that some time ago. "I'm sorry, doc, I didn't mean to get you involved. It's a curse that's been

172

hanging around my neck for a while. I know too much about some things, I guess."

"Well, I'll bet you don't know this!" the slight man chortled. "I'll bet you will not now—nor ever—guess what I know that you do not know...no sir...that you do not know....nor, without my showing you, will you ever, ever, ever know. Are you ready?"

"Ready for what, Teddy—I'm not here for Twenty Questions and I don't see what this might have to do with Lily—"

"—everything, you little chisel-chin detective, you! I know something that every greedy paw in the world would kill for—and I have it! In fact, I have invented it and live with it daily. But some suspect. Do you know why they suspect? Because one night in a great excitement and supreme stupidity I showed Lily my secret *singular greatest invention of all time*—and quite by accident she happened to mention what she had witnessed, to her stage godfather old Mr. Bruckner. Another man was seated not far away and took that information to someone else—oh, how shall I say it—someone irredeemably *diabolical, horrid, evil, deceitful, greedy, powerful, without conscience, deadly...*" He got this wide-eyed look in his eyes. "He killed my partner, thinking it was I—and thinking he killed the secret, he seemed to disappear for a while. But now he is back, in the shadows, in the streets late at night—perhaps haunting Lily to get at her, frighten her, pursue her until she cracks and forces her to confess that she, too, has seen the Great and Most Powerful—I'm a Frank L. Baum fan, you know—and then bring a great woe upon my dear niece."

"Now you're telling me something, doc. No wonder...damn, she's in plenty of danger! So...what have you to show me? And if you do, will I place myself in jeopardy forever—like poor Lily?"

"Yes...yes, and yes! You will be haunted, flaunted, shunted, bunted and blunted by those who would themselves give their lives for what I have in that room." He pointed a finger to the circular door I noticed when I first came in. "In there...in there, Denning, lies what modern man has been seeking and will continue to seek until or unless I confess my stupendous, marvelous, exhilarating invention to the mere mortals who toil in the sands of time for naught. That's why I do not display it with neon and banners and marching bands to the world. I have yet...to see one worthy man whom I believe deserves to know and benefit from my wondrous prize."

"And you want to show me? The only reasons I'm going to say yes to you, Teddy, is because I need to see what Lily saw, I'm already a dead man, so I'm not worried about my person—and then, because I really think you're nuts and I need to see for myself that you're on the level with this 'greatest invention of all time' thing."

He tilted his head to one side and smiled a rather sick-honey smile. "You're right—I *am* nuts, as you say, Denning. But only a crazy man could have brought through what you are about to see. There are dimensions I tapped into. I once knew a very powerful East Indian who was his own kind of chemist. He issued me some herbal hallucinogens one evening—and everything became clear to me. It had been teetering on the edge of my consciousness for a long time. I did not realize I had to access it dimensionally by going to it in *its dimension*. Then I could bring it back onto this three-dimensional plane and manifest it as the greatest invention the world will ever know. If I choose to share it, that is." Then he brightened up. "But then you know how eccentric and tempestuously angry a crazy old doctor can get, right?"

I was beginning to think the guy was not quite as nuts as I thought, even if he was eccentric in a curious unorthodox way.

"Lead on, doc. Let's see this best kept secret in the world..."

He approached the circular door. He tapped on each of the individual pie slices, not in succession, but in what appeared a random order. But he tapped a different number of times on each painted panel. Then there was a slight roar and a hiss of air and the huge, heavy door swung open, much like a gigantic bank vault entrance. We stepped into a world of blue-green light. In the center of the room was a brightly lit glowing triangle about the size of one of those played in a marching band. There appeared to be thousands of little lights built into the domed ceiling and they sparkled like little colored stars. "Now you never will, I say—never have before, never will again—see the likes of this, Denning. My invention supersedes all the intelligences heretofore on the planet."

"So what does it do besides just sit there?" I asked naively.

"Anything I want it to do," Dr. Teddy Norwood answered. He had a small silver piece of metal in his hand that had small buttons on it. He pushed one of the buttons. "Now...hear my voice...suddenly it is lower...isn't it? I have slowed down time...speak, Denning..."

I was amazed. "Well, doc, I am impressed. What else does it do?"

He pressed the same button on the little thing in his hand and our voices returned to normal. "It's original intent?"

"Yeah, something like that." I noticed the huge door close behind us. I was thinking it would be a hell of thing to be in here with no way out. Things that depend on electricity were at best a risk.

"What is before you, Denning, is the world's first and only *fusionator*. Fusion is a process by which atoms are collapsed in on themselves by the joining of two or more atomic nuclei. This agitation creates the release of limitless energy—enough power to light ten thousand cities the size of Los Angeles for a million years for the cost of not one penny!"

"I don't get it," I said, too overwhelmed and amazed to figure it.

"That's why I had to take the hallucinogen trip. You see, I had to visit a solar sun, for an active star operates by the compression of the items inside the atom and thereby creating that incredible light we see as solar light—the light from faraway suns. My old crazy chum, Dr. Oliphant, gave me the bug. He had separated out the fusion of hydrogen isotopes—"

"—hey, doc! You're talking through your hat here—I haven't got a clue about what you're saying. All I see is pretty colors in a dark room that can make our voices get deeper."

He looked down, obviously dejected. "Then it is useless. Even you, Denning, having seen what you have seen, cannot see this potential miracle before you—running the entire planet's energy from one simple source—lights, automobiles, factories, universities, every home in all the world. Alas, you are the reason I shall keep my secret. In the wrong hands, it shall be used either as a weapon to destroy or as a way for the greedy rich to control the earth. Blat! You'd better go now, I am disappointed in you—and all like you, shallow little human man."

I laughed. "Well, that might be truer than you say, doc, but you know, you're ahead of your time and I agree with you. Humans ain't worthy of such a knowledge. They'd abuse it, just like you say."

"You do believe me, then? For that, the least I can offer you is a consolation prize." He went to a wide drawer that was constructed into a wall and opened it. He withdrew a large paper bag that was taped shut. "Denning....take just one thimble full of this and be enlightened. Know what I know. But be careful. Do not abuse it. For once you are addicted, it will take you years to get it out of your blood system."

I took the bag and thanked the man. He made a phone call and led me to the door. "And Lily? I know, foolish man, you are concerned for her, and were probably paid by her to protect her precious self. And she is precious. But if *they* want her, they will get her. You shall not now, today, tomorrow or ever be able to stop them. Good luck, Denning. I have told you all I know."

I shook the doc's hand and left. The security guard was waiting and we took the elevator up to street level. My head was swirling.

The Trouble With Pheromones

Sometime later I was at Lily Norwood's door. She was happy to see me and we walked down the hill from her house to catch a streetcar. We traveled in relative silence since there was much I needed to share with her in private. The Red car took us right to Los Angeles Street and 5th near Crazy Jack's four-story digs, the old *Panama Hotel* now a defunct and dilapidated housing unit for the rejects of the world. Jack lived on the top floor. Lily seemed a little uncomfortable, but she trusted me, and that's all I needed. I banged on Crazy Jack's door. There was no answer. In my business you just never knew when you had seen the last of someone. People came into my life and then left this world faster than the traffic at the downtown train station. Lily was completely out of place. She wore a lovely white skirt and peach blouse with a light-straw hat with a flowered band around it. She looked exquisite.

"I'm sorry, Lily, but I don't have any other way of contacting Jack."

"It's okay, maybe just as well. Maybe whatever he'd have to say would be so unpleasant that we wouldn't enjoy our evening." She looked at me. "And I want to enjoy our evening together."

178

"Yeah, me, too," I said, thinking of how it might feel holding that dancing doll in my arms as we twirled around the room.

As we descended the stairs Crazy Jack was coming up. He wore a dirty black coat and his hair was disheveled as usual. "Jack! I brought someone for you to meet."

"I don't know! I don't know! Jack feel pooped. Policeman hit Jack with blackjack hard!" He took my hand and made me feel a bump on his noggin. "Jack do nothing—but I don't know! I don't know!"

"This is Lily, Jack. She is being pursued by someone who isn't very nice and I'd like you to use your special gift to tell us if you see someone or something that may be causing her to be menaced."

Jack looked at Lily. "Pretty dancing lady! Oh! Dancing lady hurt...Jack say be far away! Hide away, today! Ha! Jack say, but I don't know! I don't know."

Lily looked at me. "Do you think, sir, that my life may be in danger? Or is it some prank to scare me or—"

"—I don't know! I don't know! Dancer stay, dancer die. Crazy Jack see no more. Jack hurt on head...go now, Cable...nice man...Cable...help Jack—cigarette! Cigarette!"

As per our ritual, I got out a cigarette and gave it to Jack, lit him up and tucked the rest of the pack in his coat pocket. "Thanks, Jack. Sorry to bother you. Hope you recover. Do you want me to take you down to a clinic for them to look at your bump?"

"Jack good! Cigarette good! Jack thank Cable. Lady, love...love Cable...he good...but I don't know! I don't know!"

We left Jack smoking at the top of the stairs. I could tell Lily was shaken a bit. "I told you he'd pop out with anything that came to his head. But I also told you I never knew Jack to be wrong."

"Oh, Lord, Cable—what shall I do? I can't leave rehearsals just because some old crackpot says I should. Would you?"

"It's not my call, babe. I can't decide for you. All I can tell you is if it were me, yeah, I'd be outta town, hiding out somewhere until you could figure the whole thing and maybe stay alive a little bit longer."

She grabbed on to my arm and walked to Broadway where we found *Llewellyn's* restaurant. It was nice with private booths and round tables with white tablecloths and fine silver. There was a big chandelier with electric candlesticks that gave off a warm yellow glow over the dance floor. It was too early for the band.

We ordered a lime soda each and I took out my little flash of gin and poured some into both our drinks. It wouldn't be until December when alcohol would be flowing freely after the long siege of Prohibition. Lily and I toasted. "Here's to you, dancing lady. And to some wise decisions to preserve your life and beauty."

She toasted back. "And to you, my fair protector, may you find the culprit who haunts my daily life."

I was now prepared to get to the gist of things. "Uh, Lily...I went to see your Uncle Teddy earlier this afternoon. You hadn't quite prepared me for his—"

"—crazy eccentricities? Sorry, but he's my uncle and I love him with all his warts and faults and genius."

"Well, toots, you left out a couple of pertinent facts when I asked you what you knew. Now, I don't want to get pissed at you for withholding from me because maybe you weren't clear as to the rules of the game. But you conveniently left out a couple of things, one being you were a foundling, a backstreet orphan adopted by the Norwood family. Second, that you belong to some kind of religious sect called *Remoh* which certainly could implicate you in why you are being pursued by an unknown party or parties—oh, yeah, and last but not least—Uncle Teddy showed you what was behind the big circular door, you told Bruckner, but someone else heard you spill the beans and things kind of got around to the wrong parties. Sounds to me like you've gathered the perfect storm around you, lady. What've you got to say for yourself?"

He eyes were wide with surprise as I spoke and tears came as she took her hat off and placed it quietly on the seat next to her. "You should fire me as your client. You're right, I did keep those things from you. May I explain, please?"

"I think you'd better, Miss Norwood, because if you want that dance later, I've got to be convinced that you're the real thing. I don't want a phony dame stiffing me for dinner and not delivering the whole truth and nothing but the truth."

"You're absolutely right. So here goes. Frankly, I didn't think being adopted really mattered. But I got involved in *Remoh* with a man I trusted. I only have Sundays off, really, so he convinced me some spiritual or metaphysical higher knowledge would be good for me. Since I wasn't your common garden variety of Christian, I agreed. But in time the rituals turned darker and I realized there was a kind of erotic, satanic side to this

181

movement. For example, my friend wanted me to go naked and dance at some of the rituals to some kind of pagan flute and drum music. I admit the rituals were mesmerizing and the music lulled us into a kind of hypnotic state. But I later learned that the cup of water we all drank from as we entered the temple was laced with some kind of drug, perhaps an aphrodisiac. Many of the women gave themselves freely behind curtains, all in the name of *Remoh,* who was supposed to be the dark brother of Jesus Christ of Nazareth."

"Who said there was a sucker born every minute— and two to take him? How does that fit?"

She frowned. "It wasn't quite that simple. I'm not stupid, Cable. I was lonely and longed for a fraternity of like-minded people. Since I'd seen Uncle Teddy's unbelievable invention, I felt I could no longer associate with the everyday type of person. I no longer fit—if I ever did."

"So you go for exotic erotic, eh? Well, I guess there are worse things. But go on, babe..." I lit up a Lucky Strike and blew the smoke away from where she sat opposite me.

"So I quit the temple. But it wasn't that easy. It seems I hadn't finished some rituals and their bylaws state you must do so before you can terminate with them."

"So, let me guess, part of it was you naked on the altar having sex with the head mucky-muck, right?"

"Well, sort of. But I had the option of just dancing, which I chose. So I finished out my obligation that way and left the organization."

"So you thought." I was searching all the dark corners for answers. "So as I see it, if you don't mind me getting right to it, you could have your stalker coming from three possible sources. One, someone at work who is envious or whom you offended, two, someone in the *Remoh* society who didn't get into your panties but still wants to—or three, that evil someone your uncle talks about who overheard you tell Bruckner about your experience in Uncle Teddy's little *fusionator room.*"

She looked at me with those bright eyes of confidence, drying her tears with a handkerchief I had given her. "You're so brilliant, Cable. Yes, I agree. The rest of my life is work...nothing else. It's all I know."

"And you're sure now there isn't some hidden man who got some of you but wanted more?"

"Yes. I never wanted any of them. Despite what you might think, I'm a very selective woman. I don't come cheap—and I don't act cheap."

"Oh, I believe that, doll. It's just that someone else might not. You know the roll call, sex and money rule the world, huh?"

"So I've heard," she said indignantly.

"So as I see it, right now you're looking like a Dutch dyke with three major holes pouring out water. Which of the leaks do we fix first?"

The waiter brought our meals and we ate quietly. In the meantime, a small combo had set up and began playing music. They began with a medium tempo version of *Don't Blame Me* and I could tell by the time Lily had her third lime-gin drink, she was a little drunk.

Maybe she couldn't handle alcohol very well. "You know what they're playing up there?" I asked her.

"No, I'm not too up on popular music."

"It's called *Don't Blame Me*. It has some interesting lyrics. You see, for me, songs tell stories—at least the best songs. . *'I like every single thing about you, without a doubt you are like a dream, in my mind I find a picture of us as a team...Ever since the hour of our meeting, I've been repeating a silly phrase, hoping that you'll under-stand me one of these days...Don't blame me for falling in love with you...I'm under your spell but how can I help it! Don't blame me!'...*"

Lily Norwood blushed through her makeup. "Do you believe that, Cable—that sometimes it's just out of our control when certain people are brought together?"

"I don't buy into fairy tales, Lily. But I do think peo-ple are attracted to each other. Maybe it's like your Un-cle Teddy told me—it's the *pheromones.*"

"The what?"

"Pheromones...the smell of a woman or a man, that either repels or attracts. It's on the skin. You know, like when you dance, some people might smell better than others to you."

"Yes...we sweat a lot. It's true, I got pregnant from a man who smelled the way I liked. The one I told you about."

"Well, then, I rest my case. How would you like that dance?" I asked, thinking it was about time for us to move around.

"Yes. I'd like that," she said in her soft, demure way.

I took her hand and we went out to the dance floor with three or four other couples spinning around next to us. Being a dancer, she was smooth as silk and I was afraid I would seem like a clod leading her around on the floor. But what the hell, I did it anyway. As the lights fell dim she cuddled up a little closer and put her nose in my neck. "I like your smells, Cable," she whispered to me as we came to a very slow rhythm, dancing to the tune of *In a Little Spanish Town*. Half way through the dance she drifted her pretty little nose up to my cheek and pouted those lovely lips of hers into my ear. "Cable...would you ever consider taking me home and making love to me? I mean, without destroying our professional relationship?"

I was knocked over. Where do dames get these whims? "What time is it?" I asked.

"Why...what difference would that make?"

"Because I'm more expensive after midnight."

She giggled under her breath. "Then we'd better go now..."

I took a deep breath but kept dancing with her. "It's not that I don't want to, Lily, but I'm afraid in a different way than you're afraid. You see, I keep losing people I care about. And if Crazy Jack's right, you're one of the next ones on the list. And don't you think it'd just complicate things?"

"You don't want me," she said, still a little inebriated.

"No...I just said any guy who wouldn't want you would have to have his head examined. What else can I say?"

"Dancers are known to be very tight...in private places," she confessed. "All the muscle work, you know..."

"Did you hear me?"

"No, Cable, I didn't. You must live in such a neat, enviable world. The music you listen to, the way you talk to women like me, the tough outer shell that comes from having to survive the pitfalls of your business—and girls like me...who tell you the stories of love and romance you want to hear—only those stories are the fantasies that hardly ever come true. For God's sake, it's not like I'm a virgin anymore, I'm an adult woman who knows what she wants." She took a deep smell at the nape of my neck. "Yes...and yes...Uncle Teddy was right...your smell is just the thing."

"I thought when we first met, you told me that everything I alluded to was sexual. I remember your exact words, as a matter of fact. '*Why is everything so sexual to you, Mr. Denning?*' is what you asked me that day in my office, remember? So now you know."

"I only know the way I feel...and I don't pooh-pooh you anymore—because you awakened in me what's been asleep for so long. I promise I won't complicate things for you." She became a little irritated. "For God's sake, Cable, I can't beg..."

I didn't say anything but drew her closer to me. We finished the dance in silence and I escorted her back to our booth. We sat down and I looked at the beautiful woman opposite me, her warm brown eyes innocent and longing, the alcohol taking down her guard. "I can't do it, Lily. I know it sounds stupid, but I like you too much. For me, it'd be just another notch on my gun. For you, it'd have meaning, that first step in loving someone maybe, a room for something special to grow."

She looked at me, unbelieving. "If what you say is true, you're the first man...in my life...who walked the other way. Every man I've ever known has wanted me as if I were a doll in a China shop. And here *you* are, refusing my desire..."

"Believe me, it ain't personal, Lily. If I was someone else I'd grab you up like tomorrow's fire sale. But as I told you earlier, at thirty-three I've already lived a few lifetimes and losing one more someone I might just really care for—well, a guy can only take so much."

She took a deep breath. "Thank you for the evening, Cable. I think you'd better take me home."

We walked up the hill to the little house on Westerly Terrace. It was a neutral colored stucco with lots of colorful plants around. Banana trees, other trees and greenery I didn't recognize, with flowers falling over the front wall. We climbed the stairs back to her place. She took out her key and opened the door. She had been quiet, reserved on the trip back from the restaurant. She turned to me. I gently took her arm. "Are you hurt, babe?"

"Wouldn't you be? After all, it's not every night a woman gets refused. But I'll get over it. It's rather like auditioning for a part and not getting it. I'm used to that."

"Well, that's what happens when sex gets in the way. I told you. We've got a professional relationship here and I wanna keep it. So, let's just say we looked into that room and decided to pass."

"*You* decided to pass." She went ahead of me into her house, then turned to look at me with those same beautiful eyes, that gorgeous figure and face there in the dark. "Won't you at least come in for a nightcap? I don't have much liquor around, but I have some old Champagne in the ice box, unopened, that is."

"Champagne? Yeah, that doesn't sound too bad—it's been a while. But....haven't you already had enough tonight?"

"Well, Mr. Denning. Are you my caretaker, father and overseer?" she said as she led me into the kitchen and got out the cold bottle of Champagne. She handed it to me and I did the honors. The cork popped off and we both laughed like two kids stealing something from Mom's cupboard. She didn't have Champagne glasses so we poured the bubbly into two large beer mugs she had hanging around. We toasted. She clinked her glass to mine and held it there. "Somehow, Cable, I know I'll come out of this respecting you. You're the most unusual man I've ever known. And yet I feel I don't know you at all, but thanks for the dinner and dance. I enjoyed it very much."

As I was looking at her, all of a sudden I got this funny feeling about the dame. There was something familiar about her. As if there was a hidden look behind her hidden look. If that made sense. "Here's to the most beautiful dancer who will ever do *Swan Lake*."

She smiled at me, then took a big, un-lady-like gulp from her mug. "Thank you, Cable Denning." Then she studied me as we stood there opposite one another in the kitchen. "It's funny, isn't it?"

"What's funny?"

"The more a girl gets refused by someone she desires, the more she wants him."

"Yeah, that's a perversity I've observed in human female behavior. But you gotta look at the other end of it, too. Suppose you get your way. Suppose we do it and all the bells and whistles go off in the right places. You're still stuck with the morning after and the realities of who it was you allowed into your body, into your heart. Then all those pheromones your uncle was talking about kick in and your pores smell of both of you and you get hooked on a feeling, that big itch you can never quite scratch. That kind of love is like a romantic dream that belongs in some fairy tale book, tossed together with the princess who would be queen kidnapped by the evil magician but saved by Prince Charming. And one day soon Lily Norwood wakes up to find herself distracted from her wonderful dancing, her noble profession, because now she's a woman in love and those hormones and pheromones are taking her over one heartache after another. Why? Because the man she loves is like the Prince Charming in the fairy tale, he's an illusion, he doesn't exist—and in this case he's as dead as the dinosaur at the local museum. No, Lily, take my advice, be in love with your work, it's a lot safer. Be in love with the ideal romance that can never quite take place on this level of existence but lives there inside and drives the mechanism of your heart and soul—the one that tells you something *can* be but won't happen this time out because lifetimes are like little sparks that go darting around in the night and get snuffed out by a great big unfriendly universe that doesn't give a damn because it's impersonal. Only humans are stupid enough to make love personal. And finally, when you hurt enough and your tank reads 'full' and there's nothing else to do but realize you've been your own patsy, you sit out on the sidelines and you can say 'no' to some

189

beautiful woman who wants to make love to you on a balmy Los Angeles night." I paused, taking a long drink from my mug. "And in the end, no one ever figures out who they are or where they're going or why they ever were at all. All we ever have, Miss Norwood, is love and beauty. But it's the perfect, impersonal kind...the kind that feeds you like great music, or great dancing or someone who looks at you from eyes that are *all* eyes, that represent the caring *uncaring*. Then life makes sense because you can disconnect without getting hurt..."

"*You* can disconnect without getting hurt," she answered me, having stood opposite me motionless during my tirade. "As I told you when I first met you, Cable, I never heard anyone talk the way you do. And it doesn't matter what you say *with* that voice, what attracts the woman is the voice itself, not the content. So you see how you could possibly be wasting a lot of words?" Then she brightened up. "Beside, Champagne makes you forget all the rest! Drink up!"

She led me into the living room and excused herself. I sat on her nice light green sofa peering at a magazine. Soon Lily Norwood came out barefooted in just her slip. The silk clung to her body as if it were formed around it. Any red-blooded American male couldn't help but respond. "Say there, lady! Am I in for a fashion show—or what?"

"I just wanted you to see what you're missing."

I laughed. "Oh, I know what I'm missing, Lily." She was getting more and more tipsy. "I think you ought to go to bed. Don't you have rehearsal in the morning at the theatre?"

190

"I think I ought to go to bed...with *you*, Cable. Rehearsal, piddle! I can do that any day of the week. But you're not in my house any day of the week. And I don't feel this way any day of the week..." She came to me, took the mug out of my hand and sat on my lap. She put her arm around me and brought her wet lips onto mine and kissed me hard. "Now...can you be impersonal, Mr. Universal?" she purred.

"Not if you keep that up, lady," I said, enjoying the kiss that rumbled through my body all the way to my toes.

"Then let me keep it up and you just might see things my way." She kissed me again, but all of a sudden she fainted in my arms and I lowered her to the sofa. I knew it was the booze. Some people just can't handle it. I picked her up and took her into her bedroom, put her into bed and covered her gently. I looked down at this beautiful doll. Any guy with any sense would have taken his clothes off and slipped in between the sheets with her. I kissed her on the forehead and left.

I got out the front door and all of a sudden something hit me hard on the head and splattered all over me. As I went down for the count, all I could see was white liquid everywhere. When I came to, there was a figure bending over me. "Cable...Cable...can you hear me? It's me...Joe...Joe Lorena. Someone hit you with a full milk bottle. Could have killed you, buddy, and you still might have a concussion."

As my eyes began to focus and I could feel that terrible dull ache on the right side of my skull. Joe pulled me up and propped me against Lily's front door. "Joe...you

191

old son-of-a-gun. What—what the hell happened? I was on my way out—"

"—I didn't see anyone. I got here too late. How are your motor functions?" He took a healing hand and placed it on my head. I could feel a warmth course through my head and down my body to my chest. "Hmmm...you are one durable human, I must say."

Almost instantly I felt better. I was aware that the good aliens had marvelous energy faculties, including what humans would call *healing powers*. Well, Joe had that ability in spades and it was good to see this fine man who was Honey Combes' real-life sire. "So, Joe, what brings you to this neighborhood?"

"Lily Norwood...Cable...may I ask you...did you...did you, uh, make love with her?"

"Not quite, Joe, it almost happened, but she couldn't take her booze so she fainted in my arms. Why do you ask? Do you know her?"

"Thank goodness. It might have been fatal to her. I don't know how to say this, Cable, but Lily is an exact replica of Honey's mother."

I sat there in disbelief, shaking my head, checking to see if there were any cobwebs in my ears that I may not have heard right. If it was true, no wonder there was something familiar about Lily Norwood! I could see Honey in her. "Joe, how can that be? I mean, the time discrepancy—Lily's young—Honey's mother would be—"

"—Lily was one of the first successes early on in our attempts to duplicate human DNA. Lily is an exact clone of Honey's mother. We grew her from *seed*, so to say, right from her own cell code before she gave birth to

Honey. Lily's embryo reached full term in a giant test tube solution in our laboratories."

I was coming out of my semi-consciousness but all this was making my head hurt. Now it was making sense why Lily was such a perfect specimen of human female kind. "I guess it all makes sense, Joe. Lily told me she got knocked up by some dancing partner, but said she lost the kid because she was dancing too hard and shook it loose. But what you're really saying is she would have aborted it anyhow—and being pregnant put her at risk."

"Yes, Cable, precisely. I've been watching you the minute she came to you for help. But I wasn't sure I should interfere. But since I know your proclivity for women—and it appeared poor Lily was attracted to you—you might end up making love and—"

"—whatta you mean 'poor Lily'? I fought her off as long as I could." I rubbed my aching head. "Now, let me see, I've got you, Becker, the *Oculus,* J. Edgar Hoover's boy scouts and the Vatican minding my business these days. Anyone else I don't know about?"

"I know it's a full load, Cable. But as you see, my reasons are different. Lily ran away from us and showed up on some doorstep when she was four or so. It took me years to trace her to the Norwood family. And you'll also be comforted to know, I'm not after the *God of Our Fathers.* I was simply trying to protect Lily. The last time I saw you was when that little Toggth creature was teleporting to some other dimension or something, wasn't it?"

"Yeah, something like that," I said.

"How did you leave Lily?"

"A bit drunk, fast asleep in her bed...untouched, by the way..."

"Thanks, Cable, I do know you are an honorable man. Lily was not engineered to have a great sexual appetite. Seems it must have increased upon meeting you." He got up from my side and winced as he looked out into the night sky. "It almost kills me to look at Lily. She's the perfect image of my beautiful wife at her prime."

"Does she know?"

"No. She thinks she's an ordinary mortal woman. Well, in a way she is. She will grow old and die like the rest—"

"—I wouldn't be too sure about that. You do know she's being tailed by some stalker? And I've got a few doozy candidates. A jealous competitor at the ballet theatre, a satanic religious group—and some bad guys who are after what her Uncle Teddy has invented."

"Oh, him..." Joe said, scratching his head. "Do you know what he's invented?"

"*The greatest secret invention of all time*, according to him. I'm not a science guy, but as far as I can figure, it's something about *atomic fusion* for energy to run the earth with."

"Oh? Well, fusion is old hat to us. But it won't be on the earth for a while. Too many greedy, powerful earthlings would misuse it."

"That was Doc Teddy's conclusion. So there it sits, in a vault in his lab, locked away 'til kingdom come."

"So do you know why Lily is attracted to you?"

"Oh, yeah, those damned *pheromones* her uncle's been warning me about. But Lily says it's my voice. She's lonely, Joe. A young woman like that tied to her dancing disciplines doesn't have a lot of time for fun. I took her dancing. She loved it." I tried to get up. Joe helped me to my feet. "So who's chasing her, Joe?"

"I'm not sure. Probably the same guy who hit you with the milk bottle. But I don't know what he wants."

"Seems my sleuthing ability is being challenged these days. I'm having a hell of a time uncovering the layers. I just started, though. Lily left out some important shit when it came to helping me out with a list of candidates."

"You say she's, uh, she's asleep?"

"Yep."

"Let's take you in the house and wash you up a bit. You can't go home with spilled milk and blood all over you."

We went into Lily's house and Joe guided me to the bathroom. There he helped me take off my clothes and I drew a bath while he kept guard. I rinsed out my clothes. But just as I was relaxing in the tub I heard Lily's voice cry out in alarm. I jumped out of the tub naked as a jaybird and came running into the living room where she and Joe stood opposite each other, Lily armed with a tennis racket. "It's okay, Lily—it's me—and this is Joe, my friend." I could see how difficult it was for Joe to stand there, looking at the woman who was the exact duplicate of the only woman he ever loved.

Lily looked me over. "Well, isn't this quaint? Earlier I couldn't even get him to take his clothes off. But now, in the presence of a strange man, he's naked and in my bathroom. What's going on?"

"It's simple, babe. Once I tucked you into bed safe and sound, I got hit with a milk bottle on my way out. Joe here saved my butt and helped me into your house to wash and clean up."

She looked at Joe. For an instant I thought there might have been some kind of sympathetic recognition between the two of them. Not likely, I guess. She came over and checked out my head. "I'm—I'm sorry, Cable. It's because of me, isn't it?"

"Well...it could be, Lily—but these days, for me, it's hard to tell *who* might be out to get me."

Joe was nervous. "Cable, I—I think I'll run along now. I'll check in with you sometime tomorrow. Good to meet you, Miss Norwood. I'm—I'm sorry it couldn't be under better circumstances."

Lily just stood there as Joe let himself out. Then she felt her slip and looked at her crotch area. "So we didn't...did we?"

"No, Lily. I tucked you into bed, as I told you."

"Why didn't you want me, Cable?"

"I told you it wasn't that, lady. And right now I'm in no mood to talk about it. I'm dripping naked in the middle of your floor, my clothes are wet hanging from a shower curtain rod in your bathroom, I'm tired and my head hurts like hell."

"Oh, I'm so sorry...here...let me help you. We can dry your clothes in my oven." She assisted me back into the bathtub, took my clothes and disappeared. I sat back in the bathtub thinking what a hell of a night this turned out to be!

Chapter 7

THE TRANSCENDERS

By mid-April 1933 I began to worry. Becker had told me I had three months when I saw him that night in the *Bistro Club*, after which he and his Gestapo folk would be rounding me up for a go at the *neural extractor*, their diabolical new invention for sucking out specific information from the brain. Once that was done, I could be discarded like an old potato sack.

During this trying couple of months I was no further along on my case for Lily Norwood. She was still being pestered, but sleuth around as I might, I could never catch anyone skulking around her at her house or her place of work. It was as if there was some phantom presence—allowing itself to be seen in the physical dimension only when it suited its menacing purpose. Joe Lorena had contacted me and I promised him I would keep my hands off Lily. It was hard sometimes. And so was I, around *her*. But fortunately for Lily, June Maye kept me busy in that department as our sexual relationship continued to intensify. She was singing great and packing them into the *Bistro Club*. I had told June about the bag of hallucinogens Uncle Teddy had given me that day in February. She was anxious to try them out, take a trip of cigarettes, booze and dope, so we could get lost together, and up the ante on our sexual adventures. I told her about Lama Daishi's warning about addiction and recurrence, but she didn't even want to see the yellow light coming. So for the moment I said no more about it.

My trusty secretary Mandy Foster was back on the job and proved to be efficient and quite good on the telephone with screening out who I should follow up on and who I should not. I also got her to do some bird-dogging for me on cases I knew required very little expertise, such as following a husband that was sneaking behind his wife's back and rendezvousing with his girl-friend—or boyfriend, as the case might be.

One day I was sitting at my desk when I heard a hard knock at my office door. "Yeah, come in, the door's open…" I said, my mind pre-occupied on a dozen different items piling up on my desk.

An old, grizzled man appeared before me. He wore a dirty old hat, a flannel shirt with a tobacco-stained grey wool sweater that had a faded sheriff's badge pinned on it. "Son-of-a-bitch, the goddam traffic these days. Stop and go, stop and go all the way out here on the street-car." He looked me over sitting behind my desk. "You must be your uncle's kin—we talked on the phone a spell back," his gruff voice spoke out loud enough to be heard down the hall. "I'm Boots Blake…the guy who knew your Uncle Cable Denning."

I got up and went over to shake the old man's hand. "Good to meet you, Mr. Blake. I'm glad you popped by. I was getting bored with my life, so your timing is perfect. Won't you sit down?"

"Don't mind if I do." He took out a pinch of chewing tobacco and put it in his mouth. "You got quite a fancy office here. Hell, I can remember when this part of

Franklin Avenue was dirt and buggies. Even the street-cars was pulled by frickin' horses."

He was wearing a pair of old scuffed black leather boots. I looked at them wondering if those boots had ever mounted a saddle. "I do okay, Mr. Blake—"

"—what the hell is this 'Mr. Blake' crap, boy, call me Boots. And I'll call you Cable, if that don't upset your high-minded way of doin' things here in 'Hollywood', the land of freaks, whores and queers. How the hell can you live 'n work here and still have any balls left?"

I chuckled to myself. I liked this gruff old codger. "Well, I manage, Boots. The customer base isn't all that bad here. Lots of money hidden in them thar hills above us. So, what can I do for you?"

He looked at me strangely. "Now why in damnation's name would you have to be doin' somethin' for me when I've positioned my ass down on your chair to say hello—aimed strictly at a friendly visit?"

"Oh, I don't know, Boots—I guess I'm so used to everyone wanting something from me. You see, I—I don't have many what you might call *friends*. I'm kind of...uh...'off limits' to most people because of the dangerous life I lead."

"Dangerous?" He coughed and spat up. I handed him my wastebasket and he spat in it. "Hell, *dangerous* is thunderin' your posse after Joaquin Murietta in the wild foothills of California! At any second a rifle shot could knock you off your steed, the impact tossin' you to the earth like a heavy, dead branch fallin' off a pine tree. Now *that*...was dangerous, Cable." He coughed up and spat again. "You young people today have it soft. Pshaw, in my day you didn't have electricity—runnin' water came from a creek down the way and you shit in an outhouse the size of a bathtub tilted perpendicular like"

He was an outlandish character, one of those guys like my Uncle Cable who had lived bigger than life itself, I suspected. And now he had to adjust to the modern conveniences of the twentieth century, and I had a hunch a lot of it didn't fit too well for old timers like Boots. "Well, Boots, there's a kind of trade off. Some things are better, some things are worse. But you know, as much as I'd like to visit, I've got some pretty heavy things on my plate at the moment—"

"—what's this shit, Cable? First you say you're glad to see me, then you're shooin' me out the door! What's it gonna be—you a maverick like your uncle—or some patsy joinin' up with all those pussy-footed dandies walkin' around these here parts disguised as men?"

"You're right, I did say I was glad to see you. But as you launched into your idle patter, I realized how little patience I had for the past you're talking about. You see, I—I live in another world, Boots, and have been exposed to things that you wouldn't believe if I told you. So you're old stories are like museum pieces to me, interesting to visit now and then, but of little interest to my everyday reality."

"Then I feel bad for you, Cable. Dismissin' the past is dismissin' that part of yourself. Yeah, I can get up and go, but I'm tellin' you here and now, you got no roots without understandin' the past, boy—nothin' solid to help find your way out of that Alice-in-Wonderland place you young people find yourselves in these days....in this here so-called *modern times*. Nevertheless,

I see I ain't welcome here, so I will be moseyin' along now..."

He got up to go. I felt bad. "I'm sorry, Boots. Please...stay a while longer. I—I'm just going through a lot of shit right now and I'm trying to sort it out."

He coughed and spat again, took out another wad of chewing tobacco, put it in his mouth and looked across the desk to my eyes. "Cable, survivin' this life has one secret attached to it, and one secret only."

"And what might that be, Boots?"

"You gotta have a conscious reason for hangin' around—ya gotta know why you even bother gettin' up each day. Otherwise, it's all for nothin'."

"So...why do you hang around, then?"

"I'll tell ya why, you young impatient horse's ass. You people are all rushin' in a hurry to go nowhere, do nothin' of consequence, leave no worthy trace of you ever havin' been at all. Most people are like that. But my secret is this, Cable. Each day I get up, I mosey into my little backyard garden. If there be one fresh rosebud, one new string bean, one turnip comin' up from the good earth, I take a breath and I am thankful in that minute, boy, thankful for knowin' I still have reason for bein'. Why does *that* give you reason, you might ask? Because when you realize you're part of that rosebud or that new string bean or that turnip you're gonna make some turnip soup out of one day, you breathe that moment-in-time right in yourself, Cable, you breathe in...and keep breathin'...until you aren't anymore..." The old man's eyes watered.

The man made sense. Yeah, it was true, we were all running around like chickens with our heads cut off, lost

201

souls with 'causes' or 'purposes' that couldn't even compete with Boots in his backyard smelling a newly bloomed rose. But I wasn't sure I knew how to do that. Like most humans, I was either regretting from the past or projecting to a future that may or may not ever be. "Thanks, Boots. I wish I could jump aboard that train and take a ride with you to that quiet, pleasant place you're talking about." Then I checked out his face. He had taken a dirty, yellowed handkerchief out of his pocket and was wiping his eyes. "Are you...are you alone, Boots?"

"If by that you're meanin' do I have anyone else in my bed?"

"Well, more or less—"

"—I only loved someone once, Cable. And she ended up dyin' in my arms. And we didn't even know each other that well. I could never be like your Uncle Cable, fancyin' that young pussy. Busy as a bee he was, goin' from blossom to blossom. Women flocked to him like he was a honey hive and after he got burned by fallin' in love with your mother, it seemed he started a- runnin' too, just like you're a-runnin'. And I'll bet you got lots of them female tongues waggin' over you, too. You look awful much like your uncle."

I was debating whether I should tell Boots my truth. Somehow I felt he deserved to know, since he was part of my family in an off-beat sort of way. "Well, Boots, I probably look a lot like my uncle because truth is, I'm his son."

Boots looked at me, coughed and spat into the wastebasket. "Well, hell in tarnation! Why didn't I figure that out? Of course! I always suspected when your Dad went back East to that clinic, your beautiful and restless mother might hook-up with your Uncle Cable. Now I can see that she did. She was plumb in love with him. And I do believe, had your uncle not killed that man in the bar that night, he would've run away with your newly wed mother, despite the fact that he loved and respected his older brother. That thing between our legs often gets the best of us, eh?"

I smiled and took a deep breath. I took out a Lucky Strike and lit it. "So now you know, Boots. I just found out a little while ago myself. My mother confessed it to me during a rather intense conversation we were having one afternoon."

"Don't judge her, Cable. I recall lookin' into her eyes when your uncle was present. She would've followed that man anywhere. Bein' young and in love is kinda like a disease, you know, and it can stay with you the remainin' part of your days."

Suddenly I was flashing back to Honey, Adora—and Zelda Blodgett. It seemed the new breed of woman was more independent, maybe less likely to follow the man she loved to heaven, hell or perdition as some of the older generation of women would have done. But I knew also there were social and economic reasons for doing so. If babies came, women were pretty much dependent on what the man could provide for food and shelter. It was much more basic then, kind of like the caveman days when a woman had to use her feminine wiles to capture a mate, breed and hope he hung around for a while. I wondered if Zelda would have followed me, if it weren't for the child she carried in her womb now. I don't know, maybe there was danger in the woman who thought too much—and pursued a career like Lily Norwood. Of course, Lily wasn't even human in the traditional sense, so what the crap was I talking about? On the other hand, a woman was a person as well, and deserved her independence as a human being. Yeah, I thought, that would be the new woman of the twentieth century. That didn't mean they weren't good in bed. I could vouch for that. Hell, I was the luckiest guy in the world, having tasted of some of the most delectable womanhood any man would ever be privy to.

"Oh, I didn't judge my mother when she told me. I looked into her eyes, Boots, and saw the pain, the missed years, the love forced to get buried deep down there in her heart. No, I felt sorry for her. She got a rotten break. And there's no way it can be made up."

"Yep...them's the sad, dark corners of bein' human, Cable." He looked me over, picked up the wastebasket and spat into it again. "If I ever come this way again, I'll have to bring a spittoon," he laughed. "Hell, I've been chewin' tobacco since I was twelve. Got the teeth to prove it." He sat across from me, checking me out. "You know, I got this feelin' you're in deep somewhere, Cable. Is this private detective thing more than you can handle? Some men ain't cut out for it."

"No, it's not that, Boots. A couple of things are bothering me. One, I've got these really bad guys after me—you know, the life and death kind—and I'm working on a stalker case I seem unable to get a handle on. It's the damnedest thing...I show up in all the right places, but can't find a trace of this guy who's threatening this beautiful young ballet dancer."

Boots thought for a minute. He took his dirty, sweat-stained hat off his head and twirled it around in his hands. "Maybe I can help, Cable. Maybe I can be a silent backup for ya. I always say look at the most obvious to find what's not. That's how I did my sheriffin' in those days when the bad guys thought they had the edge on me—and didn't. I ain't as stupid as I look."

I smiled. "Yeah, Boots, I'd welcome any help I can get. So, what do you think about a mysterious stalker who's never there, yet leaves all kinds of ominous hints and threats, including hitting me over the head with a loaded milk bottle?"

"Well, if I was you, I'd be lookin' at the history of the victim. Or whatever it is you call them who hire you these days."

"Client...we call them clients. People who hire me to do the work the cops either can't do or wouldn't do. Especially when no major crime has been committed. You know how the justice system works. Without evidence, there's nothing anyone can do."

"Yep. I call it *crime with no fault*. Nobody's to blame until someone is dead."

"Damn, I like that, Boots. 'No-fault crime'...I'll have to paste that up in my stupid little brain."

"Son-of-a-bitch, Cable...let me help you. I haven't been trompin' around the crime world for fifty years without learnin' something of value. Besides, there ain't much excitement in my life. Even as a young man, I liked the chase. So, how about it? Want my help or not?"

I smiled over at this ancient relic of a man. "Yeah, thanks, Boots. Consider yourself my silent partner, okay?" I reached over and shook the unshaven rotund man's calloused hand. "Shall we have a drink on it?"

"Why not? Got any good whiskey in this dry land of ours?"

"Well, only some rotten gin from bootleg." I opened my right-hand desk drawer and took out a bottle. I got up and procured my one extra glass from the bathroom. I poured us both a generous shot of gin, then lifted my glass to Boots. "Well, may we have much success as crime-busters."

"Here! Here!" he growled. He drank the whole shot down and made an awful face. "Shit, Cable, this crap will kill you! I got a fellow who makes good whiskey. I gotta get you some." He wiped his mouth. "So, where do we start?"

"I don't know, Boots. For the first time in a *long* time, I'm stumped."

"Well, when that happens, ya start lookin' for cases of precedence. Was there a similar case? And if so, what was its outcome?"

Just then the phone rang. "Yeah, Cable Denning here..."

"Mr. Denning. This is Maybelline Appleby. I received your kindly send in the mail this morning. And I must declare to you first-off, sir, the man in that picture fiddling with that hussy is irrefutably not my husband. I'm afraid, sir, you have sent me the wrong photographs."

I looked on my desk at the Appleby file. "Well, let me see, Mrs. Appleby. I've got an original picture of your husband. Five-foot nine, two-hundred pounds, short shock of hair over his forehead, right?"

"Yes, that resembles Ashby."

"The fact that the man in the photographs I sent to you is wearing a Halloween mask without any clothes on—does the body still not look like your husband Ashby? It certainly matches up to your recent photo of him, including the shock of dark hair over his forehead. On what, may I ask, are you basing your dismissal of the evidence?"

"Ashby would never wear a mask—it is beneath his dignity."

"Even if he's attempting to conceal his identity from the friendly woman in question? He's also riding a hobbyhorse. Is that out of line for Mr. Appleby as well?"

There was a pause at the other end of the line. "I am benevolently insulted, Mr. Denning! My Ashby is an upright, church-going gentleman. Never known to cavort with cheap women and the like."

"What about the cigar in his mouth and the glass of alcohol in his left hand?"

"Lord strike him dead for doing such a thing!"

"And is his voice rather high and wheezy?"

"Ashby is not known for the deeper, masculine qualities of a boisterous male voice."

"Well, I heard him playing games with the lady in question, how about 'Howdy Heidi, I'm going to whip your heinie' spoken several times in a high, nasal voice that was followed by 'I'll dress you in Mable's sable, if you let me put you on the table!' Are you indeed sometimes referred to as Mable, Mrs. Appleby?"

Again, there was another pause. "Pure coincidence, detective. My dear husband would never address me by my abbreviated name when he was not in my adoring presence. You have photographed the wrong man, I say."

I thought for a minute, looking down at the Appleby file. Boots Blake was snickering to himself and fidgeting in his chair. "Well, then what about this check receipt made out to Lorraine LaMar for one hundred dollars, drawn from his very private bank account—in his name only—on the very day I snapped those photos I sent you?"

"I know nothing of such an account, and suspect you are trumpin' up accusations against my beloved Ashby to confuse me. That is, after all, how you make your livin', is it not, Mr. Denning?'

"No, that's not how I make my living, Mrs. Appleby. I make my living by putting up with people like you who live their lives with their heads in the sand, who live on Elm Street in a house with a white picket fence, an avocado tree out in front and a mail box that reads *'sterile, do not open until death do us part.'* You don't get it, do you, Mrs. Appleby—your husband is going nuts—no, maybe dying—from that suppressed empty nest you supply him with. And for whatever reasons, it stopped happening in the bedroom between the two of you long ago. What do you expect a forty-three year old man to do when he starts hankering for a warm, live and pleasure-giving woman?"

Boots winked at me with a big smile on his face. I quite expected the woman to hang up the telephone and I would never see my two hundred plus bucks I had coming from working on the case. But instead there was a tearful whimper on the other end of the phone line. "I—I just...I just could not confess it myself. I could not believe nor accept my husband would betray the vow of marriage he made to me fifteen years ago. Hearin' you speak as you do...forthright and revealin' of truth, and I...knowin' those words to be faithful from your lips...to be delivered from your own sense of professional duty... therefore, I must not sully your honor, sir. I thank you for all you have rendered...even if it has resulted...in...in a sad revelation. I will be slipping your check in the mail on the morrow, Detective Denning..." Then she hung up.

Boots' eyes were glued to my face. "I'll be a son-of-bitch, Cable—in all my years I never heard a man talk like that! Only your uncle had a similar gift of gab like that. He could sell you California over breakfast!"

"Now you know the truth, Boots. This is *mostly* what I do, collect naughty pictures of moral America breaking the rules of sexual propriety. It doesn't matter who, husband, wife, boyfriend, girlfriend, butcher, baker, candlestick maker. We all take our pants down on the restless occasion when the God of Horny calls to us. It's like kids playing post office in the back lot—boys and girls still like to explore each other."

"Anyway you cut it, Cable, I'm impressed. Now...if you can be that brilliant in solvin' this dancer's case, we'll be in the ballgame."

Brotherhood of Shadows

My visit with Boots, the phone conversation with Maybelline Applegate notwithstanding, was rewarding and left me with a feeling of male camaraderie that had been lost for some time, out of the equation of my life.

Probably ever since my childhood friend and partner Mario, was killed. It was almost as if a lawman father figure had been sent to me and I knew I would come to love that crusty old man who swore, chewed tobacco and looked like a leftover from the old west. I would look forward to our association, to be sure, but most of all, simply the warmth of his friendship and the gut knowledge inside of me that he really cared. Sometimes blessings come in strangely wrapped packages.

It was a warm April night. I thought I'd visit the *Bistro Club* and surprise June Maye in action. She had been singing great lately and as I walked down the stairs I could hear her finishing up a grand interpretation of *Nice Work If You Can Get It*. I kept in the dark of the room as I made my way to the hatcheck girl and gave her my hat and trench coat. I was wearing a nice dark-brown pinstripe suit with a silk tie and shiny black shoes. I made my way toward the bar and sandwiched in between a couple of people. On my left was some older fellow with a smile on his face and he was keeping time as June launched into a very fun version of *My Heart Belongs to Daddy*. As I twisted around to the right I accidentally grazed a rotund woman's very large boob with my elbow. "I'm—excuse me, Miss," I said as I finally got both hands on the bar counter. "Nothing personal." She was medium-short, quite hefty and wore a blue and white polka-dot dress.

She felt her breast. "You vant you should burst my balloon? Or is it such a crude vay of feelink a lady down?" she said in a decidedly Yiddish accent.

"I think it's feeling *up*, lady. Yeah, it's true, some men check out a babe's anatomy that way. But it was truly an accident on my part." I got the bartender's attention and since the *Bistro Club* had already lifted its Prohibition restrictions on its own volition, I ordered a honeyed whiskey in a hot snifter. I was watching June. She had on a very sexy shiny blue dress that clung to her in all the right places. And believe me, she had all the right places. That was something I could report first-hand, and knew in my sleep, so to speak. I knew her body so well by now, every curve, the texture of her velvet skin, how her nipples stuck out when I touched them with my finger-tips, those marvelous thighs of hers that led up to an over-active mound that brought me constant pleasure.

I glanced back over at the heavy-set gal next to me. It seemed she was with a short, thin man with wire-rim glasses. "It's crowded in here, Rose, I'm sure the man meant no harm."

I smiled and acknowledged the man. "Yeah, thanks, mister." They were both looking at June and enjoying her immensely. Especially the man, because I'm sure like any other male, it wasn't her song alone that was entertaining him.

The woman said something to the man in their native tongue. "I don't know if Cole Porter is Jewish or not—could be," the man answered in English.

"It's a naughty song, Abraham—dey should not be singink '*da boys who maul*' or sellink da body for a millionaire. Ha! She tinks I do not know dat hidden meanink—'*dining on my fine fin and haddie*'—I make da stew, and no way it tastes like dat! Dis Parisian, Porter...ha! I tell you, Abraham, I'll go for Uncle Irving any day!"

The man leaned over toward me. "You'll have to forgive my wife, mister, but she is a bit prejudiced, I'm afraid. She is related to Irving Berlin, who really is a cousin, twice removed."

"*Vonce* removed," the lady insisted.

"*Twice*," her husband persisted.

"*Vonce*—vy do I alvays have to remind you, Abraham, Elda vas married to cousin Zachary who den divorced her and married Irving's cousin, Sasha. Such a ting with your memory."

"That makes *twice removed*, I keep saying, Rose." He looked at me and came around in front of his wife and extended his hand to me. "I am Abraham Gertfelter—please call me Abe—and this is my wife, Rose."

"Pleased to meet you two, I'm Cable Denning, and you can call me Cable," I said, quite intrigued with the definitive characters their ethnicity brought out. They reminded me of Abe and Golda Sachs...the jewelers I purchased Honey's ring from. Seems so long ago, now. "So what brings you two nice, respectable folks to a smoky dive like this?"

"This 'smoky dive', as you put it, is like a 'birthground' for great American music. You see, without lovely young things like our singer up there, there would be no way to communicate the popular folk song of our proud United States of America. It is akin to the native drum, resounding throughout the jungle—a new sound, a new beat, a new melody. Of course nowadays, we have radio, we have the phonograph—God knows what they'll come up with next."

212

I really liked what Abe was saying. "Well, Abe, it's strange you should say that. I've always kind of felt that. I just never quite had the words. But, yeah, you got it right—it's the new sound of the twentieth century, isn't it? Or at least this part of the twentieth century."

"A culture cannot predict how long a music may last, Cable." He edged his way between his wife and myself.

"Now she's makink a play for da caddie!—vat's a caddie?" Rose Gertfelter inquired, trying to figure out Cole Porter's rather risqué lyrics.

"It's a man who follows a golf player around the course, carrying his clubs, tees and things."

"Never heard of such a person," she answered. "Such a silly ting to talk about naughty caddies and haddie and '*tearing off a game of golf*' and such tings—vy? Soon she'll be tearing off her clothes! I alvays tell Abe, since da Depression, da young girls are all going hayvire—drinkink, smokink—and other immoral activities—my grandmother Elsie vould turn over in her grave knowink vat *ve* vitness on a daily basis."

Abe and I more or less just bobbed our heads up and down to acknowledge Rose's outrage. "I am a musicologist, Cable, and study the wonderful cultural influences of European classical music on our modern American popular song. So much of it is Russian, German or Hungarian Jewish music adjusted to our American appetites for love and romance. Even the motion pictures are heavily influenced by our wonderful Jewish composers."

"Well, you don't have to sell me, Abe, I'm a big fan. That's the main reason I come to places like this. It's always been the *music*...you know, it kind of transports a person."

213

"Oh, yes...the Jews were among the first, very early on, to establish the tradition of song and dance. Now we have brought it to America. Our ancestors also brought their 19ᵗʰ century legacy in the form of their classical and operatic backgrounds. Sigmund Romberg, Friml, Victor Herbert, Emmerich Kálmán—they are still popular. But now a new generation of more accessible music comes. Rose's Uncle Irving and Jerome Kern in the early teens joined by Oscar Hammerstein, Richard Rodgers, the wonderful Gershwin brothers, Arthur Schwartz, Harry Warren and all the rest of those hard-working men from Tin Pan Alley."

I was being educated. It was great to hear a knowledgeable man talk about what I loved. "Well, indeed, Abe, you seem to know your composers. Where do you think it will all end up some day? My hunch is that there may be a war in a few years—will that end our great American legacy of popular romantic music?"

"Ha! It is *sex musik*—my Aunt Hedwig says you should know by a good conscience, dat up dere is fornication music—ya, boy meets girl, boy talks girl into spooning on da porch—pretty soon dey're on da lawn, wrestlink. Such a ting dat music does to da young!"

Abe and I looked at each other. Abe smiled at me and nodded his head. "What's life without a difference of opinion?" Then he glanced up at the stage. "Do you know the attractive young lady singer?"

I nodded my head with a half-smile on my face. "I guess you might say that. We, uh, we are sort of dating..." I left it at that.

Rose was recalling an earlier evening listening to June. "You see, Abe, dose sonks—vat is it I heard her

214

sink last time ve vere here—*Love for Sale*? You vant I should faint ven I heard dat? A whore sellink her vares in a song—oy vey iz mir! Dat's vat's comink, such tings ve have to listen to nowadays? Da radio, movies, live cabarets—all dis bringink and bringink of love makink and love makink—like to influence everyone to have babies!"

Just then June began to sing the third song of her set. If any of us thought June Maye was sexy, outrageously sensual or just plain suggestive before, this song set a new high-water mark. The song was another Cole Porter tune. *I've Got You Under My Skin* began with just June and her bass player. The entire room quieted a bit as June built the tune into a *tour de force* of sensuality and fine vocal gymnastics. By the time she ended, Rose Gertfelter was red in the face. A wild applause followed and we all looked around at the appreciative audience. Yep, June was at the top of her game.

"Such a ting—I don't know...see vat I mean?" Rose asserted. "All da time sex—vat is dere room left for? Sacrifice vat? She vants to sacrifice her skin because da man lives under it—or vat? Dat lady singer must be brave to sing such thinks. I couldn't!"

"Sometimes we call it *talent*, madam," I said, defending June.

"You know, Rose, like an *actress*—she has to put the song across to the audience. How else will they know what she's singing about?" Abe explained to his rather uncomfortable wife.

"It, uh, it so happens, as I said, that lady is a special friend of mine. I think I need to go up there and congratulate her for a great set."

"Great set, already—great set of vat? Seems to me she has a great set of—of vatever is popping out of her dress—"

"—Rose! Please...we don't make with bad remarks because she is a well-endowed young woman."

"Endowed, sheesch! Look at me, I'm heavy upstairs and vell endowed—but I don't look like dat!"

"May we meet the young lady, Cable?" Abe inquired.

"Sure, why not? June enjoys her fans—can't live without them, you know. The regular audience is her bread and butter."

"So now ve get to meet dee endowed singink lady?"

"Be kind, Rose. She works hard to interpret those songs, I'm certain. Let's be kind and compliment her. She's done a lot to prepare."

"Vat has she done? Varbled a few notes in a sexy dress about dining on her fine fin and haddie because she has him under her skin?"

We started to make our way to the stage to congratulate June when she spotted me. "Cable! I didn't expect to see you tonight." She ran up to me and hugged me.

"Hiya, babe. Great combo of songs! June, you have two new fans here, Abe and Rose Gertfelter. Abe is a musicologist and knows and appreciates every measure of your music. This is June Maye..."

"How do you do?" June said in her warm, sultry way.

Abe extended his hand to her. "My wife and I enjoyed your singing very much, Miss Maye. I am a big fan of Porter, the Gershwins, my wife's cousin twice removed, Irving Berlin, Jerome Kern—well, I don't have to tell you—you know the list."

"It means a lot to me to know you're also able to approach the songs from the inside out, Mr.—"

"—Abe, please..."

"...Abe...even some singers never get those layers. But I do try..."

"And you succeed most admirably. To truly interpret, one must never disassociate from the tune and lyric—and of course, the proper rhythm and tempo," Abe declared, displaying his expertise.

"Yes. And sometimes that poses a problem. I always try to imagine what the composer had in mind when he wrote the song," June said, obviously very engaged with Abe. She looked over at me. "The emotion necessary to tell someone you desire them, sometimes, uh, takes a lot out of a singer. So often I take the romantic ballads up-tempo a bit, or even do a convertible tempo, thirty-two bars slow, thirty-two fast. I think it helps to balance some songs so they don't get too mushy."

"Couldn't say it better myself, my dear," Abe said. "Sometimes a singer learns those lessons too late and once it is a habit, it's hard to unlearn. But for many, I'm certain it's better late than never, eh? But you, young woman, are truly talented."

"I don't know if I'd go that far, Mr. Gertfelter. I just love what I do, work at it hard and hope it makes a few folks feel good. Sometimes, though, I think I was born too late." I was puzzled by her last sentence.

"I am not as musical as my husband, but if Abe says dere's quality in you, believe you me, young woman, dere's *quality.*"

"Well, I second that," I said, smiling at June.

Rose stepped forward and started yanking on her husband's arm. "And talkink about late—it is past our bedtime, Abe. You should vant to be out here like dis—staying out all hours?" She gave June a rather snide smile. "I'm sure ve vill see you again, young voman. Don't be surprised if Abe flirts with you—he's a regular flirting Cameo, he is."

"That's *Romeo*, Rose," Abe said a little impatient with his wife.

"Vatever...see you again, Miss Maybe."

I laughed. "It's just *Maye*, Rose, like the month."

"You should vant I be perfect? Who's perfect, I ask you?"

Abe shook June's hand once more. The two women exchanged nods. I was relieved when they left.

When they were gone, June pulled me to a dark corner of the room. "God, I've missed you for the past couple of days. Will you come home with me afterwards?"

"Sure, babe. Loved your songs tonight. That nice Jewish couple hung on your every note and enjoyed your delivery. In fact, as you heard, Abe is a fine musicologist and felt that songbirds like you played an important role in transmitting the Great American Popular Songbook to the world."

"Oh, that's nice. At least somebody appreciates my music—and not just my body."

"How can you say that, babe? Can't you tell by the applause how much your singing is enjoyed—by men and women alike?"

"I guess," she said rather sullenly. Then she got close to my ear. "What I'm really interested in is that bulge in your pants when we get home—topped off with a ciga-

rette and some of that hot honeyed whiskey you introduced me to."

"Whoa, lady, that's pretty bold talk!

"I'm hooked on you, Cable. That's all I want—is to
fuck you and be fucked by you. I can't wait for the feel of
your touch on me—all of me," she whispered in my ear.

June had brought me into a world of unadulterated
sensuality I had never experienced. Sure, I'd known a lot
of dolls in my time, but she topped them all as far as
pure physical experience was concerned.

The evening ended and June and I took the short
ride to her place. When we got in, we went through the
usual ritual of her loading us both up with drinks and
cigarettes. I noticed she was getting tipsy more and
more often these days. I wondered if she was drinking
during the day. A bad sign—I ought to know. Whatever
eats at us that we can't or won't deal with, we have a
tendency to numb. What was June numbing inside of
her that was buried so deep that it kept her from being
able to love? As she unwound from her night, she slowly
drifted into that rhythmic, sensual flow of hers that
oozed sex. She would always start by making out, touching me all over with her fingers and the palms of her
hands like she was creating a finger painting. Soon she
was pulling me into her bedroom.

I didn't know why then, but I was restless that night.
After June and I made love, I lay there for a while. I
could feel my buttocks tingle like something was up but
I couldn't identify it. About three in the morning I got up
and got dressed. I kissed the sleeping woman adieu and

walked out into the cool early morning. I didn't get very far. As I stepped off of the last stair leaving June's bungalow, suddenly two men approached on each side of me and grabbed my arms firmly before I could draw my .38. So far no one had started slugging me.

Then I heard a familiar voice. "Cable Denning, I apologize for this unorthodox manner of seizing you in the middle of the night. I'm Father Tortelli. Remember me?

"What the—? Tortelli, how could I forget? You saved my life and my family jewels all in the same evening. Why the strong-arm tactic?"

"Sorry about that." He nodded to the other two priests to let me go. "You remember Father Banducci and Father Grandino, yes?"

"Oh, yeah—the Flying Priests, how could I forget that? Hello, guys, thanks for not mussing me up," I said, nodding to them.

"Cable—I'll get right down to it. *His Holiness* Pope Pius XI has requested an audience with you. He looks small and gentle, but carries a big stick and is quite concerned with the prolific entrance of alien presences on our planet."

I shook myself off as the other two priests released me. "So what does that have to do with me?"

"Well, Cable, it's like this. *His Holiness* knows you know some of them and are being pursued for your knowledge of the *Fen de Fuqín*. He also realizes none of their other dimensional properties are derived from this earth. Will you let us take you home to your office?"

"Wasn't I a cop when last we met, Tortelli?"

"Uh, something like that. It doesn't matter. You've always been involved in police work, as well as in the middle of life, death and dimensional anomalies."

"You got that right. Yeah, thanks, you can drive me over there."

We got to my office building and I invited the Flying Priests up. I sat in my comfy chair with Father Tortelli opposite me, while the other two priests stood on either side of Carlo. "So now that it's getting on to four a.m., it does occur to me that I have to work tomorrow at some point. So...how do you propose *His Holiness* and I get together—*if* I agree to go along with his bidding?"

"You must come with us to Vatican City, Roma. There is no other way, believe me."

"And if I refuse?"

He smiled at me. "Cable...who could refuse an audience with one of the most powerful men on earth? He was born during troubling times, in Desio, Lombardy-Venetia, then part of the Austrian empire. He knows what greed and corruption do to people—and nations."

I sat back, took out a Lucky Strike and lit it. "Even if I agreed to go, Carlo old boy, how would I get away? I've got a business to run here. I'm in the middle of a baffling case, I've got a girlfriend who's insecure, I have my regular clientele—"

"—the Church will make it worth your while, Cable, let me assure you. We *have* been watching, you know. Seems to us that you could afford a couple of weeks away by allowing your competent secretary to take over as she did when you were chasing dreams in Kathmandu."

"So you know about that, too, eh?"

"Mostly. But your old acquaintance—Mr. Blake—could he not keep a detective's eye on things for you in your absence?"

"So that leaves June…my girlfriend…"

"Keep her busy at the nightclub she performs at. Tell her it's part of your job and you'll be back soon."

"Nice work if we can pull it off, Father. But you
You know, I haven't forgotten you saved my life that night when that witch doctor, Schumacher and Ravna almost got away with—well, you know the story. I owe you a debt, Carlo. So…I guess it's a green light."

"That's swell, as you Americans say. We fly to New York on a special *mail airplane,* designed to deliver important missives to the different dioceses here in the states. From there we will go by passenger liner on to Naples. Once there, we will be flown by special airplane, built for Vatican use only. We can leave in two or three days, yes?" He checked out my face. I was squirming a little because I really didn't have the stomach for another long trip and it wasn't my favorite thing sitting down and chewing the fat with a deeply politically religious man, even if he was the Pope!

"Yeah, I guess so. I'll start getting my affairs in order tomorrow."

Father Tortelli got up, and came around and extended his hand to me. "Cable, I am glad to see you. You've matured a bit—and frankly, I'm surprised you're still alive. But we're all glad you are. Let's say we'll pick you up next Saturday morning, four a.m. The plane leaves around five-thirty for the mail run. That way, we'll take the ocean liner out of New York Harbor by Monday morning. How's that sound?"

222

"Good as any plan," I said, grinding my cigarette out in the ashtray. Then I looked the three priests over. "I've always been meaning to ask you guys—who are you really—what are you called and how does the sanctimonious church justify murder and mayhem, that must certainly come from your most expert means and devices?"

"We are called *The Brotherhood of the Shadows*, a special department of the Church. I say 'shadows' because we must remain relatively without notice or identity to most of the world. What the Church cannot handle through ordinary channels, we handle with *our* very special approach."

"Yeah, I'll bet. By the way, Carlo, do you guys believe in God?"

He shot a glance at his two accomplices. "Yes...it's just that you might say, we follow the prescribed procedure of *God helps those who help themselves* when there is no other way. If, for example, we did not intercede the night you were to be castrated by Dr. Schumacher, today you would lead a very different life, would you not say? Actually, had we not intervened for *'God'* you would most likely be dead."

"Good enough for me," I said. I stepped out from behind my desk and shook each priest by the hand. "Well, fellows, once again, Cable Denning, Master Detective, is in your hands." They smiled and left.

The next day I was sitting in a theatre seat watching Lily Norwood perform a scene from *Swan Lake*. For thirty minutes I watched, as this beautiful nymph of a woman mesmerized me there in the darkened auditorium. At three p.m. the stage manager called a break. I found Lily backstage in a dressing room with several other ballerinas. They were all standing before a huge fan and wiping the sweat off their lovely slim bodies. As soon as she saw me, she approached me with a big smile. "Cable, what a wonderful surprise! Have you been here long?"

I hugged her. "Long enough to realize how wonderful you are—and how I hold your talent in the highest esteem."

She kissed me on the cheek and pulled me out into the hallway. "Oh, Cable, I've missed seeing you. I'm actually through for the day. Perhaps we can go for a long, late lunch?"

"Sure, why not?" I answered, taking a breath deep inside because my stomach did a turn and that taboo of desire for Lily Norwood suddenly came bubbling up into my libido.

We went to a place just up the street. The walls were lined with paintings and comedic sketches of famous theatrical scenes from dance to drama to grand opera. It was easy to see why Lily would have chosen this particular joint. We sat in front of a big picture window where one could watch the sidewalks filled with busy, scurrying people and the endless, snarled traffic of exhaust-belching machines called automobiles. We ordered and sat across from each other...neither or us sure of what to say. I began. "So, I guess, no news is good news. Anything more from our shadow man?"

"Just those three letters," she said. Our stalker had resorted to the old newspaper clippings type of communication. Most of the content was about the same, some form of warning to keep her emotionally distraught and off balance. It was the last one, in the form of a riddle that bothered me most. It read: *"In a field of motion, Deserat met her end, lined with trees and hidden things, lurking behind the rocks, forbidden and plotting the ever-coming darkness...'* Cryptic, to be sure, but what did it mean?

"I've tried to figure the riddle, Lily. My gut tells me *motion* could mean your dancing, maybe even the gal meeting her end while dancing? Do you know if this *Deserat* was a real person?"

"I don't know. If so, I never heard of her. I'll go the library and look her up."

"Good idea. Someone you know, perhaps is plotting behind the scenes? I'm afraid I've been a lousy detective on this one."

She grabbed my wrist across the table. "No, you haven't, Cable. You've just had so little to go on."

"Yet I spend all kinds of time hiding in shadows looking for this guy, even under your bedroom window one night."

"I wish you had knocked," she said rather coyly. Her face was pure and filled with a woman's most haunting expressions. Those brown eyes of hers glowed in the late afternoon sunlight at me. "Why not, Cable? I practically threw myself at you that night you got hit on the head—and that strange, nice man, Mr. Lorena, came to your rescue. I'm safe for you, Cable—so safe I could even fall in love with you."

"Well, that's the kind of safe we need to avoid, lady. I can give you lots of reasons not to get involved with me. First there's June, then there's the fact that you're my client and third—I need to tell you I'm going to Rome in a few days."

"Rome?" she said as her eyes brightened. "I'd love to go with you to Rome. I love Italy. We could have a wonderful time—"

"—I'm a dangerous man, Lily—I might not even be coming back."

She froze where she sat as the waiter brought us our food. When he left, she quietly put her napkin on her lap. "You scare me when you say things like that. As if it weren't enough to be frightened half to death by this creep who's stalking me—now I worry about the man I could so easily love—and secretly do..."

She checked my eyes out. I had to harden them. "Please, Lily...you don't know how many times I've had second thoughts about walking out your door the night I tucked you in bed. Do you have any idea how hard it was for me to not take my clothes off and slip under the covers with you? But then, that would have opened another can of worms."

"I wish you would have, Cable. Then I would have awakened to you touching me. Do you know what it's like going long periods of time without being touched? Especially with someone you feel is right and good for you and you're willing to take the chance?"

"I can't even think about it, doll. I just wanted you to know it was no cakewalk that night after dancing with you and feeling your kiss bore into my lips, even as soused as you were." I cleared my throat. "But I'm not leaving you high and dry, Lily. There's a crusty old ex-sheriff named Boots Blake. He's going to take over in my absence and you can reach him and trust him the same as you would me."

"Oh, God, Cable—why do you have to go *now*—I've got a Summer Prevue of *Swan Lake* in June. When will you be back?"

" A couple of weeks, tops," I said, hoping I was right.

"What choice do I have? Please keep safe, Cable, and come back to me in one piece—I mean, come back to finish the job I hired you for. Maybe your Mr. Blake can dig into his case experience and see things from another perspective."

"Yeah, you never know." We left the restaurant, and I rode with her back to her place and we walked up the Westerly Terrace hill and to her front door.

"Won't you come in?" she asked as she turned the key in the door.

"I'm afraid, Lily, if I do, I might not come out for a long time. I know it looks like I come on strong, but as far as you're concerned, there's a soft spot I can't afford to give in to. You know the old saying, don't look a gift horse in the mouth."

"What's wrong with my mouth?" she teased.

"Nothing...that's the whole trouble...right there, between your lips, a guy could get stuck," I retorted and in that second I hugged Lily Norwood as we stood there in the doorway. It was one of those pregnant moments where you teeter on the brink of a whole new direction in your life, when a split-second decision can change things for an hour, a day or the rest of your life. She pulled her body into mine, pressing her loins against my you-know-what. I had to pull away or pick her up into my arms and carry her off to the bedroom. It was that close. "I'll call you and get things straightened out with Boots." Then I turned and left. I dared not even look back at that beautiful creature standing there wondering why I wasn't continuing to hold her, touch her, make her part of the Cable Denning collection of perfect sexual conquests.

Dealing with June was another matter. She had grown so dependent on our intimacy that once she was through at night after singing at the club, she found her life empty without my presence and of course, our ritualistic intimacy that included increasing amounts of booze and cigarettes—and possibly one day some of those hallucinogens Uncle Teddy had given me. Finally I convinced her I'd be back in a couple of weeks and we'd spend a day at the beach. She cried as much as June Maye could cry and I spent the last night I was in L.A. with her.

Mandy was a little put off, but understood Rome was a business trip and she was being paid during my absence and was grateful for that, since the economy was still shaky in 1933—in fact it was worse than in 1929. Boots relished the opportunity to meet Lily Norwood and work on her behalf. She and I told him all we knew about the stalker and after a few more details regarding clients and the usual, I was at least prepared to brush up on my Italian—which amounted to the slang and offensive words I grew up with in the East Los Angeles ghetto, across from Little Italy.

Chapter 8

AGNUS DEI

It was the morning of April 19, 1933 when Father Carlo Tortelli, the other two Flying Priests and I got onto an eight passenger, two-motor job at a remote airport in southeast L.A. Once again I had beaten Becker and his thugs at their own game and I was buying some time.

The air-hops were just that, stopping off at key American cities, changing planes until we finally made New York. From there we boarded an Italian liner, the *SS Conte di Savoia.* We made good time and once we arrived in Naples, we again hopped an 'aeroplane' and made our way to Rome.

In a half-sleep I could hear *Atropa, The Goddess of One's Calling* talking to me. "*You now experience the test, the challenge of your chosen pathway of work upon your plane of existence. You shall lose, but you shall win, and lose again. Yet...you will prevail, for in this lifetime you will be taken to experience loss and defeat, triumph and achievement. Remember those who fall and perish do so without consciousness. My sister Aluza, will come to you after you live out the days that shall have ending. Answer to your own being, Cable, answer to what impels you to this calling, for you have chosen it and must dwell within it until the end.*" None of what she said thrilled me all that much. It was like threading yourself through the eye of a needle when you knew part of you would never fit. If *Regini* had taught me the cycle of birth and death, and in Nepal the steady push of *Innioma* had taught me initiation—what more would I learn from *Sinleila, the Goddess of Passion*? It seemed to me that June Maye's existence in my life was teaching me that just fine. What else could bring more passion than falling into addictive-compulsive sex that enslaved me to the anatomy of an attractive young woman who wanted only that and eschewed love for the sake of sensation and pleasure unending? Isn't that what most men wanted—sex without all the strings and obligations that go with being accountable, being able to walk away having delivered your sperm into the woman?

A few hours out of Italy, Carlo Tortelli sat next to me, debriefing me as best he could to prepare me for the audience with Pope Pius XI. "Now our present pope is one who embraces *Agnus Dei*, Cable, literally the lambs of God, his people. He believes all people to be descended from God, Catholics or no. Therefore he will greet you as one of his own. But do not be deceived. His stature is great and he is highly honored in the world, although he appears to be a simple man whose English though broken, always gets his point across. He will ask you questions he already knows the answers to at first. Then he will query you as to what he does *not* know and hope you will have the answers he seeks. You will be paid $5000 American dollars for your trouble and the opportunity to become a devout Catholic." He laughed. "Now, I realize that last part doesn't sound anything like the Cable Denning we all know and love, but it is part of his compulsory salesmanship. Be patient, keep your words simple."

"Five-thousand bucks, eh? Not bad for a paid vacation. I've always wanted to visit the Vatican. I would like to see the Sistine Chapel, if you don't mind. For whatever reasons, I always thought Michelangelo a great genius. I've read some of his poetry and been impressed. I think he questioned the Church a lot. I recall a few lines that stuck out in my brain. I don't know, I was always touched by it. *'My fate too early here would have me sleep, I am not dead, although I change my home, since one in love takes on the other's form, I stay alive in you, who see and weep.'* That was a stave, I even remember that—192 in his sonnets."

Father Tortelli looked at me with a huge grin. "I am impressed, Cable. Yes, I shall set you loose in the Cappella Sistina to have your moment with peace and great art. I hope you won't be disappointed. Michelangelo's work has faded somewhat through the centuries and it is very high up in the vault of the chapel. It's where new popes are selected and voted on."

"Oh, I didn't know that. Thanks, Carlo."

Mortalium Animos

The splendor of the Vatican was overwhelming to a boy raised in a ghetto when the richest thing one ever saw was a colored picture from a library book at school. One cannot be prepared for such an awesome experience as walking down the corridors looking at paintings, maps and statuary, set off with gilt on either side, complemented with incredible bejeweled ceilings with classic paintings of nudes, cherubs and angels. I thought how decadent these people lived and maybe didn't even realize it was at the expense of millions of stupid peasants who dropped their hard-earned money into the coffers on Sundays.

The day after our arrival I was scheduled for an audience with ol' Pope Pius Xl. A special envoy picked me up, but I was always shadowed by the three Flying Priests. I was led into a huge chamber and asked to sit. Soon, a solemn looking little man approached me and summoned me into yet another chamber that had a big throne at its far end. There sat a medium sized man with cape and cap, smiling as I approached. Although I was told I should kiss his ring, I said to hell with that and when the Pope motioned the little guy to leave, I simply stood there, awaiting his next gesture. He wore a deep-red cap and cape, was dressed in a white robe of some kind and sported a huge golden cross on a long chain. He motioned to me. "Signor Denning. Please to come..."

I walked up to the foot of his throne platform. "How do you do, His Holiness. Thank you for seeing me so soon. I thought I—I might have to wait a bit for this audience, knowing how busy you must be."

"No, Signore, you are *il mio prioritá* thisa day." He stood up, took my hand with both of his. His hands were soft, warm, comforting. Just then a couple of other priests brought in a huge red-velvet chair for me to sit in. "*Per favore, Signore*, pleasa to sit." I did so. He looked me over. "You are so young to 'ave—such heavy *carico*—a burden on your head. My son, we speak *solo veritá*—only truth to one another?"

I nodded my head. "Yes, Holiness, I am known as a truth kind of guy. That's part of the reason I'm in such hot water out there in the real world."

232

He studied my face. "Sì, I know... is-a so un-aafortunate that all of these terrible evils—how you say—*converge* upon you all in-a one *momento*."

"Yeah...that's about it, isn't it? So...I believe in cutting the red tape and getting down to why you had me travel a few thousand miles to come see you."

He smiled at me as he withdrew his hands and sat back down on his huge, gilt throne. "I lika that. As many doing the Lord's work, you also coma from humble be-ginnings, eh? Sì...I lika that. I too, was but simple librari-an in Venetia. Now I am old...and a Pope. Who could guess...eh? *Ma, la dolce vita* is not always so sweet, eh? I am enagaged in God's fight day and night, lika you—ina my owna way. Ever since my *Mortalium Animos*, which speaks—of *libertà di l'anima*, freedom of de soul—I am fighting de communism and now devil himself in Ger-many—Hitler and those *demoni dementi* which sur-round him." He stopped and took a sip of water from a glass on a little pedestal next to him. "You lika somating to drink...sì?"

"No, thanks, Holiness, I'm fine." Even though I was itching to light up a Lucky Strike and down a quart of fine gin just about then, I kept my attention on this nice man who seemed an okay bloke in my book so far. "You look a lot like your photograph on the cover of Time Magazine the year I became a cop in Los Angeles, 1924."

"Sì...suddenly, as I tell you, I was the Pope. But were prisoners here at Vatican until 1929, whena we re-gained our sovereignty—did this you know? We 'ave young upastart in Italia—ona most pompous Signore Mussolini. Not a man for God, I am afraid."

"I guess you have quite a time finding men of God in politicians. At least that's my experience in the good ol' U.S. of A."

He chuckled. "Sì! you are right, my son. *Mi despero*— I despair the world, Signore." Then he motioned to me to draw closer to him. I got up from my chair and approached the throne. He leaned into my ear. "Soon, another conflict will arise, my son. The world willa war against itself in days to be. But so you are....privy....to certain...knowledge, you know this already, sì?"

"Yes," I whispered.

"That is why I calla you...*male diavolos* are among us—but they are, how do we say to each other—they are *estraneos*—strangers...stirring the boiling cauldron...of...of, uh, war and tension. But, my son, you also know *quelli buoni*—the good ones. So...who...*are* dese creatures? What you know about those called *Transcenders*?"

I leaned back and he motioned me back to my seat. Although I had heard the term, I wasn't clear exactly who they were. I knew that beings like Toggth, Eli and his kind could travel between dimensions at will. I didn't know this to be true of others, like Joe Lorena and those who took on human form. "I have met a few who can change their shape, Holiness, called shape-shifters that is, change into other forms of beings or creatures, most of these are benevolent—but I have also encountered others like *Cronus-Gor*, who, as you must realize, runs by proxy the *Oculus Pyramidis Mandatum*. I'm not sure, but I suggest Hitler is at least half-alien—the bad kind—and so the Germans are led by these terrible forces."

He checked out my face. "Ay...the *Pyramidis Mandatum*, most powerful—after de Church, of course. Sì...I know you speak *la veritá*. They believe...big cana devour small. Question remains, Signore, can we get good ones, *l'decente*—these you speak of, on our side? Your opinion—will the kind *Transcenders* help us bring peace to this world before great war ravages all civilization?"

"I don't know, Holiness. Even some of the good ones don't want to interfere in human matters. They seem to see us as primitive, a long way from developing into worthy beings."

"Sì...one true God...over all things...and all people— so we must include...all *beings* as well, eh?"

"Well, there you got me. See, I'm not one for religion—so I'm not the right guy to address that question to. If you and I were standing on top of a hill and watching the human race from above, I'd wager these aliens have a good laugh at our stupidity because some of our behavior is just too far below them for them to even consider us as worth the trouble of saving. Look at the trouble I've brought on myself just because I happened to see the right thing at the wrong time..."

He smiled wryly. "You mean *Fena de Fuqína*, gold container for great knowledge—sì? Is obvious through Father Tortelli...'ave been seeking it for quite some time. You know where it is...sì?"

I chuckled, nodding my head. "That would be telling, now wouldn't it? But I can hopefully put your mind at ease. It's no longer hanging around here on the earth plane."

He checked out my eyes and the old man squinted. "I see...I see...so you are forcing a seventy-five year old man, eh? So I am not to ask that question again. You not to answer any more thana you 'ave now." He smiled and lightly laughed. "Is too bad 'ave no more the Inquisition...sì? Maybe then we...*force* it from you, Signore." Then he looked deeper. "Maybe no. You are a *risoluto*, and not a man who crumbles...under torture...eh?"

"Take my word, Holiness, the Inquisition is still alive and well—it's just under a different name now."

"So.....would they force you...the *Pyramidis Mandatum*?"

"Yep, that's the thorn in my side alright. So, you see, I don't consider my presence on this earth being for that long a duration. In fact, if and when I get back to America, my days are numbered and someone's counting them out, as we speak."

A great look of sympathy came over the Pontiff's face. "*Terribile*... I say, you so younga, my son. But, we do notta know God's way for us. I will pray on your behalf."

"Thanks, Holiness." I looked around the vast spaces of luxury. "So...I'm afraid I haven't been of much help. What can I do to further enlighten you?"

"Perhaps, I can further enlighten *you*, Signor Denning. Have you ever seen *the diavolo*—the devil, as you call him?"

"No, I can't say that I have, as a matter of fact. Maybe people who said they were. But one never knows for sure." I thought the guy was putting me on, so I went along with it. "Do you happen to have him hanging around somewhere in the Vatican?"

He laughed. "*Ha! Rido!* You make me laugh—how you say in America—so...funny man, eh?"

I smiled back at him, glad I was at least amusing the Pontiff, if not being of great help in other, more serious, departments. "I'm just a simple private eye. Do you know what I really love?"

"No...but I want to know...tell me your *secret*...eh?"

"What makes me happy is a few cigarettes, a good gulp of English gin, stepping into some smoky dive nightclub and watching and listening to some beautiful babe in a low-cut red sequined gown singing her heart out to the tunes of George Gershwin, Jerome Kern, Cole Porter and the like. That's what makes me happy."

"Afraid am too olda fashion this days. Am still man of old classical music—Pergolesi, Bach, Rossini, Verdi, Beethoven, Mozart and even Puccini or Monteverdi now and then."

"Nothing wrong with those guys. I heard a Brahms second piano concerto not too long ago and it impressed me so that I can still hear some of it my mind's ear."

He paused, took another sip of water. "So, then you are, I am told by Father Tortelli, a.....*lady's man*, eh? I 'ave little experience with fairer sex—what—what—" He summoned me out of my chair once again so he could whisper in my ear. "—what is like? To be embrace, and love by woman's body? Bible is clear, to be sure, that sexual union may notta take place without sanction of the Church—yet...we botha know...it is done anyway...eh?"

"Oh, yeah—and then some, Holiness."

He smiled at me with affectionate light-brown eyes. "I'm gonna tella you now, Signor Denning, I lika you. You a real man...and do not, uh, break with ease, eh?"

"Well, it might depend on who's trying to break me, I guess."

He pulled once on a golden cord. In walked the two priests who had brought my chair in. He spoke to them in Italian. "You very sure you to want see the devil, huh?"

I thought for a second. Was he really on the level? "Well, I suppose I couldn't miss a once in a lifetime opportunity like that, now, could I?"

"Ah hah, sì! I knew it!" This time he pulled twice on the cord and Father Tortelli and the Flying Priests entered, kissed the Pontiff's ring and then turned to me. "I want to come with Signor Denning...we have good—good, uh, what you say? Uh...something like—"

"—rapport?" I suggested.

"Sì, the word of the French."

The five of us ventured through an opening in the wall of what was known as *The Map Room*. There a secret panel was opened and we all followed the Pope through it. There was a short corridor, at the end of which stood an elevator door. Father Tortelli stepped forth and helped the aging Pontiff in. We followed. "Six floors down, Signor Denning."

When the elevator stopped and the door opened, we were facing three very long, wide corridors. We took the one to the right. Soon we were led to another panel in the wall, cleverly installed behind a huge gold-framed painting of what looked sort of like *Boticelli's 'Venus on the Half-Shell'*. As soon as we entered this new hallway, everything was warmer and there was an odor in the air that seemed putrid and sweet at the same time. Half way down this hallway we stopped in front of a massive

238

black iron door with no markings. The Pope pointed to Father Tortelli and the latter pulled down a red lever at the side of the huge door. We heard the sound of escaping steam and the door grinding open. Only Pope Pius XI, Carlo Tortelli and I were allowed to proceed. There was only the glow of very dim red lights to see by. Then the Pontiff extended his hand to stop Tortelli. The Pope and I continued on alone. Now it was beginning to get mysterious. Finally we got to a large cell, a cross between a jail cell and a recreation hall. Then, to my horror, a seven-foot creature stepped out of the shadows and approached hefty bars that separated us. He was just as spoken of in mythology: a tall, gaunt creature with tight yellowish skin, cloven hooves for feet, skinny shoulders and a hideous human-like face with extralarge glowing red eyes. Oh, yeah, and the pupils went sideways. He also possessed a very long, sharp nose, and claws where his fingernails should be, strong enough to rip a bear apart! I was flabbergasted!

"*Eh, diavolo*," the Pontiff spoke. "I 'ave brought to you a guest. He was nota sure you existed. But here you are...eh?"

The big creature looked down at the Pope and me. His voice was deep, resonant, but not unpleasant. "Humph! Maybe *you* can talk some sense into his Assholeness, Mr. Guest. I have tried, but in vain. I keep telling him I am a formed apparition—there really *is no such thing as the devil*—but he doesn't get it, just like *there's really no such thing as a God in anthropomorphic form*! I hope you're not one of those devoted Catholic types."

"No, buddy," I answered. "I'm just a simple bloke visiting with His Holiness. We kind of enjoy each other's company."

The big being looked down at us, first to the Pontiff and then to me. "Simple? You say you are simple? No simple man would be allowed to visit here. I suggest you are either being set up to die, or his Ass-Wholeness here is bored. Which is it? But you, stranger, could set me free. All you have to say is, 'Satan, I wish you free...' Hell, that's all it takes, one set of fun words, free of charge and you let me walk out of here. I could even tempt you with money, women, a nice house in a country of your choice—and a motor boat for weekends on the lake."

I thought this creature to be very funny, whether it was deliberate or not. But I sensed he was desperate. I looked at the Pope. He was definitely in earnest. "You see, my son, how the *satan* does tempt a man, eh?"

The creature brought his big red eyes to the bar. "Everyone gets forgotten. Look at me. Yesterday I was delivering ice cream to orphans—suddenly I'm the devil pacing in a cell." Grabbing the bars, he slid down to his knees in front of me, his expression filled with supplication. "Please...won't you simply say it...how would *you* like to spend eternity in a prison when you could be sitting in a gleaming white castle on the Italian Riviera with servants, a beautiful woman sitting at your feet. *You* could have all this and for you, I'd even throw in an ocean view bar none, a honeymoon chalet in Switzerland for winter getaways, a pair of magic skis, a Rolls Royce and an unlimited bank account—and an exclusive mail man so you could write your Mamma whenever

240

you like. All you have to say is, '*Satan, I wish you free...*' Now, you tell me, is that too much to ask for *all that*?"

"Heh!" the Pope exclaimed. "He even does not know who his Mamma is—ha!"

"I do, too! My Mamma is the same as my Papà."

"Tu sei pazzo! How can your Mamma be the same as your Papà eh?"

"Because my Papà and my Mamma come from the same place—His Holy Poopiness!"

Not only was I highly amused at the two of them, but I began to suspect Pius XI was right about this guy not being quite the innocent victim he said he was. "Well, gentlemen, if you'll pardon my saying so, it seems to me, Mr. Prisoner—whoever you really are—that you can't *help* yourself from tempting people in your desire to get out of the scrape you're in here. If my Biblical history is in the ballpark, then I seem to recall old Satan, Lucifer or all the other names one such creature might be called, had a telltale sign about him: he couldn't help himself from tempting others in order to get what he wanted. Does that make sense, or am I hitting zero in the batter's box?"

The Pope laughed, as if he were taunting the giant behind the bars. "Ah Ha! *Il Diavolo*, Signor Denning is a private detective in the United States of America—too clever for you, eh?"

The creature's eyes lit up. "Hmmm...the United States, you say?
It would be terrible to die forgotten there," he said sadly. "In a land of capitalism—emotion, the caring kind that is, is swept under the rug at the entrance to the local bank. I could be envious...that money is worshipped

more than my alleged namesake. But then again, who invented money—who dazzled the eyes of the greedy? Was it not *moi*?"

The Pope leaned over toward my ear. "You see, my son, he is very *stupido*—he knows not he conafesses to the One God, Our Lord Jesus Christos, every time I—ha! ha!—I talk to his face, eh?"

The creature got up and paced across the floor behind the bars. "Just *five words*, Denning, and I will give you the world. Hear how that pretentious prelate prattles on? Sure, his Jesus Christos is not really a bad guy—but we disagree on major points. And that displeased *his* Papa—so he banished the brother *–not* some silly angel those books talk about—whose name was beautiful, *Lucifer, Bringer of Light*. Now, I ask you, how can someone like that be all bad, even if smooth-face here tells you I don't know who my Mamma is."

"You cannot 'ave mamma and papa same...sei pazzo! It is.... ...*impossibile*!" Then His Holiness, Ambrogio Damiano Achille Ratti looked at me. "You see why I cannot let him go, huh?"

"I—I, uh, think I'm beginning to, Holiness," I said, getting a little wearied at the constant bickering between these two odd-fitting characters. But, I thought, where else on earth would you get a show like this? Good versus evil? I wasn't so sure about that, either.

The creature came forward again and grasped onto the thick bars with his huge clawed hands. "Who consecrates the Holy See? Is it not men for the sake of controlling men? Five words, Denning, and I will show you glorious things, riches beyond your imagination—tell me, what is your very favorite thing—the one you

242

covet and most desire in the world? That gleaming white palace on the hill? Walking into your vault each morning to count your millions of golden coins? A dozen dazzling young women, all yours, all devoted to your every wish for as long as you wish. Tell me, what is it that you desire? For you see, *desire* controls all things...expresses itself like a chimera, a changeling in the night, calling to you, commanding you to possess everything the desire asks of you—and then..." He paused and tipped his head in an odd fashion, looking at the floor. "...then...you are *mine.*" Suddenly he was ripped out of his reflection. "Oh! Did I say that?—my, my—must have been influenced by the Devil!" He gave out with a roaring laughter that almost shook the cell and the rock on which we stood!

The Pope was chuckling out loud. "Again, he is *fame*—hungry to tell us who he really is. He cannot help himself, eh?"

"Please! Denning!...five little words and the world is yours! So many worlds, too...so many beings in so many dimensions...I can give you immortality...you see, I will never die, no matter how long they think they can keep me here. In time, this stone around me will crumble, the spell will be broken, and I shall be freed unto the Universe once again!"

Now I had no doubt that this creature was who Pius XI said he was. "Well, you kind of gave yourself away there, that time. You know, if I was betting on a sure thing, it'd come awful close to where you're standing. Why would I take such a risk of releasing more evil in the world? Isn't there enough already?"

He looked disappointed. He took a deep breath and looked directly and deeply into my eyes with those huge reds. A shiver went through me because the expression was so sympathetic. "Evil? Who knows what evil is? That definition, I'm afraid, is only in the mind of he who perceives—or does not—what balance is in the cosmos. You cannot have one without the other. Ah, but you didn't tell me, Denning, what it was that you desired most in the world?"

"You really want to know? Well, I'll tell you...what I love most of all in this cock-eyed world is walking the damp streets of L.A. late at night, hearing that lonely sax waft through the tenement houses, then stepping down into a noisy nightclub filled with reveling people talking and shouting and laughing while some gorgeous babe in a red-sequined gown sings her heart out with a small combo. I like to stand at the bar, being the secret voyeur, smoking Lucky Strikes, drinking good English gin or a honeyed whisky in a hot snifter. And aside from that? I like to see every decent guy get his fair shake in this world—yeah, the man of the street who isn't corrupt, who isn't attached to the world of power and greed, someone who delights in a fair wage for a good day's work, who comes home to a little woman who loves him, maybe some children who see the model of their parents as good and simple and filled with caring—and when the time comes for people to evolve to that next place—the dimensions and states of being I've seen that ramp us up closer to our original, sacred and respectable origins—then let them be ready for that. But in the meantime, leave them alone, let them live the simple life, let them live by that golden rule that you'd not do to the other guy what you wouldn't want done to you." I stopped as I heard the echo of my voice down the corridor where Father Tortelli still stood keeping watch. "So, Mr. *Diavolo*, or whoever you are, *that's* what I desire..."

There came a silence. Neither the creature nor the Pope spoke immediately. "For a speech like that I'd even throw in Bank of America, Sears & Roebuck—and Sheik Abdul's two-hundred virgin harem!" the creature said, nodding his head up and down quickly, looking at me. "Only those five words...and I would give you more than your puny little mortal imagination can conceive."

"I'm afraid it's too much for too little in the long run, and I've got a feeling those dice are loaded. Maybe some people don't have a price."

"Everyone has a price, Denning. Don't fool yourself."

The Pope remained silent. He gently took my arm and led me away. I turned once more to look at the towering figure. "You never mentioned your name, creature," I said.

"Who do you *think*...I am? Let your mind play with *that* question."

We joined Carlo Tortelli and made our way topside. At the entrance to the Pope's private chambers we stopped. The pontiff looked at me with kind eyes. "You are stronga man, huh? I lika that. So, now you see—and again, you 'ave coma to know too much. But I look into you, my son, and though maybe nota liva long, you will liva true. *Grazia,* I thanka you for coming. Father Tortelli will taka you to nice hotel in Roma, eh? 'ave a safa journey back to America..."

"Well, did I help in regard to the *Transcenders* you inquired about? I told you everything I knew about those other dimensional shape-shifters and the like."

"I know, Signor Denning. Buta we do not 'ave all the pieces. Many—how you say—layers...of *cose misteriose* yet remain. You, however, will be paid well for your co-operation...*addio*, my son...*pax et tecum* ...peace be with you, Signor Denning. And you know, eh?—I tink I lika you." With that Pope Pius Xl would walk away from me and into history. Six years later he would be dead.

Chasing Venus

Francesca Rimini was a beautiful, tall and slender young woman with long auburn hair and very blue eyes. She wore a white blouse with a light-blue skirt and white high-heeled shoes. She greeted us in the lobby of the *Hotel Stella Italia*. After Father Tortelli introduced us and informed me she was to be my hostess and guide for two days until they could return and take me back to Los Angeles, he and the Flying Priests departed, leaving me alone with the gorgeous babe.

"Signor Denning, I 'ave the key to your room," she said with an abbreviated Italian accent. "*Per favore,* to follow me." We went up to the 17th floor in an elevator, walked down a corridor and stood before Room #1701. "You look tired. I will let you rest, eh? I am instructed to pick you up for dinner ata eight o'clock. Shall you meet me in the lobby? We shall go from there to a nice quieta place to eat, eh?"

"Yeah, that'd be swell, Miss Rimini," I said, checking out the two unbuttoned buttons that bared a most ample cleavage. "Eight it is."

She said no more and left. I was tired and soaked in a bathtub for a long time. As the water began to cool, suddenly I found myself in a dream state that ripped me out of my watery lethargy and thrust me into a forbidding, frozen land. There was a blizzard all about me and sleet hit me in the face like little razor blades. I was driven onward by a coiled snake at the back of my head and its dark, deathly eyes made me not look back at it but continue trudging on in this ice field I found myself in. Soon I came to the edge of very high precipice, below which surged a restless, half-frozen sea with huge chunks of ice bobbing up and down in the water hundreds of feet below. Then I heard a voice. *"This is what it is like to live with me, Sinleila, the Goddess of Passion, without my sister, Love. There comes an unforgiving coldness that penetrates everything in your existence, then hurls you off the Cliffs of the Forsaken. Amorti brings balance, calmness from the cold and storm of mortal strife. Do not think your trials or my lessons for you are over...they have barely begun. You will experience passion until you have lost all that has had meaning to you in your earthly pilgrimage. Then you shall walk the dark night of your spirit's desolation and only after that suffering has taught you that the sensual without love leaves a vapid, longing emptiness, shall you resurrect yourself and be cast out of the abyss and deserted by the uncaring world of men."*

Something was pushing me over that terrible ice shelf cliff and I screamed as I felt that snake strike just as I fell. I woke up in the cold bathtub shaking like a child withdrawn from a frozen lake—that moment before a blue body succumbs and blanks out to oblivion. My forehead was dripping with sweat and the rest of me was cold. I reached for the towel and dragged myself out of the tub. Slowly I dried myself off and still naked, fell onto my bed, losing all consciousness.

Somewhere in the back of my mind I heard a knock on a door. I slowly came to, glanced at my watch and realized it was after eight o'clock! Still wrapped in a towel, I opened the door and there stood the lovely creature I had met earlier in the day. "I'm—I'm sorry, lady—I must have overslept! Please, come in..."

She checked my body out and smiled. "Father Tortelli is known to be wearing on people—so did he exhaust you?"

"No, it wasn't that. I had a terrible dream."

"*Un sogno*, eh? You call them horses in America—female horses or something—"

"—yeah, nightmares—don't ask me how that got named—"

"—sì! *Nightmares*...we call it *il sogno cattivo*."

"Will you wait—I'll dress and shave quickly."

She laughed. "I do not know, Signor Denning. We 'ave eight o'clock reservations. But I sit on your nice bed and wait."

I shaved and dressed, re-emerging a little more refreshed. "I hope I present myself a bit more respectfully," I said, showing off my grey pin-stripe suit, shiny brown shoes, trench coat and fedora.

She did a double take. "Signore! You are a handsoma man. Do American women, uh—how do I say?—*flock* to you like sheep and follow you around in the United States?"

"It ain't quite like that, Miss—"

"—Francesca...call me that. Let me hear you pronounce my name."

I cleared my throat. "*Francesca*...how's that sound?"

"Hmmm....," she sighed and said with exaggerated breathiness, "*romantico,* Signor Denning."

"Well, since we're being less formal here, call me Cable."

"Cable? What a strange name, eh? What does it mean in your language? I 'ave never heard such a name before."

"I don't know. My people are originally Celtic, mostly Irish, I think. Shall we go? I'm getting quite an appetite," I said as I looked the woman over carefully. She was wearing a light-peach, very low-cut dress and a single large gold pin in her hair. "By the way, you're quite a dish yourself, lady. Do you have a husband or boyfriend?"

She blushed. "No, Signore, I am not allowed those things in my position. However, I am not certain we still 'ave a reservation at the ristorante, though."

She was right. We got there and had lost our place. It would have been another two-hour wait, so Francesca Rimini suggested she drive us to Sorrento in her little 1932 Maserati convertible. It was a balmy night and little did I know that Sorrento was at least three hours away by automobile. We sped along dirty, bumpy roads part of the way. Finally I told the lady I was too famished to continue much further, so we stopped off at a tiny village at the top of a hill. "From 'ere, we can see the

Bay of Napoli—and beyond on top of the other hill, Sorrento."

We found a little restaurant-tavern and got seated at the rear near a dilapidated old radio that was playing Italian popular songs. I let her order and soon we were imbibing the best Chianti I think I'd ever tasted. "Where—where, uh, do you come from, if I may ask?"

"Oh, here, there, everywhere. I was born on one of those steep hillside 'ouses on the rocky cliffs of *Capri*." She lifted her glass to toast me. "Here is to 'aving no more *'sueño malo'* as the Spanish would say."

I toasted her back. "And here's to the best looking doll I've met so far on my Italian sojourn."

She smiled at me and lifted one eyebrow in a very sexy way. "We do speak some of the same *linqua*, eh? *Grazie, Signor Denning*."

We both drank three-quarters of a gallon of that Chianti before our order of fried fish and pasta arrived an hour later. "What'd they have to do—catch the fish?"

I loved Francesca's laugh. It was like carbonated Chianti as it bubbled from her inviting mouth. "You are funny. I like the funny man. You make me laugh—I give myself to you all night—if I like you, that is, Signore, if you are not a strict Catholic. Are you?"

"No, are you?"

Ay, *no!* I am an outcast, as your cowboy movies say."

I liked this intriguing woman more and more. "So are you a cowgirl? Do you ride bulls or sit on the sidelines?"

She blushed. "No, I am without doubt...one who likes the musica...how do you say?—the rhythm."

250

"Hmmm...sounds like my kind of woman," I teased, finishing off my glass of wine. "So why did you kidnap me to come way out here?"

Her face grew taut. Then she smiled again. "I want to sing to you in *Surriento*, as it is said in Napoli. If there is moonlight, maybe take the boat out to Capri, to show you where I was born, above the blue-green waters of the sea."

"Sounds romantic to me. So let's finish up and go." We had both eaten little but put away a lot of that Chianti. "Are you sure you can still drive? That Maserati of yours is fast, you know."

"I am fine," she answered. Then she scooted her chair closer to mine and took my arm. "I find you dangerous—and very attractive, Cable. I should not be doing this, because I am 'on the job', as Father Tortelli would say."

"How did you get mixed up with the Flying Priests? They're a pretty wild lot themselves, you know."

"The Vatican trains several women like me to host visiting dignitaries. But you are different. You are not one of those old, stuffy men come to fabricate stories in the ear of the Pope, eh?"

"I don't know. Am I different?"

There in the semi-lit room she kissed my cheek. "Something in your voice, in Italian we would say, *una voce pericoloso al cuore*...a voice dangerous to the heart. Sì, you are different, Cable, but I am fighting to not love you—we have so little time together."

"Why fight it? Take me to Sorrento, we'll find a little roadside inn and spend the night and you can road test my dangerous heart."

She was fairly drunk by now. She drew serious. "I am pledged to do my job. Italy is not a rich country. It is difficult for a professional woman to find something she likes to do."

"Do you like what you do?"

"Tonight I would like to do—no, I would like to *be*—another woman, not the one I am everyday which I do not like—but someone misterioso with you...and let you *trovare la mia femminilitá*."

"Can you translate?"

She whispered into my ear. "Let you find my womanhood."

"Well, that sounds great to me. It'll help me forget my bad dreams. Would you like to help an old gumshoe get rid of his nightmares?"

"You are not old," she said, tracing my lips with her finger pensively. "Sì, I could help you forget. I would like that."

"Then it's settled. Off to Sorrento we go!"

We drove for another hour and a half or so. Francesca put one of her hands on my leg whenever she could. It felt good and was also quite stimulating. She didn't know it, but she was prepping me for that moment when I might just yank the wheel over, have her turn the engine off and take her right there in the middle of nowhere. "You cannot see in the darkness, but up there to the left, is Mt. Vesuvius the volcano."

Finally we drove along a treacherous road that curved around the outside of the mountain and let out in a town square. It was late and few people were about. Suddenly, Francesca stopped the car and I could feel her hand start to shake. "Run, Cable, run! I am supposed to take the *pistola* out of my purse and shoot you in the arm. Then they will take you away. *Per piacere, correre!*"

I was still a bit relaxed from the Chianti and had a hard time registering what Francesca was saying. "Hell, Francesca, I'm too damn drunk to run very far—but why would the Catholics wine and dine me and then want to kill me?"

She bit her lip nervously, looking around. "It is not the Church—but it is *them* I work for. Father Tortelli does not know. He trusts me. But I was paid more money and I support my Mamma and Papà—"

"—shit, Francesca. You took a bribe from the *Oculus*—or who?"

"I do not know who they are. A man with no name met me, promised me lots of *lire* to bring you here—they are *banda di uomini terribili—va*! I beg you, go now!"

I got out of the car, having no clue as to what direction I should run in. Instinctively I ran west toward the cliffs. I found a little lane that led down to the harbor. There was a small breakwater and a lot of little fishing boats. I heard footsteps behind me...I turned and spotted Francesca coming around a corner in the dark with her gun drawn. She caught up with me in the shadows. "I cannot leave you, Cable—come!"

We ran to the end of the breakwater and jumped aboard a little boat with a small sail. Immediately she had me toss the anchor rope off and hoist the sail. As the night breezes caught it, we began to drift out of the harbor just as a pair of headlights came shooting through the street toward the breakwater. There was some moonlight beginning to appear out of the East and I saw three men come running down the marina toward us. I'll bet they were puzzled as to why Francesca didn't deliver the goods. The brisk night winds caught the sails like the gods blowing over the sea and we left the bad guys behind ranting and raving from the breakwater. Now I knew they were really pissed and must have had that familiar feeling of the 'double-cross'. I was puzzled at this woman who had betrayed the trust of the Flying Priests, the *Brotherhood of the Shadows,* not to mention mine as well. How was I going to handle her? Push her overboard and make a run for my life? Who in the hell was she? "So, tell me, are you *birth, initiation, professional calling, passion, love or death*?" I asked her as she steered with the rudder handle.

"I do not understand—what are these you say?"

"The *Seven Fates of Kathmandu,* the seven *Moirai* sisters, goddesses controlling each part of your fate. I sort of picked them up along the way. Ever since, my life's been a mine field of explosive events, and you're one of them."

She looked at me with genuine emotion in her eyes. "I am so sorry. I could not do it. I wanted to save your life."

"Well, I guess your heart was in the right place. So what do we do now, Francesca Rimini?"

"We must fool them," she said as she gave the tiller a hard left pull. We began to circle back toward shore. "They will think I run to Capri. But I know where we must spend the night safely."

"I'm glad you do, but I'm still not sure I can trust you. You know the old saying, 'fool me once shame on you, fool me twice, shame on me."

"I will not fool you, I promise on the safety of my parents."

"Well, that ain't much of an insurance policy, Francesca. Look at it this way...you're in deep shit either way you turn. You've pissed off the Flying Priests for betraying the Church's trust in you, and you created a lethal hornet's nest by stiffing those bad guys who will kill you as soon as they see the whites of your eyes—or before!"

A shudder went through her. "Oh, don't tell me that! I am *pazza stupido* for accepting their money. But as I said to you, Italy does not have an easy economy. Most are poor and struggle much."

Now we turned away from the breakwater at Sorrento and headed up the coastline. In about an hour we were approaching the city of Naples. A short distance from it, however, Francesca piloted the little boat into a calm, sheltered area. We ran the boat right up onto the shore, got out and dragged the little sailboat up onto the beach as best we could. Then she took my hand. "Come, I know where it is safe for the night." Along the beachhead were lots of little caves. She went to one she obviously was familiar with. There was enough moonlight to see into this particular cave a few feet. "These are the lava tubes of Herculaneum. When Vesuvius erupted centuries ago, the people from the village above ran for shelter into these caves. They did not know that the molten hot lava would rush through these underground tubes with the pyroclastic wave in advance. All peoples were incinerated. Still there are many remains of people in there encased in death from heat and lava so long ago."

"Wow!" I said, having no clue as to the extent of the volcano's reach in the distant past. "How do you know so much—and suddenly your English has improved? Just who in the hell are you, Francesca?"

"My Papà was a geologist and I fell in love with being a *volcanologist*, but the Italian government had no money to pay for my years of education. So I train with Father Tortelli and the Brotherhood."

"So, if I may ask, just how old are you?"

"I am thirty-three years—what about you, Cable?"

"Well, we're even on that score. For a change I'm not dating an older or younger woman than myself," I kidded her.

She stopped and looked into my eyes. "You do not hate me for what I have done? I would if I were you. I am not one to trust any longer for you, Cable. Accept my apologies, *per piacere*."

"Naw, I don't hate you, kid. But you're not exactly on the top of my favorite people's list, either. So, let's get it together. One, we spend the night, two, you get me back to Rome in your little race car tomorrow, if it's still there, that is, or isn't being watched by the bad guys. Then, I'll tell you what...I want to see the Sistine Chapel...I promised myself that if ever I got to Rome, I would visit that famous little enclave. I'm a big Michelangelo fan, not just his sculpting and painting, but his poetry. Did you know he was a great poet, in my estimation, at least?" We were out of breath and our voices echoed in the cave as we began to relax.

"Sì...I became in love with Michelangelo when I was seven. My parents took me to hear a reading of his poetry, it was read by a man who looked like Michelangelo—in Napoli." We found a little gravel knoll about fifteen feet in from the cave's entrance and sat down together. "I saw my sadness in him. I memorized one poem in the original Italian, and translated it into English. I hope I never forget it. *'Lady, while you are swerving your beautiful eyes near me, in them myself I see, just as yourself in mine, you are observing...for all the years of slaving, whatever I am, they render to me fully...'*" She stopped, her eyes misting with a little moonlight in them. "Oh, I do not remember now...the last line—"

"*—as mine do you to them, more than bright star,*" I finished it for her. "It's from a madrigal he wrote. I also fell in love with Michelangelo's poetry, you see."

She looked at me with great wonder. "How—how could you, an American tough guy, feel Michelangelo? Maybe that is why I am falling in love with you, Cable. Your beautiful eyes, your melting voice, I see me in them as I see you..." Suddenly she reached for me, clasped her arms around me and drove her lips onto mine in a kind of desperate passion. "Will you make love to me, Cable, here...now?"

It was early dawn when we awakened, wrapped up in each other's naked bodies. The pea-gravel had indented our flesh and our clothes made poor cushions from the little rocks. But we both had smiles on our faces when we first looked at one another. "You know, toots, today I want to visit the Sistine Chapel—how about you?"

257

"Sì, Cable, sì!" she said with much enthusiasm as she pulled me on top of her once more. Our bodies were stiff and aching from little sleep, and we smelled of sweat and stale breath. But we made love anyway.

When the sea began to glimmer outside our little cave with the morning sunlight from the east, I gently tapped the lady on her head. Her hair, fallen upon my chest, concealed her face and in that moment I felt such softness for this unusual woman. "Hey, there, sleepy head...I think we'd better stagger out of here, get your Maserati and check into my hotel to clean up and change clothes."

She stirred slightly. Then she parted her hair and I could see her blue eyes smile at me. "*Ay, arrendersi*...I 'ave surrendered to you," she whispered. "Cable...*ma, ero perso in te*, I was lost inside of you. It is *vergogna*— a shame—that we must face this day and part."

I looked at her and smiled. "You know, despite all the shit that's happened, and the fact you almost got me killed—there is a sweet something about you, kid." I took a deep breath. "So I'm not sure what to do with you. Turn you over to Carlo Tortelli—or give you over to the thugs?"

Her eyes widened. "*Per piacere*...you would not do that! Father Tortelli must never know. The others who paid me well, the *Occulatti*, will kill me *certamente* now. I am frightened, Cable!"

"You should've thought of that before you got in-volved. Yeah, they might get rid of you after they have their way with you. You're probably just a tad too old to end up in the white slave market—but I'm sure they'd find use for an intelligent, beautiful woman like your-self—in and out of their bedrooms."

"*O mio Dio!* Do you think I'm am *bella*, Cable, really?"

"Yes, Francesca. You're not only *'bella'* but I think I'm a bit enamored of you myself." I was thinking of the soft tenderness that was the nature of this woman, I thought what a contrast to the desperate, hard passions of June Maye with all its rough edges. Francesca had refinement and despite the fact she had made passionate love to me during the night, she was somehow still a lady about it. I don't know— you figure it. It probably doesn't make all that much sense, but what does when it comes to inti-mate human relationships?

We pushed the little sailboat into the tide and made our way slowly along the banks close to shore. Finally we saw the breakwater at Sorrento. We ditched the boat several hundred yards from it, so we would improve our chances of not being seen by the mugs I'm sure were combing the town looking for us. We found a wooden stairway that led up to someone's very nice home. A big dog greeted us with barks and licks as we sneaked our way past a hedge and finally into the street. When we reached the square where Francesca had left her car, we discovered the Maserati was gone.

We stood there in the shade of a building looking at the place from which we had fled the night before. It was that feeling one had when you realized you were up a creek without a paddle. Then a light went on in Fran-cesca's head. "My Uncle Abruzzi—he has a car we can borrow!" she explained. "Oh, you'll love him. He is my favorite uncle. He lives in the outer district. Come!" But life has a funny way of cramping your style just when you think you've made it to the other side of the road. Two fast-moving thugs came out of a building behind us and drew their guns as one pulled me into a narrow alley and the other grabbed Francesca and held her at gunpoint. She cried out..."Lasciami va! Let me go! Bruto!" Lasciami va!

The medium-sized slim man who stood facing me in the shaded alley had a very hooked nose and beady dark-brown eyes and hair slicked down like Rudolph Valentino's. He spoke with a definitive Italian accent. "Well, well, boy! Eh? We gotta you now!" he chattered nervously, as if holding a gun on someone wasn't his favorite thing to do. "You pretty tricky, eh—you and Miss Rimini thought you did us—whatta you American private eyesa say?—you did us-a de 'slip', eh?"

"It's *gave* us the slip—not did us—you slippery wops should learn the language before you put your stupid mouths in gear," I said, purposefully taunting the man in order to test his limits.

"I once kill a man for saying *'Wop'* to me," he threatened.

"So shoot—wop! Wop! Wop! There! That's at least three shots, you dim-witted gangster!" I continued to pull his chain.

"I *ama gonna kill you, you basso indegno!*"

"What's that mean, you piece of unflushed toilet mess?"

"Thatta means you are unworthy, crude, less than my mamma's garden *insetto*—a pesty bug."

"Oh," I said. "Mind if I smoke? I'm really exhausted from running all night from you guys. But I have to say, you guys are good—you know your stuff and you found us. What are you gonna do with Miss Rimini?"

"You keep your hands up, stupido. Francesca Rimini? I donno...maybe shoot 'er, too, eh? But first, before I kill you, Dr. Becker has a message for you. He wants me to tell-a you dey have found *it*—what he call it?— *oro noce*—de golden-a nut, strange-a name, eh?" Then he addressed me in a teasing tone. "And now, guessa what? You, Signor Denning, are no longer *necessario*." He began to half-sing. "*Addio, Signor America...Signor America...addio...addio*—do you like-a de opera, eh? *Puccini, ah bella!*" as he kissed his fingertips. "*Madama Butterfly*, the *tenore* sings his-a little heart out when he has to leava the pretty little Japanese lady—his lover...ah....such *musica*...you Americans have okay folka music—lik-a the poopa songs...you know—"

"—that's *pop songs*, you dumb shit!"

"No matter...eh? Hmmm...I think I tolda you everyting..."

Suddenly my world came to a stop. I couldn't believe my ears. If Becker and his band of hooligans had stolen the *Fen de Fuqín* from the Cave of the Seven Truths—*in a dimension removed from this one*—that meant they had outside help from supernatural forces like Cronus-Gor or maybe someone even worse, if that's even possible. Then there was the very bad news that now I was expendable and killing me would be like swatting a fly off the wall as far as they were concerned. I had to think fast. "You know, signore, I am really very tired—if I could put my hands down—"

"—no! no! You badda man!" He looked up at the blue sky between the two buildings. "It's a nice-a day to die, eh?"

"Yeah!" That was all I needed. Lightning quick I chopped the gun out of the thug's hand, punched him a hard right to the face and he went crashing against the old stone wall. Just then the man who was holding Francesca raised and aimed his firearm at me. "Cable! Attenzione!—he shoots you!" Francesca shouted to warn me. I instinctively dove to the pavement toward the stunned man I had just k.o.'d and grabbed his legs. As he fell forward and as the other man's .38 discharged, his accomplice took the bullet that was meant for me. The shooter, realizing his error and that he was probably in deep shit for shooting his boss, pushed Francesca into the alley while I grabbed the downed thug's gun and was about to shoot when suddenly he panicked and ran off. Francesca came running to me and collapsed in my arms.

"*Oh, Caro, ay! Molto pericoloso!* The life becomes so dangerous!" She began to sob.

I comforted her in my arms, rocking her gently until her tears subsided. "We've gotta get out of here quick, babe, before the local cops drag us in for questioning. Remember, we've got a date with Michelangelo—you haven't forgotten?" I lifted her chin and kissed her mouth gently. "Are you still my girl for one more day?"

She grabbed my neck and held on tight. "I am your girl—*la tua ragazza, signore.*" Then she looked at the fallen man next to us. "Is he—is he *morto*?"

"Naw, I don't think so. He's got a shoulder wound. He'll live to shoot at people like me another day. Let's go…"

She took my hand and we walked briskly for about a half hour. We were both hungry and thirsty. Soon we climbed a steep little hill and saw a clothesline coming out of a window with green shutters. "He is a player of the mandolino…very good. He will make you cry, he is so good…"

It must have been about ten in the morning when we knocked on Uncle Abruzzi's door. A little man with a wide black moustache that curled up on the ends greeted us. He wore dark trousers with maroon suspenders and a dark burgundy shirt that had seen better days. As soon as he saw Francesca he smiled. *"Francesca Mia! Ho pensato a te!"* he said in Italian. I gathered he did not speak English, but I was wrong. After he hugged his niece and looked her over, he checked me out. "And who…might this *uomo* be?"

Francesca spoke rapidly in Italian to her uncle, while most of that time he was looking at me. He knew the score and from the looks of us, he became somewhat alarmed. But he urged us to bathe immediately and change clothes, especially as we were in danger. Uncle Abruzzi was also hopeful that no one followed us to his humble little house. He turned over an extra bedroom to us, tossed me some clothes that were too small for me and Francesca got to wear her deceased aunt's old red and white polka-dot dress, with nothing underneath, which looked quite fetching. Francesca washed herself in the bathroom tub while I made good use of the basin in the kitchen.

Uncle Abruzzi took out his mandolin and sat down while I washed. "I play to welcome you...to *Surriento*, signore." He began to play and my eyes began to water. Then he really did it. Just as Francesca came out in that tight-fitting polka-dot dress, the older man must have thought it was his wife resurrected. He began to speak brokenly to us. "This-a song...*mia moglie*, my wife, this was her *canzone favorita*. Francesca know it...from a little girl..." He wiped his eyes. "It is the story of a beautiful young woman who is ill...but once a week, a young man who loves her very much comes to stand beneath her *balcone* and speak to her. Her Mamma has tol' the young man, when a candle is lit in the window, he may stop by, for she waits with impatience for him... So for many months the candlelight guides the young man to her window. She comes out, smiles at him from above and tells him of her saved kisses...only for him. They fall in love, but only as she stands on the *balcone*, and he on the ground below. Then, one night...when it is time for the young man to summon his beloved to the *balcone*—there is no candle in the window. The beautiful young thing has been called home by the *angeli*..."

During all this time, Uncle Abruzzi was playing the tune of this haunting song. I later learned, it was called *Fenesta che Lucive*. I would always remember that moment: the little man sitting on a stool playing his mandolin and speaking, Francesca standing frozen in the middle of the floor with tears in her eyes—and me, moved by the scene *and* the music.

We thanked Uncle Abruzzi for his hospitality and the promise Francesca would have his car returned from

Rome pronto. "If I didn't lov-a my niece so much—you could not loan la mia *Fiat*. Francesca, no bigga bumps, eh?"

"*Promessa, Zio,*" she answered as she hugged the affectionate old man. We walked to a special garage down the street where we found a spit-and-polish version of a 1922 Fiat convertible. Uncle Abruzzi prized the car, so I understood. It was immaculate with its olive green color highly waxed, golden radiator, and black wide-spoke wheels. "I swear, Cable, this car takes the place of any woman in my uncle's life. This one is now eleven years, looks new, eh? It is called *Il Torpedo*."

Despite the fancy car, it was still a bumpy ride back to Rome, punctuated by my putting my hand up Francesca's dress and playfully taunting her as she drove—a move I would not recommend while needing one's attention on the road. "Cable, I do not know why we met now...and that you are going away soon. I do not allow myself to feel these things. And what am I going to tell Father Tortelli?"

"You let me handle that. In a nutshell, I'm going to tell him that we were sightseeing in Sorrento when these thugs approached us—I made quick work of them, we got away, went to your uncle's and made it back here. Now, I fear, you, my beautiful Francesca, are in danger. Let him take it from there."

"Do you think it will work, eh?"

"Yeah. I know Carlo...he's okay. He'll, uh—he'll probably reassign you or something—and never suspect that you were involved with the *Oculus*. Otherwise, they'd have to kill you, lady, you do know that."

She squeezed my hand. "Grazie, Cable. I think I love you, Signor Denning. Maybe I will always love you. I 'ave never met such a man. You are completely a woman's man, and that thrills me."

I smiled and chuckled. "Well, we aim to please..." I said that, feeling the unsettled life I led and the unknown that lay in hiding around the next corner. Had I suspected when I entered the world of private investigation that things could twist and turn the way they did in my life, maybe I wouldn't have signed up. But you don't see those things coming. How can you? Most of the blokes who wore the moniker of private dick were far more simple and less adventurous and content to stay on the sidelines—chasing down those whose missteps in a moral society kept him snapping photos and presenting meaningless cases in court, and if not for the money, none of it would have meant anything.

"Thirty days hath September, April, June and November..." It was April 30, 1933. When Francesca and I got back to my hotel, we went directly to my room. I changed into clothes that fit me and then we drove to Francesca's apartment on *Via Stradella*, not too far from the Vatican. From her place I called a special phone number Carlo Tortelli had given me. When I finally reached him, I told him we needed to meet. He told me he had just gotten back from another assignment and said he'd meet us that evening. I told him I wanted to see the Sistine Chapel before I left the city and he said he'd arrange it, as long as we got there before Vespers at five o'clock that evening. Just ask for Father Piero at the reception office inside St. Peter's, he instructed me.

266

One is never prepared for some of the grandeur humans have produced in this world. When Francesca and I walked into the great Mother Church, I could not get over how diminutive I felt, looking at the vastness of the space, the ornamentation, statues on pedestals bigger than life—but above all, an astoundingly massive, high dome that reached to the sky and allowed a diffused sunlight to mystify the place even more. That incredible dome was also designed by master architect *Michelangelo Buonarroti* years after he had painted the frescoes in the Sistine Chapel. Francesca took my hand as we walked. It was as if I was walking in another life, and this was my woman, this was the girl I had chosen to be at home with for my mortal existence. Maybe it was the magic spell of Rome, I don't know.

Soon we met Father Piero and were guided personally by him down a series of corridors and hallways until two huge doors faced us. He quietly led us in and told us to maintain absolute silence and said he'd be back in about a half hour. Suddenly I was looking up at the great master's work done in the very early 1500's. Unfortunately, the smoke from torches throughout the centuries had dimmed and faded much of the master's work, but somewhere near the middle, seventy or eighty feet above our heads, I saw the famous fresco of God touching Adam's finger to give humans life. What a pile of crap, I thought—something went wrong somewhere. Humans weren't worthy of all this art and beauty! Michelangelo must have been an idealist, a dreamer, a hopeless artistic genius with a romantic twist.

"He was in love once, you know," Francesca said softly.

"Yeah, I know about Victoria Colonna. A married woman who adored him as well—I think they were also involved in some political intrigue together and their letters are legendary."

"How you surprise me—how would you know of such things?" she said, checking my eyes out. "Were you born Italian?"

"Maybe...no...I just liked everything the man ever created with his mind *and his hands.*"

Francesca kissed me. "He said to her, '*I had no strength before...your face within mine can well be seen...by your good will and kindness, for one who cannot see you for too much brightness...*' "Francesca turned to me. "Your brightness also overwhelms me, Cable."

"Thanks, babe. That's beautiful. I didn't know he wrote that. But I knew she died long before he did—and that he missed her."

"Sì. As I will miss you, for even though we consummated, we are still empty."

"What do you mean by that?" I asked, observing she'd suddenly become quite sad.

"So little of romantic dreams come true...there is a high season, like now with you, when my womanhood is alive and wild. Then there comes differences, children, arguments, infidelity, career conflicts, maybe even spiritual differences. 'ow can we expect another to be as we are?"

I checked out her face. She was in earnest. "Now I know why an attractive doll like you isn't married with a bunch of scrambling *bambinos* pulling at your apron strings in the kitchen. You don't believe in marriage. So, now, that means we're not only the same age, but of the same disposition—only my reasons might be different. I always doubted my ability to love...I mean, really love..." I looked up at the magnificence around me. "Like *this* guy loved...a Michelangelo, who can love so much that he can create an unforgettable world of art and beauty."

"Oh, Cable, I adore you," she said putting her arms around my waist. "The way you speak...I want to live inside your voice..."

I kissed her deep right there in the middle of God and Church and Michelangelo. "Thanks, Francesca..."

We roamed slowly the long large cavern of a room with its high arched ceiling. I knew the painter fought insufferably to crane his neck on scaffolds high above the chapel floor. From 1508 to 1512 he struggled against all odds to complete the daunting task, fighting fatigue, the poisonous paints, incompetent workers, jealous competitors—and last but not least, Pope Julius II, who, although a great lover of art, was a thorn in his side, demanding the impossible.

I was looking at the concentric yellow marble circles on the floor. "I don't think human hands could build this today, Francesca," I said. "So much of this is a lost art. Craftsmen and great artists with inspired genius stand worlds apart here. What do you think?"

"I think I can't wait until night comes when we can be alone together. Will you let me stay with you to-night?"

It was hard for me to understand how anyone could not help but be awed at the spectacle before us. Then I realized she had seen it many times and it's true that the familiar becomes commonplace when we live amongst it, regardless of its great and lasting legacy to the world. "Yeah, I guess...as long as you let me get some sleep."

"Ah...not very likely," she whispered as she gave my buttocks a little Italian pinch.

As we left I could hear the voices of the last evening mass which had started at 6 p.m., echo through the hallways of the Vatican. We exited onto St. Peter's square and walked to a separate building where we would meet Carlo Tortelli.

The head of the Flying Priests was in a good mood. "Francesca, Cable...come...here, into my office." We sat opposite the priest. "Now, tell me what happened for you two sightseeing lovers."

We looked at each other. How did he know? "Father—" Francesca began to speak, but Father Tortelli cut her off.

"—do you think I do not know that blush upon your cheek, young woman? Mr. Denning is, shall I say, hard to resist. He is persuasive and it is easy to fall for a man who lives on the edge of danger, eh?"

I smiled at Carlo as Francesca backed up a few steps, her face red with embarrassment. "Aha! So my secret's out, eh? Well, our personal lives aren't really what this is about. In a nutshell," I began my planned fabrication, "Miss Rimini was showing me the sights, Sorrento being one of them. We had even planned to visit her island home of Capri. But soon after we arrived in town, these goons came out of nowhere. We escaped in one of those little sailboats Francesca knew about down there at the marina, but once out to sea a mile or so, we circled back to spend the night in a cave in Herculaneum. Then we made our way back to find Francesca's little racing Maserati this morning. It was gone. Then probably the two thugs from *Oculus*—I'd guess—showed up again, drew their guns while one pinned me in an alley while the other held Miss Rimini here at gunpoint. I looked for a slipup in my opponent and found it, leaped at the dummy who was wanting to kill me and knocked him cold. At the same time, the other man holding Francesca shot in my direction and hit the other guy instead—but didn't kill him. The shooter panicked and ran. Francesca and I then made our way to her uncle's place, cleaned up and borrowed his car to make it back here to Rome. Then I called you—and here we are."

"Does that sound accurate to you, Francesca?" Tortelli asked.

"Yes, Father Tortelli—it is as he says."

Carlo looked into my eyes. "So, Cable...what are you *not* telling me? I know you too well. There was a reason these guys were so willing to kill both of you, knowing that you still possess valuable knowledge."

"Not anymore," I said, taking out a Lucky Strike and lighting up.

"Oh?" the priest asked.

"Yeah, seems the *Oculus* somehow got a hold of the *Fen de Fuqín*—it seems my services and my life—for that matter, are no longer needed."

He raised his eyebrows. He looked over at Francesca. "My dear, would you be kind enough to wait outside?" She got up, glanced at me and left. "Now...how do you think they managed that, Cable? If what you say is true, that means multi-dimensional creatures were somehow involved assisting the *Oculus* in procuring the priceless object back to the earth plane. Does that sound about right?"

"Don't tell me that ol' devil made them do it—I might just believe you," I laughed, recalling my recent conversation with, presumably, the old *Diavolo* himself.

Carlo began to chuckle, nodding his head. "Oh, Cable, how you find humor in these dark hours—ha! ha!—I do not know!"

"Yep, what's life without levity?" I said, tipping my ashes into the priest's wastebasket. "So, you see, the game is changed, Carlo. What do we do now?"

"Well, it's obvious Francesca is in danger. The men who accosted you—they saw her, and they'll recognize her. These guys are trained to remember. I will need to transfer her to another country. I've been thinking of a post in Switzerland. The Germans have some new underground activity there." Then he looked at me. "And you, my friend? It looks like you are indeed no longer of use to the *Oculus* or Becker's German spy ring. Whether they work together or not, they both know who you are, where you live. The question is, will they bother killing you if you are of no further interest to them?"

"Good question," I said, a tad uncomfortable realizing my life once again hung in the balance. "The fact remains, according to them, the memory of the contents of the *Fen de Fuqín* is still imprinted on my brain cells up here somewhere," I chuckled, pointing my finger to my head. "Yeah...good luck, Cable Denning, I keep telling myself."

Carlo Tortelli laughed. "Damned if you do, damned if you don't, eh, Cable? I do not envy you your return to the States. Speaking of which, we'll be prepared to get you on a mail-drop plane to Genoa tomorrow evening."

"Genoa? What happened to Naples, direct connections from the airport to the docks, smooth boarding, minimum hassle and all that?"

"It's the best I can do. Times are tough. You'll need to meet me here about seven and we'll take you to the airport outside Roma. I'll also pay you then, if that arrangement is agreeable to you." Then he studied my face. "There is a curious question circulating around in my brain, however. If neither you nor Francesca had made contact with the criminals who threatened you two yesterday, how did they know where you were—and they just happened to show up in Sorrento?—when they could've done a neater job dispatching you in your hotel room here in Roma."

I knew Tortelli well enough to know he doubted the story Francesca and I had agreed to fabricate. But I didn't want to push it. "Maybe they followed us from my hotel in her Maserati. After all, you can't miss the thing—you know, lightning fast, red convertible, loud motor and no springs. And I'll bet you dollars to donuts they stole the damn car after they lost us. I'd wager one of those guys wants to become a racing driver or something. Or, it'd make a hell of a getaway car."

"*Dollars to donuts?*" he asked me with a curious expression on his face. "Maybe they did follow you. I don't know, Cable. Something's fishy somewhere. Regardless, Miss Rimini is being reassigned, and you are catching a plane tomorrow night. You'll take a small aircraft from Genoa down to Salerno. There you'll be driven up to Napoli by a Signore Baldacci, a medium sized man with horn-rimmed glasses. He'll ask you one question, '"*What time is it in Los Angeles, Signore*? Got that? Oh, Cable, and as you go out, would you ask Miss Rimini to come in?"

Francesca looked glum as she caught up with me a half hour later. I was sitting on the steps of St. Peter's square, watching people and pigeons, warm weather and May skies. She sat next to me. "I am sure you know, eh?" she asked me, locking her arm in mine.

"Yeah, how good is your Swiss?"

"Not so funny, Cable. Who will watch over my parents in Capri? There is no one except a wild sister—and she lives in Milano."

"More wild than you?" I kidded her.

She put her cheek to rest on my shoulder. "Sì, more wild than I. To her, men are to be sampled like gelato—what flavor do I lika today? She says...ah, maybe limone or cocoanut, eh?"

"How old is she?"

"Twenty-eight. She should know better. Too fast a life is not good."

"Look who's talking? You almost get us killed, we escape in a sailboat, spend the night in a cave, get shot at the next day and speed back to Rome in your uncle's car—all in less than twenty-four hours."

"Well...perhaps *mia sorella* and me are more alike than not, eh?"

"Yeah, I'd—I'd, uh, kind of say that."

We ate that night a couple of blocks from my hotel. It was an Italian hole-in-the-wall with delicious pasta and wine. Francesca and I talked and laughed and felt for each other in the semi-dark of the café, knowing it was our last night together. She had drunk a little too much wine and her words were a little loose and naughty. "If...if I had *mi vida* to live over again, would I choose you?" she mumbled quietly. "Justa because you are good in de bed—is that *a causa sufficiente* to love you and belong with you?"

"No, babe, I don't think that can ever be the reason why two people hang out together. There's got to be a stronger glue." I was thinking of Zelda Blodgett and despite myself, how I enjoyed being around her. We didn't even have to be doing something special.

"Glue...? What is *that*?"

"You know, like a *paste*, something to make it stick."

"Oh...but I am already stuck to you, Mr. Glue," she declared with a hiccup. "Take me...take me, Cable, take me home to your hotel room. I want to breathe you all night long...so I may never forget what you smell like, or taste like...or love like..."

It was a bittersweet night for Francesca Rimini and me. Even the lovemaking suffered from the knowledge we would most likely never see each other again. We got up before dawn the next morning. When I looked over at Francesca, I could tell she'd been crying. I didn't say anything but took my tongue and licked her tears. "Damn, tastes like you've got the whole Mediterranean in them there tears, lady," I whispered to her.

She clasped her arms around my neck and clung, and buried her face in my chest. "I don' lika to be a human... not a human woman...it hurts too much, Cable," she cried softly.

"All of life hurts, babe, it's just how it's set up. But there are lots of times between, too, like holding you and feeling me inside you in the middle of the night. Now, that's special..."

"You are not a woman...she carries the feelings with her...men—"

"—hey, just a minute here. I've been known to carry a few torches when someone I really cared for got erased from my life. It's not a woman's exclusive territory, Francesca—even guys feel pain, you know, especially if it's from the heart."

"Then I don't want to be a human," she said indignantly.

"Hmmm....well, I guess if old doc Frankenstein can create a monster, maybe he can create an *almost* human who doesn't feel life."

She pounded my shoulder with her fist. "You!" Then she stopped and looked into my eyes. "I do not want to leave you, Cable."

"Tell me, doll, did you ever have a long-term boyfriend?"

"Sì...Roberto and I were together for three years."

"Do you remember going through really great times and some pretty ugly ones, too?"

"Sì...he was cruel to me...and one day I found him in our bed loving a man! That was it. I left him without more tears."

"That's not my point. It's the ups and downs in relationship that happens, the stuff that forms the dynamics of most people's intimate lives. I ought to know, I take pictures of them when one can't stand the other anymore, when that person gets restless pants or skirts and goes out on the prowl, ending up with someone else's husband or a hooker or the delivery boy at the local market, or some numbskull millionaire who uses the lady while promising her the moon. And then it gets messy, it goes to court and all those nice, revealing pictures suddenly come to life as a reality that the forever-after part of the relationship just went south and we get to see the despicable side of human nature, the accusing vitriol, the anger, the hatred, the resentment that someone feels betrayed and nothing between them can ever be the same again." I stopped, catching my breath, realizing I had gone off on one of my outbursts again. Where did they come from? Why did I let them out on those I might care for? "And then you limp away from the wreck, try to paste yourself back together again because something in you makes you want to go on, even if you don't know where. And then sooner or later, someone enters your life like a breath of fresh air, a cool breeze on a summer's night—and you take her in, hold her desperately because she may be the one, she may be the prize, the ideal romantic partner who will love and adore you and take care of you and feed you and support you and be there when the rest of your world falls like ashes to the floor."

Francesca's head was still buried in my chest as I spoke. Now she broke away and looked up at me with such love I know I'll never be able to describe it to myself, let alone someone else. "That would be me, Cable...if I could..."

I looked at her and smiled. "And it might be me...if *I* could..."

"No one, Cable, I mean *no one*...has ever spoken as you have...like that, when my ear was to your chest and I hear the rhythm of your voice in my head, my woman and my heart fall to pieces."

We embraced one more time and decided to wash up, and go downstairs. Good-bye was difficult afterwards. You know, life is a series of events and we tend to piece them together as the total summation of our lives. But we forget most of it, in time. I knew one day I might even forget Francesca Rimini. Not that I would want to, but because life happens and the soil of memory gets plowed under for the next crop of experiences. I used to think I was a pretty simple guy. But it seems, I'm not. There are too many turns in the dark alleys of my mind, too many heartaches and tragedies that have been shoved down deep, in those recesses where all is hushed. But the unconscious is sneaky. Every once in a while one of those memories comes bubbling up and paralyzes you, makes you think what an empty worthless piece of shit you turned out to be, despite how the world might look up to you, praise you for deeds well done, or a good lay well performed in the middle of the midnight sheets.

My last sight of Francesca Rimini was watching her standing in the middle of St. Peter's square as Carlo Tortelli drove me out of her life forever. But I knew she was an unreachable woman, hidden deep down like me, unavailable for love. I mused that just behind those walls a few hundred feet from us, Michelangelo's work would go on—vibrant and alive until the end of our world, that art, that beauty—and one of his last words I memorized as a very young man: *'I am inside this fire that burns in my body…a secret thought will show me and will say…I await you seeing her…another time.'* I mean—after all—I was only chasing Venus.

End Part 1

Old-timer
Sherriff 'Boots' Blake
helps solve –

Murder at the
Ballet!

The Seven Fates
of
Kathmandu

Part
II

CONTENTS
Part II

Chapter 9

INCOMING WHISPERS

Returning to Danger

Oddly, I was left alone for the return trip. As far as I could tell, there were no tails, no suspicious looking characters, or for that matter, not even a pleasant babe to pass the time with. But something else was happening. Increasingly, I was feeling a certain frequency in my head, and some days it seemed it was getting a little stronger. At first the sound was like the frequency variations when someone's tuning in a station on the dial of a radio. What I was receiving wasn't the radio station, but the sounds in between. Yet I also felt that as the days passed, the strange sound was becoming somehow more focused in my brain. It had a subtle something to it I couldn't explain. It wasn't ominous, but quite the opposite, as if some friendly voice was on the other end of a phone transmission, on its way to me and I needed to listen up. I know, it sounds nuts—but that's the way it was!

I had noticed faint signs of it just before I left for Italy. At the time I paid little attention to it. But then as it was constant, I thought maybe something was going haywire in my head, or worse, something was heralding a disease of some sort in my body. But I felt fine for a banged up thirty-three year old private dick. I also felt I needed to share this phenomenon with someone I could trust. But who? A psychologist? A biochemist? Perhaps one of Joe Lorena's aliens could help? In the end, it was Toggth's name that kept coming up. But how would I get a hold of the little creature from the Cave of the Seven Truths? He had disappeared and he came and went at will. I hadn't seen him since before my Nepalese adventure.

For a few days I moped around, missing Francesca Rimini. Her warm feminine qualities attracted me and I sensed she was a lot more intelligent than she let on. When I closed my eyes, I could feel her nose touching mine as she moved in to kiss me. How I enjoyed those warm, moist lips that grabbed mine and woke up a heart that had been sleeping since Zelda Blodgett. In a way, I wish I hadn't become so damn sexually hooked on June Maye. Sure, she was a lovely doll and sharp in her own way. But it wasn't as if we were life-committed or anything, there was just that groove we both fit into. Smoking, booze, lots of intense passionate sex—and maybe some night I'd even slip us both a few pinches of those hallucinogens Lily's uncle had given me—for an extra kick. I was aware of the possibility of recurrence, but it had been sometime since Nepal and I seemed to be okay. So what if my dreams were a little weird and intense on occasion? Maybe I picked up a tropical fever or something else—like a premonition of death.

There *does* come a time, though, when it all stops. Everything. I knew deep down in me somewhere, where my guts got wings and my head became a part of everything else—that place—where all things human cease to be and some other awareness takes over. That was the place where all our stupidities and ignorance were forgiven, where *'Father forgive them for they know not what they do'* became an oath of office, a pledge to re-member that these earth children were slow in awaken-ing to the knowledge of their own ignorance. I knew this to be so. The immature juveniles playing at being gods frolicked in the streets of darkness, ego, and self-importance, distorting natural intention. Sure, why not rape the world and pretend not to be accountable? If humans were really accountable, they wouldn't breed like rats or allow one single malnourished child to die in poor and undeveloped countries—let alone for us to let the distended bellies of our own American babies be-come the anthem of death and dying along the impover-ished roadsides of the Deep South.

But you never know when that moment comes. Yeah, you can lie in the grass like the American Indian and say to the sky, "It is a good day to die, O Father of All," but I'm not sure it always works. I guess some can sense their deaths ahead of time, but most of us are driven along the cattle trail worth only so much on the hoof until we drop off, one by one, into the abyss. Some-times remembering can be a curse. So can thinking too much...which I figured I was probably doing.

By May 14, 1933 I was back in the saddle at my of-fice on Franklin. Mandy had held down the fort in her usual style of care and efficiency during my absence. The ten grand in my bank account felt pretty good, con-sidering how much I had been gone from my office. That, plus I had some dough left from the loot Toggth had relieved the armored truck of on that day before my journey began. First there was Nepal and the outra-geous adventure of everything from signing up for the

Moirai and the *Seven Fates of Kathmandu*, who now haunted me. I kept having to go over the sisters in my head. And when would they be through with me? I think I'd experienced *Regini, the Goddess of Birth* okay, and then in Kathmandu I met *Innioma, Goddess of Initiation*—and the shit I went through on that one! Now, as far as I could gather from their infrequent communiqués to me, I was experiencing two for the price of one: *Atropa, Goddess of One's Calling*, was challenging my choice of career and livelihood and the Lily Norwood debacle was a case in point. So far I was batting zero for her. The other Moirai I was being taught by was a twin, *Sinleila, Goddess of Passion*. Her sister, *Amorti, Goddess of Love* was part of the missing lesson, that I would be sandwiched between the two of them, experiencing one now, and the other later. June Maye was teaching me pretty quick what it felt like to have passion without love. The remaining two goddesses were yet to make their appearances. I was told their respective fields of influence were *Consciousness* and *Death*. Oh, yeah, was I anxious for them!

Then there was this fairly new development, the humming frequency in my inner ear, like *incoming whispers* from some other dimension or the like. Maybe I was just going nuts and that was that, and I'd have to live with the slow decay of my brain until all that was left was a kind of abstracted presence like Crazy Jack. It's funny, but you know, we're all really left on our own in the universe punching out our own way. Nobody comes to you with a complete set of instructions of *'Here's How: The Complete Manual of Human Existence.'* So most of us fake it as we go, taking the punches, giving out a few, and hoping some fun times and a little happiness come drifting down on us in the form of stardust. I don't know. I used to think the worst it could get in the domain of unpredictability was one day at a time. Hell, nowadays it's more like one hour at a time, if you're lucky!

Roses From the South

It was late morning and I was in that state when my eyes were just beginning to focus and I was barely dressed, still trying to shake a case of bad breath and the shakes from too much gin and too many cigarettes the night before. Mandy was humming over by a file cabinet. She was happy. I enjoyed seeing her in an element that fulfilled her. I was lucky to have her. She had turned out to be one of my best business investments.

I was sitting at my desk taking a drag on a Lucky Strike when the phone rang. "Yeah, Cable Denning here."

"You should see my husband, already, taking inventory vis Miss Schnabel. Late at night he stays and stays, dere at de varehouse countingk, always countingk...now I tell you, vat he is countingk vill be de big shnookers on Miss Schnabel's chest!"

I couldn't help but snicker about the shnookers and the lady's heavy Yiddish accent. "Well, suppose you tell me who you are first, lady. I don't want to play Twenty Questions on the telephone with you." I held the receiver out some, so Mandy could hear better.

"Oh, so I'm begging your pardon—I am Mrs. Rosenbaum—*Vos machstu?*"

"I'm fine, Mrs. Rosenbaum, pleased to meet you. Now, before I do anything, I want you to know I receive thirty-five dollars a day plus expenses—non-refundable except in the event of death—or for some reason, I cannot deliver for you."

"*Vu ken ich dos opshikn?*—I vill remit two-hundred of ze dollars if you show me *fotografye* of Axel und Gertrude Schnabel doing whoopy-doopy!"

"It doesn't quite work like that, Mrs. Rosenbaum. You see, I need a deposit of at least one hundred dollars for two or three days' work—in advance."

There was a pause at the other end. "Advance—vat? You mean I should pay money before?"

"That's, uh, how it works, Mrs. Rosenbaum."

"Vell, I am not having fun already. Charging me money...when I didn't do anyting—it's Axel who is having all ze fun...in ze back room yet, viz dat cheap chippie."

"Then send *him* the bill," I said, with my tongue in cheek.

"Den he should know already I am trying to hose him."

"I think you mean *expose* him, lady. Look, I'm a pretty patient man, but we have to come to an agreement here. I'm not sure I even want to handle your case. So....uh, can you answer me a few questions?"

"Ya...such a ting I have to do...vell, so Mr.—Mr.—"

"—Denning, Cable Denning."

"So shoot viz de qvestions..."

"Okay, thanks. First of all, we've gotta look at the letter of the law here—"

"—vhat? You should vant I send you a letter?—now dat's—"

"—no, Mrs. Rosenbaum, I'm pre-qualifying our approach to the legal implications involved."

"You sound like great-uncle Sigmund—he is a liar, you know...always in court defending terrible people."

"I think you mean a *lawyer*, ma'am." I looked at Mandy who was doubled over, laughing and holding on to the file cabinet.

"Vell, vhat's de difference? Liar, lawyer—dey all ze time say de same ting. No vonder ze judge goes on de bench to sleep. Dat's vhat Sigmund's vife says—de judges sleep on ze bench. I vonder if dey're long enough to sleep on—no pillows, no blankets. Very hard, you know, to sleep on vood."

I was having a tough time staying serious. I cleared my throat. "As I was saying, Mrs. Rosenbaum, the first thing I must be clear about is that your husband is innocent until proven guilty. So at this point it's simply your word against his."

"He has no right to vords, in Yiddish he is an *eklhunt*—a disgusting dog who is—how ve say?—who *humps* his employee."

I chuckled. "That's a pretty intense charge, Mrs. Rosenbaum. So that's about it. You send me a hundred dollars if you trust me, and I'll get to work on things right away, but I need some information first."

"Ya...already you tell me dat. Vhat!"

"Okay...here goes...give me your husband's everyday habits. When he goes, where he goes, where he works, with whom he works and who the lady in question is."

"Lady—you have already ze nerve to call her a lady? *Tramp!* Tramp! Tramp! Tramp! You should vant more names? I have other names—"

"—no, that's fine, ma'am. And may I ask, who recommended me? It's good to know those who might be kind enough to refer you to me."

"You should be so lucky. A beautiful lady...someone my Axel und his company make costumes for—at the ballet."

Right away I thought of Lily Norwood. I also learned that Axel Rosenbaum owned *Hollywood Costume Designers Co.* and provided many of the major movie studios with rented apparel. Apparently it also applied to the opera and ballet—and we can't forget Halloween. I hung up with Mrs. Rosenbaum's promise to send me a hundred bucks in the mail tomorrow morning.

Mandy came over to me, still laughing even from just hearing only my side of the conversation. "Oh, Cable, I have not laughed so hard in years! How brilliantly you handled that delicate situation," she said in that wonderful southern accent of hers. Then she looked at me with very affectionate eyes. "I undoubtedly admire your ability and it's so good to have you back again. You were sorely missed, sir."

"Well, thanks, Mandy." I opened my arms to receive her hug, but she put her arms around my neck and kissed me right on the smacker! "Hey! what was that for?" I asked, quite surprised.

"That's for all the times, dear man, I wanted to do that but didn't have the courage. Please, don't take it for any more than my unswerving fondness for you, Cable. I know you have many damsels of female persuasion in your busy life—and I would never be able to compete with those beauteous feline creatures you put your particular stamp of approval on. Plus, you know, it *is* unethical for a boss and his secretary to become romantically conjugated."

"Conjugated, eh? So that limits our kisses to Christmas, New Years, Birthdays, maybe Easter or Fourth of July—but definitely not Valentine's Day, right?"

Her face grew serious and I saw a loneliness in Mandy's eyes. "Definitely, sir—not Valentine's ....."

Mandy's southern manner was so refreshing to me—and even a bit romantically appealing. But why ruin a good thing? We got on swell as boss and secretary, so why upset the applecart? "I recall, Mandy, when first we met and you took me to hear Arthur Rubinstein..."

"...the Brahms Second Piano Concerto, if I do remember correctly..."

"Yes...I looked at you that evening there in the dark, checking out your profile, the way you had your hair up, your wonderful lips and turned up nose, the way you smiled and how you filled out that blouse of yours just fine. I also remember telling you that the terms of your employment hinged on you never judging my lifestyle, my boozing, my excessive smoking, all the skirts I chase and all the beds I end up in when I don't sleep here. And you know? You've been faithful to your word to never interfere, though God knows, I realize from time to time you wanted to." I looked in my schedule book on the desk. "I also realize you've turned thirty-six during my absence—I write silly little things like that down. So, what I'm saying, Mandy, is that I'd like to take you out for a belated birthday dinner. Will you accept?"

She looked at me with her eyes misting. It pained me to know how lonely this very attractive young woman might be in her private life. I knew she wasn't a sleep-around and a certain shyness kept her from reaching out for the rougher sex. She seemed delighted and surprised. "Out of your own kindness, you would do that for me, Cable?"

"You bet—and then some, kid."

"I must, in earnest truth, however, remind you I am your senior by almost three years—and on our splendid occasion out on the town, I would have the right to request certain favors of a distinct nature?"

"Absolutely. It'll be your night, lady."

"Dare I ask if it would be appropriate to collect one of those birthday kisses to which you previously referred?"

"You bet. Goes right along with the dinner—even dancing, if you like."

She lit up. "Oh—I have not stuck my foot to the floor in the light fantastic for such a long time, sir. May I dress for the occasion?"

"I insist." I took out a Lucky Strike and lit it. "Oh, there's one thing I've neglected to tell you, Mandy. I think you're a very lovely woman, inside and out. In a way, I've always felt a little below your station—"

She lurched toward me, then stopped. "—Cable, you mustn't! I have never considered you lowly or beneath my highbred station. So please never consider that as a factor—"

"—please—let me finish, lady. Anyway, I was going to suggest we resume a modicum of classical music appreciation together—I mean, if that's alright with you."

She looked at me with a deep fondness. "I have never...never expected this, Cable...and I am delighted and privileged to be your hostess in selecting fine performances of great music."

"Then it's settled. Now...let's look at your birthday dinner..."

We settled on a plan for the following Friday evening. We would have an early dinner and get in some dancing, I would take Mandy home to her little apartment and then I'd catch June Maye's last set of the night.

When Mandy Foster Simpson opened her door that Friday night to greet me, I just stood there looking at her. She was wearing a low-cut pink dress, white heels, a pearl necklace and had her hair up like those southern girls do in a swirl with wisps on either side falling over her ears. "What in the world is the matter with you, Cable Denning?" she finally said as she came out to greet me, carrying her off-white coat.

"You're beautiful, Mandy...I just—I just never noticed. And I've never seen you dressed up like this before. You look wonderful."

"Indeed? Well, I thank you, sir. Shall we go?"

We rode the streetcar downtown to a block or two before *The Rhythm Room*, a place that had decent food, and a great dance floor. It was located in the basement of the Hayward Hotel at 6th and Spring. We descended the marble steps into a spacious dining room with black and white checkered marble floors, along with a spacious dance floor, which we would certainly sample later on. I could see that Mandy was impressed with what she saw, as we were seated and we ordered lime sodas and I took out my handy gin flask. "Would you like some in your soda?" I asked.

"I should not be imbibing your decadent alcoholic beverages, Cable, but all things considered, this being my birthday celebration and all—I reckon we are safe to make an exception on this special occasion."

I poured abundantly into her lime soda. I dumped some in mine and we lifted our glasses to toast. "Here's to your getting younger, the beautiful young woman across from me—and the best damned secretary a guy ever had," I pronounced.

She touched my glass. "And, may I say, this...to the kindest man I've ever known, the most generous—and surely, the most handsome private detective I have ever had the privilege to know."

We were having a wonderful time talking and laughing. The more I listened to Mandy, the more I was enamored with her wonderful accent. She didn't, however, handle her alcohol all that well and soon I began to hear a Mandy Foster Simpson I'd never heard before. Funny, when a woman feels safe and unwinds with a little libation, a lot of the outer wrappings come off and there it is—the real woman beneath all that insulating protection she carries around most of the time. "That was a mighty fine cuisine, Cable. Did you enjoy yours?"

I had had a big lobster with scalloped potatoes in a white sauce with stringed beans. "I am, lady, full and satisfied as a fat pig in a corn bin," I grinned.

She laughed. "Oh, that indeed, dear man, would be a most familiar Southern expression, which I so dearly appreciate." Then she adjusted her dress so that her breast cleavage showed a bit more obviously. "So, sir, you like my costume tonight, do you not?"

"I do, ma'am," I said, checking out those lovely white breasts of hers.

"I am glad...for you see, I dressed for *you* tonight, Cable. And I'm still clingin' to the hope you might be moved to dance with me."

"Oh, sure, what's the matter with me? I was so busy staring at you tonight, I forgot. Shall we?"

I took the lovely woman's hand and led her to the dance floor. With her high heels she was almost as tall as I was. The band was playing a slow version of *June Night* and Mandy stood there with me on the crowded floor looking into my eyes. Then she slowly opened her hands to me and I just as slowly took them, as if we were mesmerized and suddenly in slow motion together. Very soon her body was clinging to mine and her cheek pressed against my ear. She whispered to me. "Darlin' Cable, I have wished for this more nights than I can tell you. You have been the only man in my dreams. I must confess this to you, not in expectation...for what we might do later...but just to tell you of a part of my loneliness as a woman. Sometimes when we just understand...know how another feels, we are not so lonely. Can you hear me, Cable...?"

It's funny at moments like these because part of you is surprised and the other isn't. "I hear you, Mandy." I didn't ever want to hurt this lovely woman's feelings, so I dug up some half-truths. "I wouldn't want it any other way, lady. I owe you a lot for holding down the fort while I was in Nepal and then Italy, and for keeping the home light burning at the office."

"Sometimes I wish it was the home front porch light, Cable, the one you were coming home to...and I was at the other side of the door, longin' and anxious to greet you with my body and my heart."

Now I was getting in a little deeper than I wanted to. I didn't answer her directly, but kissed her softly on the cheek as if to acknowledge her tender words. But I knew I couldn't be the one who came home to her and that porch light. We danced until late and in the back of my head I was listening to June singing. I realized I wasn't going to get back to the *Bistro Club* in time for her last set.

About 11:30 p.m. we arrived back in Hollywood and I escorted my date to her door. She turned to look at me, the light from the street lamp casting a lovely glow on her face. "I had a most delightful time, Mr. Denning," she purred in my ear. "I shall be watching out for a suitable classical music program we can attend together."

"That'd be swell, Mandy. I had a fine time, too. I didn't get you too drunk, did I?"

"You *are* a sinful man, sir, and to be sure, I am slightly inebriated due to the courtesy of your fine English gin." Then she licked her lips. "Now, may I collect that promised midnight birthday kiss?"

I opened my arms for her and she glided into them as smooth as silk. Her warm, wet lips sank into mine as if she'd been doing it for a long time. I would be lying to say I wasn't stimulated. Maybe it was her Southern perfume, a kind of mild Magnolia scent. Or maybe it was just the feeling of kissing her because it felt so damned good. We both took in a deep breath when the long kiss was over. "Whew…I, uh, have to admit, Mandy, you sure know how to kiss…"

"…kiss *you*…only you…please…won't you come in for just a short while? I do not want this evenin' to end—I think you know that, Mr. Detective. Therefore, it bein' my birthday and all, I insist that I serve you one nightcap of honeyed whiskey in a hot snifter before your unrequested…departure…"

What could I do? I suppose if I had to do this ritual once a year it wouldn't be so bad. She was worth it, every penny of it. "Honeyed whiskey—in—in—"

"—I have observed your alcoholic preferences and some time ago realized that English gin was not your only favorite alcoholic entertainment. Like the females in your life, Cable, you do relish variety now, don't you?"

It was the first time I had ever been inside Mandy's little bungalow that she rented in back of a house off Bronson Avenue. She had me sit and quickly boiled some water and soon she was facing me with two hot snifters containing boiling water. A bottle of honeyed Canadian whiskey already sat on the table. "You can see, as any schemin' female creature might do, I had planned on corrallin' you this night with one last drink."

"And why would you want to do that?" I inquired.

"Because I needed to know, Cable...I needed to know what it felt like...how I would respond...having you in my very presence within my humble abode. And now I feel it...now I know..."

"So, uh, what's it feel like?"

She put her snifter down, came over to me, took my drink out of my hand and wrapped an arm around my neck, kissed me deeply with the taste of warm whiskey on her mouth. "That...is what...it feels like...Mister...it feels like that deeply buried feelin' of desire I seemed to have lost along the way, some years back..." She began to cry quietly. I gave her my handkerchief. "Do you know, sir, what will truly make my tears evaporate...?"

"Yes," I said, feeling her desire and pain at the same time.

"...to touch you...and never have to stop touching you...so that my woman's desire may come to life in your embrace, sir. Then finally my tears...they shall subside...and I will be contented experiencin' that rarest of flowers." She picked up the glasses once again and gave mine back to me. "Drink up, Mr. Private Detective, drink up with me—and tell me to send you home—*now*, in this moment...or else I shall become foolish and embarrass myself in your kind presence."

I gulped down the rest of my hot whiskey. "Then I guess you'd better send me home."

She shook her head. "I cannot," she whimpered quietly. "I confess it is not in me to do so. Nor can I keep you here unfulfilled—or perhaps from another late night appointment with your fine lady singer."

She gulped down the rest of her drink and reached over her shoulders to unbutton the back of her dress. I just stood there, transfixed—a typical male, fascinated, intrigued, attracted to a woman's body. Her pretty dress fell to the floor at her feet and she stepped out of it. She took off her heels one by one. Then she pulled her slip up over her head. That maneuver tussled her hair and it fell down in a sexy series of strands. Left only in her bra and panties she stopped to look at me, swaying to and fro a bit from the effects of the alcohol she had been drinking most of the evening.

"Mandy, please, I don't think this is going to—"

"—no, Cable—see it all!" she pleaded. "*Then* make up your mind." She undid her bra and two lovely white breasts came into view, solid and quite ample. Before I could say anything else, she walked to a wall switch, turned the lights off and lit a candle on the table by the sofa. Then very slowly and tentatively she peeled her panties off. "Now...please understand...I am compelled to do this...if only this one time, whether or not you accept or refuse my ardent advances...because my chest is beating so and my tears can no longer hold the sorrow...of not havin' love in my life...do you...do you understand that, Mr. Cable Denning?"

I sat down on the sofa with my empty glass. "Yeah...yeah, I understand it, Mandy. All too well. But you yourself have said how messy it can get when boss and secretary get involved. We can never look at each other in the same way—there'll always be that tinge of desire hanging around—or worse, expectation. And you know, I'm the last guy to choose for dependability in the bedroom, kid. If we did it, it might be a one and only time...and, uh—"

"—then let it be that, Cable...but if it is to be just once, I implore you to stay the night in my arms and make love to me repeatedly...until I am no longer responsible to myself."

"What do you mean?"

"That at last I will stop thinkin'...I shall cease to worry about not bein' desirable...that a thirty-six year old woman can open her...her most powerful female self...and satisfy the man she adores." She came over to me and sat down beside me on the sofa. "And I do adore you...and respect and admire you. I cannot, however, force you into my bed nor hope that I could be the only woman in your life." She tipped her head onto my shoulder. "Pretend, Cable...*pretend*, I beg you...make believe with me...make believe that I shall lie in my bed awaiting you, alive and filled with desire...and you, sweet Prince, will enter my chamber and mount me like the man I know you are. Make me delirious until I have lost my breath, and do not be polite with this Southern lady, nor mock her—but in silence, dear man, simply...love her..."

She got up and walked slowly into her bedroom. I could see another candle go on from the sofa where I sat. I had never heard a woman speak like that in all my experience. In a way it was sad, that a woman of lesser stature than Mandy who might be ten years her junior would not have to say a word, but like several women I've known in my life, simply kiss me and undress. No more said. But I knew this was a lady, and this was her way. She had established protocol deep within her and I knew she had bent the wire as far as it could go without it breaking. Truth was I was feeling desire for her. My apprehension was about tomorrow and the day after that—I didn't want to lose my most capable secretary—nor end up servicing her on the basis of expectation. Yet there was something in my heart as well as my balls that went out to Mandy Foster Simpson. What the hell, I thought, you'd be doing her a favor and satisfying yourself at the same time!

With that in mind, I walked into Mandy's bedroom. She lay on her spacious bed completely naked, her arms outstretched to me. I took off my clothes and kneeled next to her bed. "Well, I'm here, doll, just don't take this beyond tonight, okay? That's all I ask."

"I promise..." And that was enough for me. I joined her on the bed and slowly lowered my lips to hers. She anxiously came up to meet me as her arms and legs wrapped around me. Sometimes lovemaking takes on a special rhythm all its own. It doesn't taste, smell or feel like anything else you've experienced before. This was the privilege I felt as the lovely woman beneath me began that timeless ritual of union.

I didn't get back to the office until after noon the next day. It was Saturday and I told Mandy I'd call her later to see how she was. I no sooner stepped inside my office door than the phone rang. I walked over to answer it. "Yeah, Cable Denning here..."

"You didn't show up last night, Cable. I called and called when I got home. Were you out?"

"I—I, uh, forgot, June. I'm sorry I didn't make it over, but it was my secretary Mandy's birthday—you know the gal who's been watching over Cable Denning enterprises during my absences?"

303

"Yeah, I know who she is. So...?"

"Well, she just turned thirty-six, so I took her out to *The Rhythm Room* downtown."

"Yeah, I know the place...so?"

"So we ate, danced a little and I took her home."

"Did you take her to bed as an extra-added benefit— or was that her annual bonus you gave her?"

"You want it sunny side-up or over-easy, June?"

"Over-easy, but tell me the truth."

"Yeah...it'd been a long time for her...I felt sorry...I-I was okay with it, you know? It was like a...a...like a—"

"—mercy fuck? Is that what you're saying, Cable? I know you're good to a lot of people—and you can be kind...maybe too kind..."

"Are you angry with me?"

"No, Mister. It makes me want you more...when can we get together? I'm wet for you just thinking about what you did last night."

Sometimes it was hard to figure June. She never seemed to be jealous, no matter how competitive she felt she might have to be to keep me around. But then again, no one was as near pure sex as June Maye. I always got drawn back into that itch for her, some scintillating passion that pulled us together in the darkness. "Well, I suppose I can come see you sing tonight—and then we can go to your place..."

"I'd like that, Cable. I might even have a new song to sing to you. What time?"

"Oh, I suppose around ten or so?"

"Okay. Oh, don't forget to wash up—I don't want to smell some other woman's juices on you."

"It's not necessary to say that—damn it, June—don't start dictating my life, okay? I'm a clean guy and I wouldn't do that to you."

"Why not? *Some*times I might like it. But I want you pure for me tonight—spic and span and swelling in your pants when you see me."

"Yeah, okay, babe...see you tonight..." We hung up and I was thinking how depraved sex can be when it's without love. June was proving the *Goddess of Passion* to be right on schedule. The comely figure of *Sinleila* had warned me that June and I would slide down the beanpole of carnal desire. I touched myself and could still feel the warmth of Mandy's wet womanhood wrapped around my penis. I could also feel the love she pumped into me last night along with the rest of her released desires. I was once again reminded of the huge gap between a woman who loved you and one who was content with pure sex. A feeling of appreciation arose in me for Honey, Adora—and most of all, Zelda's giving—all loving women.

It was early but I needed a shot of gin...maybe even two. I took out my bottle of rotgut from the right hand drawer of my desk, poured some into my trusty old water glass, took that first needed gulp and lit up. As I leaned back in the chair, I held up my glass...watching it catch the light...and thinking...how do the pieces of life fit together? How do you figure the stuff you can't see on the surface? How do you deal with the subtle shit that comes in like the tide at Malibu and floods your head, then goes back out, leaving the debris that humans cause in their own lives? I was drinking, smoking

305

and trying to solve that dilemma when there was a knock at the door. "Yeah, the door's open—come in!" I said from my comfy chair.

All of a sudden I was looking at the face of Helmut Becker. "Herr Detective Denning! It hass been some time...may ve speak a few minutes? I trust I haff not vorn out my velcome..."

"Yeah, Becker, you did that a long time ago, but have a seat and tell me what new tortures you've been planning for me."

He took his hat off, sat down opposite me on the client's chair and leaned toward me. "Vell, vell, vell, no need for hostility." He looked out the window. "It is such a perfect Los Angeles day, eh? Varm sunlight, cool breesses from ze sea—und all seems vell in ze vorldt."

"Maybe in *your* world, Mister, but mine's still stinging from the pain of being in the human condition and watching you Krauts make corrosive inroads into the American way of life."

"No race, no nation iss meant to last indefinitely, I belieff I haff told you on prefious occasionss. Our superior mindts und organization, uniting vun people, vill make Germany ze home off ze Master Race for at least a sousandt yearss. Your so-named *United States* iss a divided experiment und financed by Jews, whose only concern iss profit at ze expense off your sleeping citizens, ze puppets who march to ze cadence off your bought und soldt politicians und hidden millionaires."

I had about enough of this insidious character. "So what do you want, Becker? I was enjoying the day until you came traipsing in."

"Oh, vell, I haff both goodt und badt newss. First, let me assure you zat your Italian escapade vis Pius XI und zat comely little voman from Capri—uh....vhat vas her name now?"

"Francesca...you probably have her measurements in your briefcase since she was bought and sold by you and your Gestapo shitheads."

"Now, no need for vitriol, Herr Denning. Cable...if you don't mindt. Vell, anyvay, it iss true, Miss Rimini's life iss in danger. You see, double spies are at greater risk off coming to an unfortunate endt, simply by ze nature off zeir choices. So, Miss Rimini's life expectancy, shall ve say, iss somevhat diminished."

I took a big gulp of the rest of my gin. "You don't say? Well, easy come, easy go, huh?"

He raised his eyebrows. "I am amazed at ze lack of emotion you display, Herr Denning. But, zat iss goodt. Ze Führer vould be delighted. Ze strategic, intellectual life must proceed vizout emotional interference, don't you sink? Vhich brings me to your visit vis Pius XI. I haff little curiosity regarding him, because he iss impotent to stop ze German advances in ze European Axis. Little Mussolini vishes to ally vis my Führer, zerefore allying Italy vis Germany. Und for all intents und purposes, zat makes ze Pope Italy's enemy. Aren't ve clefer?"

"Oh, yeah, so as you Krauts take over the world, it'll be the emotional ones who will succumb first—you know, those with families, national pride, artistic sensibilities, humanitarian concerns, etc."

"I could not say it besser, Cable. Pius und hiss little Catolic brozzerhoodt vanted ze golden capsule for zemselves. But, as you can see, zey failedt. "

I was thinking of *Diavolo* down there in a fourth floor basement cell. Now I'll bet *that* was something the Krauts didn't have. "You know, I've always wanted to...uh...ask you...what is your connection with the *Oculus*—in your words, if you don't mind?" I knew the answer, but I was unsure if Becker knew it. "Hissler" became Hitler who was half-alien, Cronus-Gor's cruel and conscienceless star-blood."

He looked at me with wondering eyes. "I do not know vhat you are talking about. Ze Sird Reich iss ze true undter-pinning, ze secret ruling power off ze vorldt to be. Vhat you speak off, I haff no knowledge."

Whether or not he was lying, I decided to let it drop. "So...what's the good news, since obviously the bad news was the imminent death of Francesca Rimini?"

"Goodt news for you, as you vere informed in Sorrento. Ve now haff ze *Fen de Fuqín* und you are, for all intents und purposes, as you might say, *off ze hook*."

"Does that mean I can go home now, teacher?" I chided Becker.

"It meanss if indeed ze object secured iss ze *genuine article*, as you Americans say, zen ve vill no longer holdt you undter surveillance. Isn't zat nice? So for ze time being, consider yourself *reprieved* und you may continue to liff out your dismal little existence."

"Oh, that's swell of you, Becker. But I think I know you Nazis better than you think. What are you really saying?"

"Fery obserfant, Cable....Herr Denning...vell, if you insist, ze vay in vhich ze invaluable artifact came to us seemed...vell...seemedt almost *too eassy*. Ve are considering it suspect until ve haff deciphered its content,

308

vhich vill reveal its authenticity." Then he looked into my face with a scowl. "Or not...in vhich case, guess vhat?"

"Let me see...now, don't tell me—I'll be back on your shit list for memory removal using your new nifty *neural extractor*, right?"

"Right! I am alvays pleasantly surprised at your hidden brilliance, Cable...not to mention your sense off humor. In fact, I haff come to admire you."

"I still don't trust you, Becker. You originally came to me about some stupid anti-gravity device I knew nothing about, then you offer me money to work for you, I throw it back in your face, but you force me to eavesdrop on that meeting between Roosevelt and Schock. Then your higher-ups hang me from a spire in Chicago hundreds of feet above the ground, trying to get information out of me I still maintain I don't have, except maybe in my dreams. And of course, you killed a lot of nice people, some of them I felt close to."

He quieted his voice and leaned toward me, ignoring everything I just said. "May I remindt you...you still haff experience vis ze multi-dimensional creatures...und zeir advanced wayss off getting aroundt, perhaps making ze hyper-driven gravity machines out off date. Zat...you might vun day share vis us. So you see, ve cannot completely dissolved our partnership now, can ve?"

"That's funny, Becker, I don't recall us ever *being* partners. I still remember you from *The Grand House of Pleasure* and your killing my little friend Sylvia Alexander."

"I told you zen as I tell you now, Cable, I abhor ze killing off people who did nossing to deserff to die—but it iss life—little people get in ze vay off big sings. Ya...so svallow hardt und take it, detective."

I looked at my bottle of gin, then picked it up and poured another shot. "I think your time's up, Becker. From now on, unless you're bent on killing me on sight, I don't want to see the sight of you. Am I making myself clear, or do we have to draw pictures for you?"

He got up and put his hat back on his head. "I am sorry I repulse you so, but again I must see you as a moral man of peasant stock who iss cursed vis conscience." He walked to the door. "But take care, Cable, you haff not seen ze last of ze effects of Ze Sird Reich—or me..." With that he left and closed the door behind him.

I was nursing my gin, thinking about how my gut always ached when Becker was around. Maybe I had an ulcer or something and he stirred it up. Then the phone rang. "Yeah, Cable Denning here..."

"Cable, it's me, Lily. I'm happy you're back safe and sound. I haven't heard from you for a while. Mr. Blake, by the way, was delightful...but I missed *you*. Can you see me? I think Mr. Blake dug up some new information, if he hasn't shared it with you already."

"Sorry, Lily, but it's been a madhouse since I got back. It's good to hear your voice. Boots and I haven't been much in contact either since I got back from Italy. I need to catch up."

"The rehearsals are going well...you will be in the audience, won't you?"

"A pack of wild horses couldn't keep me away, Lily, you know that."

"I—I just wanted to be sure. I'll be dancing for you tonight, especially as the white swan."

"What about the other one—isn't that the sensual, out-of-control babe, that causes the white swan to be lured to her death by the bad guy or something?"

"Yes. But I don't see us like that. I see us as good and pure. Even as much as I wanted to make love to you the last time I saw you, I realized for us it could only ever be two wholesome people in love and me coming home finding you in the kitchen, preparing a snack for us."

I laughed. "Boy, have you got the wrong number there! But thanks, Lily Norwood, you're okay in my book. I've already told you, in reality I'm perverse, I push the wire to the max all the time, things like booze, babes and smoking too much are my calling cards."

"Those things are self-destructive because you don't have a caring woman who balances you. It's like me being up on my toes when I dance—I think all of life is a balancing act, don't you?"

"Yeah, you might say that." I was getting a little uncomfortable about all the domestic lingo the lady was tossing my way. "I'll tell you what, kid, I'll call Boots, get updated and maybe we can meet after you're through with rehearsal—what time?"

"I'm through about six. In fact, I'm late now. Where, Cable?"

"I'll pick you up at the theatre and we'll go for a bite, okay?"

"Yes, thank you. See you then." We hung up and I could still hear her soft voice in my ear, purring in there somewhere, tinged with sexual whispers that came from this beautiful ballerina.

I picked up the phone and Boots answered. "Yeah...I hope this is who I think it is..."

I smiled. "Yeah, Boots, it's me. Sorry I haven't gotten around to spending some time with you. Lot of damned stuff happened when I got back."

"For instance? I'm a thinkin' you got them balls of yours a bit horny while you was gone and you were out makin' up for lost time with all those babes you seem to be constantly beddin' these days."

"That's only part of it. There are a lot of loose ends I gotta tie up. Also, I had an uninvited visitor from Hitler's Third Reich a little while ago. He informed me I'm currently off their shit list—at least until the next crap hits the fan."

"I can't think like that, Cable. In the old days we woulda shot a son-of-a-bitch like that or hung 'im, not pussyfoot around talkin' to him like you was havin' tea and sympathy together or somethin'."

"Yeah, well, I've been tempted, Boots." I lit up another Lucky Strike. "Now...Lily Norwood tells me you uncovered something that might be a decent lead on this stalker thing of hers."

"Yep...I did. Somethin' you overlooked, Cable. The last threat the lady received in the form of a news clippin'—you know, with the letters cut out and all—contained a mighty important clue."

"And just what was that?"

"*Lint*, Mr. Private Dick. *Velvet, burgundy lint.* I might be an old son-of-a-bitch, but my eyes are still pretty damn good and with the help of my trusty magnifyin' glass, I found the tell-tale sign. I'll bet you didn't even think of that and even though the damn British are pansies, ol' Sherlock Holmes knows a thing or two."

Even as a detective, I was stumped. A million people could have left lint tracings on a threatening note like that. "I don't get it, Boots."

"You don't get it, boy? When was the last time you saw a *man* wearin' velvet burgundy? That means it's a *woman*, Cable. You're lookin' for a woman killer here…"

I thought for a minute. "Now, that's a pretty narrow premise to go on, Boots—and don't forget this *is* a ballet company, you know, and with costumes, both men *and* women could be wearing the velvet. I'll run it by Lily, though, and see what she thinks. Thanks…and maybe next week we can grab some lunch together or something, huh?"

"I could be way off base here, but I noticed a couple of small blotches from a liquid that might have been spilled on the newspaper."

"Now you're at pie-in-the-sky here, Boots. It could be anything. Also, isn't that a bit sloppy for an intelligent killer?"

"Who says she's intelligent, you young wet-behind-the-ears, pretendin' to be a private detective? She might be obsessed with the lady herself and not the brightest pin in the box."

"Let me think about that. How about me coming over to your place with some lunch a day next week?"

"If you have some time you might be disposin' of. I know you're in a…lobster pot and it's heatin' up, so I'd be careful out there if I was you."

"Yeah, I know, Boots, thanks. I'll let you know what Lily says about the lint on the warning note."

We hung up and I knew my next step was to call Mandy Foster Simpson and check in with her. After a genuinely affectionate woman like Mandy gives herself to a man, I was thinking, she's very vulnerable and maybe even a bit overly sensitive. I heard the phone ring at the other end. She picked it up, but said nothing. "Mandy...it's Cable...how...are you doing?"

There was a pause. "You are one of best things that has ever happened to this ex-Southern Belle, Cable. You...and your manly gifts for love makin' thrilled me, Mister, more than I shall ever be able to say. And I thank you, sir, for stayin' the night, as I requested of you."

Listening to that wonderful accent of hers, I took a deep breath and remembered what a wonderful lover she turned out to be. A guy can always feel how much a babe gives when she's got her legs wrapped around him. And Mandy was no slouch, once she trusted me she gave out with all she had, I thought. "So...uh, how's the rest of you, Mandy?"

"You mean emotionally, I gather. To be sure, I am a woman and I must come to battle within me that I do not—and I repeat, that I do *not*—find myself fallin' foolishly in love with a fantasy. You have been clear to me, dear man, and I shall fulfill my promise to you. As compromisin' as it might be from time to time, I shall not fall into the trap of expectation."

That relieved me somewhat. "Thanks, Mandy. Of course, you never know what might happen on your next birthday—or Christmas, Easter or the Fourth of July."

She laughed lightly. "I do succumb to your charm, Mr. Denning. And that's comin' up right over the horizon, you realize."

"What's that?"

"The Fourth of July. Why, you might be wantin' to show me some fireworks of your own, Cable Denning. Not that I'm expectin', mind you, but one never, never knows..."

"Yeah, you're right about that, Mandy. But as we have already agreed, definitely not on Valentine's Day, right?"

Her voice saddened and softened. "That definitively...must never be mutually celebrated by our persons in a conjugal togetherness."

"You said it much better than I could, Mandy. Will you be coming in Monday?"

"Of course. I have informed you I would not abandon my professional responsibilities and you will find my disposition and efficiency top drawer."

"Thanks, beautiful lady, that's—that's, uh, reassuring. By the way, I want to tell you again in case I forget, you looked completely and disarmingly gorgeous last night."

"I am flattered, sir. May I tell you a woman's secret?"

"Sure, shoot..."

"After you left early this mornin', I came to realize how sore I was in certain parts of my feminine anatomy. But, Cable, I love it...as I love you, my dear man, and ever will."

"Thanks, Mandy. I'll—I'll see you late Monday morning." I hung up having a hard time dealing with the way she was working around the fringes of falling for a guy

315

like me. It also dawned on me at that moment how our delightful romp in the hay was transacted without any protection. Neither of us had said anything, though I think she may have spoken up if there was a risk of pregnancy on her part. But you never know...

Chapter 10

THE BLACK SWAN

Manikin Man

Lily Norwood was so glad to see me that she ran off the stage all the way up the theatre aisle to greet me after the rehearsal. She flew on her toe slippers and glided into my arms, embracing me. I didn't think it was such a hot idea with the cast and crew looking on, but it was too late for that. "Cable!" She kissed me on the cheek. "It's so good just to *see* you, to know you still exist in this world. From what you tell me, one never knows—"

"—good to see you, too, Lily. What do you feel like eating?"

"Actually, I'm not hungry, but I could sure use a drink. I've got to change real fast, will you wait?"

"Sure, it's nice and quiet in here...I'll just sit in one these theatre seats and pretend you're the white swan. When you're ready, I know of a speakeasy where most of the booze is the real thing—will that do?"

"Sure, as long as I'm with you. Will it be safe?"

"Not as long as you're with me," I kidded her.

"Then I'll hurry." She ran off as quickly as she came.

I was sitting in the dark of the theatre minding my own business when a slight little man with a nervous walk approached me. His voice was restless, effeminate. "I see you know Miss Norwood. Do I have the pleasure?" He extended a sweaty, limp hand. "I'm Axel Rosenbaum, her costume designer, sewing master and fitter. Oh...so many roles..."

"I'm Cable Denning, pleased to meet you. Yeah, I'm—I'm a friend of Lily's—also a big fan." At all costs, I needed to keep my professional capacity in Lily's life under wraps.

He looked in the direction of the stage. "She is...wonderful, is she not? Lily harkens back to the old school of discipline in dance. That's why I work so hard for her. Art and beauty like that need to be protected, don't you just feel? This harsh world is—is simply not a place for such exquisiteness. Do you not agree, Mr. Denning?"

"Well, it's hard being a full-time artist, especially with the Depression on and all. I think in America, the great classical arts always hang from the cliff by their fingernails anyway. I suppose you depend on wealthy sponsors to keep the oil lamp burning, so to speak."

He looked at me curiously. "Yes...I guess you might say that. But Lily already has an international reputation, you know. Monte Carlo, Russia...she's a true star." Then his voice trailed off, as if he were speaking to himself. "Almost too precious...to be at the mercy of this cruel and thoughtless world..."

I needed to change the subject. "So you not only design Lily's costumes, but you select the material, sew them together—and *then* do the fitting? That's quite a task," I said, checking the little man's facial expression. He seemed nervous, pre-occupied, and he turned his neck back and forth in a manner that suggested he was trying to straighten a kink out of it.

"Yes...who else can do it? I alone am most qualified to touch the hem of my dancing goddess..." He made a swipe with his hand in a very effeminate gesture. "No ordinary man should ever touch her. He would soil her, defile her magic, rub the butterfly's magic dust from her wings—so I—I, uh, *watch over* her with guarded eyes. Devotion to the great is also an art, did you know?"

"No, but I guess I do now. I never looked at it that way."

"You should." He made a restless gesture with his body. "If I may ask...are you...are you involved or interested in Lily in a romantic way? You do realize she has neither time nor space for an ordinary mortal male in her life's pathway...it would be sacrilege to defile her womanly endowments. Sex always ruins...beauty." Then he went off somewhere in his head as he spoke. "That is the illusion, you know. For a short while, like the white swan, she is pure yet has longing and desire...but as she dances she knows she is best being the elusive butterfly, dancing with the nymphs of the invisible world. Then the crude human man comes with his carnal desire, seduces her, makes her ordinary—but she is not made for such defilement—and so she dies...she dies....she must die...because she cannot regain her purity."

Yellow caution lights went on inside me. This guy was not only eccentric, but maybe a little nuts. I'd have to keep my eye on him. "Well, thanks for the synopsis of *Swan Lake*. I'm planning to attend the Summer Prevue here."

He looked at me oddly. "You are? May I ask, then, what precisely your role in Lily's life might be?"

"Yeah, you can ask, Mr. Rosenbaum, but frankly, I kind of like to maintain certain boundaries of privacy, and that's one of them."

"I see," he said coldly. "Of course, that is your privilege, Mr. Denning." He nodded his head. "I will look forward to seeing you at the performance. Remember...*Lily must be viewed from a distance*..." He turned and walked away with a slight leaning forward, his head leading his body.

Lily and I walked out of the theatre, down Broadway. "Are you okay?"

"Truth be known, I'm exhausted from endless costume fittings this morning. My designer Axel Rosenbaum is a very determined perfectionist. He's trying to fit this implausible Black Swan costume on me so that it's more integrated with my body. That means sewing in very close quarters, with quilt liners to stiffen and conform to my particular anatomy."

"I sure like your anatomy, lady," I teased her. "By the way, I just had the dubious honor of *meeting* Mr. Rosenbaum. He seems quite devoted to you." So far I hadn't received Mrs. Rosenbaum's deposit, but I was beginning to question whether or not I had a case inasmuch as Axel Rosenbaum definitely did not fit the profile of the philandering male animal. So I wonder just who is this Gertrude Schnabel?

"Axel? He actually talked to a common mortal?" she laughed.

"Yeah, mostly because he was checking me out—you know, a stranger sitting in a dark auditorium talking to *his* prima ballerina."

"He's very protective. He doesn't want anybody to want me."

"You can say that again. Did you ever suspect old Axel boy?"

"No, he wouldn't hurt a fly. He's in love with his world—and himself a little, I think. Costume design, sewing, fitting, music, dance—he adores the whole performing arts scene."

"I hope you're right. I'm—I'm, uh, keeping an eye on him just the same." I put my arm around her as we walked. I liked the way my hand fit around her shoulder. I glanced at the front of her body, the way she walked, smoothly as if she was gliding. Her white blouse was open at the first three buttons level. Yeah, she was a tight package, okay. "Yep, as I said, I sure like your anatomy, Miss Norwood."

"As if you ever really paid much attention to it," she complained. "As I said before, isn't it ironic that the man a girl would like to notice her doesn't, and everyone else pants after her."

"Yeah, it's known as *lovers' perversity*, like a law in the cosmos or something."

We went to a joint on lower Broadway, the kind you step down into, that was located behind a butcher shop. We walked down a hallway where the floor was covered in sawdust two inches thick and the smell of roast pigs' feet or the like caught the nostrils. Then I rapped on a huge door that looked like a meat locker. A face peered out from the little sliding peep-hole door three-quarters of the way up. "Yeah?" a gruff masculine voice demanded.

"Ninth Division, Four Up," I said.

The door opened. A big bald guy looked us over. Then he smiled as he recognized me. "Officer Denning! Son-of-a-bitch, man! I thought you were dead long ago." Then he looked Lily over. "But I'm glad you're not. You know, this here operation's gonna be prehistoric in a few months. It won't be no fun anymore buyin' your liquor legal-like, will it?"

"Hello, Ronnie. I haven't been a cop for quite a while. I'm a private dick these days. This is Miss Norwood. She's a famous ballerina. I'm protecting her presently and would appreciate it if you gave us a booth with a little privacy, okay?"

"For you, Officer Denning, anything." He led us to a secluded table at the end of a row of booths. He looked at Lily. "Denning here once saved my brother's life. Frankie was mixed up in distributing bathtub rubbing alcohol to the wrong people—and the mob grew wise to it. Three men went in to take care of Frankie. Only one came out alive, and Officer Denning here beat the other guy to a pulp and crushed his balls with a wooden meat hammer."

Lily made an awful face. Then Ronnie went away, but only after he sold us on some new fancy rum from Puerto Rico. "Is that true?" Lily asked, shivering inside. "Has your life really been that harsh and violent? I can hardly imagine your doing such a thing!"

"Yep, and then some. That's one of the reasons besides June Maye, that I didn't carry you off to your bedroom that afternoon. My past hangs around me like a group of vultures waiting to do clean-up duty."

She smiled at me and took a deep breath, then let out with a sigh. "I still wish you would have, Cable. I'm finding out that life can be very lonely without touch, if you know what I mean."

I was thinking about Mandy. Those were almost the exact words she had spoken to me last night before I joined her in her bedroom. And Lily was right, life without touching another person or being touched now and then adds up to a pretty empty existence, I thought. "Yeah, Lily, I do know what you mean. But, please, let's not think about it today, okay?"

She looked down at the table. "Alright..."

"Now Boots tells me you had another warning note during my absence—news clipping style, right? He also informed me that using his magnifying glass, he found some *lint*, velvet burgundy in color, to be precise."

"I, uh, I didn't see any lint on the paper—at least not enough to bring it to my attention. So what could it mean?"

"Well, Boots thinks we can stop looking for any male suspects, and focus on the fairer sex as being the culprit. He says no guys wear burgundy velvet."

"I don't know if that's particularly true. What do *you* think?"

"I don't know. There are men of a feminine persuasion, as you know, particularly in the arts, like Axel your costume guy. So I haven't ruled it out."

"Neither have I, Cable. I know I don't show it, but I'm still scared inside. To have this hanging over me—like a dark cloud ready to burst at any moment."

"I'm going to work on this thing big time, I promise. Especially as you ready for this concert at the theatre. I'll keep a sharp lookout. I'm pretty good about spotting those who don't quite fit."

"I hope so." Then she looked at me and reached her hands across the table and took mine. "If we were the only two people in the world—maybe then you would want me?"

I smiled as Ronnie brought our drinks and disappeared. "You bet, lady. I'd be first in line!" I said as I toasted her. "When can I get in to see a rehearsal when all the main characters are present? I'd like to meet your Mr. Bruckner and thank him for sending you to me. Who else? Some of these folks are bound to be real characters out of a murder mystery, like Axel Rosenbaum, for example."

"I think Axel does prefer his own sex, or maybe none at all. He usually brings a very pretty, older woman assistant with him, Gertrude Schnabel, but I think she's a cover. In fact she looks a bit like me, same figure and all. She calls him *Manikin Man* because he spends more time dressing and undressing manikins that he does anything else—not to mention me."

Ah hah! Enter...Gertrude Schnabel. "Rather odd, I'd say. Are you sure Miss Schnabel and Mr. Rosenbaum don't have something going?" I didn't tell Lily about Mrs. Rosenbaum's phone call earlier that day.

"Maybe...you know, it's hard to tell, but I doubt it. They spend a lot of time together. But I think he's married."

"Like that makes a difference?"

"If I were married, it would make a difference. Especially if it was you...I would keep you too happy to ever think of another woman. I mean it, Cable..."

I looked down at my glass of Puerto Rican rum. Then I looked at Lily. "I'm sure you would, babe." I took a swig of my drink. "Not bad stuff, eh? It goes to show, good booze is still available, for the right price."

"You're avoiding what I just said."

"I asked you before, Lily, not to even entertain the thought. My plate's full right now, lady. Let's get this case of yours solved so you can have your normal life back. I don't know where June Maye and I are going. Maybe someday, but not today, Lily...plus, if Axel the gay blade is on the level, I have the feeling he would definitely not only disapprove of my bedding you, but might take things into his own hands to prevent it."

"That's sad. Makes me feel as if I didn't have a life of my own. I'm sorry for pushing things." She looked down at the table, playing with the rim of her glass. "You know, it's like the tip of an iceberg. I only show you the part of me that's up out of the water. But underneath, what I think and feel when you're not around—"

"—okay! Please, Lily!" I looked away and took a deep breath and exhaled. "So what about the rehearsal?"

"Sorry. Wednesday would be good. Everyone will be there."

"Then Wednesday it is."

I escorted Lily to her place. The ride on the streetcar was tepid, to put it mildly. I don't know where a dame gets it, that they can assume a guy's a shoe-in to fall for her just because she says so. There's no doubt that most guys are suckers for that Venus fly trap between their legs, whether it's deliberately used as a weapon or not, consciously or unconsciously. I knew Lily was a lady, but she was a lonely woman, haunted by that Goddess of the Arts who says you must have allegiance to her first and foremost.

In a way it was hard leaving Lily on her doorstep. "So I guess I'll see you Wednesday. What time?"

"Probably around 11:00 a.m. is best. Everyone of any interest will be there by then." Then she reached for my hand. "You're making me hesitant to touch you anymore...I just want you to know I have to deal with this thing in my heart for you, Cable. I'm not sure just what it is, but I know it hurts when you go, and aches when I think about you. Isn't that perverse?"

"Oh, Lily, it's not that I wouldn't want you. But at thirty-three I'm like a burned out shoe—or worse, the dark guy in your ballet, the one who brings on the black swan. I would tempt you and get you hooked along with me in sex and unreliable emotional places—believe me, you'd be a lot worse off than you are now. Sometimes the ideal is desire from a distance, because most of the dream doesn't come true."

She leaned up and kissed me gently on my mouth. "It comes true here, deep inside of me, Cable. Maybe that's enough, maybe it isn't."

We hugged good-bye and I walked down the hill to catch the streetcar.

The Lady is a Tramp

It was about 11:20 p.m. I was on my way over to see June at the *Bistro Club.* I was wearing my usual garb, a brown pinstripe suit, vanilla silk tie, my fedora and trench coat. As I stepped off the trolley, I paused at the entrance to an alley to light up a smoke. Out of the shadows of the night came a wild-eyed woman with her hand out. "Mister, before you go in there to spend your money, will you help out a lost pain-ridden lady?" I checked her out. She had silvery hair that was tied up with a red bandana. Her grayish skirt was dirty and an off-white blouse hung around her body like a thin sack. She wore no shoes and spoke with a definite English accent, as if she'd been a lady of station at one time.

"You know, lady, I hate pandering. I grew up with nothing—the hard way—but I took the punches and made something out of myself. What about you—aren't you your own victim?"

She looked at me and tried a real smile. There was a remaining trace of beauty in the lady, that at one time you could tell this was an attractive, vital woman. "I'm not a beggar, mister... Men...alcohol, other drugs. I had two children out of wedlock. My family disowned me. So I kept sliding..." She looked up at me, searching my eyes. "Sliding...have you ever slid down the *up* staircase, Mister? It could happen to anyone. Even you. Only I started real young. That's how it happens, you know. I came from money. My mother was a British socialite who didn't even want kids. My father left her with a big estate and a million bucks and went out and made ten million more. When he saw me fifteen years later, he gave me a check for ten dollars and said he'd made his fortune starting with ten dollars selling used ball bearings for trucks."

"What's your name?" I asked.

"Adeline...Adeline Pfizer. What's yours?"

"Denning...Cable Denning...."

"You look like an undercover cop. Are you here to arrest me?"

"No, I'm on my way into the *Bistro Club*, lady, to hear some great music in order to shake off the rotten world around me."

Her eyes began to sparkle. "Oh, music...I love music...I played the piano when I was young. I mean, *really* played the piano. I learned Chopin, Mendelssohn, Beethoven, Brahms—I even liked Debussy's etudes and Chopin's nocturnes."

The lady was down and out. But she wasn't drunk or slurring her words. She seemed to be one of the many thousands of street people the Great Depression had created and then forgotten. "Sounds like you're studied up pretty good, lady. I'll tell you what, Adeline Pfizer. I'm not going to give you a cent tonight. I live over on Franklin near Cahuenga. I'm a private dick and live in the back of my office. The place needs a lot of cleaning, you know, like floors, walls, my sheets washed, and so on. *If* you can get to my place at 6400 Franklin, I'll pay you fair wages for a fair day's work. How's that sound?"

"If I may ask—private *dick*?

I laughed. "It's short for detective. I'm a private eye."

"Oh, I see—thank you for clarifying that."

"Are you honest? Can I leave my place without anything being misplaced or stolen?" Of course I didn't have anything worth stealing anyhow.

"I can't guarantee I won't misplace some things at first, but I will not steal from you, I promise you that."

"That's good enough for me, Adeline. What about tomorrow night, late—say, seven o'clock or so? My secretary will be gone by then and you'll have the whole place to yourself. Oh, by the way, it's suite B....okay?"

"Okay. And you? Where, may I ask, will you be?"

"Probably over at my girlfriend's joint."

"Oh, I see," she said in a quiet, breathy voice. "Thank you for the opportunity, Mr. Denning. I will be there tomorrow evening."

She extended her dirty hand to me and I took it. "Yeah, swell...and I'll provide the soap, water, rags and mop, okay? Oh, yeah, and if you get hungry, help yourself to whatever you can find hanging around."

I guess setting things up for Adeline the way I did was my version of helping her out. If a person meets you half way, then maybe they were the real thing and really wanted to pull themselves up by the chinstraps.

As I walked down the stairs to the *Bistro Room* I could hear June singing a hot-to-pop version of *The Lady Is a Tramp* and it made me wonder, is that what *I've* become? A guy who sleeps around with different broads and now is hooked on some dame who has room only for sex, never love? The old saying, '*Tell me who you go with and I'll tell you who you are*' probably held true for June Maye and me. We screwed more than a bunch of field mice on an annual convention and just when we thought we'd reached the saturation point, that same itching reached new heights—or was it depths?—and we had to scratch it.

She finished the song and saw me wave from the bar. She sauntered up to me and kissed me on the cheek. Even though she told me otherwise, I could tell she was a little miffed at me for taking Mandy Foster Simpson to bed the night before. "Hello, lover man," she said in a derisive tone. "Like the song?" All the other men hanging around the bar were jealous, I could tell. They wanted what I had, this voluptuous singing babe in the dark-green shimmering gown with her hooters half in and half out.

"Yeah, is that my new song?"

"No, I wouldn't dedicate that to you, silly man. No, you just hang on to your hat, Mister. The next song is going make you want me right up there on the stage in front of God and everyone."

I toasted June and sipped my drink. "I can't wait, babe. I'm sizzling already."

"Well, I hope you've built your edge back up from that mercy fuck you gave your secretary last night. Isn't she like ancient or something?"

"Well, I guess from your perspective, you might call thirty-six getting on a bit. Can I buy you a drink?"

"Yeah, sure." She was already slurring a little and I knew like me June Maye started drinking at home to bury some of that deep pain that prevented her loving anyone in this world. I knew in my gut it always started with finding a place in your *self* to love first. Then maybe you could love someone else, provided they were the right someone.

We small-talked a bit and then she finally made her way through the noisy throng to the stage. I guess when you've been to the sensual palaces of a woman's many charms as often as I had, you get a bit jaded with the game of sameness. But, let me tell you, when June sang the next song for me, I could definitely feel a bulge in my pants. I knew the piece. It was Lorenz Hart's wonderful lyrics with Richard Rodgers' sensual music that made *Lover* take you on a trip to sex land in a Saturday night penthouse with clinking cocktail glasses, smoky, dark corners with some babe dressed in black velvet looking you over. June's awesome, breathy performance came out through that microphone like hot dragon's breath melting a dim candle...I became a puddle of wax like every other red-blooded American bloke bellied up to the bar, gawking at June with that dirty white-yellow spotlight making her appear ghost-like from a distance. By the time she got to *"Lover please be tender, when you're tender, fears depart. Lover, I surrender to my heart"* I was a goner. She was right, I was ready to go up there on that stage, bend her over the bass drum and give it to her right there!

I watched as the tumultuous applause broke out. Both men and women alike had enjoyed June's sensual interpretation. I couldn't wait, so I went up to her and stood below the bandstand. I summoned her close to my mouth and whispered in her ear. "You were right, babe, let's do it behind the curtain, now!"

She giggled. "Damn, I would if I didn't have to sing again. Can you wait?"

"I don't know...that bulge in my pants is getting pretty *big*."

"Oh, I think you'll survive, Mister, let me finish this last song and we can go home—and then you can have anything you find, anywhere you want.

I swallowed hard, smiled and walked away. I had to admit my sexual addiction to June had crowded out other sensibilities in me, made me a creature of that craving, lost feeling that you're not in control anymore and it's some other thing that drives you, even though you know in your heart that there'll always be a piece missing because after you have sex with someone, no matter how passionate, no matter that you fall off the edge of eternity, you always wake up afterward and find it missing. *Love* would always be missing between June and me.

I lit up a Lucky Strike and tucked the packet back into my shirt pocket. June now launched into a song I knew little of, so it sounded refreshing coming from her experienced singing voice. It was *I'm Through With Love* and as she sang it, I began to feel maybe I was wrong to generalize about love. The lyrics said, *"I've locked my heart, I keep my feelings there, for I must have you, or no one...and so I'm through with love."* Maybe sex was June's only safe way she could show she loved me. But deep inside she could never face the general route to love because she was too damaged inside, wounded from some major thing that was missing somewhere back in her past. What I learned that night was that everyone might have a different take on this thing called love—and as elusive as it was to know or define—and though often it appeared to tear people apart...when all was said and done, it was still the glue that held people together.

Toggth x Two

We arrived at June's place around 1:30 a.m. and proceeded to take our clothes off as we locked the door behind us. It was getting so that we didn't even bother with the drink or smokes anymore—let alone talking—and simply launched into that lusty place between the sheets. As she promised, she was wet and hot that night and we went a few rounds into that sensual ecstasy po-

332

ets write about but maybe had never experienced themselves.

About five in the morning I got restless and put on a robe and walked out on to June's porch for a breath of fresh air. I sat on the stairs and lit up a cigarette. "Where do you think you're going, Cable?" Spoke a very familiar voice from behind a nearby bush. It was a voice I hadn't heard in a long time.

It was the little creature with the pointed ears and elfin nose that appeared. I got up to greet my little buddy. "Toggth! You son-of-a-gun! Where in the hell have you been? Crap, I haven't seen you since that armored car heist you pulled off before my Nepalese adventure— which didn't turn out as I expected, by the way."

"My brother Eli never guaranteed a good time, Cable. Noda and the blue-light folks are also dimensional creatures who are not all that interested in human affairs. For them, with no insult intended, it's like you going to your local zoo and staring at the chimpanzees for a while. It is the way with things. So, getting back to Nepal, lessons are learned where we least expect them. Like now, with you and the young lady...you must learn moderation. I must caution you to take no more of the *brain altering substances*—they will do biological damage."

"How in the hell did you know about them—and why didn't you help me out while I was going through hell in Nepal?"

"Eli tells me you agreed to accept the *Moirai*. They do not enjoy being trifled with. I tried not to interfere. So, I suggest, it's best to get through as many as you can while you can. Let me see, you've had *Birth, Initiation,* you've now begun *Passion* with Miss Maye...*Love, Consciousness* and *Death* will come to you in many ways later. Pay attention." He looked at me with those wonderful warm golden eyes of his. "When will you be able to love, Cable? It was right on your plate and you put it aside. Zelda showed you love. For that matter, so did Honey, Adora—even the lovely stately dancer, and your work employee with the strange accent."

"Yeah, well...you know, Toggth, it isn't that I'm ungrateful, but there's a part of me I guess that isn't completely selfish. Each one of these women is endangered. Except June...I don't get it."

"I see your point, Cable, but sooner or later, come what may, you will have to face love and what goes with it...a different kind of giving."

"I guess I'll cross that bridge when I get to it."

"Operating here as you do on Level 1, there are many subtleties that are missed."

"Whatta ya mean *Level 1*?"

"On your plane of existence, there are two of everything. Two governments, two militaries, two secret services, in the future two separate space exploration programs, two incoming generating money systems and so on. Alas, you operate on the primitive level of human emotion. The other level is cerebral—and mostly absent on your planet, is what you would call *spiritual*—which is the consciousness that pervades in all things....on all dimensions."

I sat back down on June's steps. I was nonplussed. Toggth's words felt like someone had just hit me with a ceramic bowl, then lowered it over my head. But down deep inside me, somehow I knew he was right. We are primitive chimps, striving for some sense of meaning to this whole crazy thing called life. I breathed in deeply and sighed. "So to what do I owe the honor of this visit, my friend?"

"You may not like this one, Cable. To buy you time, I synthesized the *Fen de Fuqín* but left out the unlocking mathematics to decipher the symbols."

"You didn't! That's why it showed up all of a sudden and Becker, Hitler and the rest of the mob were jubilant. I should have known."

"It will be quite some time before they discover they cannot decode the symbols. Foolishly, they will play with the existing hieroglyphs, thinking they go in some different order than they appear. Truth is, they are exactly in the correct order—but the object is useless without the mathematics. *That* is what was in the inner shiny golden tablets." He smiled as he came to sit next to me. "I did a fine job of it, if I say so myself. You'd be proud."

I patted him on the shoulder. "Thanks, guy. You're one of the few beings I know whose heart has always been in the right place. I don't know how to repay you, but I'll always remain grateful."

"They *will* catch up with you, eventually. Then they'll try to extract what you read on the genuine golden capsule with their *neural extractor*, which of course, will never work. They also do not have the *Blue Light of Noda*, by which one can read the capsule so much more clearly. My brother Eli mistakenly gave the formula to what you would call a mercenary, a creature named *Blinthe*. Then also quite by accident, it ended up in Dr. Sandor's hands." He paused and looked at me with sympathetic eyes. "But the extractor could kill you, Cable. I'll try to think up something in the meantime, but give yourself a couple more of your earth years to re-gain an orderly life."

Toggth always left me with a changed life, one way or another. Now a new wrinkle in the fabric of my life appeared. So I was buying time again—what else was new? "So where are you off to now?"

"Back to the Caves. I am preparing to elevate my being to a new level of consciousness. I will no longer require a body to be able to completely manipulate three or four-dimensional matter."

"That sounds nifty. Kind of like graduating, huh?"

"Yes, sort of. I am looking forward. I am not all that crazy about my physical appearance. I think I might be more appealing being invisible."

"Oh," I said, laughing to myself that I was even here talking to this wonderful being from another dimension. "So...are you leaving me now?"

Just as I said that, Toggth disappeared behind the bush again and June stepped out onto the porch, nude as a jaybird. "Did I hear voices, Cable? Were you talking to someone?"

"Naw...I—I, uh, I'm just replaying some of my day yesterday—telephone calls, what to say, how to say it...my kind of rehearsal, babe," I said, covering my butt.

"Oh, okay. Are you coming back in? Guess who's warm and still wet—and quite perky?"

"Yeah...I'll...I'll be in..." She went back inside and I looked up at the stars. I could always tell when Toggth was gone. I always felt a kind of empty place.

Wednesdays

If one has never attended a full rehearsal for a major ballet, my advice would be to, *prepare your self.* Amidst the cacophony of chattering people, symphonic instruments warming up, directors and lighting people yelling out orders and the general mayhem of last minute adjustments with some people in costume and others not...Lily Norwood was the shining light. The music was dramatic and passionate with a twist of sadness—ala Tchaikovsky, I was told...and for a young gumshoe from the ghetto, a completely unique experience.

Lily glided through the role of the White Swan this late Wednesday morning. Frederick Bruckner sat next to me about fifteen rows back in the darkened theatre. He was a stout man with bushy white hair and thick white eyebrows, penetrating large brown eyes and a face of general kindness. As I listened to him speak to me, I was looking for tell-tale clues. Was this my man? Or was it, as Boots indicated, a woman? "You realize Lily is the magnet of the whole company, Mr. Denning. She has secretly told me you are not her boyfriend, but a private investigator looking into those terrible threats."

"Do you have any clues that could help me, Bruckner? I've been striking out lately, and I don't like it."

"I have spent nights awake trying to make sense of it, Mr. Denning. Lily has no enemies in the company that I know of. Everyone seems to adore her. She's a pro— and professional dance people appreciate a pro."

"Yeah, I can see that when she dances. Stupendous...that's my word for it. I understand you're kind of like her ballet company godfather?"

"I wouldn't say that, but I love Lily like a daughter. I knew her many years ago when she studied here in Los Angeles as a child. She was good then. She's superior now."

The dance segment ended and Lily went backstage. I was looking for Rosenbaum. Bruckner said he'd be in the main dressing room with the dancers. I excused myself and wandered backstage. At the entrance to the main dressing room stood an attractive woman who could have been Lily's older twin! It must've been Gertrude Schnabel. I approached her, trying not to let on who I was. "Excuse me, Miss, I'm looking for Lily—did she come this way?"

"Who wants to know? She's a busy lady," she said in a low voice.

"I'm Cable...a friend...I just wanted her to know how great she was this morning on the stage. That lady can dance, eh?"

"I'm Mr. Rosenbaum's associate, Gertrude Schnabel. She's not exactly a Pavlova, but she'll do," she answered. I thought the comment quite strange coming from a cohort. She checked me out. "Are you a boyfriend? If so, it's rare...Lily's life doesn't allow much of a personal life."

"For right now you might say I'm an admirer. I realize she's a busy gal and probably doesn't have a lot of time for candlelight dinners, walking in the moonlight and the like."

"If I were you, Mr. Cable, I'd make sure first if she's interested in men. She might be of the other persuasion. I wouldn't set my hopes too high."

Now I happened to know first-hand that Lily was a man's woman from head to toe, so it struck me odd that this woman would be trying to deflect my possible romantic interest in her, in that way. "Well, as I said, for now it's the thrill of seeing the lady dance her little heart out up there—we'll see what happens off season, I suppose."

"I know what will happen. She will be off to Europe. I think you'd better drop your line off of some other pier, buddy. L.A.'s full of lovely young women who would find you very attractive, as I do."

"Well, that's the first nice thing you've said. You think I'd do in a pinch, eh?" I laughed.

"Yes...Mr. Cable...how old are you and what do you do?"

I thought about that one. "I'm—I'm thirty-three and I'm a photographer," I said, knowing the last part was only part true.

"Oh...are you going to take photos of the performance?"

"No, that's, uh, that's not my specialty. I do nature and stuff like that."

"Oh, I see." Then she looked at my lean body. "Looks like you're in pretty good shape. Do you dance?"

"Yeah, but only to big bands, combos and pretty little songstresses who warble out Berlin, Kern or Porter."

She smiled. "Ah...an appreciator of popular music—the music of the peasants," she crackled with an edge of insult in her voice.

"Yeah, that's right—peasants like me, weeds grown up from the east side of the tracks where life ain't worth much if you can't fight or steal when nobody's looking.

Some of us actually come out alive and well, Miss Schnabel. And, gee, we even appreciate art—how about that?" I'd had just about enough of the dame.

"I'm sorry, I offended you, didn't I? I can be brusque. But I sure like the way you talk, Mister, your voice carries an authority. I've got the feeling you've been knocked around a bit, both on the street and in the bedroom. Am I right?"

"Well, you know now, Miss Schnabel, I'm pretty much a private person—so I think we'll just leave it at that."

"Okay. Lily's back there, in that side room marked 'A'."

I thanked her and went to find Lily. I knocked and Axel Rosenbaum opened the door. "Oh, you! You can't come in, Miss Norwood is half undressed and it would be—"

"—let him in, Axel," Lily said from behind the door. The first thing I noticed when I entered was a foreboding costume with shiny black feathers hanging up on a rack. Lily was wearing only a slip and for an instant I wished I *had* taken her to bed that afternoon. But her voice trembled and she was shaking. I looked at her and then at Rosenbaum. Lily pointed to her mirror. Written in red across the entirety of it were the words, "*SOON THE WORLD WILL KNOW YOU ARE DEAD.*"

I went up to the mirror, studied the writing and conjectured on the instrument that might have written it. "It's definitely not been done by a lipstick tube—the writing's too fine and detailed. Lipstick writes wide and blurry. Now, if we could only get every single person in this cock-eyed theatre to write the same thing on a mirror—we might have our stalker." Lily came up to me and wrapped her arms around my waist. Her arms were trembling.

Strangely, Rosenbaum observed this but showed no sign of resentment. "This sweet lady can't continue to fight off these threats—whatever shall we do?"

"Whatever it is, we've gotta do it soon. But today, I gathered a few good clues."

"Oh? That's good to know," Rosenbaum said, looking at Lily.

"I know you two have met. Excuse me, I'm going to shower and get dressed—and we can go. The rest of the afternoon is ensemble work, so they won't be needing me," she said, sort of re-composing herself.

"Great," I said, looking around the room. I took a gander at the shiny black-feathered outfit. "I suppose this is the Black Swan, huh?"

Rosenbaum went over to it. "My pride and joy. You see, I've sewn in actual bird quills that will be specially fastened to Lily's body. Ingenious, if I say so myself. For all intents and purposes, she will all but become the Black Swan." He showed me the bird feather quills up close. "Dangerous if they should happen to puncture the skin. But I've made sure each and every one has been wrapped in a soft, protective cloth—I've been very thorough...so?"

"Yeah, it's a masterpiece, Rosenbaum."

"You think so?" He studied it. "Yes! I concur—audiences will long remember this *Swan Lake*, I can assure you that."

"Okay, Rosenbaum," I said, addressing him in my business-like voice. "If you've got any great ideas about this shit on the mirror—speak up now—because things are gonna start getting real serious real soon, I've got a feeling."

"Oh, dear, I hate violence. Why? Why do people do such things?"

"Because of a lot of reasons, Rosenbaum, love, hate, someone's in the way, mental illness—you name it and it all stinks."

"Oh, my, I like the way you talk when you're angry, Denning," he said with a wide intonation of the effeminate in his voice.

Soon Lily came out just as Gertrude Schnabel called Rosenbaum to attend a distressed dancer elsewhere. "God, I'm glad you're here, Cable."

I held her and smiled at her. "So am I, kid."

Shivering Timbers

Lily and I walked out of the theatre into a noisy world with the afternoon sunlight poking through a smutty sky. Compared to the quiet of a theatre when all is hushed, it was a shock. She took my arm as we walked. "Cable, will you take me to a movie? I just need to escape."

"Sure, why not? I'll call Mandy and tell her I won't be in until later. I have to be back around seven because I have a cleaning lady coming."

We settled on a brand new Sylvia Sidney, George Raft crime drama entitled *Pick Up*. As the romance between the man and the woman grew, Lily held on to my arm tighter and tighter. Somewhere between a few gunshots and one of their kisses, she tilted her face up to mine and kissed me like there was no tomorrow. There in the dark of the movie house I felt for her body, my hand moving up her waist to a breast. She sighed and in that minute I knew there was no turning back. Lily Norwood and I would make love at some point.

Just then there was an ominous rumble and the damn theatre began to shake. Plaster was peeling off the ceiling as I grabbed Lily and pulled her to the floor, under the fold-down seats. People panicked and ran for the exits, trampling one another. I figured our chances were just as good or better staying put. The ground heaved for about thirty seconds. Then it was over. We never got to see the last fifteen minutes of the movie. Suddenly the electricity was out and we lay there in the dark, my arm around Lily. She was strong and remained calm although her body trembled a little. Little did I know this was the infamous 1933 Long Beach earthquake which devastated a lot of rickety buildings, ruptured water pipes and toppled power poles. "Damn, I didn't know a kiss could do that!" I finally said, trying to break the tension.

She chuckled nervously and hugged me tighter. "*Your* kiss..." she whispered.

Finally, an usher opened the rear exit doors to the theatre and shafts of sunlight streamed in and made us squint in the dust-laden air. I took Lily's hand and we got up and made our way out to the street. There didn't seem to be a lot of damage on the streets of central Los Angeles, but I could see the trolley cars had come to rest where they were and the electricity must have been out all over. I hailed a taxi and we rode to Lily's little house on top of the hill. Far in the West we could see smoke billowing and the sound of sirens wailing in the late afternoon. We got into her house and looked at each other. We were covered with white powder from the flaking plaster of the theatre ceiling. "We—we should take our clothes off and bathe, don't you think?" she said, checking out my eyes. "I wonder what else could happen today." She came to me and held me tight. "I'm not being soft, Cable, but it's been a rough day."

"Yeah, babe, you're right. It's always the unexpected, isn't it? A rigorous dance workout, that lousy threat on your mirror—and an earthquake—all in one day, not bad," I quipped. I took my hat and coat off. She began to unbutton my shirt.

"Do you mind?"

"I'd mind if you didn't," I said, allowing her to do what she needed to do. Some things you can't hold back anymore, like their hour has come and you gotta recognize it for what it is and go with it.

She took my shirt off, untied my shoes and helped me off with them. "You've got holes in your socks," she remarked.

"Well, you know how bachelors are. I don't pay much attention to those things. One day the socks just shred and I throw 'em away."

She smiled and left to run a bath. When the water was running, she issued me a towel and I went into the bathroom, disrobed and climbed into the bath. I knew what was next. It had been building all day. The sun was starting to set and Lily came in carrying a candle. Only that was all—the rest of her was completely naked!

"May I?" she asked in that gentle, soft voice of hers.

"Sure, the water's fine..." I said that watching her lithe and beautiful body move toward me, that long, slim waist, the firm, tight breasts—and for the first time, I beheld the dark mound that lay between her legs.

She stepped in to join me as she twisted her body around to sit between my own legs. "Are you sure you're okay with this?"

"Absolutely," I said, bringing my hands around to cup them around her breasts. She sighed and reached both of her hands back to hold my upper legs. "Are you all right otherwise? I wonder how much of Los Angeles got damaged. I'd better call my mother."

"You never spoke of her before. Earthquakes are terrible. The feeling that all of a sudden there's nothing solid underneath you anymore."

"Yeah, it sounds like my life. I've been through a couple of those. Mom lives at the top of Vine Street in Hollywood." I took a washrag, soaped it and began to wash her back. I could tell she relished it. The water got dirty fast, so we drained it and started all over again, only this time she was facing me in the tub.

"I keep pretending I don't want you, Cable, that I'm making up stories for myself, so I might believe that what I'm feeling for you is part of some fantasy I'm dreaming up. You know, the ideal woman in her ideal world, loving her ideal man?"

"You said it before, Lily. Nobody should live without *touch*. And you know what? I'm gonna touch you everywhere tonight, if you'll let me."

She perked up with a big smile. "*Let you!?* I'll guide you with my own hands to every place on my body that's been aching for you ever since—"

"—say no more, lady, please...I don't want to spoil it or even have to think about it. In a way I saw myself in George Raft on that screen, and I saw you in the Sylvia Sydney part—he was such a chump...he didn't know how beautiful and faithful this babe was who loved him, until maybe it was too late. I don't want that to happen to us, Lily."

She got up on her knees in the tub and poured her body over me, rubbing her breasts all over my face as I licked them and lightly sucked her nipples. Wet as we were, we got out of the tub and she took my hand and led me into her bedroom, the same one that only weeks before I had put her to sleep in. "Tonight, Cable," she whispered, "I'm going to dance for you, until we find that perfect rhythm together—"

I put my finger to my lips. "—shhh...." She became quiet and began to do things to me I was surprised she knew! In a frenzy of desire, the international ballerina, Lily Norwood, was spreading her legs and wrapping those wondrous limbs around my body until her yelps of ecstasy took her over the border to that strange passionate land of almost death-like insanity where intense lovemaking sometimes takes you when you can let go of the walls and fly.

Somewhere memories rattle around in us like tin cans, and we kick them down a forgotten alley because we want to be rid of them, we want to keep them from seizing our days and nights and owning us like an unredeemable pawn ticket. Our psyche tries to keep them hidden— hidden down so deep maybe they can never be retrieved. So they think. But life is never like that.

Those brains cells up there are living sparks of light, igniting a cosmos of amazing things like thoughts, action and reaction, memory and desire. And maybe once in a while, *love*. But love means *giving*, and too few of us are willing to give up our selfish ways so we can come up for air long enough to heal. So we let the chasm grow as we get older, feeling—what the hell!—nobody really cares anyway, not in the end.

A couple of hours later, as I got up from Lily's bed and went into the bathroom, I looked in the mirror and saw a haggard private dick with not too long to go before he ended up in a ditch along a roadside somewhere like poor Mario Angelo. What did women see in this philandering, reckless and intense man? Although Lily made me feel great, the restless specter of a hopeless insomniac haunted those eyes looking back at me, and maybe the only thing I had going for me was *truth*—even if it was my own brand of truth—the kind that tells it like it is as long as it really doesn't hurt anyone you care for. I went into the living room and sat on her sofa. I lit up a cigarette and watched it glow in the dark.

I picked up the telephone. "Hello, Mom?" I said. "Just checking to see if you're okay. At least the phone lines aren't all down."

"Son—are you safe? Where are you? Oh, that was quite an experience. I'm okay, just a little nervous still. They talk about after-shocks and the like, you know."

"The important thing is that you're alright. I'm at a friend's house. I'm about to go back to the office." I just thought of my seven o'clock appointment with Adeline Pfizer. Hell, it was past nine! "Did your place suffer any damage?"

"I don't think so. Just a lot of rocking and rolling, but I hear the center was near Long Beach—a lot of damage there and southern Los Angeles."

"I need to come see you soon. You going to be around Sunday?"

"Where do I go, Cable? You're mother's getting older, son. My bones have been creaking a lot lately."

"What can I do for you, Mom—what can I bring?"

"Just come, Cable. And write Zelda once in a while. You'll have a son born into this world pretty soon, and I'll have a grandchild. That part makes me happy. Zelda loves you so and misses you, but she'll never admit it to you—"

"—Ma, please! Let's save it for Sunday. Whatta you say about two in the afternoon?" I was feeling uncomfortable.

"Yes...of course, Cable. That will be wonderful. I'm looking forward to our visit, son."

We hung up and I glanced over to the entrance to Lily's bedroom. She stood there in her nakedness, with only a nearby streetlamp lighting her luminous body. "The electricity's back on," she said softly. She walked over to me. "Was that your mother?"

"Yeah. I'm going to drop in on her Sunday. I don't see her very often. I don't know why...she's a fine woman and did a good job raising me and my office is close by now."

She sat beside me and patted my hand. "I know she'll appreciate it a lot." Then she took my hand and pressed it between her very wet legs. "There...it feels so good, Cable. It's like a dam burst loose inside of me when I

348

climaxed. To feel you enter me...it was everything I anticipated it would be...and more."

I took her hand and kissed it. "Thanks, lady. You're quite a woman, Lily Norwood, probably the best kept secret in all of the ballet world, huh?" I laughed.

"For your eyes only, Mr. Detective. Cable...thank *you*, ...for making love to me."

"You're welcome...and don't ever think you're not a complete woman, because you are. And another thing, I don't take it casually—you're giving yourself to me. Sure, I entered that bedroom like a savage beast with no other thought than to get you off, I admit—but then I found *you*, Lily, and I remembered the other side of tenderness."

"And what's that, Cable?"

"It's called love. You see, lately I've been caught up in pure sex without any of the trimmings. June wants sex without love."

She kissed my cheek. "Funny, isn't it—I *want* your love when I give myself to you. Do you think she's incapable of loving someone?"

"I don't want to talk about it, Lily. We're all lonely hunters and obviously I'm no better than she is when it comes to that. So let's leave it, okay?"

"Yes, Cable, as you say. Are you going now? I can feel you're restless. I hope it isn't me, is it?"

"No, I'd stay for a second round except two hours ago I promised to break in a new cleaning lady...some derelict I found on the street who says she happens to play Mozart and Beethoven on the piano."

"Oh...well, be careful she doesn't steal from you. Vagrants often can't help themselves."

349

Glo Man and the Life of Plants

I said goodnight to Lily and promised I'd call her the next day. I had begun trying to piece together the mysterious mosaic our demented stalker had put together. With the *Swan Lake* performance a little over a week away, I thought I'd better figure it out fast.

It seemed strange as I walked toward my office on Franklin that I was really all but casual about screwing Lily Norwood earlier, contrary to what I told her. Any other male animal would have panted and fought for her. Maybe that's what happens when too many babes line up on your list. Right now there was June, Mandy— and now Lily. How ungrateful of a chump can I be?

As I climbed the stairs to my office, I sensed something wasn't quite right. I drew my .38 and made my way carefully to the top of the second floor landing. I noticed two things immediately. Adeline Pfizer was on the floor sound asleep at my door and second, a pulsing, nebulous luminosity was hovering in a corner over by the next door. I moved cautiously toward it, but I knew that my earthling weapon would somehow be useless against whatever it was hovering above me. "Okay, whoever or whatever you are, what do you want?" I said in as threatening a voice as I could muster.

Then with a rather un-natural but not threatening voice, the thing spoke to me. "You wanted to know a *Transcender*, Cable Denning—just as your stupid religious man at the Vatican. Well, behold one...I am *your kind* forty-five thousand years into what you would call a *future*. But you see, time is an illusion also. Let me ask you this...*if you can remember the past, why can't you*

350

remember the future? That is your lesson of the day, primitive one." He snickered. "That worthless piece of metal in your hand—a weapon? Ha! if you could see from my perspective, you wouldn't even want to be alive here on this planet in this time zone."

"Well, I already feel that—so there, you melodramatic thingamajig. I figured out long ago that this earth thing ain't such a hot idea after all, like someone was experimenting and it got out of control or something."

"Not completely ignorant," the voice commented. "The cosmos delights in creative games, experimenting itself on itself. Some creations are successful, others not. Humans are a dangerous mixture, half beast, half god. It was an unfortunate thing they did, coming here and cross-breeding you. So now you live within a twenty-million year discrepancy, neither fish nor fowl, I would say."

"So you still didn't tell me, *Glow Man*—to what do I owe this visit? I've learned that everybody wants something. What do you want, creature?"

He continued. "'*Glow Man*...that's inventive. That stupid Pope thought he had some kind of Judeo-Christian '*devil*' imprisoned, didn't he? It was only another *Transcender*, like me, only he was magnetically trapped by some invention the *Ylpzoo* came up with. They are an alien group that is employed by your estimable religious institution. That's how he was imprisoned. He shape-shifted into the fearful human visage of some imaginary creature you call the *devil*. I assure you that evil exists, but not in *that* mythological form."

"You're ignoring my question, glowing thing—whatta ya want?"

"To have permission to live in your body for a day—just one day."

"What? Why in the hell would you wanna do that?"

"*Transcenders* are amazing beings, Cable Denning, capable of multi-dimensional travel using *time-space Continuum Gates* at will. But there has been a price to pay for 45,000 years of difference between us. A feature component has been bred out of us, and that component is the ability to feel feelings, experience sensual delights of a flesh and bone body with a primitive nervous system tuned to a three-dimensional world. In other words, if you give me permission to inhabit you for only one day, I will reward you many times over. Shall you consider this?"

I was astonished. Here you had a being capable of incredible feats practically begging to inhabit my body for the sake of experiencing what it felt like to be human 45,000 years before! "Do you have a name, stranger?" I asked.

"No...only a very high vibrational number. So it would be useless to attempt to call me anything you could possibly recognize. Even though I have to admit I like *Glow Man*—it adds a touch of heroic class, don't you think?"

"Maybe, I say if the shoe fits, wear it, buddy. And you need my permission to inhabit my body?"

"Yes. No creature can forcibly inhabit another's body without dire consequence. It is, what you might say, a universal law. So, will you consider?"

"I don't know," I said. I didn't want any tricks, let alone being faced with the experience of some other creature, or whatever it was, taking over my physical body. "How invasive is your presence?"

"You will hardly notice I am present in you. My vibration is very high and fast, so it would register lightly upon your own rather slow and heavy vibration."

"Give me some time, Transcender, to think it over. I have a lot on my plate just now. And why in the hell would you wanna inhabit *this* body, full of booze, cigarettes and sexual restlessness?"

"Exactly..."

"Exactly what?"

"Exactly why I would *want* to choose you to experience a decadent, self-destructive human male, his habits, the way he treats his physical three-dimensional temple."

"Temple?"

"Yes. Your body is like a temple, to be attended with reverence. Quite the opposite as you do, I fear."

There was a perverse part of my nature that relished in experimentation. And since I figured my days were numbered anyhow, maybe it wouldn't be such a terrible thing. "Will I benefit from your presence is my body?"

"Yes."

"How?"

"Clarity, accelerated learning, other dimensional experiences—increased sexual potency—in exchange for being allowed to feel your feelings empathetically along with you."

I thought it over for a minute. "Well, give me a little time. You come back, stranger, in a couple of my earth days."

"I shall do that." Then the glowing light disappeared and I spun around to see a trembling Adeline Pfizer sitting up against my office door. "You heard?" I asked her.

"Yes—yes…it woke me up, I—I—what—what *was* that? It was rather frightening, don't you think? What *was* it?"

"You got me there. Some other-dimensional creature, no doubt. Once you let one into your life, it's like they follow the vibe-trail to you or something. Are you okay? I'm sorry I wasn't here earlier—got delayed."

I came over and helped the older lady up to her feet. "Oh, that's okay. I was tired, so I slept. I hope you don't mind my falling asleep at your door? "

"Naw…so what? Come on in. Did that earth trembler bother you earlier this afternoon?

"Earth trembler? Oh, you mean an earthquake. No, I was so tired I must have slept through it."

"Do you still feel like doing some cleaning, Adeline?"

"Yes. I'm sorry all I have is me. But I am a good worker."

"Well, that'll have to do." I looked her over. "Before you start cleaning up my place, I think you need to clean yourself up. Now, I strongly suggest you go into my bathroom, make a nice tub of hot water for yourself and scrub until you sparkle. I'll leave out the rags, soap, mop and bucket. I think I'm going to take a walk." I looked around the room. There were some vases Zelda had left that contained new little green things and some flowers planted and arranged by Mandy. Zelda's plants had died long ago. I wondered if relationships suffered the same fate. Had Zelda and I died, long ago? "So, tonight, Adeline, begin with the floor. If you have time to beat the big

354

rug outside, do that—otherwise maybe you can clean the bathroom."

"Yes, Mr. Denning, thank you. I will."

"Call me Cable. You can sleep on the waiting couch over there tonight, if you wish. Maybe then we'll make other arrangements for you. You can't stay out there on the streets."

Her face brightened and she smiled with worn out grey eyes. "Oh, you are so kind. I promise I'll be no bother, and everything I said I would do, I will, honest."

"That's good, Adeline. Now, do you want to play the piano again?"

"Do I!" she cried. "I would give anything to—"

"—so what are you doing Sunday afternoon?"

"I don't understand—I'm not sure what you're asking..."

"I'm going to visit my mother up there, at the top of Vine Street on Sunday. She has a fine upright piano that no one's playing much anymore. Would you like to come and practice while my mother and I are visiting?"

"She won't mind?"

"I'm sure she'll love it. She's crazy about music."

She came up to me to give me a hug, but she stank a bit. "Go take that bath. Oh, and in that drawer across from my bed—the bottom one—I think you'll find some women's clothes that might fit you."

She looked at me strangely. "You wear women's clothes?"

"No, old girlfriends. You know how it is, through the years they leave things..."

Long Journey From the Heart

That lonely sax wafted through the air on a cool breeze that came up from the sea disturbing and shifting bits of papers and debris along the sidewalk as I strolled. My shoes clicked on the concrete like hollow reminders that it can feel like solitary confinement walking alone. I had this gut feeling that at times like these, it was as if I was walking away from my self, my heart—walking away from all the things love can bring and gritting my teeth and pushing against the wind with a runaway soul that couldn't quite figure out this earth life. After a while you've got a mouth full of it and it doesn't taste so good. Then you look around at all the other escapees, the faces behind closed doors who live alone and drink themselves to sleep like me, listen to the radio and escape to somewhere else—or look at want ads in the lonely hearts section on a Sunday morning, wondering what it might be like to meet a stranger and fall in love—I mean, really fall in love.

All of a sudden I was feeling deserted, empty, a ship without a rudder, filled with pretend and fantasy about how I thought my life should go. If I stayed away from women long enough, I might get to know myself once more, I thought. I figured that pre-occupied activity of rolling around in the hay with all these broads squeezed out all the other spaces for time with myself. A doll is a doll, and at my age, there were still plenty of them floating around, ready for the picking. But between June, Mandy and Lily, my life was chocked full of affectionate female attention and warm nights between the sheets. Why would I look elsewhere?

I realized I had walked all the way to Western, so I turned up the little hill towards Los Feliz Boulevard. As I was walking, I began thinking about Amanda Baxter. I was twenty-five when we met. She had shoulder-length ashen hair, a petite nose, full lips and a body that wouldn't stop at "Ooo-la-la!" She probably didn't know it, but she was a top-drawer roll in the hay as well. We did it over at the Hollywood Dam under a Jeffery Pine tree. That was yesterday when I was younger and stupid. Now I'm older and stupid. First loves have a way of sticking out in your brain and sometimes I wondered whatever happened to her.

I passed a building that sat up against the eastern foothill leading to Griffith Park. On the second floor there was a window with the lights on and the curtains were open so I could see a young woman dancing back and forth with a floor lamp lighting the room. Maybe life was supposed to be like that. A dance with yourself, being content to do the moves that were about what you felt at the moment, some spontaneous ritual of rhythm and inaudible song. Maybe loneliness was an illusion when the ego has nothing to reflect it and its air is being choked off. So it languishes, looking for someone in that dark night of the soul to fill in the blanks, that place where insomnia and restlessness grab you by the throat and shake you out of your everyday stupor like a puppy growling and shaking a rag doll in its mouth. But the music keeps playing, somehow, and you dance to it in a ritual of swaying drunkenness while the world continues to erode you, layer by layer until you get forgotten under a piece of cold marble in a cemetery you probably wouldn't have chosen in the first place. It was this perversity that haunted me, made me look long and hard for a deeper meaning to life. So alcohol, tobacco and babes numbed me up enough so I wouldn't have to think about it too much. If I had a big enough eraser, I'd blot out those wasted hours spent feeling sorry for myself over a cigarette and a bottle of cheap gin, I'd give back to those babes who really loved me the sanity of their lives without me, so they could find a decent everyday bloke who would be there when they needed him. It just wasn't me. As Henry Thoreau said, "My heart hears a different drummer and to that cadence I must step."

I turned around and headed back down Western Avenue and found *Ginty's Bar & Grill*. Somewhere in the back of my head I could hear that incoming signal again, a pleasant low hum that sat at the base of my skull like a vibration of warm, yellow glue, holding me together in a way I couldn't explain. But what did it mean? When people go nuts, is this what happens...they hear sounds inside themselves? Or was I tuning in to something from another source, out there in the dark cosmos somewhere, beaming its signal to my receiver?

I seldom patronized neighborhood joints, but this night I felt like it. The place was busy and noisy, the way I liked it. It was a younger crowd, my age and younger. I ordered an English gin and tonic—and got it! I was surprised that the alcohol had begun to flow again in the neighborhood joints. Prohibition's end was still a few months away.

Drinking alone isn't healthy for people, they say. But I did a lot of it. I wasn't usually bad company, but tonight I seemed to be out of sorts, for some reason. Zelda

Blodgett came floating back up into my mind. The life of plants...yeah, she was the botanist, the plain looking little gal with the thick glasses. That was when I first met her. Then suddenly she bloomed into a lovely young woman, filled with intelligence, good looks, fine body and great sex. She had comforted me after Honey died. We became close and finally one reckless night when I had just had my whole concept of sex tweaked by *Cassiopeia*, an alien doll who turned out to be a replica of a real woman—I banged on Zelda's door and she let me in. There in the dark she took my hand and led me to her bedroom. It was that night I took her virginity, the way she wanted it, gentle and strong and passionate. From that moment on it was wonderful. I loved Zelda Blodgett. I mean, really loved her. I think I fell for her because she was so damned good and intelligent, like I said, but also she was damned good for *me*. But my dangerous life style kept her a bit on edge. She would have stayed with me if that was all that got between us. But she packed up one day and told me she had to go, as it had all become too much for her. The real reason she left, I later found out, was because she was carrying my child—and never told me. My mother and she had bonded and I knew she would soon be giving birth. Sometime this year! What was I doing about it? Why in the hell was I looking the other way? What is wrong with guys like me? When they find love that fits like a glove, why do they bolt into the night of men, chase down other skirts, drink, smoke and lose themselves in someone like June Maye—who opts for pure sex alone? Yeah, Zelda and the life of plants. We were like a beautiful couple of plants together, growing side-by-side, smil-

359

ing up at the sunshine with laughter and touch, long walks and happy conversations, glad that we were in each other's lives—then bam! The plants stop getting watered and nurtured. So they die a slow, shriveling death until they are brown, broken twigs lying on the bottom of the pot.

Killing Donald

Suddenly I was taken out of my reverie by a soft female voice. "You look lonely, Mister, can I buy you a drink?" she asked. A handsome woman about five-four with dark, investigating eyes was looking at me. She wore shiny red lipstick, had her hair cut short in a pixie and sported a hefty breast underneath a peach blouse. "Hello, Mister, are you there?" She was probably a little older than I, a warm low tone carried her voice out of the tavern into a bedroom somewhere in a clandestine fantasy.

I came to. "Oh, I'm—I'm sorry...I was day dreaming—more or less taking a trip down memory lane."

"I hope they were pleasant memories. Or perhaps they were not... you look at little forlorn. As I said, may I buy you a drink?."

"It shows, eh? Yeah, thanks, I could go for one of these gin tonics again."

She left and soon came back with two glasses. One was my gin, the other a mixed drink of some sort. "May I sit a minute?"

"Yeah, sure. Thanks for the drink."

She sat with me at a small table by the jukebox. "My name is Andrea, Andrea McCardiff…"

"Cable…Cable Denning…mind if I call you Andrea? Nice name. Are you a long time Los Angeles person?"

She seemed relaxed and took a deep breath. "Oh, twelve years or so, I think." She perked up. "But it doesn't matter. Tonight I'm celebrating…will you join me in a toast?"

I lifted my glass. "And to what do we owe this auspicious occasion?" I asked, smiling at the attractive woman.

"I just killed my husband. After fifteen years of torture, humiliation and meaningless existence, I finally did it."

I sat there with the drink almost to my lips. I raised my eyebrows. I should've been shocked, but I wasn't. After all, I had been a cop before being a private dick and had seen the seedy underbelly of human relationships. Many a poor soul was trapped in a marriage he or she passionately longed to be free of. I took a sip of my drink. "Well, I gotta say, you're a gal who goes directly to the point. I like that. So…congratulations…if that's what's gonna make the lady happy."

She gulped her whole drink down. "You mean you're not upset? Don't you think most people would get panicky and call the cops or something?"

"Not me, kid, you picked the right guy. I *used* to be a cop. I've seen your kind of story unfold a hundred times and it never ends up pretty. So your secret is safe with me."

"But I don't want it to be a secret. I need to call the in-laws, his military, dictatorial brother…his snippy, mean-spirited sister and tell them they don't have to have that perfunctory Christmas Eve at their house this year. Donald is dead on my kitchen floor with my biggest and sharpest slicing knife buried in his chest."

"Oh, I see," I said, not sure whether Andrea McCardiff had left the house with all her marbles in place. "They probably *will* panic and call the cops. Why don't you give yourself a few hours before you do that?"

"You think? Hmmm...maybe you're right. I suppose if I could get rid of Donald's body, it could be a case of mysterious *disappearance* and even though I would be suspect, I might get away with it."

"Yeah, now you're talkin'," I said, feeling the drinks I had been slowly imbibing all day. "You know, you've been in prison for fifteen years, as you say—why not live a little before they catch up with you? If there's a little money, take off, you've got a nice figure and you're not too old to put on a nice two-piece bathing suit on the French Riviera and have a fling with some romantic Frenchman."

She seemed amazed. "You mean you're not going to tell on me?"

"Nope. Not my business. What you told me, you told me in confidence—I'm used to that, keeping things discreet if I have to."

"May I ask what you do professionally?"

"Yeah, I'm a private dick, that's what I do."

"A private what?"

"An independent detective—the kind you might hire to find a missing husband or something," I said, tongue-in-cheek.

"Oh, I thought for a minute you were a gigolo—you know, a guy who hires out to a woman for the night. You are very handsome and keep yourself in good physical shape. You might be a little skinny, but I could fix that up fast. I make the best pasta in the world. My mother was Italian, my father Scottish."

"Hey now!...that's quite a bloodline combination there."

She was beginning to feel the drink she had gulped down. "I sure like you, Cable. There's something about the way you talk that—that makes me want to trust you. Do you have a girlfriend?"

"Oh, yeah...try three at the moment."

She widened her eyes. "Three? Can you...uh...keep them all satisfied? If so, you must be quite some man. Want another drink?"

"No, thanks, Andrea. I'm fine. I need to go soon. I have to get back to the office. My cleaning lady's working late and it's her first night."

"Oh, I see. Well, will you stay just long enough to watch me gaggle down one more drink and talk to me, please? It's been a hell of day for me, with killing Donald and all."

I couldn't help but chuckle. "Yeah, sure...I'll wait..."

She excused herself and soon returned with a drink twice the size of the last one. She raised her glass to me as she sat down. "Hickory daiquiri dock!" she slurred. "To the end of Donald and the beginning of a most charming man—and hopefully, a life out of the clink, at least for a while. I'd hate to be locked up when I really think about it. Maybe you're right, the French Riviera. I could just disappear, you know."

363

"Yeah, I'd consider it."

"Will you come with me? I've hoarded many thousands of dollars these years that Donald never knew about. Please, Cable, come...?"

"I'm sorry, Andrea, I'm tempted—but I can't. You see, I've got a pretty full plate here in L.A. Besides, I told you I've also got three girlfriends and I can't just desert them now, can I?"

"Make me a fourth," she said lowering her voice and leaning toward me across the table. "Do you know how long—how long it's been for me, Cable? And me...ha! of all women...I'm a touchy, feely kind of gal with a lot to offer in special places. Whatta ya say?"

"As I said, Andrea, it's a tempting offer, but I can't. If I were you, I'd go home, find a way to get rid of your husband's body, reserve a boat ticket for France and have the time of your life."

Then she got a pouty expression on her face just as the jukebox started to play a fine trumpet player's version of *Stardust*. "I'm too old for you, is that it, private detective? Don't tell me, I know...good looking men like you go for the young ones, tender flesh that feels new and exciting in the night when the radio's playing softly in the background and the room is lit with only one candle." She was daydreaming. "I felt like that once. I married Donald when I was twenty-five. I'm almost forty now. Do you know what it feels like to waste your life?" Her eyes began to tear up. "Do you know what it's like to wake up in the morning and when you look at the clock on the mantle, you realize one more meaningless day of your life will go by—and the only thing that stops the misery is either a walk in the park or taking care of myself when Donald was off at work?" She checked out my eyes for reaction. "Does that surprise you? Lots of women do it that way because the slobs they're married to are not lovers, but bacon earners who satisfy themselves, wipe themselves off, get out of her bed and go back to their own."

For some reason I got a little irritated. "You know, Andrea, there are two sides to every story. You married the guy—if it wasn't working, you knew it the first year out or so—why wait fifteen years and build up the suffering inside until you're driven to kill the poor bloke? He had an equal right to live just as you do—just maybe not with you. You should've broken it off when you finally rubbed the stardust out of your eyes while you were still young and knew what intimate love should feel like. Just like the lyrics to that song, Andrea, *'sometimes I wonder why I spend the lonely night, dreaming of a song, a melody, haunts my reverie,'* you should've exited the scene long ago and put your chips on someone who could love you and fulfill you in the bedroom. People have a disease of enjoying sameness, not declaring themselves *to* themselves, spelling out their needs. So they spend their prime years locked in some ho-hum vapid nothingness, and as with this case, *'til death do you part."* I stopped.... I realized I was admonishing this woman who had gone through so much on this crazy day. "I'm sorry...I have a tendency to foam at the mouth sometimes. I would have made a good soapbox politician."

She reached her hand across the table and held my wrist. "No, you're—you're completely...completely right," she said, a little more drunk than fifteen minutes ago. "Instead I made love to myself when the going got rough, Cable. And that...I guess...isolated me even more..."

"I gotta go, kid. Pull the pieces together and get on with it. Have a life before they come to take you away. Sooner or later they just might catch up with you. Statistically, about forty percent of all murders go unsolved. So, maybe if you play your cards right, you can make it into the top forty, eh?" I laughed. "But someday, Andrea, you'll stop and something will be haunting you. It'll come like a ghost in the night and knock at your brain until you can't stand it anymore. So you'll take another drink to numb its presence."

"And—and what might that...that be, Mr. Private Dick...?" she slurred.

"Your conscience. I know your type of babe. You can bury it along with Donald's body for a while. Then it gets resurrected and you have to face whether or not it was worth killing him for your freedom—and whatever else went with it?"

"I wish you went with it, good man. Pretty please...? Take me to a hotel for the night...I'll pay for it...I need to spin off the tension I feel—"

"—can't do it Andrea, sorry."

She looked down. "Then...I shall just...just have to find my way alone...won't I? Like all the other years...alone...alone, Cable..."

I stood up, came around to her side of the table, bent over and kissed her on the forehead. "You know, lady, we're an awful lot alike, you and me. I've killed people before, too, and I've been responsible for deaths I didn't see coming—but you know what? Sometimes murder is *legal*, but I carry the same demons you will one day. So, before it catches up to you, have the time of your life, lady. And don't look back. In the end, it doesn't ever matter. You can't bring any of it back or re-do your life."

That melancholy sax started playing in my head again as I left her sitting there nursing an empty glass. Yeah, that's how it was, a woman alone in a bistro sitting by a jukebox with an empty glass late at night. I hoped she'd get a refill.

Mendelssohn on a Sunday Afternoon

The house at 2166 North Vine Street looked good. Between my mother's love for puttering with flowers and plants and Jake Oswald the gardener I hired for her, the landscape was shaping up fine.

Adeline was a bit shy when she met my mother. She had put on a nice yellow dress, with black polka-dots, she found in one of my drawers and it fit her. So I gave it to her. One could tell that at one time Adeline Pfizer was a very attractive woman with a nice figure. Even now she was nicely proportioned, if a bit on the skinny side. Adeline was crazy about the garden, so we let her go out to meander and sit while Mom and I talked about things.

"I don't know how earnestly you have taken this, Cable—but Zelda's baby is expected soon." She studied my face. "I can see you've been drinking. And the tobacco doesn't help, either. Did I raise you to have no heart, son?"

I reached into my pocket and gave her an envelope. "When you see Zelda, give this to her. There's quite a bit of dough in there. It ought to keep her and the baby sitting pretty for a while."

Mrs. Denning took the envelope and shook her head back and forth. "Do you think *money* solves it all, Cable?"

"No, but it sure as hell helps."

"Maybe we can't salvage whatever love there was between you and Zelda. But I know you. You truly loved that girl, even more solidly than Honey or Adora. What's the matter with you, son—have you lost your sense of accountability? I know I didn't raise you like that!"

I shriveled inside a little. I adored my mother and so when she spoke, I listened. I guess it's a left over thing in your head from childhood when your mother was the anchor of the family and her authority counted. "She was right about things, Mom. My life was and still is a desperate dice game. I don't even think you realize how much danger I was in for a long time."

"*Was* in?"

"Yeah, it's subsided a bit for now. But don't worry, they'll be back. So Zelda couldn't take my coming and going, disappearing for days and the fact, as she said, I might come home one day in a pine box." I stopped. I wanted to smoke, but I refrained. "And you gotta remember, she never told me about her pregnancy until *after* she'd flown the coop and went off to be with the aunt."

"I know...I asked her about that. She says now, she should have told you. She was so in love with you that she would've done anything to keep you—and your new little family together." My mother's eyes misted. "But she had to protect the baby, she said, and to get it out of harm's way meant her having to leave you—oh, Cable, why do we complicate our lives so?" She stopped and looked outside at Adeline enjoying just sitting on the grass. "I often think if your Uncle Cable would have stayed, would I have divorced your Dad to marry him? I doubt it, regardless of the pull at my heart. Your uncle is too much like you—independent, stubborn, head-strong, with a great gift of the gab, and I'm sure, pur-sued many women." She wiped her eyes. "Well, there's no reason to go on like that now, is there?" she said, brightening her voice somewhat. But I knew she was hurting inside thinking about that fearless adventurer she fell in love with so many years before.

"What was it like for you? I mean loving him...did your instincts tell you if it would last—or even could?"

"No...I knew...but he was dangerous and exciting, and when he touched me I was filled with desire for him. Yes, I had my desires, too, Cable. You ought to know, you've inherited some of both your parents' drives and need for emotional satisfaction. Older age permits us the letting go. Now we can reflect with the bittersweet of memory." Then she snapped out of it. "Let's get your piano lady in here to play for us while I get some sandwiches and tea. I think the piano's out of tune, but it plays."

Soon Adeline sat at the keyboard. At first she just sat there... unbelieving, that at last once again she was to be reunited with an old friend. She bowed her head, I think to unite with the moment...then slowly, as if in a trance she lifted her hands into position over the keys. Well, let me tell you, both my mother and I were delighted and entranced when that woman put her fingers to those keys. She said she was going to play a ditty from *Men-*

delssohn's *Songs Without Words* for solo piano. We sat there being floated away by Adeline's playing, as if after all these years she was able to summon up from the depths, everything that was inside and so dear to her, that it remained part of her. Suddenly I was imagining her playing a grand piano with a symphony orchestra and a thousand people tuned to hear this gifted woman play.

We said good-bye to my mother after she assured me she'd get the envelope with the dough to Zelda. She also invited Adeline to come play the piano anytime she liked. Adeline loved *that* idea and we walked, heading back to my office. "Thank you, Cable," she was saying. "I just found myself again—today, after so many years."

"You don't know how good that makes me feel, kid. And damn, Adeline, you're the real thing—you must have been a genuine mistress of the piano at one time, huh?"

Her eyes glowed as she spoke. "I was so young. I won a scholarship to the Curtis Institute and my professor, the famous Stanislaus Virinsky, gave me lessons on the side for two years. Unfortunately, he also gave me lessons on dallying in his bedroom and I conceived his child. I nearly died, but I put it up for adoption—all for the music, all for the promise of a successful career. Women pianists were rather rare those days. I mean, especially those that were promising. I suppose being good looking helped."

"Yeah, it always does. So then what happened?"

"After the baby I had to leave Stanislaus. But work was hard to come by and the Great War was looming. By then I wasn't a star-struck teenager anymore, so to earn a living, I learned dozens of popular tunes of the day and accompanied singers by day and played in the joints at night. Classical music was an island for the rich, I discovered." She paused as we walked. "Then I met Charles. He was what I called a *wealthy slummer*, and inhabited joints like the ones I worked in at night. He dressed impeccably, tuxedo, top hat, spats, very handsome with wavy black hair. He liked me. What was worse, I liked him. After hours he'd invite me for a cocktail at some up-scale restaurant. I started to drink with Charles—I mean, too much. So, one thing led to the other and we'd get drunk together and go home to his place and make love. I must have been a fertile gal those days, because I conceived Charles' baby. But he didn't want his style cramped, 'took away from the romance of it all,' as he'd say. So, he dumped me while I was three months pregnant. I was desperate. I tried to get an abortion. No one would risk it because I was too far along. I had a girlfriend, Monica Brown. She took me to a black man who put all kinds of moss or something inside me to make me abort. I got very sick. I had a fever and the shakes and violent spasms in my stomach. He delivered the fetus dead. My life changed on that day, Cable. So I stopped playing the clubs, I did war relief volunteering and stopped seeing men altogether. I couldn't be trusted with them. But I got lonely and started to drink. After a while, around '20, I began to drink heavily with stupid girlfriends who hung out in seedy clubs with horrible men. So for thirteen years I've been sliding down the long pole." She stopped us in the middle of the sidewalk and put her hands on my arms. "Until you, that is. You are a good and kind man, Cable. I shall be ever grateful

371

to you for rescuing me. I'm going to be fifty in December. But when I look in the mirror, I realize I look sixty-five or older."

"But that's okay, Adeline. You've earned those crow's feet. We'll work it out, kid, don't worry about it— oh, and by the way, you look great in that dress."

She took my arm and we continued walking down to Franklin.

The Adventures of Glow Man

Mandy was indeed surprised to find Adeline busy cleaning the front door glass of my office when she came in Monday morning. The once aspirant pianist was still wearing the yellow dress with the black polka dots I had given her. Mandy peaked around my bedroom door corner to see if I was stirring. The week before, Mandy and I had had quite an evening. It ended somewhere between a mystery and a homerun, depending on how one looked at it. In the process of thanking her for being such an upstanding and efficient secretary, I had offered to take her out to dinner and she accepted. But once we got home and alcohol plus deeply seated emotions in the babe contributed to one of the most touching moments of the evening, as Mandy launched into her heartfelt feelings and the loneliness an otherwise perfectly okay person can experience, when she is forgotten by the world. But that night I promised myself I would never forget such a lady, whether or not we ever made love again. She was worth putting on Noah's Ark as one of the saved.

She saw me roll over. "I do declare, Detective Denning, you keep the oddest hours of anyone I've ever known. Why, it is comin' out that you even consort with older women in the most intimate of ways," she grinned.

I was barely conscious. "Ahrrrr...*please* tell them not to squeak the glass—I can't stand the sound...who's out there?"

"I trust it is a new person you have hired to perform the heavy cleanin' that is below my station," she said haughtily, laughing.

"Oh, yeah, Adeline...she slept on my—my couch last night—I took her to see my mother yesterday, and...she played a marvelous piano—Mendelssohn, I think."

"Did she now? That is more than you have arranged for me, seein' as how I cared for your dear mother during your many adventures abroad. And speakin' of which, the lady in the yellow polka dot dress—does she always clean with such *panache*?"

I rolled out of bed, realizing I was still naked. "I gave her the dress. From my drawer...over there..." I covered myself.

"My, my, aren't we a surprise now, Mr. Denning? I never realized, sir, you might indeed be a cross-dresser. It just goes to show, one can never, never be too sure now, can one?"

I tried to crack a smile at Mandy. "Go away and let me get cleaned up and dressed. Her name is Adeline Pfizer, a street person. I picked her up and brought her home because she's....she's a worthy person. I need to find a place for her to stay. She's too good to hang out in filthy dark alleys with bums peeing on her in the middle of the night."

Then Mandy drew serious. "I am truly sorry to hear that. I shall endeavor to look into the matter of suitable housing for Miss Pfizer."

"Thanks, Mandy."

Instead of leaving, she came over to the bed and knelt beside me, lowering her voice. "I have been a very happy woman all weekend long, Cable. But I do have one request. If ever you should kiss me again, would you consider, sir, keepin' your lips directly on mine for at least ten minutes or more at a time?"

I tousled her hair with the palm of my hand and smiled. "Oh, Mandy...please, not today. Some other time, okay?" The pressure of Lily's upcoming performance had haunted me all night and I also knew that Glow Man would show up within the next couple of days. I knew *that* would prove to be a fun time at the carnival of fools, and I might end up being the fool. Why did I even consider such a favor to a *Transcender*? After all, even though I had met Lei-Tao, Eli, Toggth and all—I knew that not *all* aliens are good folks. Shape-shifters were odd beings to begin with.

Mandy departed, went out into the office and introduced herself to Adeline. Strangely, I had a feeling these two women would get along. I washed, shaved and dressed and came out into the office. I called the two women over to my desk as I took my usual place in my comfy chair, lit up a Lucky Strike and faced them. "Now, ladies, within the next day or two there will be a visitor entering through that door. But you won't see a person. Instead, you'll see a glowing ball of pulsing light. If you happen to be here at the time, do not be alarmed, he's a sort of client of mine."

The two ladies looked at each other. Adeline stated that she had indeed seen a ball of pulsing light hovering in a corner in the hallway. She also mentioned that it spoke, but the language was garbled to her.

"That's because what he had to say was for my ears only. He's a *Transcender*, shape-shifter you might say—and we have some business together."

This was the first Mandy had heard of any of this. She'd never met Toggth, so had no clue as to what I was talking about. "Cable, my dear man, I know you have been imbibin' more than your general share of late, but are you and Adeline here tellin' me there are such things as appearin' and disappearin' creatures right before one's very eyes?"

"Not only that, Mandy, but these creatures that can change their shapes to look like—well, anything they want to, I guess."

Mandy checked out both our faces. "For me, seein' is believin', so I must reserve my final opinion after I have viewed such a being."

"Good enough for me," I said.

It was about six o'clock on Tuesday evening. Gracious lady that she was, Mandy agreed to share her house with Adeline, especially after they visited my mother Monday night and Adeline played the piano for my mother and Mandy. And of course anything classical was an extra bonus. I agreed to rent a tuned piano and install it at Mandy's house, so Mandy could be treated to Bach, Beethoven, Brahms, Mendelssohn or Chopin on a regular basis. Everyone was a winner and Adeline and Mandy would stay friends for life.

I was supposed to catch June's last set that night and then we'd do the usual: go home and screw. Mandy was just finishing up and had her purse in hand when we both heard a strange humming buzz and a corner of the office lit up like a lighthouse. Mandy ran over to me and held my arm. The pulsing, glowing ball of light steadied itself and I could hear it speak to me. All Mandy heard, she reported later, was the same as Adeline—a kind of voice but no distinguishable language. "Glow Man here...have you considered my request?"

"Yep." Then I glanced at Mandy who happened to be trembling a bit. "I need to send my secretary home." He didn't respond. I escorted her to the office door and opened it. She turned to me.

"For God's sake, Cable, I shall never...I mean, never doubt you again. Had I not seen whatever that creature is with my own ever-livin' eyes—"

"—we'll—we'll discuss it tomorrow, okay, Mandy?"

She kissed me on the cheek and exited. "Is that one of your *sexual root-stirring beings*?" Glow Man asked.

"Well, that's hard to say. She's kind of an on-again, off-again stimulation model, you might say."

"So...now...is it a yes?"

"With one proviso, Glow Man— and that is, if for some reason I ask you to vacate my body, you must do so immediately. Is that clear?"

"Absolutely clear."

"Now here's how it's gonna have to be. If it's pleasure you want, you enter into my body now. I'm going to see June Maye tonight—she's a very sensual singer of popular music, with a band at a loud, dirty, smoky, decadent night club, so you can soak in some of that."

"Oh, that sounds delightful!" Glow Man chimed in.

"Now, the real meat of the matter, so to speak, is that after June is through singing, we're going to her place to indulge in some pretty hot sex. Think you can handle it without blowing out some of your circuits?"

"Surely you jest, earth creature. I am so advanced of you that I will be operating at about one ten-thousandth of my normal field energy."

"Oh. Well then, I guess we have a deal. Remember what I said, though—when I say out—it's *out* and there will be a good reason for it, so no questions asked."

"Yes. Fully comprehended. May I call you Cable? After all, we are going to be part of each other for a while."

"Yeah, swell. Shall we be able to communicate verbally while you're in my head or wherever you're going to be?"

"Certainly. Even if you whisper—which you probably should do anyway—I will hear you clearly."

"Ready, then?"

He asked me to stand in the middle of the room. As I did so, almost immediately I could feel a tickling, pulsing energy going through me like a low current of electricity. But it felt good and even stimulated me a little. Then I heard Glow Man's voice coming from within me.

"Safe and sound, Cable. Can you hear me?

"Yeah, just like you're inside me or something," I joked.

The *Bistro Club* was jammed for a Tuesday evening. Somehow I could feel Glow Man's excitement in my own body as we walked down the stairs to the tune of Cole Porter's *I've Got You Under My Skin*, an appropriate song if I ever heard one, considering Glow Man's present location. June's style and approach to musical interpretation was growing all the time and the sparkling arrangement made the house come apart when she was through.

When June saw me at the bar, she waved and I waved back. She stepped down from the bandstand and headed towards me—or was it *us*? "Now, don't do any fluttery stuff when she kisses me or anything, okay?"

"Why would I do that?" Glow Man retorted, a little miffed.

"Because you're new to this, buddy, and you may not know how to respond to human nervous system actions and reactions at first—"

"—I'm not an ignoramus, you know—"

"—I didn't say you were an ignoramus—"

"—Cable?" June said, looking around and then at me strangely. "Did I hear you talking to someone?" She upped and kissed me. I could feel my skin jump like I was having a minor spasm. "What was that? Are you okay?"

"Yeah, babe...I was, uh, just rehearsing what I'm going to have to say to a client tomorrow. And the...uh, nervous jumping thing, I, uh, I ate some chili for lunch and I guess it's sort of repeating itself."

"Oh," she said, apparently satisfied.

"That arrangement of the Cole Porter song was stupendous. Yours?"

Mandy was indeed surprised to find Adeline busy cleaning the front door glass of my office when she came in Monday morning. The once aspirant pianist was still wearing the yellow dress with the black polka dots I had given her. Mandy peaked around my bedroom door corner to see if I was stirring. The week before, Mandy and I had had quite an evening. It ended somewhere between a mystery and a homerun, depending on how one looked at it. In the process of thanking her for being such an upstanding and efficient secretary, I had offered to take her out to dinner and she accepted. But once we got home and alcohol plus deeply seated emotions in the babe contributed to one of the most touching moments of the evening, as Mandy launched into her heartfelt feelings and the loneliness an otherwise perfectly okay person can experience, when she is forgotten by the world. But that night I promised myself I would never forget such a lady, whether or not we ever made love again. She was worth putting on Noah's Ark as one of the saved.

She saw me roll over. "I do declare, Detective Denning, you keep the oddest hours of anyone I've ever known. Why, it is comin' out that you even consort with older women in the most intimate of ways," she grinned.

I was barely conscious. "Ahrrrr...tell them not to squeak the glass—I can't stand the sound...who's out there?"

"I trust it is a new person you have hired to perform the heavy cleanin' that is below my station," she said haughtily, laughing.

"Oh, yeah, Adeline...she slept on my—my couch last night—I took her to see my mother yesterday...and...she played a marvelous piano—Mendelssohn, I think."

"Did she now? That is more than you have arranged for me, seein' as how I cared for your dear mother during your many adventures abroad. And speakin' of which, the lady in the yellow polka dot dress—does she always clean with such *panache*?"

I rolled out of bed, realizing I was still naked. "I gave her the dress. From my drawer...over there..." I covered myself.

"My, my, aren't we a surprise now, Mr. Denning? I never realized, sir, you might indeed be a cross-dresser. It just goes to show, one can never, never be too sure now, can one?"

I tried to crack a smile at Mandy. "Go away and let me get cleaned up and dressed. Her name is Adeline Pfizer, a street person. I picked her up and brought her home because she's....she's a worthy person. I need to find a place for her to stay. She's too good to hang out in filthy dark alleys with bums peeing on her in the middle of the night."

Then Mandy drew serious. "I am truly sorry to hear that. I shall endeavor to look into the matter of suitable housing for Miss Pfizer."

"Thanks, Mandy."

Instead of leaving, she came over to the bed and knelt beside me, lowering her voice. "I have been a very happy woman all weekend long, Cable. But I do have one request. If ever you should kiss me again, would you consider, sir, keepin' your lips directly on mine for at least ten minutes or more at a time?"

I tousled her hair with the palm of my hand and smiled. "Oh, Mandy...please, not today. Some other time, okay?" The pressure of Lily's upcoming performance had haunted me all night and I also knew that Glow Man would show up within the next couple of days. I knew *that* would prove to be a fun time at the carnival of fools, and I might end up being the fool. Why did I even consider such a favor to a *Transcender*? After all, even though I had met Lei-Tao, Eli, Toggth and all—I knew that not *all* aliens are good folks. Shape-shifters were odd beings to begin with.

Mandy departed, went out into the office and introduced herself to Adeline. Strangely, I had a feeling these two women would get along. I washed, shaved and dressed and came out into the office. I called the two women over to my desk as I took my usual place in my comfy chair, lit up a Lucky Strike and faced them. "Now, ladies, within the next day or two there will be a visitor entering through that door. But you won't see a person. Instead, you'll see a glowing ball of pulsing light. If you happen to be here at the time, do not be alarmed, he's a sort of client of mine."

The two ladies looked at each other. Adeline stated that she had indeed seen a ball of pulsing light hovering in a corner in the hallway. She also mentioned that it spoke, but the language was garbled to her.

"That's because what he had to say was for my ears only. He's a *Transcender*, shape-shifter you might say—and we have some business together."

This was the first Mandy had heard of any of this. She'd never met Toggth, so had no clue as to what I was talking about. "Cable, my dear man, I know you have been imbibin' more than your general share of late, but are you and Adeline here tellin' me there are such things as appearin' and disappearin' creatures right before one's very eyes?"

"Not only that, Mandy, but these creatures that can change their shapes to look like—well, anything they want to, I guess."

Mandy checked out both our faces. "For me, seein' is believin', so I must reserve my final opinion after I have viewed such a being."

"Good enough for me," I said.

It was about six o'clock on Tuesday evening. Gracious lady that she was, Mandy agreed to share her house with Adeline, especially after they visited my mother Monday night and Adeline played the piano for my mother and Mandy. And of course anything classical was an extra bonus. I agreed to rent a tuned piano and install it at Mandy's house, so Mandy could be treated to Bach, Beethoven, Brahms, Mendelssohn or Chopin on a regular basis. Everyone was a winner and Adeline and Mandy would stay friends for life.

I was supposed to catch June's last set that night and then we'd do the usual: go home and screw. Mandy was just finishing up and had her purse in hand when we both heard a strange humming buzz and a corner of the office lit up like a lighthouse. Mandy ran over to me and held my arm. The pulsing, glowing ball of light steadied itself and I could hear it speak to me. All Mandy heard, she reported later, was the same as Adeline—a kind of voice but no distinguishable language. "Glow Man here...have you considered my request?"

"Yep." Then I glanced at Mandy who happened to be trembling a bit. "I need to send my secretary home." He didn't respond. I escorted her to the office door and opened it. She turned to me.

"For God's sake, Cable, I shall never...I mean, never doubt you again. Had I not seen whatever that creature is with my own ever-livin' eyes—"

"—we'll—we'll discuss it tomorrow, okay, Mandy?"

She kissed me on the cheek and exited. "Is that one of your *sexual root-stirring beings*?" Glow Man asked.

"Well, that's hard to say. She's kind of an on-again, off-again stimulation model, you might say."

"So...now...is it a yes?"

"With one proviso, Glow Man— and that is, if for some reason I ask you to vacate my body, you must do so immediately. Is that clear?"

"Absolutely clear."

"Now here's how it's gonna have to be. If it's pleasure you want, you enter into my body now. I'm going to see June Mayc tonight—she's a very sensual popular music singer at a loud, dirty, smoky, decadent night club, so you can soak in some of that."

"Oh, that sounds delightful!" Glow Man chimed in.

"Now, the real meat of the matter, so to speak, is that after June is through singing, we're going to her place to indulge in some pretty hot sex. Think you can handle it without blowing out some of your circuits?"

"Surely you jest, earth creature. I am so advanced of you that I will be operating at about one ten-thousandth of my normal field energy."

"Oh. So then it's a go. Remember what I said, though—when I say out—it's *out* and there'll be a good reason for it, no questions asked."

"Yes. Fully comprehended. Maybe I can call you Cable? After all, we are going to be sort of part of each other for a while."

"Yeah, swell. Shall we be able to communicate verbally while you're in my head or wherever you're going to be?"

"Certainly. Even if you whisper—which you probably should do anyway—I will hear you clearly."

"Ready, then?"

He asked me to stand in the middle of the room. As I did so, almost immediately I could feel a tickling, pulsing energy going through me like a low current of electricity. But it felt good and even stimulated me a little. Then I heard Glow Man's voice coming from within me.

"Safe and sound, Cable. Can you hear me?

"Yeah, just like you're inside me or something," I joked.

The *Bistro Club* was jammed for a Tuesday evening. Somehow I could feel Glow Man's excitement in my own body as we walked down the stairs to the tune of Cole Porter's *I've Got You Under My Skin*, an appropriate song if I ever heard one, considering Glow Man's present location. June's style and approach to musical interpretation was growing all the time and the sparkling arrangement made the house come apart when she was through.

When June saw me at the bar, she waved and I waved back. She stepped down from the bandstand and headed towards me—or was it *us*? "Now, don't do any fluttery stuff when she kisses me or anything, okay?"

"Why would I do that?" Glow Man retorted, a little miffed.

"Because you're new to this, buddy, and you may not know how to respond to human nervous system actions and reactions at first—"

"—I'm not an ignoramus, you know—"

"—I didn't say you were an ignoramus—"

"—Cable?" June said, looking around and then at me strangely. "Did I hear you talking to someone?" She upped and kissed me. I could feel my skin jump like I was having a minor spasm. "What was that? Are you okay?"

"Yeah, babe...I was, uh, just rehearsing what I have to say to a client tomorrow. And the...the, uh, nervous jumping thing, I, uh, I ate some chili for lunch and I guess it's sort of repeating itself."

"Oh," she said, apparently satisfied.

"That arrangement of the Cole Porter song was stupendous. Yours?"

"No, we have a new band member. Larry Brooks, he arranges and plays drums. Drummers are crazy. He's a little wild." I watched June's eyes look over toward the bandstand, watching the drummer play. "He's cute, too. I have to admit I'd like to screw him sometime—I just don't want it to ruin what we have, lover man."

I cleared my throat. "Well, you know, I did it with Mandy. I couldn't very well judge you for making it with Larry boy, now, could I?" I said that partly because in a way it would be nice to relieve some of the sexual pressure I felt making it with June all the time. After all, a guy like me is used to calling his own shots and this expectation thing on her part wasn't exactly my cup of tea.

"Yeah...but I doubt if I will. Your big and constant, *ahem*, takes care of me just fine."

I guessed that was that. June soon walked back to the bandstand and launched into a wonderful version of the Gershwin's *Embraceable You*. June sang with all that was female in her and the sex just spilled out like a waterfall of sensuality. "Oh, my, this pleasure female creature is stimulating us, isn't she?" Glow man said.

"Yeah, she's good at that. Look around. Every male in this room between twenty-one and seventy is privately fantasizing just about now. That's one of the reasons she packs them in. Even the women like her. I suppose a lot of them would like to be able to do what she does. But they don't know the other side of it."

"What's that?"

"Oh, you'll discover that when we get to her place. Gees, in a way I feel like I'm betraying June's trust with you hanging around in my body. You're like an alien voyeur...kind of perverted, really."

"You promised."

"Yeah, I know, so fasten your seat belt in there, you're gonna need it."

When we got to June's place, she immediately took her clothes off and paraded around in the kitchen completely nude. She fixed us a couple of drinks and sat with me on her sofa. "What—no hurry to do it tonight?" I asked.

"I've been thinking, Cable. I'd like to get away with you somewhere. You know, for a couple of days at the beach or something. I've always wanted to do it in the ocean. Feel the waves splash over us, the sand run through our bodies as the water goes out. How about it?"

386

"Yeah...how about tonight, Cable, so that I can go along...tonight. Yes...tonight," Glow Man said, his voice very enthusiastic.

"Not tonight...it wouldn't be good tonight," I answered Glow Man without thinking.

"I didn't mean tonight," June said, looking rather surprised at me.

"No, I—uh, I know you didn't. I was just thinking out loud—"

"—you seem awfully weird tonight, Cable. Is there some other woman you've been thinking about—or what?"

At the moment I was thinking of Lily Norwood and how pleasant a change that was from June's insistent sexuality. "I—I've not been sleeping lately...thinking about the Lily Norwood case and how close that performance is next Saturday night."

"Oh...well, that's understandable, I guess. You do become obsessed with your work." Then she felt up my leg and held my crotch in the palm of her hand. Glow Man winced inside and my body jumped. "Are you too tired to do it tonight?"

"I don't think so. You might have to get me kick-started, though."

"Oh, that's easy, lover man. Take your clothes off and follow me."

"Now your pulse rate and blood pressure are elevating, Cable. Is that a sign the pleasure model is stimulating you?" Glow Man observed.

"Yeah, something like that," I whispered.

I walked into her bedroom. She was sitting on the bed holding a small white jar. "This stuff is called *Hot*

Cherry. You rub it on your hot, erect penis and when you enter me, it's supposed to send us both up and away. My sometimes girlfriend Edna suggested it. Seems she and her boyfriend reached a stagnant plateau of some sort."

I sat down next to her. "Is that what's happened to us?"

"No, not really. I just wanted to go to new places with you, try new things. The minute I see you walk in, my whole life gets centered between my legs, and that's all I want to do—"

"—what's in the stuff?" I took the jar. The label didn't say much.

"Oh, a bunch of hot chili peppers, some other herbs to make the blood flow harder and faster, so Edna told me."

She had me lie down on the bed and quickly had her mouth around the head of my penis. Soon I was erect enough for her to rub the *Hot Cherry* all over my dick. I could feel Glow Man getting all excited himself. I think he was already getting his money's worth. The damn stuff seemed to work and though it stung a little at first, soon I swelled beyond my usual penile girth. June got onto her back on the bed and opened her legs as I eased into her. She flinched at first and I could tell the gel was burning her insides. But soon the excitement overcame the pain and she started going nuts with orgasms. Glow man got so worked up that he had me doing spasms like a hot Mexican jumping bean. It must have lasted for at least a half hour until June's body was exhausted and she couldn't come anymore. Interestingly, whatever the *Hot Cherry* gel did for my penis size, it did nothing for my ability to orgasm, so in the end, the score was June 12, Cable 0.

We were both sopping wet as I rolled off of her. "Oh, God, Cable...I want to go there again!" she whispered still out of breath.

"Yes, Cable, can we go there again?" Glow Man spoke up somewhere in my head.

"I don't think so," I muttered softly. "*You* try it. It's physically exhausting without a lot of pay-off, at least today."

"What did you say?" June asked, again looking at me curiously.

"Nothing...I've been talking to myself a lot lately, I guess..." I said, trying to cover how stupid I was to keep answering Glow Man.

"Something about a pay-off?" she persisted. "Weren't you satisfied? Lord, buster, any man would be in heaven just about now with a woman who came so many times on his cock in less than an hour."

I kissed her. "You're right about that." She drew me back to her lips and kissed me strong.

"I don't kiss you enough. We fuck so much...I—I forget how much I enjoy kissing you. But then again, I always start feeling deeper feelings when I kiss you—ah...I don't know, someplace I don't want to go, I guess."

"Yeah, I remember, June...never love, just do a lot of screwing."

"Well, don't you think I'm right? It's so less complicated that way. If I could fall in love with you like so many other girls must have in the past, I would be a mess. Plus we would end like a wreck on the side of the

389

road. And all those pieces can never be put back togeth-er again."

"Well, you sure make sense, babe. Yeah, you're right on the money, uncomplicated, straight to the sex and keep it that way, right?"

"Yes, Cable. That way we'll keep each other..."

June slept like a baby in my arms that night. It was late Wednesday morning by the time I washed up and got dressed. "Why is it that I had to wait so long while you humans regenerated your apparently spent ener-gies?" Glow Man complained as I looked in the mirror shaving.

"Because, like you saw, they put out a lot of energy, especially all that hot-pistol energy you witnessed last night. Hell, that's why I don't gain any weight. I must lose three pounds every time June and I have a sweat-session like the one we just did."

"Anyway, it was a long wait. But the experience was well worth it. Except I missed the—the, uh, *male orgas-mic* part."

"Well, that chemical shit—cayenne hot peppers and the like—kind of numbed my member, Glow Man. It in-creased my stimulation and size and all, but had a downside to it, I discovered."

"What can be done about it? Can we go back in there and release all that pent up spermatozoa in your body?"

"It doesn't go quite like that."

"Please?" Glow Man pleaded.

"I've got to get to work."

She was still sleeping, so I quietly went over to her and kissed June good-bye.

Glow Man and I got back to my office just in time to catch the mailman. He handed me my mail and I went inside. Immediately Mandy was hitting me with several professional demands. "And you still haven't gotten back to Jason Arnold—the young wife whom he suspects of havin' a clandestine affair with his neighbor's wife."

"Why is it when a woman commits adultery with another woman, the rules seem to change?" I asked as I went to my desk.

"Whatever do you mean, Cable?"

"Exactly what I said. Okay, so I catch them in bed with my Kodak. I show hubby the photos. What's he gonna do—take her to court and cause a whole can of worms to open he can't control? And what does she do, pay him a settlement, alimony or what?"

"I see your point...but Heavens, Cable, that should not prevent you from pursuin' the case. Mr. Arnold's money is as good as anyone else's."

Yeah, I suppose. I'm telling you the outcome of same-sex philandering—especially between two women—seems to get swept under the carpet more times than not. Unless she's a zillionaire...then all the lawyers jump on board like vultures to reap the bounty."

"I do like the way you talk, sweet Cable. May I kiss you good morning with just one lingering little kiss?"

"Yes...yes," Glow Man insisted. "Ask her if you can release in *her*—so I can feel your orgasmic jubilation."

"That's not the way it's done, one needs to work up to such things, and for God's sake, it's the middle of the day."

Mandy seemed indignant. "Well, I never...all I was askin' for was a spontaneous good morning kiss—and it's not barely past the middle of the day. And I can't imagine why you would have to work up—"

"—I'm sorry, Mandy, I wasn't talking to you—it's Glow Man."

"Glow Man?"

"Yeah, the ball of light, remember? Well, I gave him permission to inhabit me for one day. He says he wants to encounter human experience first-hand."

Mandy looked at me strangely. "I see. You understand why I might find that rather odd, Cable?"

"Do it and I'll super-charge you with *jolt-microns*," Glow Man whispered to me. "I promise she will respond as she never has. Just think, you'll be making us both happy."

I opened my arms and Mandy came slipping in. Her warm lips clung to mine and they did feel damn good. Again, there was *love* in this woman, and though part of it may have come through her pussy, the under-layer was still love and caring. "My...my..." she said as she began to feel Glow Man's charging me up. My whole body felt tingly all over and I could feel everything swell in my crotch. "You are indeed *electric* this day, Detective Denning. May I have one more for good measure?"

She kissed me again, only this time her lips stayed longer and I could feel Glow Man rooting us on. All at once Mandy pulled me up by the hand and lead me to my bedroom. She pulled down the age-discolored shade and sat me on my own bed. "May I remind you lady, this is a work day," I said, knowing full well she was under Glow Man's spell.

"In this extra-ordinary moment, I'm asking your permission to lock the front office door." She questioned my eyes.

"Only because I promised Glow Man—it's his fault," I affirmed.

Mandy left the room as Glow Man stirred in me. "Just a few more hours and you'll be rid of me, as promised, Cable. But I've a feeling the best is yet to come!" he said as my body jolted with his energy.

Mandy came back into the room. Only this time no more words were spoken. She had me stand and began to undress me, item by item. I was a bit worn out from June's *Hot Cherry* assault the night before, but Glow Man's energy was doing special things to my sexual chemistry. I began stripping Mandy of her clothing just as she finished with mine and by the time she slipped out of her skirt, my hand was down her panties and she let out with an ecstatic cry. We glued together like a couple of lost pretzels who had found the perfect fit and once again she wrapped those wonderful legs of hers around me. "Oh, oh!" Glow Man was saying, "Why couldn't they have preserved this when our evolutionary modifications took place?"

Just then Mandy Foster Simpson let out with the biggest orgasmic squeal I think I ever heard. Her entire body went into spasm and for a minute or two I felt I was astride a bucking bronco or the like. She seemed to come and come until her body could no longer sustain the intensity and she grabbed me with her arm and squashed my pubic area even more violently into hers. At that instant I finally let go and squirted every ounce of my essence into her womanhood. Glow Man's presence made me plunge deeper into Mandy than I had ever gone and finally we lay there together, trembling.

Finally Mandy had enough presence of mind to kiss my mouth ever so gently and look up into my eyes. "Thank you, Cable...I do believe I have been to Heaven and back..."

"You're welcome, kid, but I was really built up...so thanks, too."

"My pleasure. Now I shall have the privilege of carrying you around in me all day."

"Yeah, and speaking of carrying someone around—time's almost up, Mr. Glow Man."

"How about one more day?" Glow Man requested.

"That's a definite 'no'. A deal's a deal."

"Are you addressin' me?" Mandy asked, looking perplexed.

"No, hon, I'm sorry. It's Glow Man here. I want you to know he amplified our sensual delights this afternoon, enabling us to experience a super-charged act of sexual union."

"However it happened, an engagement to be relished and re-visited, I should say," Mandy said. "I have read about girls and their climaxes—but with you—and a little help from our friendly alien person—I cannot dare speak it, how sensually fulfilling it was—my womanhood has never, I mean never, not even in my imaginations, come close to such an ecstatic response of nerve endin's and the like."

We washed up, dressed and went on with our day. I knew after about an hour that Mandy was daydreaming and still in la-la land from our very hot physical exchange. So I sent her home with my blessing and just told her to come back to work the following day.

Around dusk I finally prevailed on Glow Man to exit my body. When he did, it was almost a letdown, as if the air had been taken out of my tires. "That...was an experience! Thank you for your co-operation," he exclaimed as he reformed himself into a swirling ball of light on my ceiling. "Now...true to my word, I am in a position to grant you *three wishes*, just like the genii of old. It is true some things I may not be able to grant....but try me."

"A guy has to really think about it, Glow Man," I said. "You know, when I was a kid I used to think about shit like that. What would I wish for if a genie appeared out of a bottle, and with his magic offered me those three wishes?'

"Now is your opportunity. Boy, did I have a fine go of it, as your English say. Talk about wishes, I wish I could capture that marvelously raw and sensual experience and share it where I come from."

"And just exactly where is that?"

"*Adnos Prithix*. Hard to explain, but it's not in a three-dimensional world, you see. It's more like consciousness with mathematics as one's entertainment. Yes, very difficult to explain to a primitive."

"Well, it doesn't sound very exciting anyway. We can skip it."

"Well...your wishes...I'm waiting..."

"When I was young it was *money, the perfect babe* and *truth*. But I think two of them have changed."

"Yes?" he elongated the word.

"Now I think it'd be *truth, meaningful friendships* and *love*—only love ain't just a babe anymore, more of a *universal love.*"

"That is stupid, but I suppose to your way of thinking, it's noble. Is that what you desire, then? Remember, once the wishes are granted, they are set into your psyche and you or I cannot reverse them."

"I *could* opt for super strength, a million bucks and a lifetime supply of cigarettes and booze."

"What would make you happiest, Cable?"

"In the long run?"

"Yes."

I took a deep breath and let the air out. "I guess I am who I am, Glow Man. I'm like a warrior in this world, and truth sets everyone good free and destroys the bad guys eventually. You really can't live without friends. I don't have many, but I treasure those I do have. And love? I don't even know why I would choose it...I don't even know what it is. I call it by its name, but I haven't got a clue. It's something you feel, I guess. Or you don't. But I would like to think it's like a healing, caring extension that comes from deep within your self. How's that?"

"Insipid, careless, outlandish, smacks of the hero's quest—but you know, you might just be one of them."

"One of them who?"

"The *Justine Celestias*, a group of beings spread all over the universe, designed to bring truth and justice to ailing, primitive societies like the one you're in."

"How would I know I'm one?"

"That thing you call *'soul'* has it etched on it. Your true heart allows it to be known to your consciousness."

"So far I haven't detected anything like that. I was just born with the desire to seek out the truth, no matter the cost."

The ball of light that was Glow Man began to dissipate. "I must go now, Cable. Are you certain, this is what you want? You could have so much more, if you desire it."

"Not for me, Glow Man...maybe for some other guy, but I'd be tempted by money, destroy myself with women...hell, I'm already addicted to one, not to mention what smoking, drinking and who knows what else would do to me?"

"So be it." An invisible impact hit my body. "Goodbye, Cable. I enjoyed myself immensely. I might be back one day to check in on you to see how truth, friendship and love are working out for this lifetime."

The light began to shrink down to a pinpoint and then disappeared right before my eyes.

Chapter 11

AT THE BALLET

The evening of June 11, 1933 was calm and balmy. Hundreds of theatre patrons waited in line to see one of the world's great and most popular ballets, *Swan Lake*. The musical score was written by a homosexual Russian composer, a guy named Peter I. Tchaikovsky who, I later learned, was considered one of the great masters, right up there with Bach, Beethoven, Mozart, Schubert and Brahms. He had written other famous ballets, *The Nut-cracker* and *Sleeping Beauty* that gained worldwide fame. His passion was opera, but he was never too hot at that medium, I guess. He wrote five symphonies and died before he completed the sixth from a bad case of cholera by drinking contaminated water.

It must have looked like a strange assortment of bedfellows as Boots, Joe Lorena and I walked into the lobby of the theatre. It would be the only time in our lives that we would come together as a trio. Sad, now that I look back on it. Boots had some old field glasses from the Great War and Joe a small but nifty single lens deal that resembled a small telescope, but magnified the figures up on the stage to a crystal clear presence.

I decided to drop backstage and wish Lily the best but I was stopped at the entrance hall to the dressing rooms. I guess it was considered bad luck to wish a ballerina *bon voyage*, good luck, happy tip-toeing and all that stuff as she went through her paces on stage. I was just about to go back and join Joe and Boots in the auditorium when a very disturbed Frederick Bruckner came rushing up to me. "Mr. Denning...Mr. Denning...please..." he wheezed, out of breath and obviously exasperated. He took me aside and withdrew a small piece of paper from his pocket. It was a note. "This...this was found...in Lily's make-up case as she was preparing this evening. She's terrified..."

I yanked the note from Bruckner's hand and opened it. *'He carries a very sharp knife and you will never know when...beware!'* Furiously I looked around. Right about now every man, woman or child in the place was a suspect. "Bruckner, I need to keep this—I have a couple of other sleuths with me already out in the lobby and on the job."

"Yah, sure...please...please protect Lily tonight, Mr. Denning!" he implored.

"I'll put everything I got into it. See you later." I made my way back out into the lobby and found Joe and Boots. "We've got to find someplace where we can talk, pronto," I said.

Both men looked at me with their eyebrows raised as they followed me downstairs to the bathrooms. There in the semi-lit hallway I showed them the note. Joe was visibly alarmed, but Boots was sniffing out something other than the note.

"It's a ruse, I tell ya. You weren't listenin' when I told you about that lint, now, were you. I'll wager my badge on it, Cable, it ain't no man. This here scribble was meant to confuse and detract and nothin' more."

I thought frantically. I had only a couple of hours to solve this mystery that had been eating at me like a consuming fever. I was sure about one thing. Whoever was pulling the strings was clever and on the inside. But *why* kill Lily Norwood? I couldn't find a motive in all the heaps of crap I'd dredged up on the case. Joe Lorena took his fingers and felt the paper, the writing. Then he crinkled it in his hand while he held it to his ear. "This was written two or three days ago, gentlemen. Cable, it's now or never, who do you suspect?"

I brought the men in closer to me until our heads were all but bumping together. "That queer costumer, Axel Rosenbaum fits it better than any I can come up with. Boots was worried about the purple velvet lint found on the last written threat from that news clipping, insisting it was a female. But think about it, a costume designer uses all kinds of material, male and female—if it matters—and Rosenbaum could have easily been trimming costumes or whatever when he pasted together that note."

"Makes sense, but again, I'm not familiar with the case," Joe said, fidgeting where we stood.

"Ain't good enough, Cable," Boots insisted. "Did you ever figure, how's Lily gonna get it? Now, if what you say is true—that the killer intends to do his dirty work during the stagin' of the play—he can't just run out there up to Lily and knife her now, can he? Less he's wearin' a costume. He'd get caught sure as hell, and I'm a thinkin', like most killers, this person does not want his crime betrayin' him. So...I repeat, just how's he gonna do it?"

Joe and I looked at each other. "Joe, can you use some of your other worldly talents to help us here, buddy?" I said.

"Otherly what?" Boots guffawed.

"Oh, I didn't tell you, Boots. When I met Joe he was the head mouthpiece for Jack Dragna's syndicate, but turned out to be the sire of my fiancée Honey Combes—who one of Dragna's men shot to death in a jealous rage one terrible night. As it turned out, Joe is pure alien in human form—and Honey was half-alien, and Lily Norwood an exact biological clone of Joe's wife, who died from childbirth complications days after Honey was born." I could see Joe was uncomfortable.

Boots gave us both the once over. But the old man couldn't handle it. "Well, that—that was before my time, I'm afraid," he said, looking away and tucking some chewing tobacco in his cheek.

Then a light went on inside of me. "Boots—damn it! Why didn't I get it? You said unless the killer was in costume he's bound to get caught. What if he's one of the cast? What if he's got it planned to the nth degree and he'll knife Lily at just the right dramatic moment in the music?"

"I always tol' you, Cable, I'm smarter than you and twice as fast when it comes to figurin' out the criminal mind."

I had to act post haste. "Joe, will you sit in the audience. Using that telescope of yours, you can watch every face, every hand—anyone who even comes within earshot of Lily—can you do it, buddy?"

"Of course I can, Cable. I've got a lot at stake here, too, you know."

"Thanks..." I turned to my old silent partner. "Boots, you watch from stage right, that's to your left, facing the stage. Do you have your badge with you? Otherwise they may kick you out." The old cowboy was wearing a

1920s double-breasted grayish suit and black tie with those old western boots he must have been born in.

He reached in his pocket, withdrew his old tarnished Sheriff's badge and pinned it on his suit above the left pocket. "Yep...always prepared, Cable, every lawman worth his salt always comes prepared."

I went to cover stage left where I knew Lily would come in and out. I had seen the rehearsals a couple of times and knew just about all her entrances and exits. Now I had to keep my eye on everyone. At a time like this, no one is friend, no one is foe. Everyone is suspect. I went backstage and was stopped by the same man again. I flashed my P.I. identification to him and this time he let me pass. I stood at the wing of the curtain where I knew Lily would have to enter onto the stage.

It was quiet backstage, despite the last minute bustling. I was checking out the set on the stage when I felt a tap on my shoulder. It was a highly painted woman in a white costume with very red cheeks, dark, dark eyebrows with lots of mascara, matching red lips and a smile that made me feel I wanted to take her up into my arms and carry her off. "Cable, thanks...for being here," she whispered into my ear. "I feel a lot safer now. Did Mr. Bruckner show you the note?"

"Yep, I have it in my possession."

"So?"

"How do you feel? Can you go on with it? If you can last the evening, I think we might have your stalker by the end of the performance."

"Yes—really?"

"I'm pretty damn close. Joe Lorena, remember the man you met up at your place that night who helped

402

me? Well, he's out in the audience with a nice little tele-scope so he can see everyone up close and personal. Boots is opposite me at stage right, checking all those blokes out with the tight, see-through crotch panties."

She squeezed my hand. "Cable? When this is all over, will you take me away with you for a couple of days—anywhere, just to be alone with you and feel safe and warm and loved..."

"You bet, kid...if anyone's ever been brave about this thing, it's you, Lily Norwood. Hang in there..." As the music started up, she quickly kissed the top of my hand and danced away into the bright lights.

Lily danced like a sacred nymph of the forest prime-val, hopping here, jumping there, twirling round. When the white prince picked her up, it was as if she was weightless and floated like a Terpsichorean goddess. The audience loved her so much that when she made her first exit, people clapped and yelled out to her loud-ly like Saturday morning at the Italian opera.

The particular version we were all watching that evening was the story of a beautiful young woman, Odette, who had been transformed by an evil magician into a white swan by day...along with her friends. Only a pledge of true love from a virginal prince would bring her back into a human form again and break the spell. The prince meets her and is immediately smitten and they dance their dance of love. At the palace ball, the vil-lain has transformed his daughter Odile into a swan very closely resembling Odette except that she is a black swan. The prince gets confused and thinking it is Odette, proposes to the wrong young swan. Odette is looking on from a distance and seeing this, flees back to the lake as she thinks she has lost her true love and the only chance to break the spell. The prince realizing what has happened runs after her and explains to her, pledging his love. The evil magician says he must make good his proposal to his daughter, Odile....he says he would rather die with Odette...and they jump into the lake together...their true love breaking the spell. End story.

Everything went like clockwork the first half. Lily ran passed me on her way out to strip and dress for her role as the Black Swan. It was at this time that I expected the killer might take the opportunity to act. I wasn't even certain of that. What if he was a cowardly sort, a stalker with a lot of hot air in him, full of bragging, circling around the ring, but with no Sunday punch?

During the intermission, I crossed the busy stage flittering with stagehands and crew changing the sets. I was looking for Boots. He wasn't where he was supposed to be. I went down into the auditorium and made my way among the masses of people looking for Joe. I finally found him outside of the theatre, pacing. "Have you seen Boots, Joe?"

Joe looked at me oddly, as if he were coming out of a trance. "Uh...no, Cable—isn't he backstage with you?"

"No."

"He'll show up." Then Joe Lorena looked up into the L.A. night sky, checking out the dim and sparse stars that appeared above. "This is harder for me than I imagined. Seeing Lily up there is seeing *Lorena Brockmore*, Cable, the features, the special looks, familiar movements of my lost beloved, Honey's mother. I don't know if I can go back in there."

I put my arm around Joe's shoulder. "It's okay, Joe, I understand. Go home if you think you need to. Lily doesn't even know you, or at least who you really are. And from my view on top of the hill, I think it's just as well—for both of you."

"Yes...maybe you're right. But then, who will watch from the audience? I'm divided. I guess I should stay. You know, I really don't think, in the end, that I'm cut out to take on human form after all. Some of us do it better than others. I may not be one of them."

"I'll tell you what. If I can borrow your looking glass there, I'll see if Bruckner can take your seat and he can watch. He's highly motivated to see to Lily's safety. He loves her like a daughter, I suspect."

Joe handed me the little telescope. "Here. I'm sorry, Cable. Lily's such an incredible dancer—I wonder where she got the talent?"

"Oh, us humans are kind of weird like that. Maybe a great grandmother was a dancer and then those genes come popping up in subsequent generations." I hugged Joe. "I'll call you—"

"—no, I can't leave! Just let me stay out here. Bring Boots and Lily with you after the performance. I have a wonderful surprise for you."

"Suit yourself, Joe, see you later." I went back into the theatre looking for Boots again. I knew it was almost time for the show to start, so I darted backstage, borrowed a flashlight from a set manager and went searching for my old sidekick. Just then I heard the music start up for the next act and I went frantically searching for both Bruckner and Boots. I found Bruckner at stage left where I had been hanging out and he agreed to take Joe's place in the audience. I scooted around between costumed swans and leotards until I got to stage right. I finally found Boots Blake, but he was out cold on the floor behind a piece of a set. I flashed the light on him and saw a little red blood trickling from a cut on the side of his head, just above his left ear. "Boots! Boots!" I called to him. I felt his pulse. He was okay. I picked up his Stetson hat and told a stagehand my friend had been clobbered. There was a buzz of activity and two men carried Boots to Lily's dressing room with me in tow. Desperately I looked around for the black swan, but she had donned her costume and was on stage dancing by now. I poured some water on Boots' face and he revived slowly. I told him the performance had already started and he looked up at me with those old grey eyes.

"It's—it's too late, Cable. The son-of-a-bitch who conked me is the killer, alright, but I didn't see a thing."

"So now you think it's a man?"

"No, I don't think so, Cable. But I'm too goddamned dazed to think straight just now. You better get to your post. Look for that little knife...just in case I'm wrong and the note was on the level."

I ran out until I was in the wings at stage left again. I could see Lily as Odile the black swan dancing around the Evil Magician conspiring to seduce the prince. My eyes were in a thousand places at once as I looked for a costumed man or woman who might be concealing a weapon. I saw nothing that looked questionable. As the dance moved to the seduction of the prince and the prince now fully deceived, they danced a passionate du-

406

et— and for a minute I flashed back to our evening in the bathtub at her place. How wonderful and genuine that lady was, how honest to give herself to me, a bum, glued-together with hollow dreams and street violence, dirty dives with women who kept forbidden hours behind alley doors. I was a pretender, a drinking, smoking gumshoe thrown like a pair of bad dice into the ring of chance, and just like a prizefighter with a glass jaw, I couldn't take the best punches because I would shatter before the fifteenth round.

Just as the prince was vowing his undying love, he lifted Lily high in the air, his hands tightly around her waist, as he lowered her slowly, sensuously back down and close to him. I saw her body flinch and her face wince. Something was happening! I drew my .38. Lily began to waver where she stood. The conductor noticed but kept the orchestra playing, thinking it was part of the play action somewhat altered. Now her dance partner began to go for her, I went flying out with my gun drawn as Lily collapsed in his arms and the music stopped. The audience rose to its feet with sounds of alarm as I conked the prince over the head with my gun butt and caught Lily as she collapsed on the floor. Lily was wet with perspiration and trembling. Her eyelids were fluttering and she fought for breath. Someone came rushing out with a sharp knife and cut her out of the Black Swan's costume. But it was too late. Lily Norwood was pale, limp—and dead in my arms.

They carried Lily's body to her dressing room. A kind doctor in evening dress rushed back stage to attend her. Her naked, white body was discolored around

407

the ribs—*just where the feather quills had been taped to her body!* Now both the house doctor and the other man inspected her carefully. They looked at each other, then at me. I was kneeling beside Lily's body, tears streaming down my face. "It appears she's been injected with enough poison to kill ten people, the way her body's beginning to bloat and fill with these spreading rashes," the doc said.

I got up and spun around. "Rosenbaum!" I shouted. The little Jew presented himself, his face red with tears and mourning. "If it wasn't you, who was it?"

He was bawling. "I...I...I don't know...I adored Lily...I would never have killed beauty—only a *beast* would kill her."

I knew by now it wasn't her dancing partner that I had conked on the head just in case. "Where's that *bitch*, Schnabel?" I was almost screaming.

Everyone in the room looked at each other. I went flying out. Bruckner met me in the hallway. I grabbed the older man by the shoulders and shook him. "Schnabel, Bruckner—where is she?"

"I don't know—why? Is Lily all right? She fainted on the stage—what do you think—"

"—Lily's dead, Bruckner. Go say good-night—it's her last one!" I shouted at him...I'd lost control. "Now, tell me!...where can I find Gertrude Schnabel?" The old man sank to the floor, sobbing.

"Her—her car is a bright red Lincoln convertible in the back parking lot," said a young ballerina in costume. "If it's there, she might still be around."

I ran to the rear exit and out into the parking lot. The red Lincoln was still there! I ran toward it, but as I did, a gunshot rang out from the dark shadows behind the staircase. I fired back blindly. "Schnabel—I was too stupid to put two-and-two together—why?....you scheming bitch! What did she ever do to you?'

I dodged behind another car as a second shot rang out. Then I heard a cry from behind the staircase and I made a lunge for the location of the sound, rolling over until I was almost on top of the first step. Then I looked up to see Joe Lorena carrying the wriggling body of Gertrude Schnabel in one hand! He was walking like a zombie, emotionally numb, staring straight ahead as he lifted Schnabel's body high and was about to crush her neck with that one powerful hand. "No! Joe! Don't! You did it to Laggore—that's enough. Let the law take over from here."

"Law?" he snickered. "Law? You humans are without law. Just as you have no heart, no conscience...no love in you." He dropped Gertrude Schnabel's body hard onto the concrete and walked away lost in his tears. I never saw Joe Lorena again.

I bent over the fallen woman's body, checked her out for any more weapons. She was stunned from being dropped and almost choked to death by Joe Lorena's grip. "Why, Schnabel?"

I rolled her over on her back. She was dressed in a red dress, black heels and a black onyx necklace hung around her neck. "Axel...Axel wanted her for his own...she had everything I ever wanted—but he never wanted me...no matter how hard I worked—worked for him. She was too perfect...too beautiful to live..." She swallowed hard. "Now we don't have to worry about any of that, do we? And you...you phony detective...you killed her, too...you screwed her...you...*you* took away the white swan...desecrated her with your hot sex and fancy talk..."

I took a big breath. "I figured it...but I figured it out too late. You poisoned the quills. When the coast was clear, you undid Rosenbaum's taped ends, injected poison into them. You also knew that when the prince lifted her into the air that first time, the pressure of his hands and her body position would force the quills to puncture her skin and release the poison into her."

"And kill her," Gertrude Schnabel hissed with a terrible smile on her face. "You lose, Denning..."

I could hear the familiar sound of the sirens, their haunting screams piercing through the night as they approached. A breeze had come in from the sea causing scraps of paper and debris to dance their own kind of maudlin ballet in the parking lot around me. "We all lose..." I said half to myself as I picked myself up and walked away from the woman. By then several other people with mixed pathos and anger on their faces were looking down at Gertrude Schnabel. Soon the cops were taking her away and the ambulance loaded Lily's body for that trip to the County Morgue.

Boots Blake was sitting on the stairs smoking a cigar. He had a bandage wrapped around his head. "Sorry, Cable...we didn't get there soon enough to save her."

"Are you okay, Boots?" I asked.

"Yeah, whippersnapper. I told you it was a female skunk, didn't I? It was them damn quills that did it, wasn't it?" He looked around. "What the hell happened to Lorena?"

"Oh, he...he, uh, had to leave. This time for good, I suspect."

"What the hell are you talkin' about? I swear, boy, you don't make much sense sometimes."

"It's been a tough night, Boots. I'm...I'm just not in the mood. In fact, I'm gonna walk for a while before I go home. I need some fresh air."

Life can leave you with a bad taste in your mouth. Failure goes by a lot of names, names that can't always be picked out of the hat that's been worn too long, just because you're used to it—and after a while you get numbed to the feel of it on your head, so you start to wear it on the inside, there, in your craw, until it seizes up your guts like when you pass over someone's grave and know the occupant ain't comin' back because wherever they are, it's final. So they get to wear that tombstone fedora forever, hanging out in a forlorn cemetery, forgotten.

That damned music of *Swan Lake* was still going on over and over inside my head and I was watching Lily open her arms in one of those wonderful ballet gestures when the arms sweep back as the dancer tip-toes backward. She was smiling at me and it hurt too damn much, because I knew I wouldn't be congratulating her tonight for a marvelous performance—and she and I wouldn't be going away for that little rendezvous she had asked for. That music played in my head until I finally had to change it into the comforting sound of that familiar sax, that old friend that haunted me whenever I walked the lonely streets late at night. And tonight I would walk—I'd walk all night until the pain had woven itself into

every part of me and then I could punish myself sufficiently to smoke and drink myself into oblivion with a
whole bottle of English gin. And June? She'd have to
wait. After all, that hot, wet place of hers would be open
for business again tomorrow night and the night after
that. And soon my restless addiction to her would turn
into a bottomless sorrow of booze and regret, seductive
words spoken in a drunken slobber and sweating bodies venting life's loveless ironies on each other. Now
there was no place to go except down.

Love and Death

Instead of going home to bury myself in that bottle
of gin that sat waiting in my office desk drawer, on some
insane impulse I hopped one of those red and orange
streetcars out to Temple Street and the County Morgue.
I couldn't figure it then, but somehow love and death fit
together like a hand-in-glove and there was no place
else I wanted to go except to that creepy, cold room
where all the one-way trips end up with rigor mortis. I
had to see Lily one more time.

The streetcar was empty except for a young couple
teasing each other and a motorman and conductor. I got
off and hoofed it over to the coroner's office. As a cop a
few years back, I had visited that house of the dead too
many times, checking out cases so terrible that even a
twenty-four year-old tough guy from the ghetto of East
L.A. could hardly bear up under the horror. What humans did to each other challenged even the wildest imagination. My young partner and childhood pal, Mario

Angelo, and I had witnessed the best and worst of humanity when we were cops. Now he was dead, ending up in a ditch as a young cop because he defied the underworld *and* the powers that be, down at city hall. Broken lives came in all forms, from the derelict drunk who died forgotten in a dark alley, to the beautiful dame whose boyfriend decapitated her because he never wanted anyone else to have her. And the list goes on. If you can think of it, it happened somewhere out there in the L.A. jungle of dreams and nightmares, human and otherwise.

The door clicked open and I approached the night clerk. He was smoking and reading a dime novel. He wore thick glasses and peered at me as I flashed my P.I. identification at him. When I told him who it was I wanted to see, he looked at me strangely. "Oh, the new one...dancer got shot on stage or something?"

"Yeah, something...where is she?"

He told me which room Lily's body was stored in and I went there with a sinking feeling in my stomach. Why in the hell was I torturing myself? Slab rooms are notorious for being dimly lit and smelling of chemicals mixed with a little death. They keep the stiffs air conditioned to delay putrefaction and usually have run out of individual slide-drawers, so a lot of the corpses lay on tables with a simple white sheet over them. But when I entered the slab room I wasn't alone. There was a youngish woman checking out toe tags in the far corner. She looked up when she saw me. "May I help you? Regular hours are over, Mister. You might want to come back tomorrow."

"I'm a private investigator, lady, and I was with Lily Norwood when she got it tonight—"

"—oh..." she said in a soft voice. Then she looked me over carefully. "I'm Dr. Stretcher, assistant head of forensics."

"The last head guy I remember doing business with here was old Dr. Sandor."

"Unfortunately, he's passed on. Dr. Okamura is our new head pathologist under Coroner Nance."

I checked the dame out. "Aren't you awful young to be in this line of work? Usually it's the old one's who have earned their merit badges for entrance into this elite social club of misfits and stiffs."

She looked hard at me. "You know, *that's why I hate the living*," she flashed at me. "People like you, hard, insensitive cops, always coming out with some stupid comment, thinking the dead don't deserve anything decent anymore, just because they're gone from *your* world. Well Mister, they're in *my* world now and I happen to like the dead. Like Lily Norwood. I've seen her dance and she was the best. And just because she's gone from your world, it doesn't mean—"

"—lady," I interrupted. "Please...just show me Lily's body, give me a few minutes and then I'll leave you alone to your world, okay?"

She pointed to an area a few slabs from me. "That's her, over there." She went back to what she was doing, and ignored me.

I approached the toe tag that was tied around Lily's beat up dancing feet. Her toes were cramped and bent, as if dancing had distorted them through the years. I hadn't noticed that before. Carefully, I drew the sheet

414

back from Lily's body. There she was, that once gorgeous face, pink now and bloated from the deadly poison Gertrude Schnabel had used to kill her. "Hello, babe," I said under my breath. "I'm—I'm so sorry I let you down. It was my fault. I should've been with you all the time—I should've never let you dance tonight."

I felt I needed to say something, so I went back into my early memories for some kind of prayer or poem that might do. Emerson came to mind: *Though I loved her as myself, as a self of purer clay, and though her parting dims the day, stealing grace from all alive, heartily know when angels go, the gods arrive.* Then I put both my open hands to my face and sobbed like a child over Lily's body. I was here, but I had no reason to be any longer. She wasn't like me anymore, she couldn't take my hand and kiss it as she had done tonight before she leapt out onto the stage, filled with spring and spritely leaps. She could no longer take me to her lips and her bed, nor embrace me with those lovely arms that danced the dance that lovers dance. I'd seen it a hundred times, but now somehow it was different. Yeah, dead was dead and I knew that—but a beautiful young Odette lying dead among the thorns of the old and abused didn't fit somehow, didn't belong to those whose mouths lay agape in rigor mortis, and whose skin was tightening around their cheeks in death's beginning victory over the living.

Next thing I knew Dr. Stretcher was standing beside me. She saw my tears and knew my feelings, somehow, as best as one could who came in during the ninth inning of the ballgame. "You loved her?" she asked quietly.

415

"Yeah," I sobbed. "I loved her too late...and failed...to keep her—I...I was hired to protect her...and...and—"

"—it's not always up to us, Mister—Mister—"

"—Denning...remember that name, never hire a bloke named Cable Denning—he's poison to his clients—he brings death under the pretext of hope."

She touched my arm with her hand. "It's probably not a good idea for you to stay here. It only hurts more. I promise I'll take good care of her. After all, you're right—she was special...I'll talk to her...and tell her you came by...and I'll remind her that you loved her...that'd mean a lot...I'm sure..."

I walked out into the midnight air, searching the skies for redemption, forgiveness, some place to run where I'd never have to face something like this again. At thirty-three I'd fucked up my life plenty good, lived too hard, too much...maybe even too long...

Chapter 12

FALLING TO OBLIVION

During the ensuing months, I sank down into a world of sex, booze, smoking and anything else I could with June Maye. As often as possible I escaped into the safe bosom of Never Never Land, consumed with remorse and addiction to the Goddess of Passion without love. *Sinleila* had told me this day would come, but somehow when it does arrive coming down the tracks like a fast-moving freight train, it hits you head-on and you get caught on the cowcatcher, plowed along on the tracks of misery and sameness. June continued to sing well and reminded me it was our sex that kept her singing alive with sensual expression—so at least, I was good for something. My business began to slip and I took on less clientele. Mandy saw the deterioration, and both she and Adeline tried to pull me up without success. Boots was constantly disgusted by my listless lifestyle and warned me to straighten out or I'd end up in a gutter somewhere, unrecognized and forgotten by the world. Maybe he was right, but something drove me to continue abusing every part of my psyche and body.

It was Christmas Eve, 1933. June was singing at the top of her form and had found some kind of happiness between what we did behind closed doors and how she sparkled up there on the stage in front of her little combo. The *Bistro Club* was filled to the brim with Christmas celebrants and as I came in around ten that night she took the house with a couple of sensational numbers.

Every guy in the joint was hanging on to her every sen-sually expressed syllable. There was a blonde babe be-side me wearing a sparkling low-cut blouse. She had thick lips and very blue eyes and earlier, I noticed, she had had a difference of opinion with her date, who had gotten so annoyed with her, he left the club in a huff. "Are you celebrating alone, too?" she asked me. "Merry Christmas."

I turned to look at her. "Well, I'm not really one to celebrate holidays, lady. I spent too many of them in a patrol car weeding out drunks and prostitutes from street corners."

"Are you a cop? I like cops. Especially young ones like you." I could tell she'd already been drinking too much booze.

"Used to be...now I'm a private dick..."

She laughed as she put her glass down hard on the counter and looked at me. "You're *what*? You'll pardon my saying...but shouldn't they *all* be private?"

"That's short for *detective*, lady. I have an office up on Franklin and I play that joke on all babes who look like they might appreciate the double entendre."

"Double who? Ah...mysterious private eye, huh?"

"Yeah. What do *you* do?"

"Well, Mister, until tonight I was screwing a pretty nice guy who took good care of me. So I didn't have to work. But I don't think Randy's coming back for me. You see, all good things must come to an end." She burped. "So...that's that, now, isn't it?"

"I don't know. Guys are known to have a change of heart. From the looks of you, he'll start missing you in a day or two and want you back."

"Maybe," she said, looking me over as a possible candidate. "But it might be time...hic! to—to move on. Are you with anyone tonight? Seems impossible that a hunk of a guy like you wouldn't have some pretty dame panting after you."

"As a matter of fact, you see that babe up there singing? We're, uh, kind of an item these days."

The lady looked up at June. "Damn, she's a looker too. Even *I'd* like to do her. Have you ever...ever done it as a threesome?"

"No, I've pretty much kept it at a one-on-one basis..."

"Too bad...maybe a fine—fine—hic!—Christmas present for her would be *me*. Maybe all three of us could go home to your place. It's fun, like when we were kids, you know..."

"Well, I wasn't a kid in quite *that* way, Miss—"

"—Dolly—call me Dolly Haynes. I love singing. I have two younger sisters who sing. They've formed a—hic!—a duo. They want to go into show business."

"It's a tough way to go."

"I think it's a tough way to *come*, Mister, Mister—"

"—Cable...just call me Cable." I could tell the babe had 'good time' written all over her. June had launched into a third tune of the evening, one of those naughty Cole Porter songs that grab you from the first note. *I Wanna Be Loved By You* was a June Maye special and she always did it with sex and class at the same time.

I was already a little drunk. Mandy Foster Simpson had registered her discomfort with me before I left my office that night. She was complaining of the neglect of my professional manner and clientele. But you know what? I didn't give a shit. My ship was sinking and I

419

knew it. I thought it was time to let all the stops out anyhow. It seemed all my friends had turned against me, Boots, Mandy, even my mother had expressed her disapproval at my life style. Piss on 'em! I thought. It's my life, and I'm not accountable to them—at least when it came to what I did in my private life. I reached over and touched Dolly Haynes on the hand. "You know, let's run your threesome idea by June—you never know, she might go for it. Whatta ya say?"

"I'm—I'm game...hell, two beautiful people like you two—and me in the middle. I could...I could probably—hic!—teach you guys a few things."

"Yeah, I'll bet."

Soon June came off the stage and approached us. "Hello, babe," she said as she kissed me and then gave Dolly the once over.

"Hiya, singing lady. Damn, that was a swell set. It never gets old for me, June...every time I hear those tunes, you ratchet them up even higher. Oh, by the way, this is Dolly Haynes."

Dolly extended her hand. I could tell June had been drinking already, but it hadn't affected her singing yet. Usually by the last set of the evening, lately I could tell she slurred more and got slightly out of tune now and then. "I am happy—happy—to meet you, June Maye. My boyfriend and I were really enjoying you until he—he—hic!—got pushed out of shape and left. So...I was suggesting...to...to your handsome beau...here...Cable...that maybe...if you were open...open to it...we could, the three of us, go home and party together..."

June looked at me and I nodded my head in approval. "Why not?" she answered with a very sexy smile on her lips. "I've got another set to go. Will you wait?"

She looked June's wonderful body over. She was wearing a peach-colored sequined skirt with a matching loose blouse—and I mean, *loose* on top, allowing her full breasts to come popping half way out. "Oh, sure, honey...I'd wait for—for you...a long...long time."

By the time we got to June's little house, it was after one a.m. Christmas Day. Soon the three of us were naked on June's sofa, sipping booze and puffing out white clouds of thick cigarette smoke. Dolly's body was enticing, to say the least. She had very fair skin that showed two-piece bathing suit tan marks, long, lanky legs and a pair of boobs big enough for both June and I to get lost in. In fact, Dolly kicked things off by reaching over to kiss June lightly on the lips. June responded and soon the two of them were making me hotter than a shotgun in a turkey-shoot. There was something about two women fondling and kissing one another that riled up my private parts. Then they invited me into the midst of them and soon I couldn't tell whose nipples I was kissing and sucking on. June took our hands and led us into the bedroom. She lay down and invited me on top of her. Then Dolly grabbed my cock and balls from behind and started massaging them as she used her other hand to finger June's pussy.

Needless to say, it was an explosive, explorative evening and by early Christmas morning all three of us were out on June's bed like the three bears in hibernation. But you know, it was *fun* and I enjoyed every minute of it. There was something good and safe about Dolly Haynes, like a big girl who hadn't quite grown up but still had a good heart in a fully developed woman's body. I would never know how many times we came, or who came in who. But it didn't matter, because we were all celebrating, weren't we? Merry Christmas, all!

Lost Dreams

But the ensuing months didn't fare as well. By April 1934, June and I were drinking and smoking a lot more than we were eating. We had begun to lose weight precipitously, and I observed June's great clothes didn't hang on her in quite the same way they had just a few months before. Mandy had called Boots, trying to get him to save me from myself and my dwindling business. I stayed drunk for days and refused to answer most phone calls, and when I did I was often so incoherent to the prospective client that he or she just hung up in disgust.

But try as they may, neither Mandy nor Boots could bring me around and I continued to slide down that long fire pole into longer and longer periods of drinking and stupor. In July, June and I were celebrating the Fourth when I realized even our sex had gotten numb and routine. I discussed this with June and she felt the same. "Stagnant," she called it. She was right. I had to do something. Then it hit me—those little bags of hallucinogens that Uncle Teddy, Lily's pseudo-uncle, had given me that day in his laboratory.

June had sung that night and after her last set I had come over to her place from my office to be with her. As addicted as we were to cigarettes and alcohol, I was rather excited to be sharing the hallucinogens with her, hopeful that it might kick-start our waning sex life. She came in late and seemed to be in an okay mood. She undressed as usual. Only this time I fixed the drinks and lit up a cigarette for her. We sat on her sofa. She looked at me. "Aren't you going to let me see that naked, sexy body of yours?" she asked me, a little tight already.

"Yeah, as soon as I show you my surprise."

"Surprise?" she slurred. "What surprise?"

"Just hang on, babe." I had been drinking a lot of the night and staggered into her closet, grabbing one of Uncle Teddy's little bags. I didn't know exactly how much of the stuff we should be taking, but I guessed we'd chew a little of it and swallow it down with some honeyed whiskey in a hot snifter. I came back in and sat down beside her. "Prepare, baby, for a jolt—and...and a Buck Rogers trip to outer space!" I muttered.

"What in the fuck are you talking about, Cable? You're drunk. I'm not that sloshed yet. So let me catch up and then we can talk about your Buck Rogers trip, okay?"

I got up and made us both those honeyed whiskies in the hot snifters, except I put a triple dose in June's glass. We toasted and she drank it down like a fish. Soon she was on that high buzz. Now was my opportunity. "So...how're you feeling now?" I said, burping.

"I think I want you to fuck me first, lover man, so we can—you can ...rise to the occasion."

"Not yet, my pet," I chuckled. "We are going to screw royal blue tonight, lady J., but later."

"What?"

"Lady J., I said."

"You never called me that before."

"So I fucking just did now."

"I think I like it. Maybe the club should bill me as *Lady J., Super Songstress*, eh?"

"Yeah, why not?" I handed her a few pinches of the herbal looking substance and took some myself. I placed mine on my tongue and she did the same. "Now wash this shit down." I got up and refilled her drink with pure, cold honeyed whiskey. "Drink up, babe, then hang on..."

I went into the bedroom and it took me forever to take my clothes off. I was so drunk that I couldn't figure a way to pull my trousers over my shoes. Of course I didn't think about taking my shoes off first. By the time I got into the living room where my naked lady sat, the room was spinning. But it felt wonderful, as if with each spin I was going higher and everything got warmer and friendlier. June was feeling it too. But she seemed to accelerate and zoom to some place I couldn't go to.

"Son-of-a-bitch, Cable, colors—colors everywhere! I love it! Oh, Cable, what is it? Can you see them? Everywhere...rushing...rushing by me...inside me, inside my head, my chest, my pussy..." She began to breathe heavier. So did I.

It was then that I realized for the first time that one person's drug trip is not necessarily the same as another's. "I'm—I'm just...swirling...babe...swirling...ha! ha! going up, up, up...!"

She yanked me over to her and shoved my hand up between her legs. "Now, lover man, your Lady J. is going to fuck you—I mean, really fuck you—are you ready?" She looked at my still-limp member. "What—what's this? You're—you're usually as hot for me as your .38 pistol about this time of night. The colors...they're making me hot...and I'm floating with them...they're spreading my legs...can't you see them?"

My whole experience was really different from hers and I was still spinning like a top. Then I seemed to reach a plateau and my cock began to rise as June manipulated me. Then she put her mouth down onto the head and sucked me up into her. Soon I was erect as a baseball bat in the hands of Babe Ruth ready to hit a home run. But something else was happening. We were looking at each differently. She wasn't June anymore and I wasn't Cable. We were these two very young teenagers frolicking in a strawberry colored meadow, flying, floating, enjoining, uncoupling, rejoining, laughing, crying, cursing.

Then all of a sudden June went into a long speech about herself, spilling out words carelessly as if she were given a script and she had to read it then and there. "The truth....about me, Cable Denning...the truth about June Maye, Lady J. I've about had it with you, you old fuck, because I'm superior now and I don't need you anymore....I don't need your dangerous days with dangerous broads and nights of fucking your secretary! You're just a low gumshoe...but me...ha! I'm the champion singer...the only one who does the notes right and does you at the same time. You think...don't you? You think it's been all on account of your intense, attentive screwing me that's made me sing better...huh? Huh? Isn't that what you thought? Well...big ball buster private *dick*—can I—can I surprise you right here...right now?"

I was laughing at her in my own delirium. "Ha! Yeah! Right now, June Maye—tell me...tell me your...your surprise..."

"I've—I've been fucking Larry Brooks in the back room...hee! hee! That's my secret, Cable, do you like it—I *love* it!" she tittered. "I've been fucking my drummer! *And* I love it! You hear that? I *love* it!"

"Ha! so do I....it's—it's like an extra turn-on, babe..."

"But you don't know why I've—I've been ballin' his jack now, do you, Mr. Detective? You know why? Because your big cock got stale in my cunt, Mr. Man...because you never knew who I am, or who I was, and never asked...so now I'm telling you...I'm a singing whore...I do it for money...you think you get it from me for nothing, my slick, wet pussy, huh? Well, you don't—because Larry gets it for free, too—how's them apples, buddy boy? Huh? And you pay for it, Cable Denning...you pay for it with serving that hot, unquenchable thing between my legs...because it can never get enough...because you—you, lover boy with the policeman's pee-pee brain—ha! ha!—I like that...pee-pee brain...you don't get it...you dare to screw me, night after night, month after month, obeying mindless—mindlessly—what—what I commanded you to do...and you know—you know what that is? Huh? Well, I'll tell you exactly—exactly what that is. It's fucking me for pure sex...pure, pure, pure sex! Never love, never love, never love...that's what I told Larry...and he didn't

426

care...he licked up my pussy there in the dark because—because, Mr. Denning, he didn't care! He doesn't *want* love!" She hesitated and then sat back down on the sofa after having paraded around the room naked during her tirade. She lowered her voice. "But you...you, Mr. Man...are beginning to want *love*...I can feel it...and that...that, Cable, will simply—hic!—simply not do, will it?"

All this time I had a smirk on my face, listening to her words like an entertainment, like that prepared script she was reading from and I enjoyed her performance with no personal response to it. "So Larry and you got it on! Yeah! Good—good for you, chick! Good for that pussy of yours that only wants cock without love...without—without anyone...even caring...about you...ha! But what care we?"

"I'll tell you *what care we*...you male whore, you!" She grabbed my hand and yanked me into the bedroom. There she pushed me onto her bed and jumped on top of me, sliding around all over my body. She eased her sopping wet pussy over my erect male member until it slid into her with such a thrusting force that she let out a yelp. Then, like a violent animal I flipped her over and drove into her like a bulldozer taking down a mountain. The frenzied excitement brought us higher and higher until our orgasms peaked like a morning picnic on Mount Everest. Again and again we climbed that mountain together until our bodies would no longer perform and I collapsed on top of her, totally exhausted.

That night we lost all our dreams together. All that was left was the need to go higher and higher and at least once a week we went through the same ritual until all of the hallucinogens were gone. I asked around in desperation for a replacement. I went to Uncle Teddy's, but he wouldn't see me, now that Lily was dead and there was no longer a reason. I managed to beg, borrow and steal some heroin, but it wasn't the same. Whatever was in that shit Uncle Teddy had concocted was pure dream fantasy potent dope. Soon, June and I fell into a kind of tolerated togetherness. It was true that she was screwing her drummer, but I didn't seem to mind anymore—or maybe I never did. It's a funny thing about jealousy. Maybe most men have to love the dame they think they possess before that ownership thing kicks in. I don't know. Could be I just lost interest along the way.

Stardust Endings

By New Year's Eve, 1934, we had reached the bottom. Now the nightmare of recurrences began, just as Lama Daishi had told me in Nepal at the foothills of the Himalayas. Sometimes in the middle of the night, one of us would yell and appear to be swatting away evil things playing at our faces, or during the day I would go into a trance and be carried away to some multi-colored vision of floating on an orange planet with a green monster chasing me.

June was singing for a huge private party at the *Bistro Club* and she invited me that night. By then much of her wonderful singing voice had deteriorated into hot breath over a microphone. People began to notice, but she sang on with the same sensual intensity she always had. She started that night with a hot rendition of *I Get a Kick Out of You* and by the time she got to the words, "*I get no kick from cocaine,*" I knew June Maye's good singing days were over. I could see the disgust in the band members as their favorite singer slid down the ladder to that place below mediocrity. Even Larry the drummer had stopped screwing her.

She miraculously made it through her early sets. But on the last three songs, I knew in my heart, as inebriated as I was, smoking one Lucky Strike after another, she might not finish the evening. She seemed, however, to gain a fresh wind as she went into the Burke-Haggart tune, *What's New?* I felt there was also a message from the bottom of her bottle for me in that song. It was June's last good-bye to me, her unconscious way of precluding our togetherness. When she got to the words, '*What's new? Probably I'm boring you, but seeing you is grand, and you were sweet to offer your hand, I understand...adieu, pardon my asking what's new, of course you couldn't know, I haven't changed...I still love you so...*' June Maye would never be capable of saying "I love you," so she did the next best thing; she put it into secret messages in her songs, a way to let me know, despite everything, she still wanted me and cared for this old gumshoe she'd traded in for a young, new drummer—and lost.

Her professional career came to a sad ending that night. It would be remembered only as a whimper from somewhere in her horribly disfigured past, some ogre that haunted her and whose name I would never be privy to. The party was beginning to break up and some attendees were anxious for June to finish so everyone could sing *Auld Lang Syne* and go home. June's last song was the fabulous Hoagy Carmichael's *Stardust*, and June was so far gone with alcohol and haunting visions by midnight, that by the time she got halfway through the song, it was all over. She stopped, wavered for a minute, then went crashing into a music stand and fell to the floor, passed out. Yep, Lady J., just like Lady Day in Harlem, had succumbed to drugs, alcohol and head-on into a dangerous collision with a wreck named Cable Denning.

A couple of the band members poured June into their car and drove her home. I didn't even follow. I went outside into the warm night and grabbed a streetcar up to my office. I didn't even know why I was going there. Maybe there was no place else to go. When I started to put my key into the front office lock, the door creaked open. Out of instinct I drew my .38 and crept into the darkened room. Tied to my desk chair with the neon light across the street flashing on and off her body sat Mandy Foster Simpson. "Don't try to free her, Denning," a hard-as-nails voice said from the dark behind me. I felt a gun barrel in my ribs and I dropped my piece. "We have something to discuss." I turned to face my assailant. I had never seen him before. He was a fairly tall, good-looking bloke with dark, curly hair. He was well dressed but spoke like a gangster. I knew their meter by heart. Not only did I grow up with them, but my cop years were riddled with run-ins with the likes of Ardizzone, Bardini, Cuppola, Jack Dragna and his kind.

I wandered over to Mandy. "Are you okay?" She nodded her head. "So...who are you and what do you

430

want?" He put his gun away. "You know what I tell all my clients? Everyone has a story...you included, grease-ball. So spill it, life's waiting—what's *your* tale of woe?"

"I'd say you're pretty cocky for a washed up gum-shoe, Denning. Okay, it's late and it's New Year's Day and I have a party to get to. I'll make it brief. Unless you can come up with everything you and the Pope dis-cussed on your recent visit to the Vatican, you will be a dead man by tomorrow night at this time. Capisce? Now, isn't that nice and clear and to the point, Denning? I pride myself in being Jack's real pride and joy."

"You mean Dragna?"

"Who else?"

"And what if I'm not sober enough?"

"You'll die anyway. Just...for the fun of it, huh?"

"I guess that's fair enough. You know the old saying, fore-warned is fore-armed."

"I'm afraid that's not going to help you. No guns, no old sheriff's posse, no girlfriend like your charming sec-retary over there...nothing's gonna stop that ol' clock from ticking away your remaining hours."

"Sounds pretty final to me. I always wondered what early death would feel like...but you know, shithead, I don't really give a fuck. Kill me now, it'd make me feel better."

"You're drunk, Denning. Sleep it off..." He started to leave. "Oh, and by the way, Happy New Year."

As soon as the bloke had left I ran over to Mandy and untied her. "Cable!" she cried as she fell into my arms.

431

"I'm sorry, Mandy. Part of the risk of being you know who's employee. Did you know who he was—did he give you a name?"

"No, but I've got to relieve myself quite urgently." She ran off for the john. Soon she returned. Her face was filled with angst. "Are they indeed going to attempt to murder you in cold blood—oh! Cable—I could not take that! That would about kill me as well!"

"Eh...don't worry about it, kid. I've got it together just fine. I've heard their songs before. I just won't be here when they come knockin' at my door, that's all."

"But they will find you...and track you down, dar-lin'...then—"

"—relax, Mandy. I've been there a lot of times. I'm like that proverbial cat with those nine lucky lives, huh?" I comforted her.

"I sure hope you are in earnest, Cable. I became so frightened...you hear tell of people's violent adventures—but when you're face to face with evil and their terrible brand of violence—I declare, it's—it's a whole other mode of consideration!"

"Yeah, that's about it, Mandy. Want a drink?"

"Yes, sir, I would definitely enjoy imbibing in a New Year's Toast to us, Cable." I got out my bottle of gin, but my hands were shaking as I poured for both of us. Mandy noticed but we clinked glasses anyway. "To a better new year than this that has just passed." Then she looked curiously into my eyes. "Where is the charmin' Miss June Maye this evenin', if I may ask?"

"She collapsed into a music stand, fell to the floor and passed out during her last song tonight at the *Bistro Club*."

432

"Oh, dear, was—was she hurt?"

"I doubt it. She's young and made of rubber."

"Am I to assume you two are no longer an item?"

"I didn't say that, Mandy. But now that you mention it, yeah, from now on I drink and smoke alone. I've had it with broads, you included. In your case it's nothing personal, it's just that I practically begged you in the beginning when you first came to work for me, not to get involved with your boss. Now look at you. Look at *me*. A has-been on a lost weekend—see what women can do to a man?"

"I beg your pardon. The fairer sex did not cause your downfall, Cable. Your reckless, carefree and frolickin' lifestyle did you in, Mister, you're not bein' accountable to yourself nor to your profession—let alone the few friends you have in this world. Now we must add to that, drinkin' too much alcohol, smoking way in excess of your body's ability to handle all that tobacco poison—and indulging sexually with that—that singin' woman, who for all fair intents and purposes, ruined you and turned you into this drunken man who is about to lose his place of business, his secretary—and his place in the world."

I took a deep breath. "That bad, eh?"

"Yes, sir, that bad...and I have seen no actions or proposals on your part to remedy the situation, Mr. Private Detective Cable Denning ..."

"It's only temporary, Mandy. I'll—I'll get myself together here soon...you know, I gonna have to dry out a bit...that's all."

"It's never that simple, Cable." She looked at the mess that used to be Cable Denning. "And to think I love you still…lookin' at you there in this occluded light. How could a man who brought me such great happiness, choose this path to destruction before my very eyes?"

I was flippant and still a bit drunk. "Ha! It's easy when you know how. Stick around, lady, you'll see…I'll pull it together. I always do."

"Would you please escort me home? I'm plumb exhausted from the ordeal of this evenin'."

"Just out of curiosity, what were you doing in the office so late?"

She put her head to my own. "I was waitin' for you. You see, a woman who loves a man and who has given herself with open intent to continue lovin' him, however that is tarnished, awaits in the lonely night for a glimpse of his face or the sound of his voice."

I hugged Mandy. "Thanks, Mandy…" Then I took her home. As I walked out of her little bungalow, I realized I could not go back to the office. It was full of bad dreams and guilt just now. I checked out my pockets. I had about two hundred bucks, a comb, a set of keys, a handkerchief and me. I took the yellow streetcar downtown. I needed to hide until this Jack Dragna thing blew over. I found a safe haven at *The Zambia Club,* a dump off Los Angeles Street on the edge of skid row. In my cop days it was a joint where great musicians hung out. But no singers were allowed and jazz greats came in to play their souls out with their horns or fingers. I knew a few of them. And they were open all night, working themselves up to a trance of almost psychic improvisation, drifting into the realms of the abstract and elusive. But that was jazz, the emotional outpouring of what life had dealt these wandering minstrels.

I drank all night and bought drinks for everyone who was within earshot of my voice. By dawn I was broke. I asked Max Left the bartender if I could conk out in the back room. I knew where it was because cops used to take their whores back there in the 20's. I staggered down a dark hallway with Max to a lumpy couch and collapsed.

June's voice was haunting me. Her songs got all mixed up in my head. I could see her expressive face up there standing in a sequined dress, displaying her formidable talents, big tits and singing her heart out. All the songs came rushing together in a montage of sound, a cacophony of words and music. My heart missed her, but my head turned its back. I knew June Maye was gone forever from my life. I also knew she would sink, just as I was sinking into that abyss of forgetfulness where souls who live on the edge go when they've lost their way—just as *Sinleila* had said.

It must have been mid-morning when Max came back and pulled me up out of the sofa. He told me I had to go. I told him I was broke and needed to borrow a few bucks until I got back on my feet. He told me he was sorry but couldn't give me any dough. We fought and he tossed me out of the club onto the street of filth and bums, into the gutter. I hit my head on the curb and I began to black out. Yeah, *Sinleila*, the *Goddess of Passion* had finally finished with me. In that deep recess of the intuitive self, I knew for all practical intents and purposes my life was over—at least for now. Let Jack Dragna's thugs find me and work me over, let them beat the shit out of me and then toss me back into a filthy alley with the rest of the leftovers of society. After all, we were all dispensable, the outcasts who never quite made it to the top of the heap. Maybe some of us had everything at one time, but ended up with nothing. Maybe Cable Denning was a paper tiger after all, a tough guy made of balsa wood inside, running, running, running from the demons that inhabited him now, abandoned to himself and the Fates who waited on the sidelines, ready to assign the next lesson. But maybe, just maybe, I'd get to skip *Love* and *Consciousness*, and advance past Boardwalk and Park Place to the *Goddess of Death*. Then the blackness finally overcame me and I gratefully sank away from the world.

The End

Acknowledgements

Cover Images:
Cable Denning: Kenneth A. Cox Photography
Blonde with Cable: © deanpowell.com
Asian beauty with Cable: Photographer-Crystal Cartier
Himalayas: Provenance unknown
Indian Sadhu (Holy Man): © Can Stock Photo/Kadmy
Cobra: © Can Stock Photo, Inc.
Vintage Woman in b/w: © Can Stock Photo/Shmeljov
Los Angeles night scene: Public Domain – Photographer
Cable Denning shadow: Kenneth A. Cox Photography

Interior Images – Part II
Sherriff 'Boots' Blake: Provenance unknown
Ballerina – Lily Norwood: © Can Stock Photo/warrengoldswain
Swan: Fotolia – renamarie – Photographer

Original Cover Designs: Frances Walker-Moss

Editing and Research Consultant: Frances Walker-Moss

www.ingramcontent.com/pod-product-compliance
Lightning Source LLC
Chambersburg PA
CBHW051510250626
47156CB00001B/31